THE FLYING TOOTH GARDEN VOL. 1

THE JUNGLE TOMB OF THE ICE QUEEN

M HAROLD PAGE

Published by Level Up in the United Kingdom in 2021

Cover illustration by Sippakorn Upama
Cover by Claire Wood

ISBN: 978-1-83919-372-9

www.levelup.pub

Dedicated to Hugh Hancock (1977 – 2018), who once threw me through a pile of chairs.

Chapter 1: Forward the Banner!

Men fought and died at the breach. The Marshal tensed his fingers against his gilded gauntlets.

Form 3. Performing Warlord at Level 13.

"My lord?" prompted the page, proffering Peacebringer.

"He'll say when, boy," hissed Cordinus the Bannerman.

The midday heat had crushed the sound out of the battle. Blades thudded on shields, clanged on helms. Arrows crunched underfoot. The only human noises were the grunts of sudden effort and the wet whimpers of the dying. Beyond the ragged walls, Gronchard the Flayer's advancing Myrmidons kicked up a dust cloud.

Again, the Marshal's Demon spoke:

307 Medium Infantry. Standing Ground. Firm.
Uncounted Gronchardian Medium Infantry.
Assaulting.

It was Gronchard's conjurers that had sent a Hell Troll to smash the ramparts of Yinkesia, ancient seat of the Yinksi Empire. There'd been no time to build barricades, so now a mere shieldwall of soldiers and militia struggled to postpone the moment when the enemy would clamber in over the debris and rampage through their city.

For three generations, the Myrmidons had smashed all resistance, leaving only smouldering cities and skull stacks in their wake.

Defeat was inevitable. *Almost.*

Once again his Demon made the puppets dance across the Marshal's vision; ghostly figures flickering in triple time, playing out the counter-attack. It might even work. However, for now, the Marshal—he had a name, but only one person had used it in thirty years—could only watch from the portico of the Temple of Yin. He shifted his weight, surreptitiously loosened his leg muscles while the sweat trickled down his forehead. Beside him, the Queen looked on, golden mask impassive. They were both warlocks, but he knew he had seen her face for the last time in this or any life.

295 Medium Infantry. Standing Ground. Firm.

A dozen of Gronchard's archers bobbed up onto the rubble itself, black figures in the glare and dust. Bow staves flickered.

"Arrows!" barked the Marshal.

The Royal Shieldman moved to protect Queen Zenobia. The Marshal ducked so that the peak of his helmet covered his eyes.

An arrow slammed into his cuirass. The impact bruised his ribs. Another glanced off his helmet. More arrows thudded into the Queen's tower shield.

Now a return volley whirred down from the temple roof, swept the enemy archers away.

17 archers. 3 arrows left each. Standing Ground. Shaken.

"You should put on your armour, my Queen," said the Marshal.

The skin of her neck tautened, and he could imagine her smiling behind the mask: lips quirked, crowsfeet furling around twinkling eyes. "I have perhaps one spell left in me," she said. "Let it not be said it was unspent when my civilisation fell."

The Marshal nodded. His queen, with her uncanny grasp of the future, did not believe in his plan.

The Marshal shrugged against the rattling weight of his armour. He could not be other than who he was. He glanced down the reserve line formed up before the ancient temple's porch. The men of the Queen's Guard fidgeted and shifted at their posts. They were all in heavy cataphract wargear—lamellar armour of overlapping plates, small shields strapped to their arms, and double-handed lances hacked down for infantry combat.

42 Heavy Infantry. Standing Ground. Eager.

The ideal moment would come when the attackers committed their reserve. There would confusion as unblooded troops breasted the breach. The three remaining Yinksi goeticists would expend their last spells while the archers on the temple roof emptied their quivers. Then and only then could he lead the decisive counter-attack.

He looked back to the defenders in the melee.

240 Medium Infantry. Wavering.

Sure enough, the Yinksi shieldwall bowed, split. Yelling in triumph, Gronchard's men burst through. The melee became a whirl of duels and brawls, with the greater numbers of the attackers starting to tell.

235 Medium Infantry. Disordered. Fighting Desperately.

"Queen's Guard!" barked the Marshal. "Advance! For the Queen!"

They took up the cry. Armour rattling, they trotted down the steps, leaving the Queen with just the Marshal, his page, and her Shieldman.

The Guard formed a wedge as they descended, slammed into the melee, imposed a lethal order on the chaos. Yinksi defenders let themselves be swept past and joined the rear. Attackers died where they stood or retreated to the hard-won breach.

39 Heavy Infantry. Fighting well. Confident. 213 Medium Infantry. Rallying.

Even so, Gronchard's light troops were scrambling up the sides of the breach while—from the other side of the rubble—unseen magicians and archers kept down the heads of those defenders who perched on the remnants of the battlements.

47 Gronchardian Light Infantry. Eager. Unlock Mason or Sculptor?

"Ha!" *Sculpting*, he answered. The knowledge of working stone into recognisable shapes flowed through his mind.

"What is it?" asked Queen Zenobia.

"Remember I've yet to pick an additional Vocation? I've spent so much time looking at fallen masonry, my demon now recalls a past life as a statue maker."

"I can't imagine you as that," said the Queen.

"But I can now imagine capturing your grace in stone."

"Don't use the word *capture*," she said.

A dozen enemy Conclave spearmen broke free of the melee and charged up the steps toward them.

13 Gronchardian Medium Infantry. Eager.

"Excuse me, My Queen," said the Marshal. "*Boy, my sword!*" He took up Peacebringer and jogged down the five steps to the first landing where there was room for footwork. He dropped into an easy fighting stance—knees bent, sword cocked back over his right shoulder—and the aches and pains of two score years of warfare dropped away.

The Spearmen are level 5 challenges.

The Marshal grinned. Of course. Gronchard's elite troops.

The spearmen could have simply evaded him, flowed around to get to the Queen. Her death curse might have accounted for most of them. However, the shieldman and bannerman were both too heavily armoured to deal with a swarm of lighter troops, and the page was just a boy. The Queen would have been killed or captured, or chased into the temple with the same eventual response.

But an old man in golden armour…how could they resist?

Form 3. Performing Warrior at level 25.

The Demon chattered away as the Marshal did his duty.

He stepped over the bodies on his way back to the Queen.

Zenobia did not speak. She caught his questioning look. "All these years," she said, "and this is the first time I have seen you use a sword in anger."

Not in anger, he thought guiltily. "It is not how I would have you remember me," he said.

"There will not be a remembering, I think," she said, and gestured at the breach.

4

The Marshal turned back to the fight. All order had been lost except where Yinksi soldiers formed knots of resistance.

21 Heavy Infantry. Disordered. Fighting desperately. 164 Medium Infantry. Disordered. Fighting desperately. Uncounted enemy Medium Infantry. Assaulting.

"Page, see that my pyre is lit," said the Queen.

"It will not be necessary," said the Marshal, but he did not call back the boy.

"Gronchard shall not take me to the Flying Tooth Garden for flaying," said the Queen.

"Nor shall he," said the Marshal.

Trumpets sounded beyond the wall. Sandals tramped.

"At last." He clapped his Bannerman on the armoured shoulder. "Cordinus, my friend, I find I cannot order you to do this."

"I've followed you in life, Marshal," said Cordinus, "it is fit I should follow you in death."

A great sadness settled in the pit of the Marshal's stomach. His friend was no warlock. There would be no reunion of avatars. But since he had but one death to die, it would be wrong to try to take away his choosing of it.

"Stay a good few paces behind me," said the Marshal, "so—"

Cordinus laughed. "So you can use your sword. It will be like old times."

The Queen tore off her mask to reveal tear-bright eyes. She opened her mouth but no words came.

The Marshal flexed his shoulders against his armour. "It is how it is."

Zenobia stood on tiptoe and kissed him with dry lips. "Perhaps in the next life we shall love as equals. Perhaps I shall bear you a child."

The Marshal shook his head. "I am done with hurting and being hurt. The Grey Cortège will come for my body and you will give it to them." He caught a whiff of burning pitch from the pyre. He turned away so as not to see her look of hurt.

Black pike shafts appeared above the breach.

5

Uncounted Multitudes of Gronchardian Medium
Infantry. Assaulting. Eager.

"Forward the banner!" roared the Marshal. "For the Queen and for Yinkesia."

Chapter 2: Duelling Warlocks!

Gronchard's pikemen breasted the breach. Three fireballs whooshed down from the temple roof. Orange flared as human fat combusted. More soldiers pushed through the mayhem and the fear and rage braided into a noose that seemed to constrict Zenobia's skull.

Zenobia pointed her fingers and started to chant.

Current form 5. Performing Wizard at level 30. 1 of 27 Potestas remaining.

Her gaze flicked to the Marshal's armoured back as he waded through the mayhem. Their…private exercise regime had kept her fitter and tougher than the average queen.

The world sharpened even as her body ached and her shoulders sagged.

She barely heard her Demon's commentary as she went through the familiar spell.

Before her eyes, nearly two dozen men in front rank of Gronchard's legionaries dropped their weapons, clutched burst hearts or simply collapsed with blood trickling from their nostrils.

Her empathy left her naked to the splash of pain and terror.

You are Empathic.
Will 13. You have avoided acquiring the issue Guilt.

"Let me be cold hearted in my next life!"

The last of the arrows buzzed overhead and added to the disorder.

The stench from her pyre was overwhelming now. She must give herself to the flames while they were hot enough to truly consume her, otherwise her remains would end up in Gronchard's Mausoleum, and her next incarnation would see her soul flayed back to the woman Gronchard had once loved.

But she could not turn away from the Marshal.

The big man cut down any of Gronchard's soldiers in his way. There was no drama; they simply fell before him. He did not seem to defend himself, only shrug his way into attacks so that blades drew sparks from his armour and spears slipped past. Then, with an economical pivot, he would whip his sword around and dispatch the threat. It was like watching a servant prepare the table for a feast, laying out plates with brusque efficiency, tidying displaced napkins in passing.

Her Demon settled back into its usual role.

Influential Courtier. Master Diplomat. Master General. Queen's favourite. Loyal.

Behind him followed the heavily armoured Bannerman, one armoured hand on the Yinksi sunburst banner, the other brandishing a mace as he clambered over the corpses.

A champion reared up out of the press like some hellish beetle shod in gilded steel and Zenobia felt the presence of another warlock; not just the presence, the tug on her soul.

Gronchard!

God Emperor. General. Diplomat. Flayer.

Zenobia put a hand over her mouth, steeled herself to watch.

"GIVE US SPACE," ordered Gronchard, in words that rang in the mind.

The men of both sides left of fighting and formed a loose arena around the Marshal and Gronchard.

Gronchard made a sweep with his golden sword. With its spikes and flanges it looked far more imposing than the Marshal's simple blade. Then he raised his visor. He was middle aged, younger than Zenobia, but his eyes burned with passion and the hellish thing was that even in the midst of this death and horror, she felt her heart leap.

Charismatic Presence. He is a level 11 magical challenge.

Zenobia relaxed a little. The Marshal's amulets would at least protect him from that.

"Angelica my love," said Gronchard. "I have come for you."

"Go home, Gronchard," said Zenobia. "Angelica died long ago."

Gronchard shook his head. "You were stolen by a shell self before I could flay it away. Come with me now and I will keep you always."

"I *am* that 'shell self'," said Zenobia. "Marshal, my love, kill this man for me."

The Marshal raised his sword.

Gronchard took up the same stance. He laughed. "You should not be here. I have killed you before."

The Marshal came forward with all the speed of a young man.

The blades clashed, whirled, sparked.

The two armoured men switched grip to hold their swords like paddles. They hooked and wrestled, thumped with the pommel, curled legs and evaded trips.

Then Gronchard's helmet came off. Blood sprayed from his throat.

The Marshal merely flowed past, left the other warlock dying on his feet. Cordinus followed stepped into the arena, banner aloft and bellowed, "For the Queen!"

The corpse of the god crashed into the dust. Zenobia blinked, trying to make sense of what she'd seen.

The other combatants unfroze. The Yinksi men yelled and surged against the attackers.

Cordinus's banner reached the breach, and there was the Marshal in his golden armour, legs bracing and unbracing, driving the hips that in in turn drove his great sword. Zenobia had always considered her courtier lover handsome but ungainly. Now, in this fatal hour, she saw that he had been like a storm-wreathed mountain seen from the stork pond of a formal garden. Here, in his natural element, he had a terrible, elemental grace.

At first the enemy swirled past the Marshal and his bannerman, and he merely took a tithe as they passed. Then a couple of Yinksi soldiers fought their way to his banner, then a dozen, then dozens.

The flow of Gronchardian soldiers cut off. The surviving Yinksi men gathered to the Marshal's side. The priests chose this moment to come out of the temple and start ministering to the wounded of both sides.

Crowd of 154. Loyal. Angry.

For the first time since the siege began, Zenobia's heart truly lifted. A future opened up, one in which she ruled with the Marshal at her side. In a reborn empire, she could do away with masks and conventions. In the autumn of her life, she would make a consort of her lover.

The Marshal's voice rang out over the carnage. "Charge by all the Gods! Charge! Charge! For the Queen! Kill them all. *Charge!*"

The Yinksi men let out a roar made terrible by its very humanity. Gronchard's Myrmidons had devastated their homes, winnowed them as they fled, enslaved their sons and daughters. Now those same Myrmidons routed, presenting their backs to the wrath of her subjects…and thanks to her empathy, Zenobia could feel that wrath like poison in her veins.

The banner went forward, down off the breach and out of sight into the trampled pastures beyond.

Zenobia left the temple and climbed one of the bastions. She looked on as her men slaughtered the enemy in droves, overreached, fell back, job done. The worst of it was that they were laughing and brandishing heads on pikes.

They left behind their casualties, except for the Marshal, whose limp body returned over the shoulders of two strong men.

She did not go to him, for she knew it would be her unmaking and the city needed a Queen, not a woman. Instead, she managed the aftermath from her bastion, her Potestas trickling back to her.

Gronchard's army sent a priest offering a twenty-four-hour truce in return for their master's body. She knew that they would take it to his mausoleum as a bate for his next avatar, that they would capture the poor child and flay his soul back to expose the personality of their God Emperor. Even so, her duty to her people forced her to agree.

By the time they carried away her enemy's remains, the sun was sinking behind the temple, dyeing the city's marble a warm pink. It was the time of day when she would retire to her chambers to prepare for the evening meal. Courtesy of a secret passage, she and the Marshal would have a precious two hours. Sometimes they would slip out in disguise and wander the city, pretending that they might simply walk away, take on false names and buy a small estate on which to grow old together.

A pillar of fog appeared beyond the Conclave siege lines. Eerie chanting echoed through the warm evening air.

The fog folded in on itself to let in the glare from another land where it was still full daytime. Still chanting, a column of grey-robed figures emerged from the portal.

33 Humanoids. Unknown. Supernatural.

The Grey Cortège—they were real.

The late Gronchard's forces parted to let them through. Servants unpegged tents and dragged them aside. Soldiers wheeled away mobile shields.

Zenobia half-sprinted, half-tumbled down the stairs. Attendants streaming behind her, she rushed to where they had laid out the Marshal's body.

The monks were already stripping him of his armour.

33 Humanoids. Grey Cortège. Supernatural.

"Wait!"

They ignored her. She pushed between them.

Form 2. Performing Virago at level 22.

No single wound had killed the Marshal. Rather, his pale old flesh was punctured in a dozen places, his undershirt soaked crimson.

A cold hand caught her shoulder.

She twisted.

There were no faces under the cowls, just a hazy grey-white glow. She could not tell whether they were daemon, or humans in the grip of some spell.

33 Humanoids. Grey Cortège. Unknown challenge.

She decided to risk all and gathered up her presence.

Using Virago, Commanding Presence +10 5/6, cost 1 Potestas, 1 of 27 remaining.

"I know who you are," she said. "But I *shall* say farewell to my Marshal, and you shall not stop me."

The monk released her.

Result = 22 (Performance) +12 (Feat) +1 (Luck) -32 (Challenge) = Tentative Practical Response for a few moments.
Virago, Commanding Presence +10 advances to 6/6 and is secured.

The demon made no effort offer to unlock another Virago feat. Zenobia let out a bitter laugh.

Until this very moment, she had been walking in the footprint of dead selves—but then she had always dreamed of ruling over strange lands; how could she not have been a queen or an empress before? Now she had exceeded every other person she had ever been, and—despite the grief and fear—it felt liberating. She understood now why the Marshal wanted to end his cycle of reincarnation. She brushed the grey hair from his brow and kissed it. "I am sorry, my love," she said.

If her demon said something at that moment, she chose not to hear it.

Then she stood aside so the monks could finish their task. They shrouded the naked corpse. Still chanting, they returned to the portal.

Under cover of night, the Gronchard's army pulled back from the walls of Yinkesia. It could have been that they were incapable of fighting on, now their God Emperor had been temporally slain. However, Zenobia liked to think that in summoning the Grey Cortège, The Marshal had somehow saved the day.

#

Zenobia never again wore her golden mask.

Nor, though she had many lovers to warm her final years, did she again press lips to flesh; she had left her royal kiss on the forehead of the Marshal.

Nor did she plan an Imperial mausoleum.

In her next life, she vowed, there would be neither throne nor protocal.

On her deathbed, she ordered trusted retainers to bury her under the desert sky, with a book of magic, a bag of coins, and her true love's sword.

CHAPTER 3: TEMPTED!

"I am wholly present in the now!" sang Acolyte Torstag.

Unlock Scout, Forest Proficiency, Foraging? whispered his Tempter.

Torstag did not pause in his weeding. The season was turning and dusk brought with it a cold wind that whistled down the Untrodden Valley. The sooner the weeds were gone, the sooner he could warm his fingers. He continued, working in time to the words; "Present now and forever."

"As am...I," sang back Acolyte Ingar, a shrill tenor to Torstag's increasingly deep baritone. "Forever and forever."

The two acolytes were fighting back an infestation of Creeping Mandrake in the planting beds by the parapet of Middle Terrace, one of five massive platforms raised out of the towering rock walls of the Untrodden Valley.

They sang in unison: "Verily, for all Eternity, Life After Life, My Every In...car...na...tion. In accordance with the Book of Obedience."

On this cold day, the words were like stones settling in Torstag's belly, but they were supposed to silence the Tempter and if you didn't keep singing, the monks would beat you.

The sun flashed on the snow-capped peaks of the mountains making up the opposite wall of the valley. Torstag imagined standing there and seeing the world beyond.

Unlock Scout, Mountain Proficiency, Climb? whispered his Tempter.

Acolyte Ingar edged a little closer. "Even as putrefaction takes each and every of my mortal forms." He flashed a wolfish grin from under his cowl. He was a head shorter than Torstag. However, his freckles

14

gave his round face a dirty lived-in look, making him seem older. "Hey, Torstag?"

"Shush!" hissed Torstag. "We need to stay out of trouble."

"Pish and boll-ocks," sang Ingar. "The monks won't no...ooo...tice"—he made an arpeggio of that last word—"as long as we sing this blo...uh...uh...dy stu...oo...pld...song."

They chorused, "In accordance with the Book of Obedience."

Torstag glanced around the terrace. The Grey Cortège had harvested Ingar from his theatrical troupe at the advanced age of twelve, a crucial two years later than normal. Six years on, and Ingar still hadn't settled to monastic life.

Today, however, Ingar was lucky; the garden terrace seemed empty. If anybody was listening, they were far enough away only to hear the melody, not the words.

Torstag leaned closer and hissed, "We can't mess around any more." He glanced over his shoulder—still okay. "If we want to become priests."

That was the plan; to qualify as priests, get posted to some distant temple, and simply fade away into the Ten Thousand Realms.

"There are othererererer wa—ays to get ow-ow-ut of here," sang Ingar.

"Not safe...ways," sang Torstag. "The Portal To Outside is guarded day and...night."

"There must be a route...down the...cliffs," sang Ingar. "When I get out...I'm going to fuck all the women and drink...all...the beer." He added in his speaking voice, "Though not necessarily in that order."

"If we want to get out, we need to—" said Torstag. He found himself staring past the parapet and wondering, not for the first time, where the Untrodden Valley led to.

"Torstag?" prompted Ingar.

Torstag returned to singing. "-obey the rules as set out in the Book of Obedience."

"Do you even want to escape?" said Ingar.

"Yes," said Torstag. "I want to be my own man."

15

"You'll have to be your own man before you can escape," said Ingar. "You do know that, right?"

Torstag looked beyond his friend to the distant peaks.

A weed bit his finger.

He pinched the plant's head and twisted it off. "Damn."

Unlock Scout, Forest Proficiency, Foraging, or Entertainer, Geeking?

He Tempter was louder now. It helpfully supplied an explanatory vision of biting off chicken heads while carnival-goers jeered and cheered.

"I am wholly present in the now!" sang Torstag, firmly banishing the Dead Memory. He straightened and sucked at his wounded finger. His back, meanwhile, reminded him that he was now too tall to spend days stooping at the planting beds.

"Oh, really?" sang Ingar. He moved close enough to bump shoulders. *"There's a g...uh...uh...rll in the Stone Grove!"*

"A *what*?"

"A girl," whispered Ingar. "Like a boy, but with curves and other...features."

"I know what a damn girl is." Torstag stamped and rubbed his hands together against the cold. "But it's not possible." Then he sang, *"I do...not...wa...aa...ont...to know!"*

"There is! There is!" sang Ingar as he edged closer. His eyes were bright. *"A Girl. A Vessel of Ini...qui...ty."*

Unlock Homesteader, Horticulture, or Entertainer, Geeking? murmured his Tempter.

Now he had flashes of himself tending strange blooms under a canopy of greenery and while nearby a naked, blue-skinned woman pounded at a quern, flesh quivering enticingly as she—and then back to biting off chicken heads in the carnival.

A rod bit into his shoulders. "Acolyte Torstag! You stopped chanting!"

He turned but did not flinch.

Brother Neutrality, who had a way of stalking up unnoticed, brandished the implement. "You were listening to your Tempter!"

The grey-robed man somehow seemed smaller than before. When they dragged Torstag away from his family's tumbledown castle, the Grey Cortège had been terrifying giants. It had taken him a good season to throw off the memory of the white glare under grey hoods, voiceless gestures, and the cold hands taking his. It had taken longer still to lose the nightmares of his grandmother collapsing as they tore him out of her arms.

Now, eight years later, this Brother, and all the others, seemed...*breakable*. He wasn't sure that was the right world, but it would—he felt—be easy to *break* Brother Neutrality.

Unlock Warrior, Pugilism Proficiency or Polearm Proficiency, Wrath Strike?

That was louder than usual.

Torstag's gaze flitted to where they had propped wooden stakes against the parapet wall. Nearby lay a long-handled hammer. Come to think of it, swung properly...

"Acolyte Torstag!" snapped the Brother.

Torstag lowered his eyes. "Sorry, Brother Neutrality. It always comes as a surprise."

"Temptation should never come as a surprise," pronounced Brother Neutrality. "It is as inevitable as Death and Rebirth. It is why you *must* chant to silence its voice."

"In accordance with the Book of Obedience," recited Torstag. "Thank you, Brother Neutrality."

The Brother struck him again. The rod was heavy enough to smart through the thick robes.

Torstag focussed on the mountains on the other side of the Untrodden Valley.

"If you let it in..." Another blow. The Brother continued, punctuating his words with rod, "...then you will lose yourself to your past self, the dead hollowing out the living. This is not what your Past Self wanted. Is this what *you* want?"

Unlock Warrior, Disarm?

Torstag shook his head. "No, Brother Neutrality." His fists clenched within his wide sleeves. However, something prevented him from raising them in anger. "Thank you for schooling me, Brother Neutrality."

"You were trouble from the beginning," said the old man, turning away. "You'll never be a priest."

Fuck you too, Smelly Newt, thought Torstag, but the fun had gone out of using the old nickname.

Unlock Scout, Stalk Close, or Entertainer, Stunning Insult?

Torstag wasn't even sure what those were. *Shut up!* "*I am truly present,*" he sang.

"*As am I,*" sang back Ingar.

They carried on like that until Brother Neutrality was out of earshot. "*There cannot be a girl the Brothers would have ex...pel...ell...ed her,*" sang Torstag.

Ingar's hood bulged left then right—the youth was shaking his head. "They don't know yet," he said in a low voice. "Nobody uses the Stone Grove in cold weather."

"So who found her?"

"Hohan. He'd been tending to the Temple of Gronchard and I guess he wanted some privacy to...you know..."

Torstag pinched the bridge of his nose. He was getting a headache. "Really, I don't *want* to know!"

"Well, I'm going to take a look," said Ingar. He hopped up onto the raised beds and made for the parapet. "I'll be quicker without you, anyway."

"You can't!" Torstag gripped Ingar's arm.

"I bloody can climb down. Watch me."

"No, I mean, Women are Vessels of Iniquity. Epicentres of Temptation," said Torstag. He knew it was probably not true, but it *felt* true. His headache worsened. "It says so in the Book of Obedience."

"Just what I need," said Ingar. "I didn't *choose* to be here."

Torstag gasped. He grabbed the material of his friend's cassock. "But you *did*. Your Past Self had an Epiphany."

"Bugger my past self," said Ingar, "sideways, with a bargepole. I *want* me some iniquity and maybe a little temptation." He shook free from Torstag. "As far as anybody's concerned, I'm tending the Chapel of Gronchard."

"You can't."

"This may be the only girl we ever see."

"But we've both seen girls before we were taken," said Torstag. Ingar flushed behind his freckles. "You know what I mean."

"I thought you had a plan?"

Unlock Warlord, Commanding Presence or Sneak Raid?

Ingar shrugged weakly. "Not a safe one."

"No," said Torstag. "You don't even know how far down you'd have to climb to get to the valley floor. And the monks would catch you."

"Ha," said Ingar. "I'm more worried about not starving to death once I've escaped."

"Your appetite!"

"Talking of which," said Ingar. He clapped Torstag's shoulder. "Old Smelly Newt's done his rounds. He's probably toasting his feet by a fire right now. I'll see you later."

There was a scraping sound from Torstag's bucket. Some weeds were trying to climb out, so he stabbed them with his trowel.

His Tempter whispered: Unlock Warrior, Dagger Proficiency, Multiple Jabs, or Homesteader, Butter Making?

"Nice try", muttered Torstag.

"What?" said Ingar.

"I'll come with you," said Torstag. "But we'll have to take the Water Stairs."

CHAPTER 4: THE GIRL IN THE STONE GROVE

The Water Stairs were narrow stone steps that pierced the terraces to serve as run-offs for the winter rains. The Acolytes were forbidden to use them, supposedly because they were slippery, but really—Torstag was certain—because anybody using them was hidden from sight.

As they descended between towering walls, Ingar lost his footing— swore—twisted, grabbed Torstag and brought them both down.

Torstag went over on his back, scuffed the masonry, and landed on Ingar. He flinched. The blood rushed in his ears. Any moment, and weapons would batter at his armour, chip away at the gaps, drive up under the skirts of his cuirass…

> 2 point of Vitality Loss. 1 of 3 remaining.
> Toughness 1 Negated and Surpassed. 1 Wound incurred.
> Hindrance "Stunned". Form 0. No Feats possible.

He stared up at the grey sky for a few moments.

> Will 3. Hindrance "Stunned" shaken off.
> You have still have Hindrance "Wounded."

He hurled himself to his feet. His right leg gave under him. "What the Hell?"

> Unlock Warrior, Armoured Combat Proficiency?

"Fuck, Ingar, I'm sorry!" cried Ingar. The youth was sitting against the wall rubbing the back of his head through his red frizz. With his hood down he seemed soft and harmless, like the old dog Torstag had adored before the Grey Cortège stole him away.

"Not your fault," said Torstag. He helped his friend up. "The steps are slimy, that's all."

"But you looked to being ready to rip off my head and shit down my neck."

"Just the shock," said Torstag, starting to hobble down the last of the steps. "A Dead Memory, that's all?"

"Must have been a hell of a flashback."

"Let's just say there was fighting."

They emerged onto Orchard Terrace. This one was given over to apple trees. Here and there, bare branches webbed the sky like a cracked glaze, offering just enough cover from overhead observation.

A gust of wind kicked up a cloud of red leaves.

Torstag brushed some from his face.

He'd scuffed his knuckles on the Water Stair. Now they were the same red as the leaves.

"I really am sorry, Torstag," said Ingar.

Torstag shrugged. "Come on." He set off at a fast hobble.

"Hey! Slow down. You're hurt!" panted Ingar, as he caught up. "What's the sudden enthusiasm?"

He was dragging his right leg, he realised. His ankle felt like somebody had driven a nail into it. Torstag shrugged. "I guess I feel like my own man right now."

A movement made him spin on the spot, drop into a fighting stance with his knees bent, even though it hurt.

Just a pig snuffling in the leaves. Most certainly not people trying to kill him with spears. "Huh?"

"Torstag, are you all all right?"

It was probably how his father died, he realised. Yes, he was thinking about that for some reason.

Torstag limped off along the path. "How did she get into the Monastery?"

"What?" said Ingar, panting as he kept up. "I don't know. Who cares? Temptation! Iniquity! Fuck all the women!"

"Drink all the beer," said Torstag. "Yes, but nobody's supposed to be able to get in. I'm not sure she's real."

"So why are you coming with me?" asked Ingar.

21

"Temptation, I suppose," said Torstag. "It was your idea."

Another narrow set of steps took them down to the cold pools of the Rice Terrace, and thence the entrance to the Stone Grove. This was more of a platform than a terrace: a walled half-moon a level lower than the Rice Terrace. Seen from above, its stone columns formed a spiral. However, as they walked out in amongst them, the columns really did make it feel like a grove...or what Torstag, who'd grown up in arid mountains, imagined one might feel like based on glimpses of the trees carpeting the Untrodden Valley.

There was no rule preventing the Acolytes visiting the place during their meditation time, but few of them had the urge to do so. It was from here that the fog-wreathed Cortèges set off among the Many Realms, sometimes to bring back a corpse for internment in the Catacombs of Hesitation, other times to return with a weeping child.

Torstag shuddered.

Next to him, Ingar seemed to shrink into himself. "She's not here," he said.

Torstag cut through the spiralling columns. He halted at the verge of the central "clearing".

There she was, making tea using a little charcoal-fired samovar. In the cold blue winter light, her face seemed as gaunt as that of any senior monk. Even so, she could perhaps have been about the same age as Torstag.

"A g...girl," stammered Ingar, practically squirming on the spot. "I really am feeling...tempted."

Torstag frowned. He'd just started to notice the older girls when the Grey Cortège took him, and she wasn't pretty like them: sharp cheekbones, mouse brown hair carelessly tied back leaving her long neck bare to her open collar. The village girls had dimpled and giggled a lot. This one was grim and silent.

"Tempted," repeated Ingar, hopping from foot to foot.

Torstag left the stone columns behind and limped closer. Some vague memory of castle etiquette prompted him to bow. "My lady."

The girl rose to her full height. She was as tall as Torstag, but her sheepskin kaftan wrapped a figure more slender than Ingar's. Small eyes twinkled like riverstone beads. She returned the bow.

"Tempted!" gasped Ingar, behind Torstag. "I have to…I must…"
His footsteps receded into the forest of columns.

The girl made a sweeping gesture at the paved ground and started to kneel.

Torstag copied her, though clumsily; going down first on his injured leg then leaning on his bruised hands to adjust his position.

"Welcome, my lord," she said, as if he, not she, were the visitor.

"Thank you, my lady," he said.

The samovar hissed steam. The girl reached into a leather bag and brought out two bronze cups, elaborately enamelled with scenes of gryphons hunting lions. She wrapped a cloth around her long-fingered hand and poured.

Torstag waited until she reached for her cup and sipped, then took his.

The girl regarded him with dark eyes. "Cautious."

"Polite," he said.

The tea was black and well stewed—she must have prepared it earlier. It had a dry taste, and a bitter fragrance that suffused his senses.

"To our quest," said the girl.

"*Our* quest?" said Torstag.

"For the Jungle Tomb of the Ice Queen," she said.

"That's…" began Torstag. He set his chin. "…making assumptions," he finished.

Her lips quirked just a little. "Your pardon my lord if I have skipped ahead in our story. I have dreamed of this moment."

Torstag groped for the right words.

Unlock Warlord, Tea Drinking?

And Torstag was seated on a rug amidst armoured men. Around him, fallen arrows sprouted from the mud like ripe wheat, carpeting the bodies of slain warriors and slaughtered horses, and a man with a missing eye and caked blood on his cheek offered him tea in a gilded skullcup…

And he was back with the girl, feeling sick now from the pain in his ankle, and totally out of his depth. "I haven't," he said.

She raised her gaze to scrutinise him.

23

He flushed and closed his eyes to escape his embarrassment. *Go away!*

Unlock Warlord, Tea Drinking, or Companion, Seduction of the Eyes.

Some very…strange experiences jumbled across his mind's eye, one or two of them…anatomically challenging. His cheeks burned. *Damn you!* Warlord, Tea Drinking *if that will shut you up.* But the Tempter did not shut up:

You now have a 1/6 Grasp of the Feat Warlord, Tea Drinking. You have unlocked Warlord at Level 0. Using Feat Warlord, Tea Drinking 1/6. 3 out of 3 Potestas expended.

Was there a note of triumph in the Tempter's words? Surely he had just been tempted from his path, just as the monks had warned. His mind whirled. It was like rifling through the pages of a book and somehow understanding the words, but he knew now that this was a moment for formality, and all the while his hands and elbow throbbed dully and his ankle twinged as if a needle were being driven into it.

Form 3. Performing Warlord at level 3.

Torstag suddenly had a sense of how he would defend this place, how many archers to deploy and where, and how to drink tea with this mysterious girl.

"I meant, O honoured lady," he said, "that I have not had the pleasure of dreaming about this," he said.

"Of course not, my lord," she said. "Not here."

Torstag wanted to blurt, *Why?* Instead he sipped his tea, set it down. "Some statements beg questions."

The girl went through the business of sipping her tea, then setting it down. "Sometimes it is best to make up one's own mind."

"And yet," said Torstag, sensing how this game worked, "without knowledge, wisdom is as a riderless horse." He reached for his cup to indicate that he would listen.

Her eyes twinkled.

**Form 3. Performance 3. You have hindrance
Wounded.
Result = 3 +2 (Feat) -2 (Hindrance) +1 (Luck) -4 (Gorvak
Nomad Tea Ceremony) = 0
Effect = 0 (Adequate)
Tea Drinking advances to 2/6 Grasp.**

The girl leaned in over the little fire. "My lord, throughout almost my every incarnation, you have been my protector," she said. "Thus my enemy is your enemy, my quest is your quest."

Torstag looked at his own reflection in the black liquid. A grey-bearded man stared back at him and then was gone. "The monks say that to listen to past incarnations is to risk becoming hollowed out."

"My soul is like an ancient fortress," she said. "Previous owners have left behind tapestries and books, but I am not them."

"In my last life," recited Torstag, "I had an epiphany and dedicated myself to the Grey Cortège, who brought my mortal remains here, then, when I was of age, fetched my new self to begin my Holy Service, in accordance with-"

"Do you let dead people make your choices for you?"

"Hang on," he said. "You just said…"

Unlock Scholar, Debate, or Companion, Banter?

Enough!

**Unlock Companion, Banter, or Companion,
Conjunction of the Butterflies?**

What?

Lurid imagery tugged at his mind. He resolutely kept his eyes open. Enough was enough. This encounter had sent his Tempter berserk.

Shut up! Shut up!

"I am an Acolyte of the Grey Cortège," he managed.

"This is your choice, my lord?" she asked.

"As it was mine before, my lady," said Torstag. "I am my own man."

"Are you so certain?"

A dog's bark rang through the forest of stone columns. It was the hollow sound of an animal neither entirely alive nor properly dead. Somebody hollered, "This way!"

Torstag's heart lurched, but he did not rise. "I am my own man," he repeated.

She sighed. "When you are ready for freedom, visit your past selves in the Catacombs of Hesitation."

"Past self, singular," corrected Torstag.

She leaned over the fire and kissed his forehead.

Contact with Paramour of Past Lives.

"What...?"

But she was gone—along with her fire, the cups, but not the taste of the tea.

The dogs and shouting grew closer.

His Tempter went silent. More than silent. It was as if it were inhaling so deeply as to leave a tangible absence.

Torstag got up. A chill wind plucked at his robe. His ankle throbbed painfully. Wincing, he hobbled for the doubtful concealment of the forest of columns. What was he going to say to the monks? The other side of the Untrodden Valley seemed further than ever.

You have Hindrance Wounded.

Then, louder:

Surge.

Lightning coruscated up his spine, bloomed in his skull.

He stumbled.

Time stopped.

12 Advancement Points available.
Advance Warlord, Tea Drinking 2/6?

Wait!

This all seemed vaguely familiar, like one of those dreams with old friends you don't know.

How does this work?

26

> **You may advance any unlocked Feat, or unlock new Vocations and Feats.**

Vocations?

Images jumbled across his mind—past selves yelling orders, gathering mushrooms, trading insults, cutting down foes, biting the heads off chickens…

How many can I… "unlock"?

> **You may have 4 Vocations, then an additional Vocation every 4th Level.**
> **Surge enables you to choose from other recently relevant Vocations, namely Warrior, Scout, Entertainer, Companion, Homesteader.**

Torstag chewed his lip. Apart from Warlord, those were all vocations that his Tempter had been pestering him with for months, years even.

In the vision, his past self flipped back and forward between carving a bloody path with a sword as long as Ingar was tall, to climbing shear rock faces while leather-winged creatures flapped at his face.

That.

Time stopped.

The fighting images called to him, but he remembered Ingar's talk about climbing down from the Monastery. The only realistic escape was still over the edge. Now, however, he could perhaps survive the climb.

> **Scout unlocked at Level 0. 1 Feat required to advance to Level 1.**
> **Select a Proficiency.**

The Tempter offered a choice of environments.

As far as Torstag could tell, the Untrodden Valley was forested. He had, however, to get there first so…

Proficiency, Mountains unlocked.
You are Agile, so Scout feats start at 2 Grasp.
Scout, Climb unlocked at 2/6 Grasp.
12 Points of Advancement available.

Put them in Climb!

Scout, Climb 2/6 secured. 8 Points remaining.
You have a 1st Scout Feat.
Scout advances to Level 1. 3 Feats required to reach
Level 2.
Select a Proficiency.

Forest, obviously.

Select a 2nd Scout Feat to unlock?

His Tempter brought up a vision of a massive shard of slate with a tree scratched onto the surface. Along the branches, little moving stick figures performed various outdoors actions.

I just want to be able to make it to the floor of the Untrodden Valley.

Climb +1 unlocked at 2/6 Grasp.

Fine, now put what's left into it.

Climb +1 secured. 4 points remaining.

Looking at the stick figures, he realised that he had the option to move very fast indeed for short climbs.

Spider Climb unlocked at 2/6 Grasp.
Spider Climb advanced to 5/6 Grasp. 0 Points
remaining.
Potestas reset and boosted.
Vitality reset. Wound negated.

It was as if somebody had driven a rusty nail into his injured ankle and then yanked it out. Then the pain was gone and time seemed to be restarting.

You are: Torstag, Human Warlock, Youth, Agile,
Empathic, Cautious, Marked.
Potestas 6/3. Will 1.
Vitality 3. Toughness 1.
Vocations:
Cleric 1 (Learned): Meditation, Repel Shade 2/6.
Warlord 0: Tea Drinking 3/6.
Scout 1 (Mountains, Forest): Climb +1, Spider Climb
5/6.
Various General Skills.
Form 5.

Ingar appeared from behind a column that should have been too slender to hide him. "Over here!"

Torstag sprinted over then followed Ingar through the stone forest towards the outer edge.

The columns ended and there was the narrow stone parapet and beyond that the long drop through the clouds to the floor of the Untrodden Valley.

Torstag stared down at the sea of white fluff. The soles of his feet tingled. "Trapped!"

"We were already trapped," said Ingar.

"So where do we go?" asked Torstag. "No…you can't be serious."

"It only *looks* like a sheer cliff face," said Ingar. "We can take it slowly. Your Form is five. I hope you took a Climbing feat?"

"What?" Then Torstag remembered what he'd done. "I don't know what you're talking about."

"You surged. I saw it."

"Um," said Torstag.

The hollow barking came closer.

"Fuck," said Ingar. "Okay. Have it your way." He swung a leg over the parapet and started to climb down the outside.

Torstag's toes curled as if they could somehow grip the rock better. He leaned over the side. Ingar was on a ledge, a narrow one. Far below, cloud flowed down the Untrodden Valley like an overeager glacier.

Ingar grinned up at him. "Come on in," he said above the hiss of the wind. "The gazillion foot drop is lovely."

The hollow dog barked. Somebody ordered, "This way!"

29

"Damn." Limbs quivering Torstag clambered up to straddle the low parapet wall separating the Stone Grove from the abyss. He stretched his newly healed right foot and found a ledge. He swung his left out over the parapet wall to join it.

CHAPTER 5: GRONCHARD THE FLAYER

A long, shrill scream issued from the Arboretum.

Gronchard the Flayer sat up in bed. "What time is it?"

His attendant answered in measured tones, "An hour after dawn, Divinity."

The screaming continued.

"Have they *no* consideration?"

Gronchard huddled under the covers, pulled the pillow over his ears.

The screaming abruptly stopped. The Flying Tooth Garden heaved like a ship on a light swell.

Flying Tooth Garden fully sated. Ready to translocate. 4 of 4 translocations available.

Gronchard gave in to his youthful humours, shoved back the silken coverlet and rolled out of bed.

The balcony looked out over the rippling greenery of the Shrubbery.

The Flying Tooth Garden was currently located several hundred feet over the main temple complex of the Plains of Hope, a featureless expanse of fields and dutifully fecund peasants, whose tribute kept the shrubs fed for months at a time. Above the artificial horizon of the disk's edge, there was only blue sky. Today, anything seemed possible.

"Angelica!" declared Gronchard. "I *will* find you this time!"

But that was his youthful body speaking. His old soul knew that saying a thing did not make it so, even for a God. A knot formed in his stomach. A familiar headache settled in as his attendants garbed him in golden raiment and seated him in his litter.

Four broad-shouldered eunuchs carried him through the streets of Paradise. The Seraphim chanted and clashed their finger cymbals. The laity sang hymns. The din made his head hurt worse, but it was only that; a din. His people were just going through the motions.

Form 1. Performing Cynosure at level 5.

That wouldn't do.

Using Charismatic Presence +3, cost 1 Potestas. 5 of 6 remaining.
Result = 5 (Performance) +5 (Charismatic Presence) +1 (Luck) -2 (Average Will) = 9
Effect = Enthusiastic Response.

The chanting and singing took on a new vigour.
Gronchard focussed himself.

New Form 2. Cost 1 Potestas, 4 of 6 remaining.

Now he was ready.

Using Feed on Adulation, cost 1 Potestas. 3 of 6 remaining.
Result = 5 (Performance) +1 (Luck) -5 (Challenge) = 1.
Effect = 6 (Result) +5 (Hundreds) = 6.
Potestas now 9 of 6.

The headache faded. The world became more vivid. The litter passed through the gates of the Temple of Vision. The noise of the crowd faded. Now Gronchard perceived every carving, every gem, as if examining it under a magnifying glass, but all at once.

Saint Prescience waited before the bronzed doors of the Sanctuary. "Divinity!" The attendant priests prostrated themselves, but as befitted his status, the Saint merely bowed so deeply that his elderly Angel had to flap its leathery wings to maintain its shoulder perch. "Divinity, the fires are prepared. Visions of your beloved Sacred Angelica await!"

Gronchard found he had no urge to get down from his litter. "I tire of the heartbreak."

Saint Prescience flapped his hands. "But Divinity," he wheezed, "the omens are encouraging."

"They always are encouraging," said Gronchard, "and yet I no longer see my Angelica."

"A low probability event, Divinity..." began Saint Prescience.

"I know," said Gronchard, then realised he did not. The worst part of being an Immortal was the *memory* of dead memories that had yet to return.

"Go on, remind Me," said Gronchard.

The old man inhaled wetly. "A low probability event, Divinity, may be unlikely on any given day, but still virtually inevitable over the course of several days."

"Or, several years," said Gronchard, feeling the knot returning to his gut. He sighed. He had not seen Angelica since her Vessel had grown in her power and learned to detect and resist his scrying. She did not inhabit the body he remembered, but she was still *his* true love and visiting the Immaculate Hall of the Holy Concubines was not the same without first beholding her current vessel. He blinked back an un-godlike tear.

Saint Prescience wobbled closer to the litter. "The Divinity is unwell! Send for Saint Hale."

A page scurried off.

"It's nothing," said Gronchard, painfully aware of the adolescent crackle in his voice. "*You*—go after him and countermand that order."

As a second page sprinted off, Gronchard said, "The noise of the tributes kept me awake last night, that is all."

"Those shrubs!" Saint Prescience chortled. "They are never so hungry that they won't insist on having their fun, eh, Divinity?"

"Remembrancer," said Gronchard, "note that sacrifices will in future be bound or lamed before being fed to the plants. That should make things shorter."

The Divine Remembrancer scribbled on his tablet.

Saint Prescience shook his head, making his jowls flap. "Oh no no no. You tried that before, Divinity. The shrubs demand to play before they feed, and if they don't feed, the Flying Tooth Garden goes nowhere."

Gronchard bit back a retort. The fat old man was forever remind-ing him that he had served Gronchard in his last prime, and during the dotage before that. Saint Prescience had certainly been a welcome face during the post-flaying disorientation, but now he was becoming irksome. One day the old retainers would outlive their usefulness.

"Well let us get this over with," said Gronchard, stepping down from his litter.

Saint Prescience gave the signal. A gong sounded and the great bronze doors swung open, letting out a cloud of eye-watering incense.

Gronchard left behind his attendants except for the Saint and paced through pink-tinged wreaths. Deep in the interior hung a great orb.

"Show me Angelica."

Using Scrying Oracle. 3rd Circle Enchanted Item. Cost 6 Potestas, 3 of 6 remaining.

The distorted incense clouds swirled across the surface of the orb. Gronchard's heart rose. He took a step closer.

Now the clouds parted to reveal a dimly lit hall. Its windows cast bars of light over faded frescos representing a battle that must have seemed significant to the mortal who had commissioned it.

"Nothing!" said Gronchard. "Where is she?"

"Do not be downhearted, Divinity," said Saint Prescience. "The battle scene may be indicative. The angle and quality of the sunlight suggests that it is late afternoon in the Realm under observation. This considerably narrows the possible location."

Gronchard looked down at his boots. He was standing on the mo-saic face of one of his past vessels. He ground his heel on it, punishing himself for having let Angelica slip through his fingers all those incar-nations ago. "Possible location of what?"

"The Holy Angelica, Divinity."

"Yes," said Gronchard, voice shrilling embarrassingly, "but. My. Angelica. Is. Not. There."

Saint Prescience turned and seemed to see Gronchard properly for the first time. He stammered. "F…forgive me Divinity, but the orb may be displaying the Shell's point of view."

Gronchard bore down on his Saint. "If that's her point of view, then, Where. Is. My. Angelica?"

Saint Prescience paled. "I…she…the Shell as it were may be visualising this scene…"

The view shifted to show the room's floor.

"Terracotta tiles," said the Saint.

"What of it?" said Gronchard. "Look!"

A big circle was marked out in salt, with little clay figures guarding each of the four quarters and a small woven carpet in the middle.

Wizardry. Ritual. 2nd Circle Spell.

And a girl stepped *down* into it.

Step Between.

Gaunt, mousey brown hair caught up in a thong; this vessel was not the sweet blond angel he remembered…but somewhere in there *was* Angelica. His Angelica.

The vessel sank to her knees, then huddled on the rug as if exhausted by the spell.

Gronchard chewed his lower lip, thinking. Her state meant that she was powerful but not so powerful that the 5 Potestas required by a 2nd circle spell was insignificant to her.

"Her Potestas must be low," mused Saint Prescience. "Which is why she has not detected the scrying."

"Yes, yes," said Gronchard. He leaned closer to the Orb and whispered. "Where have you been my love?"

"Divinity, she cannot hear you," said Saint Prescience.

"I know that," snapped Gronchard. "But where has she been? She has just Stepped Between. Since we can see the apparatus of her Ritual, it follows that she has just completed the return leg of a journey. What does her vessel plan?"

"The Orb shows only what the etheric currents bring, Divinity."

"Leave us," said Gronchard, "I wish at least to be alone with my love."

"Divinity." The Saint bowed and slipped away.

Angelica's vessel didn't *do* anything other than doze on the rug until the vision faded.

It was more enough for Gronchard, however. Just seeing her brought back dead memories. There would be no need for a visit to the Immaculate Hall.

When he finally emerged into the fresh air, he was unsteady on his feet. He clambered into his litter. As the slaves lifted it, Saint Prescience wobbled into the courtyard.

"Divinity! Divinity!" cried the Saint. "We have her!"

Gronchard blinked. Once again, his heart rose. "What?"

"Divinity!" The fat old man rippled with excitement. "Terracotta floor tiles! Late afternoon! Images of a battle showing a mighty sword wielding champion in lamellar! She can only be in the Yinksi Republic."

Gronchard clenched his fists. He wanted to believe so badly that it hurt. "Or some other Realm, far, far away and not in your records."

"But the omens were promising today, Divinity," said Saint Prescience. "The City of Yinkesia is a mere five translocations away."

Gronchard shook his head. Judging by the emptiness of the hall, the Shell had no plans to settle down in that place. He was not going to risk running out of sacrifices during some ill-planned foray outside his Magisterium only to find she wasn't there anyway. He had a far better plan. "Take me to the Temple of Omnipresence! Quickly!"

Chapter 6: Over the Edge!

Using Scout, Spider Climb 5/6, cost 1 Potestas, 5 of 3 Potestas remaining.

Below Torstag, the rock face changed without changing.

It was like that moment as a child when he discovered he could read the inscriptions in the ruined temple that made up one wall of his castle's enclosure.

That had been, he realised, shortly before the Grey Cortège harvested him.

Now he could see every handhold, every ledge, all the way down to where the cliffs plunged into the ocean of clouds. If he fell, how *long* would he fall for?

You are Cautious.
Will 1 negated. You have issue Cowardice with 1/6 Hardening.

Ingar had wedged himself in a nook between a projecting shard of rock and the main cliff face.

Torstag told himself, "If I fall, I'll reincarnate."

Wrestling with Cowardice 1/6, cost 2 Potestas, 4 of 3 remaining.

What was that?

Wrestling with Cowardice 1/6, cost 2 Potestas, 4 of 3 remaining.

I meant, what were the odds? Tell me the odds.

Potestas loss overcomes Will 2.
You have Hindrance "Nerves".

Heart hammering in his ears, foothold by foothold, he lowered himself over the void while the wind made his robe ripple and flap.

His right foot slipped, scraping the top of his toes, then snagged another ledge. He brought his other foot down, and shifted his weight to it, and suddenly he was moving across the rock face as easily as if he were strolling.

He slid into the notch beside Ingar. Only then did his fingers and toes decide to uncurl.

"Spider Climb, eh?" said Ingar. "Show off."

Torstag closed his eyes and finally exhaled.

Current Form 5. Performing Scout at level 6.
Result = 6 (Performance) +2 (Feat) -1 (Luck) -2 ("Nerves") -4 (Challenge) = 1.
Effect = Success.
2 points of Vitality used.
Toughness 1 surpassed exceeded.
Condition "Stunned". Form 0. No Feats possible.
1 of 3 Vitality remaining.

"Are you okay?"

"Um…" said Torstag. "I…"

But his Tempter hadn't finished:

Scout, Spider Climb advances to 6/6 Grasp and is secured.
You have secured a 3rd Scout Feat.
Scout advances to Level 2.
Select a new Scout Proficiency.

Different environments whirled across Torstag's mind's eye. He thought of the girl's quest and picked the obvious one.

New Scout Proficiency, Jungle.
You have Levelled Up.
Level Up Surge.
8 Points of Grasp Advancement available.
Select a Vocation.
Scout.
Unlock a 4th Scout Feat.

Torstag dithered between Forage and Stalk, but then realised his immediate future might feature some sneaking around.

Scout, Stalk unlocked at 2/6 Grasp.
Advance or select a different Vocation?

Once he had escaped the monastery, he would need to be able to defend himself.

Warrior.

The images spiralled into nothingness then bloomed into a tree...the drawing of a tree on parchment. It bore the legend WARRIOR FEATS in several languages and more than one script, including something that looked like ochre hand prints. It was laid out much like the treasured genealogies in his family's small library—assuming the castle still stood, of course. However, where each coat-of-arms should have hung, a moving image of a warrior bestrode the parchment, smiting, breaking, slashing, goring, throwing and otherwise doing violence to one or more shadowy figures. Heads and limbs flew off, reattached, flew off again. Bones crunched, skulls cracked...

Vocation "Warrior" unlocked at Level 0. 1 Feat
required to advance to Level 1.
You may only use Warrior Feats when wielding
weapons in which you have a Proficiency.
Select a Proficiency?

A variety of weapons leaned or hung from the main trunk of the tree, among them a familiar sword and shield, a longsword, a poleaxe and a spear—all weapons he had started training with scant weeks before the Grey Cortège harvested him. There were also more unfamiliar weapons like chain maces, disk flails and whip swords...something to explore later.

Torstag's fingers curled. He'd always been drawn to the longswords in the castle armoury, especially the larger variants like his grandfather's old greatsword and his brother's new two-handed sword.

But the practical answer was obvious.

Proficiency, Brawling unlocked.

Further up the tree, warriors plied a variety of weapons, each illustrating a feat with names ranging from the evocative, like "Squinter", through to the descriptive, like "Thwart Strike".

Most of them seemed to need a weapon.

Then he spotted "Wrath Strike". Judging from the little figures endlessly punching, hacking, knifing, and bludgeoning opponents into the ground, it did exactly what the name implied. Better yet, it would give him access to four more strikes, plus Feats that let him destroy shields and weapons once he did have a weapon proficiency.

He clenched his fist. *Let's have that!*

You are Agile, so Warrior feats start at 2 Grasp.
Warrior, Wrath Strike unlocked at 2/6 Grasp and secured. 4 Points remaining.
You have 1 Warrior Feat. Warrior advances to Level 1. 3 Feats required to advance to Level 2.
Select a Proficiency.

He cast his eye over the Proficiency branch.

Once again the longsword called to him. However, what was he realistically going to get his hands on?

Probably not a real weapon. Perhaps a club, or a hammer.

There were military versions of both of those hanging next to a long war knife and a single-handed sword.

Proficiency, Sidearm unlocked.
Select a second Warrior Feat to unlock.

How about just hitting things even harder?

Warrior, Wrath Strike +1 unlocked at 2/6 Grasp

Put the points on that.

Warrior, Wrath Strike +1 secured. 0 Points remaining.
Select a 3rd Warrior Feat to unlock.

Split Shield looked…satisfying.

Warrior, Split Shield unlocked at 2/6 Grasp.

The tree faded. His muscles ached, as if he was having late growing pains.

Potestas reset and boosted. Hindrances cleared.
Vitality reset.
You are: Torstag, Human Warlock, Youth, Agile,
Empathic, Cautious, Marked.
Potestas 8/4. Will 2. Cowardice 1/6.
Vitality 3. Toughness 1.
Vocations:
Cleric 1 (Learned): Meditation, Repel Shade 2/6.
Warlord 0 Tea Drinking 2/6.
Warrior 1 (Brawl, Sidearm): Wrath Strike +1, Split
Shield 2/6
Scout 2 (Mountains, Forest, Jungle): Climb +1, Spider
Climb, Stalk 2/6
Various General Skills.
Form 5.

Torstag felt stronger, tougher. He squared his jaw and somehow that brought back memories of his brother addressing his retainers before riding out that last time.

Ingar repeated. "Are you okay?"

Torstag flushed. "Another Surge."

Ingar laughed. "Nothing to be ashamed of! Did you Level Up?"

Torstag nodded. "What does it mean?"

"You had a new vocation high score. Fuck me!" Ingar's freckled face split into a wide grin. "It's such a relief to talk about all this."

"How do I know how to do all this?"

"You remembered, of course."

"I don't remember climbing a cliff, ever," said Torstag. "And I just moved across that cliff face like I was walking to morning prayers."

"You remembered from past incarnations, you fuckwit. *Dead* memories!"

41

"Gods!" Torstag sat in silence watching the flowing cloud beneath his feet.

A hawk flew past below the promontory.

Ingar glanced up at the sky. "Looks like rain. We wait until that drives off the monks, then climb back up."

Torstag looked across the valley to the other mountain wall. It seemed closer now. "This is the first time I've been outside the boundaries of the monastery.

"How does you feel?"

Torstag furrowed his brow. "Like my own man...for real?"

"Fucking amazing, eh?" said Ingar. "When you start listening to your Tempter. You should see what else I can do!"

Torstag's heart lurched. "Oh Gods!" he said. "I'll be hollowed out!" He took a breath and wedged his fingers into a crack in the rock. "Are *you* hollowed out?"

"Out of here, for sure," said Ingar.

Torstag's voice rose. "Are you hollowed out?"

"This is why I stayed schtum before! I knew you'd freak out."

"I am not freaking out," said Torstag. "Answer the damn question."

"What does that even mean?" said Ingar.

"I want to be my own man," said Torstag, "not some dead man's meat puppet."

"I'm still me, just better at it." Ingar grinned. "Now, fuck that for a pile of metaphysical horse-shit. We can escape together now. That's the point."

"We could get caught," said Torstag.

"We're already caught."

"The punishment..." began Torstag.

"I don't care any more," said Ingar. "Not after seeing that girl and knowing what I'm missing—oh, what about the girl?"

Torstag frowned and stared over the edge. Far, far below, the white clouds foamed over the floor of the Untrodden Valley.

"Well?" prompted Ingar. "Did she...?"

"She told me that I was her protector in past incarnations. That I had to help her with her quest, and that when I was ready to escape, I should go and visit my past selves in the Catacombs of Hesitation."

"Oh," said Ingar. "That's...*cryptic*? I need to think about that. What else?"

"She gave me a cup of tea."

"I hope that was more exciting than it sounds," said Ingar. "Because that's all you'll have to remember as you grow old and wrinkly on this mountainside. I'm off to…"

"…fuck all the women, drink all the beer," said Torstag. "I know."

"Perhaps they'll let you tend the Temple of Gronchard," said Ingar. "There's a very nice statue of a lady there."

"I'll escape with you," said Torstag. "I can climb now."

"At last!" said Ingar. "Look." He squirmed and twisted in the nook, cheerfully dangling one foot over the abyss.

"Careful!" gasped Torstag.

"Wimp!" said Ingar. He thrust his hand into a crack in the cliff and pulled out a leather bag. He placed it carefully in his lap then extracted an everlight on a pendant and a small leather-bound book. He flipped it open. "Here. I was going to write up a clean copy for you when you came round but…well, fuck it."

Torstag peered at the page. It had lots crossing out, and what looked like a prurient drawing was bleeding through from the other side. "Warlocks?"

"That's what we are." Ingar braced his arm to hold the everlight steady. "Read it while I think about what the girl said."

NOTES ON BEING A WARLOCK

We're warlocks. We have a voice in our heads called a Tempter and it thinks we're a bag of fucking numbers. (Seriously, Numbers For Everything.)

We can remember abilities from previous incarnations. Our bodies change to catch up, which can hurt ~~like fuck~~. Think a year of growing pains in a few seconds. ~~Seriously.~~

NUMBERS FOR ABILITIES

We have VOCATIONS like "Burglar", "Warrior" or "Artist" They have Levels to say how good we are, like Burglar 1 is pretty basic. Burglar 6 looks to be top professional.

Vocations are built of FEATS, which help (add +2) when doing stuff like climbing or hiding. You don't need the feat to do the thing, but it's handy. (These feats have boring names like "Climb" and "Hide".) Feats cost Potestas to use, which is kind of power and focus rolled into one. (See below)

The better you know a Feat, the less Potestas it costs.

Learn enough feats and your Vocation goes up a level. Your top Vocation gives your Level. When that goes up, it's called Levelling Up and you get a Surge.

There are also General Skills that work like Feats but don't have a Vocation.

Some of this stuff is "Learned" the hard way, not remembered.

~~MORE FUCKING~~ NUMBERS FOR ~~BASICS WHO WE ARE~~ MIND & BODY

We have a LEVEL, that's our top vocation score. When that goes up, it's called Levelling Up and you get a Surge.

We have other stuff too:

VITALITY is ~~hit p how much how tough~~ pretty much what it sounds like. (Vitality = 2 + Half Level)

TOUGHNESS is how quickly we recover Vitality (Toughness = Half Vitality (rounded down)). It seems to also tell us how much of a battering we can take before we're screwed.

POTESTAS is kind of power and focus rolled into one. We burn it using Feats, but also it measures our Situational Awareness (don't ask me how I know that term). (Vitality = 2 + Level)

WILL is how quickly we recover Potestas. (Will = Half Maximum Potestas (rounded down)). Sometimes it's tested, e.g. to avoid freaking out.

FORM that's the serious biggy. It's how on the ball we are right now. Seems to range from 0 through to 4. You can grit your teeth and try to improve your form, but that costs a Potestas and doesn't always go your way.

Actual PERFORMANCE is Form + Vocation, so on a good day we can be ~~a fuck of~~ a lot better than we ought to be.

Torstag turned the page, blushed at what he saw. "Is that *it*?"

"For now."

They sat in silence. The wind picked up, bringing with it stinging rain, turning the cliffs black and shiny.

Ingar leaned closer. "I've thought about it."

"Thought about what?"

"What the girl said, you idiot," said Ingar.

"What *did* she say?" asked Torstag.

"She has an escape plan for us," said Ingar. "Obviously."

"No," said Torstag.

"How can it *not* be an escape plan?" said Ingar.

"No, as in I won't do it. I don't want to be a hollowed out dead man's puppet. And, I don't want to escape only to swap masters. I am my own man."

Ingar grinned. "So we're climbing down several thousand feet of cliffs, then escape through a wilderness of unknown type, and doing so while the monks are trying to catch us?"

"That's your damned plan," said Torstag.

"It was a stupid plan. I always knew that," said Ingar. "Ask your Tempter."

Torstag looked over the side of the promontory to rock face.

Performing Scout at level 7.

He had a memory of seeing the valley floor on a clear day.

The cliffs are a level 4 challenge and would take 2 Watches to descend, including rests, raising the total Challenge to 8. 4 Fatigue would be incurred, resulting in 4 Vitality loss.

He opened his eyes. "It's doable!"

Ingar shook his head. "Two watches is most of daylight hours, or all night. And 4 Fatigue. We wouldn't be able to move once we got to the bottom."

Torstag frowned.

Fatigue recovers at Toughness points per watch.

"We'll just have to toughen up first," said Torstag.

"That *was* my plan," said Ingar. "But two watches…do you think perhaps the Monks might be waiting for us at the bottom?"

Torstag shrugged. "Then we'll fight them!"

"Really?" said Ingar. "That is insane."

"Ha!", said Torstag. His brow furrowed. "Yes, it is. But then *your* plan is to somehow break into the no-doubt heavily guarded Catacombs of Hesitation and browse the mummies to find our past selves and somehow that will get us safely out of here? Somehow. Somehow. Somehow."

"If the girl has a plan, then it'll cover outrunning the monks."

"*If!*"

Unlock Warlord, Command Presence?

Torstag saw himself bringing a block of pikemen to attention, making them hold their ground as arrows winnowed their ranks and the sand ran red.

No! I am not ordering my only friend around.

"Torstag," said Ingar. "Learning to climb is dangerous. The skills we'd need for the catacombs—I don't know? Sneaking, opening locked doors—will be much safer to get the hang of."

"Half an hour ago you were insanely brave," said Torstag.

"Yes," said Ingar. "I had to be because my escape plan *was* insane. This is better."

"I don't want to end up enslaved by some random girl," said Torstag.

"I can think of worse fates," said Ingar, cocking his head at the monastery parapet above them. "Anyway, we can use her plan and do a runner. You don't *have* to stick around."

Torstag chewed his lip. "That seems…dishonourable."

"Just a couple of hours ago, *you* were letting an old fucker beat you with fucking stick," said Ingar. "You don't *have* any honour. Besides, what about me? I'm your actual friend."

"Damn," said Torstag. He thought for a moment. "But we can make the climbing plan work. We just have to…" A word came to him "…level up."

Ingar shook his head. "No. Not when there's a safer way."

"If you want safe," said Torstag, "then let's stick to becoming priests."

"Five fucking years," said Ingar. "And they'll probably send us to different temples…did you think of that?"

Torstag grimaced. "I…Just no. I can't."

"Well fuck you Torstag," said Ingar, "and fuck the goat you rode in on." He rose and climbed back up to the parapet leaving Torstag alone on the spur of rock projecting out into the void.

For some reason the grey-white clouds rolling past below reminded him of the girl's skin.

"No."

Chapter 7: A Visit to the Tasset and Pauldron

An oddly distorted fanfare rang out over the din of the taproom of the Tasset and Pauldron. A voice boomed, "Trophimus!"

The wench screamed and sprang from Trophimus's lap, spilling his ale. She pointed past him and screamed for a second time, then turned and fled for the door.

Trophimus leapt to his feet, reached for his dagger as he turned.

He found his business partner Cerdic already standing. "Fucking warlocks. Look what we have here."

The translucent figure of a well-dressed youth towered over the tavern's clientèle, outsized head just short of the ceiling beams.

"I didn't uncover the orb," said Trophimus.

"Apparently that makes fuck all difference," said Cerdic.

"Trophimus!" repeated the apparition.

The other drinkers suddenly started moving. They yelled and shoved their way through the door, leaving the two men alone with the apparition.

"Shit, Gronchard," said Cerdic, "did you have to do that?"

The young demigod drew himself up so that his head almost touched the ceiling. He glowered and Trophimus felt Gronchard's displeasure they way you feel a north wind. "Mortals!" boomed the divine youth. "You will address me as Divinity or Master!"

Trophimus bowed his head. "Yes, Master." How could they have been so disrespectful?

"Silence!" said Gronchard. "You will proceed to Yinkesia and pick up the trail of the Sacred Angelica."

"Yes, Master. But…"

"Do you still have the lodebone?"

"Yes Master," said Trophimus. "Safe in my coin purse."

Gronchard's face purpled. "In your purse?" he shrieked "The relic of my Angelica jostling with profane coins? You are keeping my true love's thigh bone with your petty cash?"

"Um. Yes, Master." Trophimus flushed. "I'll fix it right away. Find some more um respectful bag or container."

Cerdic nudged him in the ribs. "What the fuck, Tro? He's diddling with your mind."

A flash of rage blew away Trophimus' obeisance. Who *was* this kid to force him to abase himself like this? Just another warlock with a bag of magic tricks.

"Was there something else, Master?" asked Cerdic.

"Make haste and you shall be doubly rewarded." Gronchard raised his arms, which was the usual signal that he was about to depart.

"Master, wait!" said Trophimus.

Gronchard sighed. "What is it?"

Trophimus took a step forward. "Master, we need to know more about her."

"I am a God! Do you take Me for some kind of messenger!"

"No, Master." Trophimus bowed his head to hid his smirk. "I take you for a God who wishes to restore his consort to his side. There may be just one chance to 'rescue' her."

The apparition stared at him.

Trophimus discretely bent his knees, ready to dodge left or right—not that it was likely to help if the demigod started tossing around magic.

Five long heartbeats later, the apparition spoke. "Very well, Trophimus." The kid folded his skinny arms. "The Shell has suc-ceeded in appropriating some of Angelica's accomplishments, mean-ing she has at least some wizardly powers."

"A wizard," said Cerdic. He shook his head. "Wizards cost extra."

"Your greed will be the death of you, mortal," said Gronchard.

Cerdic shrugged. "Sure, *Master*, but then you don't get your An-gelica back."

Trophimus held up a hand. "Be reasonable, Master. We'll need to hire a bigger team."

"She is only a wizard!" said Gronchard. "She is not a goeticist with fireballs at her command, nor a necromancer with undead servants. At worst she can make your pants fall down." He smirked.

"Yes," said Cerdic. "But wizards can be tricky bastards. Slippery. We need more people. You're a fucking God, for crying out loud. You're good for the money."

"Very well," said Gronchard. He named a very large sum indeed.

"Master," chorused Trophimus and his comrade, both bowing deeply.

"Wait," said Gronchard. "I also require discretion. This blasphemous episode must be erased."

"Of course, Master," said Trophimus, jerking his head to signal his partner to be silence. "We shall manage."

Gronchard's spectre simply vanished.

Trophimus stared at the empty space, mind racing.

"We're fucking screwed," said Cerdic. "Did you hear that? Erased? How do you erase a blasphemous episode? You erase the fucking people involved. I bet the bastard was always going to do that."

Trophimus laughed. "Don't you see? We've finally got some leverage over him."

"You're talking shit. We're dead. We should just leg it down the nearest portal, and the one after that and keep going till we reach the Edge of the Ten Thousand Realms."

"No," said Trophimus. "If we tell everybody about his Sacred Angelica…"

"Who's going to believe that? A warlock god running around after some totty for a thousand years?"

"Nobody, unless he *erases* us. And the more people we hire, the more people he'll have to erase, the more it will confirm the story."

"Ten or so should do it," said Cerdic.

"Yep," said Trophimus. "Any more and we'll be tripping over ourselves. Wizard or not, it's just one girl."

Chapter 8: Axe Girl and the Kid

"No," said Axe Girl. She frowned, making her lined forehead runkle. "I've retired." She set down her gilded wine cup and flexed scarred fingers. "I've got my nephew to think about now."

"You're literally whoring him to the wives of half the city's Patricians," said Trophimus.

"And the Patricians themselves," said Axe Girl. "It's a good career. That plus my savings…" She waved a meaty hand around the parlour of her town house. "It's nice to sleep in the same bed every night and know that's not going to change. It's nice not to spend my life on a bloody horse chasing runaway slaves and defaulting peasants."

"Fuck that for a game of poke the fish!" said Cerdic. "This is *real* money."

An upper class voice interrupted them. "Did somebody say *real* money?" A man in his early prime swaggered in through the door. He was tall, with a well-trimmed beard and a ridiculous red codpiece. Trophimus had seen the type before; the by-blow of some patrician household living off a small remittance, too classy to work, too illegitimate to use his family connections to find a better living.

"This your latest piece of rough, eh Axe Girl?" said Cerdic. "Bit young for you."

Axe Girl blushed and her scarred cheeks actually dimpled. She got to her feet. "Actually, this is my husband, Dekan."

Trophimus stood and held out his hand. "Trophimus and Cerdic. Pleased to meet you, sir. You're a braver man than the two of us put together."

Dekan grinned. "Oh, I've learned to go with the flow with my Alice. No courage required."

Axe Girl swatted his rump. "Not in front of other people."

They both giggled like lovestruck youngsters.

Trophimus glanced at Cerdic.

Cerdic gave a little nod.

"Sir," said Trophimus. "We are old bounty hunting colleagues, and we have come to offer your lady a share in a particularly rich prize."

"Sacred Angelica, consort of Gronchard the Flayer, God of the Flying Tooth Garden?" said Dekan. "I heard." He gestured for them to sit. The maid poured more wine and they made small talk about weddings and the couple's plans for the town house's garden.

Eventually Dekan leaned back in his chair. "So, messirs, tell us about this bounty."

"A tragic story," said Trophimus. "And a chance to reunite true lovers separated by time."

"And make a shitload of money," said Cerdic. He mentioned what Axe Girl's share would be.

"I'm retired," said Axe Girl. "I quit while I was not dead."

"It's just one girl," said Trophimus.

"Then why are you and Cerdic recruiting?"

"She's a wizard," said Cerdic. "They're slippery, that's all."

"It doesn't *sound* very dangerous," said Dekan. "Money like that would buy us an estate, a small one, yes, but we'd be proper gentry."

"No," said Axe Girl.

"You'd be Lady Axe. Or Axe Lady. Or Lady Alice of the Axe."

"No."

"Take me, messirs," said Dekan. He flexed his fingers. "I know how to use a blade. I've killed my man before."

"No!" hissed Axe Girl.

"For us," hissed Dekan.

"No, sir," said Cerdic. He held up his hand to forestall objections and managed to speak without swearing. "I'm sure you can fight one-on-on, but you have no experience of teamwork."

"Actually, *yes*," said Trophimus, with a wink only his partner could see.

"Shit, Dekan," said Axe Girl. "You'll get killed and I'll be alone."

"Then come and keep him safe," said Trophimus. "Come on, Axe, it will be like old times."

Axe Girl sighed.

"Just one itsybitsy fucking wizard girl," said Cerdic.

"Count me in." A long-haired youth, not much more than a kid, emerged from the back room. He was beautifully groomed and wearing a white silk shirt open to show a smooth chest. He spoke with a drawl, whether from genuine lushness or affectation, Trophimus could not tell.

"Shit," said Axe Girl. "But you *like* being a Companion."

"Indeed," said the Kid, "but this sounds exciting. *Bounty hunting!*"

"No," said Axe Girl.

"If he's old enough to…put himself about, he's old enough to help out," said Trophimus. "But you'll have to make yourself useful, lad, tending the fire, fetching and carrying, acting as groom."

"Manly stuff! I shall positively enjoy roughing it." The Kid turned to Axe Girl. "And you can't stop me, Aunty. This is my chance to be a real man."

"Oh shit, shit shit," said Axe Girl. "Shit shit shit." She stopped to take a breath. "But three professionals and two newbies isn't enough."

"No it isn't," said Cerdic. "We're going to recruit another six professionals."

"She's a wizard," said Axe Girl. "Isn't she going to be impossible to track?"

Cerdic and Trophimus exchanged a nod. Trophimus extracted the lodebone from his purse and let it hang on its thread. It spun clockwise, then anticlockwise, then abruptly froze. "Made from her thighbone."

"That's sick!" said Axe Girl. She tilted her head and squinted. "But it is pointing to the North Portal."

"Exactly," said Trophimus. "It will do the navigating for us."

"A proper estate," said Dekan. "With a walled rose garden."

Axe Girl let out a long sigh that made her broad shoulders slump. "When are we setting off?"

CHAPTER 9: SEEING DEAD PEOPLE

"Torstag?" hissed Ingar, just audible over the slobbering groans of what had to be at least a dozen zombies.

A weight lifted from Torstag's shoulders. "Yes?" began Torstag, then broke off to cough. The stench of embalming fluid always got to the back of his throat. Somehow, an hour of meditation made him even more aware of the feeling.

Potestas 8 of 4. Meditation doubles the maximum attainable Potestas.

It was a month since the magical girl and this was the first time Ingar had spoken to him. "Go on," he hissed.

The weather had broken, ushering in the Winter. Now two dozen acolytes huddled together behind the chalk line at one end of the Practice Vault. Ingar and Torstag had the rope while Acolyte Hohen chanted a prayer to the Ineffable Resurrectionist and paced across the floor through the mob of zombies, which recoiled as he approached, then closed in once he had passed. The glare of the everlights cast multiple shadows, so Hohen was like a fat spider waddling out to battle.

Hohen made it to the middle of the floor. The dozen or so zombies—ethically sourced from legal executions, according to the Brothers, and thoroughly defanged—growled wetly as they shambled around him. They waved the stubs of their arms, but stayed well out of reach, like night things recoiling from a campfire in the midst of the Desert of Lenses.

Now where did I get that from? Torstag had never heard of the Desert of Lenses, let alone sat around a campfire with bearded warriors, boasting of past exploits and debating philosophy.

Ingar nudged him. "I've secured Stalk!"

"Great," said Torstag.

"I'm on Open Lock, now," hissed Ingar. "The girl's plan…"

The weight returned. "No," whispered Torstag. "I'm sorry…"

"Well fuck you too—"

The zombies emitted burbling roars.

Hohen had lost concentration. "Get me up!" he screamed. "Get me up."

Ingar and Torstag hauled on the rope, hank after hank. The pulleys squealed and Hohen—not a light young man—rose kicking above the slimy-fleshed mob. He'd hang there until one of the instructors went down to clear the way.

The zombies started trying to chew on his toes.

Hohen screamed and danced in the air. "I can't breathe! Get me down!"

"Imagine if there had been no safety rope," said Brother Neutrality. "If the zombies had teeth and hands."

The Acolytes exchanged glances.

"Acolyte Torstag," said the Brother. "Go and retrieve your classmate. Let's see if your performance improves under pressure."

"What?" blurted Torstag. "Without a safety rope?"

"Without a safety rope," confirmed the Brother. "Or are you feeling…*impure?*"

"No Brother," said Torstag.

Brother Neutrality gave him a look that set his most recent welts throbbing.

"I mean, yes Brother, right away, Brother."

He hurried down the steps and crossed the line of Blessed Salt.

The dozen zombies swung away from Hohen's feet and shambled toward Torstag.

"Get me down get me down!" yelled Hohen.

Unlock Necromancy?

His Tempter treated him to memories of graveyards and organ jars. "Hell no!" growled Torstag and started his chant: *"Ineffable Resurrectionist, who is mighty in Your Essence of Not Thereness…"*

Unlock Necromancy?

I already have four vocations. Shut up!

Up close, you could see that they had once been people. They were technically mummified zombies; they'd been allowed to decompose enough that the Soul had departed, leaving only the Shade. Only then had the Cortège morticians halted the process of decomposition. This rendered the skin a uniform wet leather, so that the puffy and bloated faces still looked human.

Here and there you could see how they'd died—noose tracks on a throat, a face missing a jawbone from a rising sword cut.

How did I know that?

Torstag wondered what state the body of his former self was in, whether it had wounds, or whether he had died peacefully. He certainly had had some adventurous past lives, judging from the skills his Tempter was dredging up.

He had a fleeting vision of a much older woman, crinkle-framed eyes as bright as any girl's, cheeks coloured, lips parted…

"Torstag!" yelled Ingar from behind him. "Look out!"

Torstag came back to the here and now. He'd stopped chanting.

The zombie of a kindly-looking man of middle years rocked closer, moving with surprising speed even as he leaked embalming fluid from what remained of his upper arms.

Unlock Warrior, Brawling, Body Slam or Companion, Formal Dancing?

Oiled bodies flashed across his memory, and pretty girls in flouncy dresses and sand and cheering crowds and cheerful music, bright chandeliers and—

—he tasted tea.

Something cold and soggy bumped his chest.

Torstag yelped and stumbled back. *"In Your Holy Absence, Your Divine Strength is Truly Manifest…"*

The Acolytes all started talking. Then the zombie groaned through toothless lips and shambled after him.

Torstag forced himself to close his eyes. He chanted harder. *"Both Inactive and Active and at once All Potent…"*

"Get me down get me down!" squealed Hohen.

Torstag visualised the Ineffable Resurrectionist, an absence of a presence, and drew the not-here into his not-hereness and chanted the prayer to the Unknowable Not-God—he didn't really understand the theology, but it had worked before.

Zombies hemmed him in. Slobber sprayed his face. The chemical smell became unbearable. His gorge rose. It became hard to breathe.

You are ritually impure. Supernatural Cleric Feats unavailable.

"What? How?"

Ingar bellowed, "Torstag! Fuck!"

Unlock Necromancy, Repel Shade?

"You win!" gasped Torstag.

Once again, he had the sensation of being out of time, riffling pages and inhaling knowledge like the scent of a musty book.

Necromancy unlocked at Level 0. 1 Feat required to advance to Level 1.
Select a Proficiency

There seemed to be several ways of doing Necromancy, some much slower than others. Torstag selected the speediest.

Necromancy Proficiency, Cantrip unlocked.
You are Empathic so Necromancy Feats start at 2 Grasp.
Necromancy, Repel Shade unlocked at 2/6 Grasp.
You may have 4 Vocations. Cleric vocation Abandoned. Supernatural Cleric feat lost. Meditation retained as a Skill.

Eight years of study gone just like that.

A zombie roared into his face, spattering him with embalming fluid.

Challenge = 2 (Zombies) +2 (Dozen) = 4

Enough! Begone!

Using Necromancy, Repel Shade 2/6 cost 3 Potestas,
5 of 4 Potestas remaining.
Form 2.
Performing Necromancy at Level 2.

Words that were not words came to him. The vault became ever so slightly fuzzier. The shadows seemed to want to rise up from the packed earth floor. There were also too many shadows.

Result = 2 (Performance) -1 (Luck) -4 (Challenge) = -3.
Effect = Failure.

The zombies pressed, their slimy cold tangible through his robes. The blood rushed in Torstag's ears. Panic clutched his vitals.
He shouted in his mind, *BEGONE, REALLY I MEAN IT.*

New Form 5. Cost 1 Potestas. 4 of 4 Potestas
remaining.
Performing Necromancy at level 4.
Using Repel Shade 2/6 cost 1 Potestas, 3 of 4
remaining.
Result = 5 (Performance) + 1 (Luck) -4 (Zombies) = 2.
Effect = Tentative Practical Response.
Repel Shade advances to 3/6 Grasp.

The pressure ceased. He opened his eyes and felt dizzy. The stench no longer seemed quite so bad. The zombies shambled backwards, leaving the floor clear except for the ghosts, of course.

The other acolytes cheered until Brother Neutrality silenced them.

"Um…*Thus Your Divine Manifest Potency is Vindicated,*" completed Torstag, as loudly as he could. Then he sang, "*As per the Book of Obedience.* "

The acolytes echoed him.

Wait a moment. Ghosts?

15 Zombies, retreating. 19 ghosts, haunting.

"Uh?"

But it was true.

Torstag counted nineteen ghosts dotted the floor of the Practice Vault. They were all robed as acolytes. Some were trying to repel zombies he couldn't see. Some just drifted around aimlessly. Yet more stood mutely amongst his living peers.

"I said, *thanks*, Torstag," stammered Hohen. Evidently, they'd managed to get him down.

"Any time," said Torstag. He frowned. "What's that thing?"

"What's what?"

"Oh nothing, my eyes are tired."

But his inner eye showed him a silken thread connecting Hohen's sternum to that of one of the ghosts, a similarly plump specimen who scurried up and down the vault as if something had gone very badly wrong.

Now Torstag knew what to look for, more silken threads linked some of the shades—for that's what he'd been taught ghosts were; not souls, but their left-behind shadows—to the living, including to Brother Neutrality, whose shade counterpart squatted on the floor rocking backwards and forward, endlessly soiling himself.

Torstag frowned. Was that how he wanted to be? Drawn back time after time to spend each incarnation rotting in this non-place?

The ghost of Brother Neutrality's avatar stared back at him with hollow eyes. The lips moved.

Torstag turned away.

Hohen's avatar leaned in and spoke earnestly, silently. Torstag could almost hear the words. *Cold...so cold...*

Unlock Necromancer, Channel Shade?

No!

Torstag shut his eyes against the dead and blundered toward the chalk safety line.

Ingar took his arm. "Are you all right, Torstag?"

Torstag opened his eyes. "Just a bit of a shock."

"Good," said Ingar. He turned away.

Slobbering snarls rose up behind them.

"Come on, the zombies are recovering."

Brother Neutrality stepped out of the way as they crossed the line of salt. "You were distracted, Acolyte," he said, and Torstag remembered the way he had plied the rod. "Were you speaking to your Tempter?"

"Oh no, Brother Neutrality," said Torstag. "I was caught up in religious ecstasy."

"Indeed." Brother Neutrality's eyes became unfocussed and he mumbled a prayer.

Cleric. Level 6.

A cold hand seemed to clutch his heart. If "Performing at Level 4" lent such insight from his Tempter, what could the monk discover about him?

How do you hide in plain sight?

Unlock Shade Cloak?

His Tempter seemed to want him to wrap one of the shades around himself. He shuddered but there was no choice.

> Unlocking second feat, Necromancer, Shade Cloak at
> 2/6 Grasp.
> Using Shade Cloak 2/6, cost 1 Potestas. 0 Potestas
> remaining.
> **Test of Will 2. Hindrance "Disquieted" shaken off.**

One of the ghostly acolytes drifted over to envelope him in coldness. Not just coldness, memories of feelings. Boredom. Sadness. A melancholy lust for another acolyte. Fear. Despair. More boredom, and the shadow memory of just standing there at letting the zombies crush him to death.

> **Result = 4 (Performance) +1 (Luck) -0 (Ghost) = 5.**
> **Effect = Several minutes concealment.**
> **Shade Cloak advances to 3/6 Grasp.**

The hairs on the back of Torstag's neck bristled. He shuddered and tensed in expectation of his Tempter once again offering him Channel Shade.

> You...

No! Really. NO!

> ...may only unlock up to 2 feats per Vocation at any
> one time.

Well he'd found one way to get his Tempter to stop pestering him: always have two Necromancer Feats on the go.

"Hmmm," said Brother Neutrality. "It seems you are progressing well toward Monkhood after all."

"Th…thank you, Brother Neutrality," stammered Torstag.

"No safety rope for you from now on. And you are almost ready for skeletons."

"Yes, Brother Neutrality," said Torstag, feeling sick. "Thank you, Brother Neutrality."

I'm buggered, he thought as he tramped down the cliff steps, passing through the ghosts of all the young men who had fallen or jumped into the abyss over the centuries.

There was, of course, a ghost in his bed.

Wrestling with Horror of the Despairing Dead 1/6,
cost 4 Potestas, -2 Remaining.
Potestas loss overcomes Will 2. You have Hindrance,
"Disquieted".
Potestas below 0. You have Hindrance "Upset".

Torstag sat on the dormitory's cold stone floor and wept until one of the Supervisors yelled at him to get into bed.

Chapter 10: A Lady Spelunker

The sea breeze plastered Millicent's heavy tweed skirt to her legs, making her fight to get close to the cliff edge. A seagull zoomed over her head, screeched loud enough to make her flinch.

She ducked, cursed, then pushed down her hat and surveyed the curve of the cliffs.

The sun was low somewhere behind grey clouds that blurred into the ocean to hide the horizon. Even so, visibility was good as far as the other end of the bay where she could make out the shard of rock—the "stack"—with the ruined tower on it. A wave splashed white at its base. A scattering of puffins fluttered and dived manically, as if flustered by the approach of dusk.

"No dragons," declared Millicent. She glanced around, but of course nobody was here to notice her talking to herself like the madwoman she probably was. "Mad *and* unlikeable," she declared, "and so, magnificently..." She raised her arms to the sky, "alone!"

Unlock Goeticist, Cantrips, Manifest?

"Silence!" Millicent checked her pocket watch. "I don't have time for you." She had perhaps half an hour before she needed to turn back for the entry portal. Even with her new-fangled "flashlight" it would not do to be blundering around here after dark...wherever *here* was.

Millicent raised her field glasses and dialled up the magnification. The ruin on the stack was round like the stub of a factory chimney, but made of unmortared slabs of stone. If the chart was correct, then those walls enclosed the next portal.

Mind you, she reflected, the chart also said *Here be Dragons*.

The stack hadn't quite detached itself from the cliffs. A natural arch remained. Millicent carefully traced the precarious path across the top. It dipped steeply from the clifftop, then rose equally steeply to where the ruins crowded onto the summit of the stone pillar.

Something big and black fluttered through her field of view. She looked for it over the top of the spyglass, but it was gone.

Perhaps a cormorant?

With a sigh, Millicent closed the glasses. She would need to return much earlier in the day to investigate further. If the Lady Spelunkers were going to use this portal, contractors would be required; men with cast-iron beams and chain railings. To justify that expenditure required that somebody verify that the tower portal opened onto a Realm *within* the Pale.

Of course, Millicent hadn't *really* verified the island she'd just tramped across. There were simply no natives to ask, and no real architecture to inspect for clues. However, the tower could have been a broch, and the landscape seemed vaguely familiar, so perhaps it was one of the northern Farm Isles? In any case, no natives meant no hazards, so…

Millicent frowned.

When had she become quite so blasé?

Probably, when she had set off from her lodgings in the dead of night.

"There's no reason why a woman in middle years cannot have an adventure," she declared.

Besides, discovering a new route like this was such a coupé! The Society of Lady Spelunkers would surely award her the Pathfinder of the Year Cup. In that context, secrecy made sense, didn't it?

Millicent fished the canary out of her shoulder bag and wound it up. It tweeted and flapped its tin wings, proof that factory-made goods worked here. Even if this were an unexplored Realm, it was still within the Pale, so that was fine, wasn't it?

Was it?

She would ponder that on her way back to the first portal.

64

Out to sea, a whale breeched and blew with a hollow snort. Oily black skin passed above the dark water like the great rubber-tired wheel of a traction engine.

One of her dream memories came to her; standing legs braced on the back of a whale as it wove between floating ice rafts.

Unlock Virago, Command Beast?

Millicent bellowed, "Silence!"

She blushed and looked around.

Perhaps it was time to take one of her pills?

The problem was that the pills would make her woozy, and woozy would just not do for what she had in mind.

Millicent frowned. Was the portal *truly* hidden amongst the ruins crowning that stack? Was it worth the risk?

She unrolled the chart and pressed it to a handy slab of granite.

Another gull soared up over the cliff edge and hovered in the on-shore wind.

Millicent used one hand to clamp the chart to the rock and the other hand to wave her hat at the bird. "Shoo! Off with you."

Unlock Virago, Intimidate Beasts?

"And off with *you* too!" This *really* was not the time for her Voice to disturb her sanity.

The gull screamed and dived away, leaving the chart safe from its droppings, and her head cold from going hatless. A pang of conscience interrupted Millicent's thoughts. Should she, a librarian after all, really be taking such a precious item out on her perilous adventures?

Why not? It had come to her by luck, tucked away in an antique desk, but it was *hers*, and carrying it felt right.

You are Self Hating.
Test of Will 3. You have resisted acquiring an Issue.

"How very nice of you to say that. I really do not want to waste more time and money on more sessions with Dr Joyous. Now, *go back to being repressed!*"

Still with one hand on the chart, she slipped on her reading glasses.

The parchment was covered in dozens of little circular maps, all webbed together by portal lines. The inner portals connected to a crudely-drawn central crown. This next portal would take her to within two portals of that prize, whatever it was. She could at least take a quick look before giving up.

Just how certain was she?

The tiny map of the island certainly depicted a tower projecting into the ocean, and this was the only arrangement remotely fitting that description. She'd read that seas like this could turn a headland into a stack in a matter of centuries, and, judging from the age of the ancient script, her chart was at least 500 years old—though the *Here Be Dragons* was in Modern Gorlakian Runes, implying a whimsical annotation by a more recent traveller from Beyond the Pale.

Besides, it *felt* like the location for the portal, as if her years of pathfinding had given her a nose for the things.

A spray of rain spattered her spectacles.

Quickly, she rolled away the chart and tucked it and her spectacles into her shoulder bag. Squinting into the wind, heavy skirt rippling against her legs, she strode along the cliff top.

A few blustery minutes of walking and there was the natural bridge, dipping away before her. It was steep, but not so steep that she couldn't treat it as a flight of steps…albeit dangerous ones.

A sensible Lady Spelunker would turn back at this point. If she fell and broke her leg, there would be no chance of natives rescuing her because there were no natives. Nor could her friends come and find her because there was no second copy of the chart—for some reason it did not photograph well—and besides, she had somehow neglected to inform anybody where she was going…a strange oversight, now she came to think about it. Her host might eventually inform the authorities that she had not returned, but it was normal for explorers of the Great Northern Nest to vanish for weeks or even months as they wandered the maze of portals left by the hypothetical wyrms.

She shook her head. "Never mind all that!"

Millicent—*sensibly!*—checked the lacings on her boots, buckled up her shoulder bag, tied her hat down with her scarf, then buttoned the deep pocket containing her father's old service revolver. *For scaring off wild animals*, she told herself, and tried not to imagine using it as an alternative to dying of exposure.

Her heart hammered in her chest as if it wanted to tear free of her corset. Holding her arms out like a tightrope walker, she stepped down onto a ledge, then got her right boot into the angle between two rocks and took a long pace down onto a sloping natural step.

Just as she landed, the wind rose under her skirt, making the fabric billow.

You have Disadvantage "Hampered by Long Skirts".

Millicent lost her balance, flailed her arms, then somehow managed to right herself. "Damn you."

Form 3. Performing Skill Mountaineering at level 6.
Cost 1 Potestas, 5 of 6 Remaining.
Result = 6 (Performance) +0 (Luck) -2 (Hampered by Long Skirts) -4 (Challenge) = 0.

She squinted against the wind. Something black loomed up out of it, like a skinny tramp in an old rain coat.

Test of Potestas 5. Disadvantage, "Surprised" avoided.

She reached for her revolved, but of course she had buttoned the pocket. All she could do was huddle down on her precarious perch.

Current Form 3. Disadvantage "Untrained."
Performing Warrior at Level 1.
Unlock Warrior, Unarmed Proficiency?

"No! Shut up! Be silent!"

Result = 1 (Performance) +0 (Luck) +4 (Full Defence) -2 (Untrained) -2 (Challenge) = 3.
Effect = Successful Evasion.

The thing wailed as it hurtled by.

Two more black shapes appeared out of the ruins; man-sized things of wings and claws…*vaguely familiar* things of wings and claws, actually…

Scholar 4. Performing Scholar at level 7.

Dragon heads and wings. No forelegs. She'd seen them in an old bestiary. "'Here be dragons', indeed. They're wyverns you ignoramus!"

They sailed the wind towards her, trailing their clawed feet like eagles fishing.

This was not the first time she had encountered supposedly mythological creatures on the edge of the Pale. "I do hope you are not endangered."

With cold fingers, she fumbled her pocket open, pulled and yanked at the revolver until it tore free.

The wyverns were on her.

Millicent turned away, huddled low but there was nowhere to duck to. Worse, one pace right or left would have her plummeting hundreds of feet into the ice water of the bay.

Claws raked her walking coat, snagged on the bones of her corset. She flinched and hunched into herself.

**Result = 1 (Performance) +1 (Luck) -2 (Untrained) -2 (Challenge) = -2.
Effect = 2 (Result) +0 (Claws) -2 (Armour) = 0.**

"Pardon? *Armour?*"

The corset covers your torso so works as Level 2 armour against thrusts, missile weapons and flying attacks, and Level 1 against anything else.

Millicent rose and sure enough, though her back felt bruised, there was no sense of blood. "You ruined my damned coat! It came from Cromerton and Frisbie!"

Black against the slate-grey sky, the wyverns soared overhead, battling the wind back out to sea.

With shaking hands, Millicent checked the cylinder had bullets in it, thumbed back the hammer. She felt rather than heard the reassuring clunk.

The wyverns wheeled over the ruins and came at her again along the line of the rocky arch. They spread out to present an intimidating wall of wings. However, only one could now attack her at a time.

Millicent extended an unsteady arm, considered kneeling to brace herself, rejected the idea because she wanted space to duck into…

The wyverns rushed closer.

**Test of Potestas 5. Disadvantage, "Rushed" avoided.
Pistol takes effect first.**

Millicent picked the one that was coming right at her. There was no time to think, just pull the trigger.

The revolver thumped like a slammed door, kicked.

A great invisible hand seemed to yank the wyvern past her. It struck the rock where it rose to the cliff top and lay there like a badly displayed moth.

**Current Form 3.
Using Skill Shooting 4. Cost 1 Potestas, 4 of 6 remaining.
Performing Shooting at Level 7
Result = 7 (Performance) -1 (Luck) -2 (Challenge) = 3
Natural Armour 2 (Halved by bullet) Negated.
Effect = 7 + 3 (Revolver) = 10.
Wyvern killed.**

The two survivors screamed past.

This time they soared left and right. They would attack from either side, and Millicent could only shoot one—*if* they weren't more circumspect, *if* she managed to pull the trigger on time.

She ran across the natural bridge, breathing hard as she hopped between lumps of stone.

Far below, the ocean surged. In the corner of her eye, the whale breached.

The wyverns stooped.

> Manoeuvring.
> Current Form 3. Performing Mountaineering Skill at
> level 6. Cost 1 Potestas. 3 of 6 Remaining.
> Result = 6 (Performance) +1 (Luck) -2 (Hampered by
> Long Skirts) -2 (Challenge) = 3.
> Effect = Successful transit + Tactical Advantage.

One wyvern managed to cone in from Millicent's left, while the other was still wheeling. She dropped to her haunches.

> Test of Potestas 3. Fail. You have been "Rushed".
> Performing Warrior at Level 3.
> Result = 3 (Performance) +4 (Full Defence) +2 (Tactical
> Advantage) -1 (Luck) -2 (Untrained) -2 (Challenge) -4
> (Enemy Full Attack) = 0.
> Effect = Tie.
> Enemy Grapples.

Once again, wyvern claws tore her coat, flapping its huge wings.

Millicent tried to bring the revolver to bear, couldn't, settled for twisting and using the weapon as a club.

> Result = 3 (Performance) +0 (Luck) -2 (Untrained) -3
> (Challenge) = -2.
> Effect = -2. Wyvern maintains hold. You have
> disadvantage "Grappled."

The second wyvern belatedly swooped in from the right.

Millicent elbowed the first beast, then with a prayer to Minerva, tugged on the trigger.

She hadn't recocked the pistol, so it took strength to rotate the cylinder, bring back the hammer.

The pistol banged, bucked.

Pistol takes effect first. Close Range.
Current Form 3.
Using Skill Shooting 4. Cost 1 Potestas, 2 of 6
remaining.
Performing Shooting at Level 7.
Result = 7 (Performance) +1 (Luck) -3 (Grappled, Pistol
Uncocked) -2 (Cautious Approach) -2 (Challenge) = 1
Natural Armour 2 (Halved by Bullet) applies.
Effect = 1 (Result) + 3 (Revolver) -1 (Armour) = 3.
Target Toughness 1 Negated. Target has Hindrances
"Stunned", "Debilitated" and "Wounded".

It flailed at her, trying to catch her with its claws.

She clouted it with the barrel of her revolver.

Performing Warrior at Level 3.
Result = 3 (Performance) +0 (Luck) -3 (Grappled,
Untrained)- 2 (Challenge) +2 (Enemy was Cautious) +3
(Enemy Stunned, Debilitated, Wounded) = 3.
Effect = 3 (Result) + 0 (Improvised weapon) -2 (Natural
Armour) = 1
Enemy Unconscious.

The wyvern tumbled away. The wind caught it, swatted it into the
heaving ocean.

The third creature still had her by the coat. It picked that moment
to flap and tug at the fabric. Buttons popped.

Millicent found herself stumbling backwards toward the edge.

Result = 3 (Performance) +0 (Luck) -2 (Untrained) -2
(Grappled) -3 (Challenge) = -4.
Effect = -4 Dragged.
Test of Potestas 3. Prompt Action has advantage.

She twisted toward the wyvern.

The screaming beast flapped harder, tore the coat free of her right
arm.

Millicent plucked the bag strap from her shoulder and over her
head, then turned the other way to let the wyvern take the whole garment.

**Result = 3 (Performance) +1 (Luck) +2 ("Prompt Action") -2 (Untrained) -3 (Challenge) = 1.
Effect = Coat abandoned.**

It sailed into the air, taking with it her torn coat, leaving her in just her cardigan, blouse and corset. Already the tendrils of cold clawed her arms.

Millicent cocked the hammer and aimed.

Medium range. Human sized target challenging at 3.

The wyvern rose rapidly, but at the greater distance she could account for that with a slight raise of her hand.

She fired.

**Current Form 3. Performing Shooting Skill at level 7.
Cost 1 Potestas, 1 of 6 remaining.
Result = 7 (Performance) +1 (Luck) -1 (Half Target Challenge) = 7. Bullet on target.
Hit Quality = 2.
Natural Armour 2 (Halved by bullet) negated.
Effect = 2 (Quality) + 3 (Revolver) = 5.
Target Killed.**

It fell out the sky. The coat detached itself from the claws and blew onto a rock at the base of the cliffs. A foam-marbled wave caught it and dragged it back into the black water.

The wind picked up. The sky darkened. The rain grew heavier, plastering her blouse to her arms, leaching the warmth from her limbs.

Millicent shuddered.

1 Vitality lost. 3 of 5 remaining.

She shouldered her bag and slipped the revolver inside.

The first portal would lead her back to a temperate Realm of rice fields and the guest room of a farmer's cottage.

However, she was already at the foot of the rocks where the natural bridge rose up to the stack proper. The path back to the cliffs was in gloom now, the bumps and edges faded together into the grey of twilight. Behind the rush of the wind, the ocean splashed and slapped the rocks.

Millicent fished in her bag and brought out her new "flashlight"—a *Mr Simmons' Patent Always Ready Explorer's Electrical Torch*, no less — and pushed the switch forward.

Nothing happened.

Not *exactly* nothing.

Rather than projecting a beam of light, the heavy tube had become wreathed in luminescence, as if the electricity were leaking…which she was sure wasn't supposed to happen.

Moreover, sparks were dancing across the surface, whirling and forming fleeting patterns.

Millicent held it at arms length so she could see it properly without taking out her spectacles.

The sparks resolved into tiny demonic figures cavorting across her expensive flashlight.

She blinked. They were gone, but her flashlight was still broken.

"Poppycock and superstition! First voices, now I'm seeing things."

Specifically, *seeing* the mythical Gremlins that were said to assail the products of engineering and industry if you left the Pale.

Millicent harrumphed. It was just too easy to become suggestible in such an isolated place. The revolver and the canary had both worked fine, so this island was within the Pale and that was that.

Besides, she had other more pressing problems to worry about. Even if she still had not lost her coat, this was no place for a lady to camp out. She should backtrack while there was still a little light…

Except…

Except, for reasons she could not quite articulate, it still made far more sense to turn seaward and scramble up the rocky slope where the natural bridge rose to the summit of the stack.

Somewhere below, the ocean crashed against the rocks.

Chapter 11: Thirteen Skeletons

Thirteen skeletons rattled and shuffled behind the bars at the other end of the Practice Vault.

Torstag's heart raced. It wasn't the presence of the skeletons. They were too stripped back to their function to tug at his empathy. Rather it was—

Form 3. Performing Necromancer at Level 3.

Once again, the vault filled up with ghosts.

Wrestling with Horror of the Despairing Dead 2/6, cost 2 Potestas, 6 of 4 remaining. Potestas loss overcomes Will, 2. You have Hindrance "Disquieted"

"Bugger," muttered Torstag.

"What was that, boy?"

"I said, 'Brother, I had better get on with it'," said Torstag. He glanced at Ingar, who avoided making eye contact.

Torstag sighed and edged toward the protective chalk line.

Brother Neutrality shoved him between the shoulder blades and he stepped over it. "Now!"

A chain rattled. The bars at the other end of the vault lifted.

The skeletons ducked under, shook out into a line, and advanced down the hall. Each carried a wooden club.

Test of Will 2. Hindrance "Disquieted" continues.

Meanwhile, the vault's ghosts carried on as if nothing was happening. Two transparent acolytes kissed in the corner, one rolled around the floor billowing phantom fumes from his burning robes. The others wandered aimlessly, or huddled against the walls.

Torstag licked his dry lips. There was plenty of space for one more ghost.

Brother Neutrality prodded Torstag's back with his cane. "Make haste, boy, before they focus on you."

"Of course, Brother," said Torstag. "Just let me settle my thoughts."

Buggered, he thought.

And it was too late to fall back on his Cleric vocation—it had literally gone, leaving him with just Meditation as a skill.

One-by-one, the ghosts turned to look at him. Mouths worked mutely.

The skeletons rattled closer, passing through the ghosts. They seemed intent on reaching the main group of acolytes. When they discovered the protective line, they would double back and focus on Torstag as the only available target.

"Acolyte?"

Go to Hell, Smelly Newt.

Test of Will 2. Hindrance "Disquieted" shaken off.

Torstag grinned. In the several weeks since he'd unlocked Necromancy, he'd learned the best way to deal with his horror was to take time to confront it. He still, however, had not yet managed to resist succumbing in the first place.

Annoyingly, he'd also only managed to advance Necromancer, Repel Shade from 3/6th to 5/6th Grasp. It seemed that after the first few times, zombies without arms or teeth weren't enough of a threat to jog his Dead Memories.

However, he *had* developed the knack of keeping the prayers going while casting the spell at a safe distance. His Tempter might have been unimpressed, but he had most certainly impressed Brother Neutrality, who had brought out the skeletons early, especially for his new star pupil.

Challenge = 4 (Skeletons) +2 (Dozen) = 6.

As a level 0 Necromancer, he really *was* buggered, even without the horror.

Another glance at Ingar.

Torstag's friend was stone faced, gazing straight ahead.

I'm buggered.

Torstag took a deep breath. *"Ineffable Resurrectionist, who is mighty in Your Essence of Not Thereness…"*

The skeletons broke into a charge.

Unlock Warrior, Disarm?

Shut up.

He put himself into it and mouthed, BEGONE.

Form 3. Performing Necromancy at level 3.
Using Repel Shade 5/6 cost 1 Potestas, 5 of 4 remaining.
Result = 3 (Performance) +0 (Luck) -6 (Challenge) = -2.
Effect = Failure.
You have failed.

"Shit!"

A club hit him in the belly.

He doubled over.

Performing Warrior at Level 3.
Result = 3 (Performance) -1 (Luck) -2 (Tactical Disadvantage) -4 (Your Neglected Defence) -2 (Challenge)= -6.
Enemy Effect = 6 capped to 1. (Light clubs.)
1 Vitality lost, 2 remaining.
Loss overcomes Toughness 1.
Condition "Stunned". Form 0. No Feats possible.

The skeleton that had hit him carried on past. The skeletons reached the chalk line, jostled against it.

Torstag stumbled away, his stomach blazing with every step.

Test of Will 2. Hindrance "Stunned" persists.

He ignored the sensation and, forcing himself to focus, kept going.

**New Form 3, cost 1 Potestas, 4 of 4 Potestas
remaining.
Performing Warrior at level 4.**

Blast! Focus you idiot!
Some of the skeletons turned away from the acolytes and advanced towards him.

**Manoeuvring.
Result = 4 (Performance) -2 ("Stunned") +2
(Retreating) +1 (Luck) -2 (Challenge) = 3.
Effect = Successful Retreat.**

A club caught in his sleeve, tore it, but he found himself beyond the gauntlet and briefly out of reach of the skeletons.

Unfortunately, they were now between him and safety. They rattled closer.

Test of Will 2. Hindrance "Stunned" shaken off.

Somehow he managed to restart the chant, "Ineffable Resurrectionist, who is mighty in Your Essence of Not Thereness…"

Mentally, however, he was yelling, *Necromancer! Necromancer!*

**New Form 5, cost 1 Potestas 3 of 4 Potestas
Remaining.
Performing Necromancer at Level 5.**

The chamber's ghosts became more solid, as did all the braided threads connecting the ghosts to the acolytes, and both ghosts and acolytes to the Catacombs.

That would be him unless he was lucky. If only he'd managed to level up…

"Oh!"

He singled out a skeleton that was in the lead.

Challenge = 4 (Skeleton) +0 (One) = 4.

Repel Shade. "BEGONE!"

> Using Necromancy Cantrip, Repel Shade 5/6. Cost 1
> Potestas. 2 of 4 Potestas remaining.
> Result = 5 (Performance) +1 (Luck) -4 (Challenge) = 2.
> Effect = Tentative Practical Response.

The skeleton simply halted.

The other skeletons simply flowed around it.

Even so, Torstag grinned like an idiot.

"Here it comes."

> Repel Shade advances to 6/6.
> Repel Shade secured.
> 1st Necromancy Feat secured. Necromancy
> advances to Level 1. 3 feats required to reach Level
> 2.
> Unlock a Necromancy feat.

Just as when he surged, he found himself out of Time, looking at a tree drawn on parchment, only this one was entitled Necromancy and showed magicians doing…disturbing things.

Little signposts with skulls on them showed that they were grouped into Cantrips and more powerful Rituals, which also needed the proficiency Ritual. There was also the Proficiency Charm, which seemed to be a way of preparing spells ahead of time, and Proficiency Enchant, which seemed to make magic items.

And he had to pick a Feat, one that he was likely to use so he could secure it and level up.

There was Channel Shade…he wasn't going to use that. Ever.

Repel Shade, however, gave him access to Manifest Shade and Command Shade.

What does Manifest Shade do?

> Necromancy Cantrip Manifest Shade. Depending on
> the Success, this enables you to make a shade
> properly visible and present for conversation and
> weak physical interaction for a matter of minutes.

That *could* be useful. Since, however, he was at the start of the tree Necromancy, he might as well leave the slot open and see what he needed.

Leave it for now.

And his Tempter dropped him back in the flow of Time.

The skeletons were almost on him.

> **Challenge = 4 (Skeletons) +2 (Dozen) = 6.**
> **Current Form 5. Performing Necromancer at level 6.**
> **Using Necromancy Cantrip, Repel Shade. Cost 1**
> **Potestas. 1 of 4 Potestas remaining.**
> **Result = 6 (Performance) +0 (Luck) -6 (Challenge) = 0.**
> **Effect = Passive Response.**

The skeletons halted.

Singing now, Torstag strode through the gaps. As he passed out of them, he sang out, *"Thus Your Divine Manifest Potency is Vindicated."* He grinned at the silent audience. "I was chanting all the time, just not very loud. Praise Be to the Ineffable Resurrectionist!"

Everybody echoed his cry.

The ghosts, meanwhile, regarded him hungrily. His mouth went dry. The blood pulsed in his temples.

> **Unlock Cantrip, Channel Shade Necromancy Feat?**

No! Shut up.

One of the skeletons shuffled forward, then stopped at the white line.

> **Chalk line, Enchanted with Cleric, Repel Shade.**

Something made him turn to look in the corner.

Brother Neutrality was regarding him oddly. He smiled stiffly. "Enough for one evening I think." He clapped his hands. "Line up, Acolytes."

He knows! realised Torstag. *He saw.*

But why had the monk not immediately restrained him?

He stumbled and realised he had kicked one of the discarded clubs.

> **Unlock Warrior, Hurl?**

Suddenly the club was more than just a lump of wood. The well-worn grip seemed inviting to Torstag's hand. For once his Tempter truly was tempting him.

That was why Brother Neutrality was hesitating. Torstag could probably pretty much kill everybody in the room.

"Shall I report to the Infirmary, Brother?" asked Torstag. He patted his bruised stomach.

"What? Oh, of course. Off you go, Acolyte."

Torstag bobbed his head in obedience. A plan was already forming in his mind.

He brushed past Ingar and whispered. "Midnight. Dormitory Roof."

Chapter 12: The Dark Tower

Current Form 3. Performing Mountaineering at level 6. Cost 1 Potestas. 0 of 6 Remaining.

Millicent reached the crest of the ramp.

Jagged shapes loomed grey-black in the gathering gloom.

She heaved herself up into the imperfect shelter of the mess of broken walls around the base of the ruined tower. The masonry blocked the horizontal rain, but funnelled the wind so it buffeted her as she scrambled deeper into the rubble.

Result = 6 (Performance) +0 (Luck) -3 (Hampered by Long Skirts, Poor Visibility) -2 (Challenge) = 1. 1 Vitality lost. 2 of 5 remaining.

She felt her way through the shadows, the stone cold on her fingers.

The remains of the drystone tower rose before her. Close to, the stub was twice Millicent's height. The entrance, however, was a narrow patch of darkness. If this wasn't an actual broch, it came from a very similar tradition. She felt for the lintel.

She would have to duck low to squeeze in there.

Being down to zero potestas—whatever that really was—always made her feel lightheaded. It also meant that any attempt at mountaineering or shooting would be pretty much doomed until she rested.

Ideally, she should wait to recuperate. However, the top of a rainswept pinnacle was not the ideal place for that.

Millicent reached for her torch, but it felt dead in her hands even before she tried to switch it on. This time, there were no dancing sparks, but nor was there a beam of electrical illumination.

That left candles, for which she would need shelter.

Millicent hunkered down and pushed sideways into the pitch dark of the narrow doorway.

Icy stone edges scraped her arms. The lintel bumped her head through her hat. She ducked yet lower, and finally emerged into what could once have been the lower storey of a round tower. Wind whistled through the ragged stones that framed the darkening sky. In the very centre of the floor, glowing white lines outlined the shape of a door.

"W…what?" exclaimed Millicent, and realised she was stammering from the cold.

The rain still pattered down inside the tower, but at least the walls sheltered her from the howling wind.

She dropped to her haunches and felt in her bag for her all-weather matches.

A quick strike and she had flickering light.

The round floor was covered in bones and human skulls in varying stages of brown-whiteness. There were also shards of giant eggshells—clearly she had found the wyvern's roost.

Millicent felt a pang of guilt. No wonder the creatures had fought so hard to keep her from it.

You are Self Hating.
Test of Will 3. Issue "Crippling Guilt" avoided.

Millicent shrugged mentally. She had other things to worry about…like the door.

In the middle of the floor stood a studded wooden door, balanced for all the world like a giant domino piece propped on end.

Millicent's match burned out. She blinked in the dark. "Now I'm hallucinating."

She brought out a candle and used another match to light that. Now she could see properly.

There was nothing she could use as fuel, unless she could get the bones burning.

The door, however, was still there and most definitely real.

She paced closer, crunching bones and eggshells as she trod.

The candlelight revealed it to be *not actually* free standing. Rather, the door was sunk into a slab of rock shaped like a massive tombstone, leaving a finger's-breadth of stone around it to act as a frame. There was no handle, no keyhole.

Millicent walked around the slab, confirmed that the rear was entirely blank stone, and returned to inspect the front. She traced the crack around the edge of the wood.

It was warm to the touch.

She bent closer, inhaled balmy air with a whiff of exotic blooms.

No wonder somebody had installed a sturdy door. Keeping out the cold wind was reason enough, even without the ferocious wyverns. Though all the skeletons suggested that the same somebody was using this portal as a way to get rid of unwanted people.

Should she knock?

1 of 6 Potestas restored.

That meant roughly twenty minutes had passed. Millicent wasn't getting any warmer. It did mean she had enough mental energy to make the climb back down onto the natural bridge. However, she'd still need to cross it and climb up again. She should wait at least another twenty minutes.

Millicent put her ear to the wood and clamped a hand over the other ear to muffle the sound of the wind.

Was that drumming she could hear?

The wind picked up, screaming across to the open top of the tower. It brought with it heavier rain that splashed the walls, ran down her face like fingers of ice, and doused her candle.

The chamber was pitch black now, except for the faint glow outlining the door, promising warmth and sunlight on the other side.

She huddled down, and with numb fingers fumbled more bullets into the revolver's cylinder.

She shuddered. Her jaw spasmed. She clenched it.

You are cold and wet. 1 Vitality lost. 1 of 5 remaining.

Millicent rose up and hammered the butt of the revolver against the door.

No response.

She put her back to the wood, tried to feel whatever warmth it held flow into her.

She shivered. Despite her clenched jaw, her teeth started to chatter.

2 of 6 Potestas restored.

Another twenty minutes and she'd be ready to mountaineer her way back onto the mainland. The problem was that she was losing Vitality. She would be unconscious and then dead before she reached the other portal.

"Bugger."

She brought out matches, dropped the packet, felt for it in the dark amongst the bones, finally relit her candle and took a really close look at the door. Judging from the lumps of fallen masonry in front of it, it had to open inwards.

Which side was the hinge?

The human remains gave no clue; they seemed scattered evenly. If they'd been propelled through the portal, then they had arrived alive.

She stooped and made out the remains of rope binding wristbones.

"B...bloody marvellous!"

Whoever lived on the other side of that door had been using the portal for murders or—more likely—executions.

"Come on young lady, focus!"

The door had to be locked from the other side. It would probable be constructed to be opened with the right hand, meaning any mechanism would be on her left as she faced it. Needless to say it would be at comfortable hand height.

With numb fingers, Millicent took a piece of chalk from her bag and tried to mark the door. The wood was too damp to hold the chalk. Instead, she scrawled a shaky X on the stone frame next to her target. Then she set the candle on a skull, stood back and drew her revolver from her bag.

The shots were appalling loud in the confined space. She put six bullets into the door where she hoped the lock would be. They didn't go through.

She reloaded—paused to enjoy the warm barrel against her hands—then, standing a little closer, pulled back the hammer for another try.

The door swung inward, blasting Millicent with daylight. Somewhere a crowd roared.

She squinted into the glare.

Framed in the doorway stood what could only be a naked barbarian.

Chapter 13: A Lethal Practice

"Let me go let me go!" yelled the beggar. The purse of coins Trophimus had given him jingled as he zigzagged between the trees. This was the perfect spot for tactical training. The trunks were thick enough to provide cover, but devoid of low branches that might limit visibility and turn the thing into a stealth exercise.

The beggar halted and addressed Trophimus. "I really don't like this."

"Look out, behind arsehole!" barked Cerdic.

The beggar turned in time to skip clear of a shield rush from Axe Girl's trio.

"Why did you warn him?" asked the Kid. "We were about to win!"

Axe Girl answered for Cerdic. "This is training, boy. Not about winning."

Trophimus frowned into his visor. She sounded just a little out of breath. Perhaps bringing her out of retirement had been a bad idea.

The beggar meanwhile was running off to the left, but this put him in the path of the Blade Bitches. The trio of almost identical blond women—Trophimus had long ago given up trying to treat one as the leader—were perfectly spaced, tempting the beggar to slip between them and get clubbed.

The beggar sensibly veered away.

Trophimus moved sideways to track him, taking his time.

Cerdic, meanwhile, was in slightly lighter armour of just a mailcoat and open-faced helmet. He jogged out to the left, pacing the beggar.

Now Rufus and his trio swept in.

The beggar spun away.

Cerdic cast his net.

The beggar dodged, tripped then rolled to his feet. He ran straight into Axe Girl's trio.

The Kid swung his club, caught the beggar in the belly.

The beggar doubled over, dropped his purse. The coins scattered. He scrambled for them.

The Kid strode in and raised the club.

"Stop!" yelled Cerdic and Trophimus in unison.

The club came down with a crack.

Blood splashed the ground.

"You fucking idiot!" shouted Cerdic,

Trophimus raised his visor. "What did you think you were doing?"

"I got him! I got him!" said the Kid. "We won!"

Axe Girl tore off the kid's helmet. It clanged on the ground. She cuffed him around the ear. "This is training, boy," she said.

Dekan dropped to one knee and examined the beggar. "Dead."

"Fuck," said Cerdic.

The Kid rubbed his ear, "It's just a beggar."

"Yeah," said Cerdic, "but where are we going to find another one?"

The others had gathered in.

"Oh well," said one of the Blade Bitches, pulling off her helmet. "I guess we're done training for the evening."

The other two also removed their helmets. The trio shook out their long blond hair as if they shared a single soul.

Trophimus rounded on them. "You ladies will have cause to regret that attitude."

One of the blonds shrugged. "It's just a girl."

"A wizard warlock girl," said Trophimus.

"Fuck," said Cerdic. "Right, Kid, dig a grave for the corpse."

"But…"

"Shut up kid," said Axe Girl, "you're not in some fancy boudoir now."

"Say," said Rufus, a cocky young man whose team Trophimus had only reluctantly included. "The kid could take a turn as the target."

Axe Girl scowled. "No. He could twist an ankle, somebody might get too enthusiastic with a club."

"She's right," said Trophimus. "Plus it's not practice if we're going easy, is it?"

Rufus shrugged. "Maybe he doesn't deserve us going easy."

"Maybe," said Axe Girl, "you want to fight me?"

"You still have the axe," said Rufus, "but you're no girl. I'm younger, faster, and stronger."

Cerdic's net draped over Rufus and tightened.

"Hey!" cried Rufus. "What the fuck?"

Cerdic yanked the rope and Rufus went down on the carpet of fallen leaves.

"Screw you, man!" said Rufus, thrashing around.

"No," said Cerdic moving to put his foot on the downed man's chest, "Screw *you*. This is our big score, mine and Trophimus', and you're not going to fuck it up for us. Once it's done and you're rich then you can fight Axe Girl if you really want, if you don't mind her probably killing you, or if you win, a knife in the dark from Dekan or the Kid."

"Hey," began Dekan. "My honour…"

"Shut the fuck up," said Cerdic.

Trophimus raised his voice. "We're all going to get rich over this, but we can't get rich if we're dead from going in against the girl unprepared, or because we killed each other because we got hot and bothered. Everybody probably owes everybody an apology, so let's skip that part and get out of here."

"What about the dead guy?" said Cerdic.

Trophimus shrugged. "What's one murdered hobo, eh?"

"Okay!" said Cerdic. "Pack your kit…"

There was a familiar disembodied fanfare.

"Shit fuck," said Cerdic.

Gronchard the Flayer manifested in their midst.

The spectral boy looked around him, eyebrows raised. "Trophimus! Who are these people? I told you *discretion*."

Trophimus' mind raced. "This is my normal team, Master."

Out of the corner of his eye he saw Cerdic nod encouragingly at the others.

Everybody mumbled things like, "Yes…Usual team…Absolutely. Always together."

Gronchard moved forward. It was a disquieting effect because his big legs passed through fallen trees and the occasional bush.

Everybody shifted back, like jackals staying clear of a lion.

Gronchard's gaze lowered to the corpse. "And who might that be, Mortal?"

"Oh," said Trophimus. "That's Tom Loosetongue. It turns out he told everybody about your quest for the Holy Angelica, and we were so shocked…"

"Absolutely *fucking* shocked," said Cerdic.

Everybody muttered, "Yeah, shocked."

"…so we executed him," said Cerdic.

More murmurs of confirmation.

"Told everybody my secret?" grated Gronchard.

Trophimus flinched. Could the demi-god work destructive magic via his manifestation? He'd seen no sign of it. Even so.

"Yes," said Trophimus. "But I swear nobody really believed the story…there are so many rumours about the Powers of the Ten Thousand Realms. Once we have all returned from our mission, it will all be forgotten…."

"Hmm," said Gronchard. It would have sounded more impressive if his voice had been lower pitched. Also, the demi-god seemed to have been suffering from acne.

"Oh!" said Trophimus.

"What?" said Gronchard.

"Well, I suppose if we *don't* return from our mission, then people will talk about the fact we've disappeared and *that* will keep the story alive. So it would be in your interest, Master, to ensure we go get home safe, perhaps by providing some kind of magic item."

Gronchard's out-sized face frowned. "You have the lodebone. That should be enough. Do not trouble me again."

He vanished.

Everybody looked at Trophimus.

"You shouldn't have gone and embarrassed him," said Axe Girl. "If he could reach us to deliver some magical dodads, he wouldn't need Bounty Hunters. He could just drop his own people on the ground."

"Yeah, asshole," said Rufus. "I thought you were supposed to be the diplomatic one?"

Trophimus chuckled. "I thought asking for favours he couldn't supply was probably better than straight up blackmailing him." He cleared his throat. "Oh Mighty God, if you eliminate us, then rather than quash the rumour about you being a whiny little bitch who lost his girl toy, it will confirm it."

"Fucking genius," said Cerdic.

"I guess that was pretty smart," said Rufus. "But it didn't *sound* smart."

"Best kind of smart," said Trophimus. "Gather round everybody— not *you* dead hobo guy…"

Everybody laughed.

Trophimus waited for the uneasy silence to settle. "You've seen one half of the problem—Gronchard the Flayer. I think I convinced him not to eliminate us, not least because my reasoning was honest."

"Except you're the wanker that spread that fucking rumour," said Cerdic.

More laughter.

"Yes," said Trophimus. "However, if Gronchard finds out he's been played, he'll probably come after all of us and our families and our neighbours. The same goes if we mess up and don't bring him back his precious Angelica. You saw him! For all that he's an immortal, he's stuck in a pimply adolescent body. Imagine what happens if he reverts to type and has a tantrum."

"Crap," said Rufus.

"Indeed," said Trophimus. "Now the other half of the problem. Anybody here met a warlock before?"

"Not counting Phantom Pluke Face," added Cerdic

Much shaking of heads.

"Well, I have," said Trophimus. "I once teamed up with a Warlock girl who was down on her luck. The thing is they all have this voice in their head that tells them how good they are…I don't mean it praises them, I mean it literally gives them a ranking for their skills. So, you've all—most of you—seen me fight. How do you think she rated me with a sword?"

"A *pork* sword?" said Rufus. "About a one."

Everybody laughed.

"A gentleman," said Trophimus holding up his hand to silence them, all the while grinning to show he shared the joke, "does not speak of some matters. Let's just say I was not deficient in that area and move on to considering martial matters. Fighting with a sword, how did she rate me?"

People called out random numbers: "Fourteen...One hundred...Ten..."

Trophimus shook his head and everybody suddenly sobered.

"My worst," he said, "is a six, sometimes I can manage seven or if I'm on really good form, eight. It took me something like twenty years to get this good. Now bear in mind that a warlock is remembering skills from past incarnations, how did you think my young warlock whore rated?"

Uncomfortable silence.

"She was young, might have been eighteen or nineteen, but her worst was four. That's as good as most professional fighters, you folks included."

He gave them a moment to absorb that.

"It gets worse," continued Trophimus. "Once we got in a bar brawl and she just killed everybody in the room. I asked and she said she was fighting as a nine. It turns out that, whereas us ordinary mortals can *sometimes* fight a rank higher on a supremely good day, Warlocks usually fight at least two ranks higher. Stop and think about that for a moment."

"So when we going to train some more, Trophimus?" asked the Kid.

"Soon as we find another hobo to murder. Now let's mount up and get going."

Everybody laughed as they gathered their stuff.

"You scared them, Tro," said Cerdic, once they were back in the saddle. "But you brought them together as well."

91

"Indeed," said Trophimus. He was checking the lodebone. "We'll have to double back to the other portal. She's obviously moving around."

"We'll catch her though?" asked Axe Girl.

"Sure," said Cerdic.

Trophimus surveyed his little army and nodded. "You'll have your rose garden."

Chapter 14: Poltergeist Rodents

The wind whistled behind the shutters. The lamps flickered.

Torstag rolled over on his narrow bed and stole a look across the Dormitory.

From the outside, the building looked like a massive beehive, the stonework tapering in to form a roof. However, the inside was hollow with shallow sleeping cubicles lining the walls like giant nesting boxes in his castle's dovecote. The central observation tower rose almost to the vaulted ceiling, blocking his view of Ingar's sleeping place. From the tower's top, the monks could monitor the Acolytes as they slept. There could be no succumbing to the Tempter, not without a beating or worse. Nor could there be any wandering around at night…which reminded him.

He checked his Conscience.

The crude terracotta statuette had started to weep blood, as it did whenever his Tempter manifested itself during sleep hours.

Of course, even if the Monks saw the blood from their watch tower—they had a big spyglass for when they *really* wanted to monitor an acolyte—they would not intervene until it had trickled down in sufficient quantity to tip a delicately balanced pair of scales, causing a cascade of marbles to hit a drum.

Torstag wrinkled his nose. Now he had stopped meditating, the sickly sweet stench of dead rat become overpowering. This was the result of his new Forage feat.

Unlock Warlord, Goblin Rat Eating Ritual?

Seriously, shut up! How much Potestas do I have?

Meditation had worked then.

What about everything else?

> Torstag, Human Warlock, Youth, Agile, Empathic, Cautious, Marked.
> Potestas 8/4. Will 4. Cowardice 1/6. Horror of the Unquiet Dead 1/6.
> Vitality 3. Toughness 1.
> Vocations:
> Warlord 1: Tea Drinking.
> Warrior 1: (Sidearm, Shield): Wrath Strike +1, Split Shield 2/6
> Scout 2 (Mountains, Forest, Jungle): Climb +1, Spider Climb, Stalk 4/6, Forage 2/6.
> Necromancer 1 (Cantrips): Repel Shade, Shade Cloak 3/6.
> Various General Skills including Meditation.

Torstag checked that the twine was still where he had tied it to the shutters.

Next, he checked on the pair of Monks on the tower. Were they keeping an eye on him? Hard to tell. Certainly not using spyglasses yet.

What fate did Brother Neutrality have in store for him? More than a severe beating. Being forced into some boring vocation such as Gardener. No, they would execute him or—worse—perhaps wall him up alive. It definitely happened from time to time. 'Immuration', they called it.

Now the monks were both looking the other way. His Conscience, meanwhile, had one drop of blood half way to the scales, but was otherwise almost dry. He should—probably—get away with what he was about to do.

Necromancer!

Form 4.
Performing Necromancy at Level 5.

His heart lifted. That was a brilliant start!

Then he was aware of bleak thoughts and mounting despair.

He sprang out of bed, and there was the ghost of a slight looking boy. As he watched, the ghost spasmed, racked by a long-ago cough.

Torstag flinched, then the blood rushed in his ears and his fists clenched. The boy had been killed by homesickness as much by disease. *Was I that young and frail when they took me?*

Wrestling with Horror of the Despairing Dead 1/6. Resisted. Hardening advances to 2/6.

Even better!

He stumbled off and used the bucket in the back of his cell. When he turned, he could also see plump spectral rats snuffling around under his bed near where he had slung the sack of their corpses.

To manifest the ghosts of a dozen rats to poltergeist level is a Level 6 challenge.

MANIFEST!

**Using Necromancy Cantrip, Manifest Shade 2/6. Cost 2 Potestas. 6 of 4 Potestas remaining.
Challenge = 1 (Animals) +3 (Dozens) +2 (Poltergeist) = 6.
Result = 5 (Performance) +1 (Luck) -6 (Challenge) = 0.
Effect = Shades manifest as poltergeists for 1 hour.
Manifest Shade advances to 3/6 Grasp.**

The rat ghosts...*solidified* and started squeaking.

Rat poltergeists, a dozen. Invisible with normal sight.

Perfect! Got it first time!

He *had* planned to repel them, but could he save some Potestas? Again, he glanced at the observation tower. Nobody was watching.

He moved briskly back toward the bed, flapping his arms and hissed like a cat.

One of the Night Watchers called over, "Acolyte Torstag? What *are* you doing?"

Torstag froze. A beating now would...complicate matters. "Rats, Brother," he called back. He clapped hard.

The ghost rats squeaked and hurried away.

"Go back to bed, Acolyte Torstag," ordered the Night Watcher.

That would have been a warning to him just on its own. It was unheard of for nocturnal misbehaviour to not result in instant punishment. It followed that the Monks were just waiting until he fell asleep to seize him.

Torstag got into bed, felt the endlessly dying boy seep through his consciousness.

Wrestling with Horror of the Despairing Dead 2/6, cost 2 Potestas, 4 of 4 Potestas remaining.

You have hindrance "Disquieted".

He shivered.

Come on come on come on. Behave like live rats.

A Conscience drum went off in a cell somewhere to the right.

"Acolyte Hohen!" roared the Chief Watcher. "Stop this instant!"

"I'm not doing anything, Brother!"

A ghost rat must have scented blood weeping from the eyes of Hohen's Conscience. As it climbed the statuette, it would have had just enough physical presence to tip the balance and set off the drum.

From the direction of Hohen's cell came yelps and pleading, then protests punctuated by the thwack of wood on flesh.

Another drum rattled. Sandals clattered as a second monk ran to administer punishment.

And another drum. And another. The ghost rats must be fleeing to a different cell every time they heard approaching footsteps.

Will 2. Hindrance "Disquieted" shaken off.

Torstag rolled off the bed, landed on his hands and knees.

To fully manifest a single human ghost is a Level 5 challenge.

MANIFEST!

Using Necromancy Cantrip, Manifest Shade 3/6. Cost 1 Potestas. 3 of 4 Potestas remaining.
Result = 5 (Performance) +1(Luck) –5 (Challenge) = 1.
Effect = Shades manifest as poltergeists for 1 hour.
Manifest Shade advances to 4/6 Grasp.

Torstag cursed under his breath. That feat had burned two Potestas!

A child whimpered, half aloud, half in Torstag's head.

He suppressed a guilty qualm and rolled over the floor.

There on his bed was the ghost boy, softly solid and twitching. Beyond him, the watch tower was empty save for a single monk who was looking to Torstag's left from where more drum sounds were coming.

Torstag rose and walked over to the window. He leaned into the narrow aperture and pulled back the shutter to reveal a square of night.

Once—perhaps in the ghost boy's time—it been barred, but the iron had long since rusted away. Only a few Acolytes jumped each year, so perhaps the Monks hadn't thought it worthwhile making repairs.

He vaulted up and wriggled through the cramped passage in the thick masonry.

His face emerged into dark. Hailstones stung his cheek. He squirmed around onto his back. Fingers tingling, toes curling, he very slowly eased himself to stand upright on the window ledge, pressed against the sloping masonry with the hundred foot drop just beyond his bare heels. The stone chilled his soles, the cold air prickled his bare legs. The icy pellets bounced off the masonry and stung his face. However, he couldn't make himself move.

Wrestling with Cowardice 1/6. Resisted.

Torstag grinned as the fear receded. He'd beaten the odds twice tonight. But had he truly slipped out unnoticed?

He stood for a moment, heart hammering in his chest.

The cold breeze made his nightshirt billow. He teetered, flailed his arms, then somehow managed to lean in even closer to the masonry.

With shaking hands, he drew up his shirt between his legs and tied it into a makeshift breech-clout. Then, shivering, he felt for gaps in the gently sloping stonework. Once, the outside wall had looked forbiddingly perfect. Now, he could feel plenty of handholds.

You have Scout 2 (Mountains, Forest, Jungle): Climb +1, Spider Climb, Stalk 4/6, Forage 2/6.
Current Form 4. Performing Scout at Level 6.
Climbing the exterior to the top is a level 9 Challenge and will take minutes.

Doable, as Ingar would say, with Luck. At least his Tempter wasn't complaining that this wasn't actually a cliff.

Using Scout, Climb +1. Cost 1 Potestas. 2 of 4 Potestas remaining.

He squeezed his fingers into a crack, lifted his right leg, found a toe hold and pulled himself up above the level of the window.

Now it was just a matter of feeling for where the mortar had crumbled away.

About half way up, he was probing with left foot when his right began began to slip.

His outstretched foot found crevice. He levered himself up another six feet or so.

The stone in his left hand came out of the wall. It bumped down his arm, rattled off down into the night.

His weight went onto his right side and for a moment he was flapping like a prayer banner in the wind.

Result = 6 (Performance) +3 (Feat) -1 (Luck) -9 (Challenge) = -1.
Effect = Climb about halfway.
Test of Potestas, 2. Fall avoided.

Torstag clung on with the fingers of one hand while the ice wind plucked at his robes, clawed hail into his bare legs. "What…what were the odds?"

Silence.

"Okay, you know what, perhaps I'll go back and surrender myself to the monks. Tell me the odds!"

Was that a sigh?

With Potestas 2, it would be typical to avoid a fall 2 out of 6 times.

"Six? What in the Thirteen Hells? Is this a thrice-damned game of dice?"

Then the thought hit him that when his climbing failed, he had had a better than 4 in 6 chance of simply falling off the wall.

What was he supposed to do now?

A bleak determination seized him. There were no choices left anyway.

Using Scout, Climb+1. Cost 1 Potestas. 1 of 4 Potestas remaining.

Limbs aching now, he swarmed up a few hundred feet. After that the going was easy. The stonework curved in until at last he was more crawling than climbing.

Result = 6 (Performance) +3 (Feat) +0 (Luck) -9 (Challenge) = 0.
Effect = Success.

He stood up on the domed roof and resisted the urge to whoop into the wild weather and pretend he was flying. He walked toward the very top of the Dormitory, the wind like ice knives on his bare legs. As he reached the summit of the dome, his muscles shuddered and gave. He sank to his knees and gathered his robe close.

1 Vitality Lost.
2 of 3 Vitality remaining
Toughness 1 surpassed.
You have condition Stunned. Form 0. No Feats possible.
Hardening towards Issue "Cowardice" advances to 2/6.

His Tempter tested his Will three times before he felt better.

99

Slowly, he rose again and turned on the spot, taking in the arc of stars, the moonlit peaks, the darkened valley between the mountains, and the black mass off the cliff where the dormitory half merged with it. This was the first time he'd been truly alone since he was ten winters old.

Though perhaps he'd never really be alone again. Maybe the monks of the Grey Cortège were correct and he risked being hollowed out…but if they were correct, then why were they lying to him about whatever it was they were lying about?

"Fucking hell!" said Ingar, completing the last part of his climb. "You took your time changing your mind!"

Torstag took a step toward him, checked. "I didn't. Brother Neutrality spotted me."

"Spotted you escaping?" said Ingar.

"Spotted me succumbing to my Tempter. I think they were just waiting for me to fall asleep."

"Fuck," said Ingar. "Well let's get you the fuck out of here."

"You're not angry with me?" said Torstag.

Ingar shrugged. "Brave isn't your thing." His teeth flashed in the gloom. He closed he distance and hugged Torstag. "I can't believe we've gotten this far!"

"Not by good planning," said Torstag, returning the hug. "I'm down to one Potestas."

"Nine," said Ingar, letting go. He bowed. "Ingar Ingridson, Third Level Burglar at your service, and possessor of a mighty maximum Potestas of five, ten after meditation."

Torstag nodded. "How did you make it look like you were still in bed?"

"I smuggled in some wicker hoops from the garden. Set them up under the covers. I've been planning that for weeks."

"Cunning," said Torstag. "I had to burn Potestas."

"What?" asked Ingar. "To make an illusion? Can Necromancers do that?"

"In a way." Torstag turned and tried to pick out their route in the dark. The Dormitory, along with most of the monastic buildings and guest temples, was on the highest of the five great terraces. However, their destination was the final stretch of the Dedicant Road that ran along a wide ledge that overlooked the rest of the monastery.

It was impossible to make out anything.

What does Necromancer show me?

Form 3.
Performing Necromancer at Level 4.

Scores of silvery threads stretched out from the Dormitory and from the Monk's cells, braided together and extended up the pitch black cliffs to what had to be the location of the Catacombs of Hesitation.

Pale light illuminated the way ahead.

Torstag's heart leapt. He spun around.

It was only the moon rising above the mountains on the other side of the Untrodden Valley.

A vision of the girl's pale face flashed across his mind's eye. He shook his head.

"Perfect timing!" Ingar clapped Torstag on the shoulder. "Don't worry, I'll take it from here."

CHAPTER 15: TRAPS!

The hailstones drummed the back of Ingar's hood.

The cliffs glowed in the moonlight, all except for a square of black; the entrance to the Catacombs of Hesitation.

Ingar chewed his lip. Since he'd started to level up, his dreams had been full of scything blades, sprung spikes, explosions of flame and other traps.

1 Vitality Restored. 2 of 3 Remaining.

"I just got one Vitality back," said Torstag. "And I'm already back to two Potestas."

"Me too," said Ingar. "The Vitality at least. I'm still have a cushion of extra Potestas from meditating."

"I've got two," said Torstag.

Ingar grinned. "A good job I'm doing the work from here."

Ingar strained his ears, listened for an alarm bell. Nothing. "I think we got away with it."

The two acolytes were clinging to the crags just below where the winding Dedicant Road reached its destination. It had cost them a Potestas each, but it had been an easy climb, with Torstag using his ability to see threads to keep them on track.

"And I just got a Potestas back."

1 Vitality Restored. 2 of 3 Remaining.

"Hang on," said Ingar. He half closed his eyes and thought, *OK Doofus, where am I at?*

You are: Ingar, Human Warlock, Youth, Quick Witted,
Nimble Fingered, Hedonistic, Sensitive.
Potestas 9/5. Will 2.
Vitality 3. Toughness 1.
Vocations:
Burglar 3: Hide, Climb, Fall, Spider Climb, Move
Silently, Stalk, Pick Pocket 3/6, Open Lock 5/6.
Cleric 1 (learned): Meditation. Repel Shade, 1/6.
Entertainer 2 (Learned): Tout, Recite, Acrobatics,
Sing.
Artist 0...

Ingar blushed. *Enough!*

"Can we still do this?" asked Torstag. "We've not really had time to level up."

"Fuck it," said Ingar. "We've got all those past lives to steal from." He started to climb. "There's nobody around, we might as well get on with it."

Together, they pulled themselves up onto the Dedicant Road and, hunching low—as if that would make a difference if somebody looked their way—scurried the short distance to press themselves against the wall either side of the doorway.

Well, more of a gate than a doorway.

An iron grating blocked the entrance. From somewhere beyond came the echo of sporadic clattering, loud enough to be heard over the hiss of the hail.

"What's that sound?" whispered Ingar.

"No idea." Torstag sniffed. "What's that smell?"

Ingar inhaled and caught the Practice Vault scent of tar and embalming fluid. "Just mortuary pong."

"No, more than that."

Ingar moved to press his face against the bars. A dry breeze warmed his face. Behind the mortuary stench was the scent he remembered from when work took his band of strolling players to the Palatinate of Sandilands: herbs and dust with the promise of better fragrances if it rained. "The desert," said Ingar. "*How?*"

"Portal," said Torstag.

"Of course," said Ingar. "It would be a good source of dry air for the catacombs."

"Bastards," said Torstag. There was a new edge to his voice. "They had this, but they kept us shivering in our dorm."

"I could have told you they were bastards when I arrived here."

"You did," said Torstag, "frequently."

Ingar dropped to his haunches and palmed his everlight so that it was exposed just enough to illuminate the lock.

"Hey?" said Torstag.

"Oh," said Ingar. "I've been practising my Burglar skills."

He took out his tools—a pair of bent wires harvested from the Mortuary Temple workshop—and set to work.

> Form 2. Level 3 Burglar.
> Performing Burglar at Level 5.
> Using feat Burglar, Open Lock 5/6. Cost 1 Potestas. 8
> of 5   Potestas remaining.
> Result = 5 (Performance) +2 (Feat) -1 (Luck) -8
> (Challenge) = -2. Failed.

"Crap!" said Ingar.

"Is something wrong?" asked Torstag.

"No," lied Ingar. "Everything is fine."

> Using feat Burglar, Open Lock 5/6. Cost 1 Potestas. 7
> of 5 Potestas remaining.
> New Form 1. Cost 1 Potestas. 6 of 5 Potestas
> remaining.
> Performing Burglar at Level 4.
> Result = 4 (Performance) +2 (Feat) -1 (Luck) -8
> (Challenge) = -3. Failed.

"Crap!" repeated Ingar. He screwed up his eyes and focussed on feeling the interior of the mechanics.

"Crap! Crap! Crap!"

He tried again, this time concentrating the way the monks had when they taught him to meditate.

> New Form, 4. Cost 1 Potestas. 5 of 5 Potestas
> remaining.
> Performing Burglar at level 7.
> Using feat Burglar, Open Lock 5/6. Cost 1 Potestas. 4
> of 5 Potestas remaining.
> Result = 7 (Performance) +2 (Feat) +1 (Luck) -8
> (Challenge) = 2.
> Effect = Lock Opens.

The lock clunked.

> Open Lock advances to 6/6.
> Open Lock Secured.
> You have Burglar 3: Hide, Climb, Fall, Spider Climb,
> Move Silently, Stalk, Pick Pocket 3/6, Open Lock.
> You have 7 Burglar Feats. 10 Feats required to
> advance to the next level.

Ingar's head started to hurt.

"At last!" said Torstag. "Come on, before they start searching," He took a pace forward.

Something seemed wrong about the corridor.

"Wait!" said Ingar, grabbing his friend's arm. "Traps!"

"Oh…" said Torstag.

They both stared into the gloom. "I think my Tempter warned me," said Ingar.

> Possible traps.

"Yes," said Ingar. "When my form is good, it tells me stuff."

"Likewise," said Torstag. His brow furrowed. "Relying on you makes me feel blind."

"Thanks a fucking bundle, mate," said Ingar.

But Torstag didn't seem to hear him. He had screwed up his face and was muttering, apparently to his Tempter, "*Come on! Come on! You're not telling me I never robbed a tomb in a past life…*" He sighed. "Apparently not."

"Perhaps your Tempter is tired," said Ingar.

"I'm an idiot," said Torstag. "I've got four vocations on the go."

A horrid thought struck Ingar. "What? There's a limit?"

"Didn't you ask?"

"Fuck."

> **You may have 4 Vocations then an additional Vocation every 4th Level.**

"What *did* you pick?" asked Torstag.

Ingar flushed and wished he could stop just blurting out his thoughts. "We can talk later," he said. "Let me do my Burglar thing." He shone his everlight down the darkened passage.

> **Unlock Burglar, Detect Trap?**

Hold your horses, Doofus.

With Performance 7, he might not need to burn Potestas on a feat.

"What do you see?" asked Torstag.

"Nothing." Or at least nothing his performance would let him spot.

"Well?"

"I'm going to need a Feat."

> **Burglar, Detect Trap unlocked at 2/6 Grasp.**
> **Current form 4. Performing Burglar at level 7.**
> **Using feat Burglar, Detect Trap 2/6. Cost 2 Potestas.**
> **3 Potestas remaining.**
> **You are Detecting Traps at = 7 (Performance) +2 (Feat)**
> **= 9.**

"Phew," said Ingar.

"Well?" prompted Torstag.

"Shut up." Ingar dangled the everlight lower so that it cast long shadows from any irregularity in the floor. Something was not quite right about a crack running across the passage a body's length beyond the threshold.

> **Success   = 9 (Detecting Traps) +1 (Luck) -10**
> **(Challenge) = 0**
> **Possible pressure pad or trapdoor.**
> **Detect Trap advances to 3/6.**

"See that crack? We're going to have to jump past it."

The leap is a Level 4 challenge...

He backed off a few paces.

Unlock Feat Burglar, Leap?

He shook his head. His Form was good enough he didn't need to burn Potestas. He took a running jump...

Success = 7 (Performance) + 2 (Boldness) -1 (Luck) -2 (Challenge) = 6.

...landed fine, then got out the way for Torstag.

The taller acolyte launched himself over the obstacle. "Shit!" His front foot slapped down just short of the crack. He dived forward and collided with Ingar.

They both ended on the floor.

Ingar's everlight rattled away across the flat rock.

Ingar rolled over to sit up and reach for the enchanted orb. "What the fuck Torstag?"

Something whooshed past at chest height. His topknot fell to the floor.

They both stared at the ball of red hair.

"What the hell was that?" asked Torstag.

"You must have clipped the um...*pressure pad?*" said Ingar. "Holy Shit Torstag! It was *only* a Level 2 challenge!"

Torstag looked away. "I um, have this personality trait that kicks in from time to time. I'm *cautious.*"

"Nice timing," said Ingar. "Do I need to worry about this 'trait'?"

"Worrying is my job," said Torstag.

"Literally," said Ingar.

Torstag shrugged. "Is it safe to get up now?"

"Buggered if I know. Let's go on hands and knees first."

Ingar used a foot to hook his everlight closer.

Side-by-side, they crawled into the teeth of the warm breeze. Every so often he halted and held the light low to cast those tell-tale long shadows.

"Hang on," he said. "I think we *can* get up." He helped Torstag to his feet. "Now look—" He lowered his everlight again.

It cast shadows from a big crack that ran across the tunnel, and from a second one a good dozen paces off.

Success = 9 (Detecting Traps) +1 (Luck) -6 (Challenge) = 3
Effect = Tilt Trap Identified.

"This section tilts."

"Seriously?" Torstag squinted at it. "Which way?"

"Along its length so people can get past. But is it left or right…?" Ingar crouched. "Let me see where the wear patterns are."

"We don't have much time." Torstag raised his foot.

"No…!" began Ingar.

Torstag stomped the floor.

It tilted left, and it was clear it was finely balanced lengthways along its middle.

"What happened to 'cautious'?"

Torstag shrugged. "Doesn't always apply."

"Come on," said Torstag.

Keeping to the right, they edged past the trapdoor. The tunnel opened out further ahead. The warm breeze grew stronger and the stench of embalming chemicals overwhelming, as did the clattering sound.

"Almost there," said Torstag, striding out. His foot swung over a row of dents in the floor.

Success = 9 (Detecting Traps) +0 (Luck) -9 (Challenge) = 0
Effect = Possible Trap Detected.
Test of Potestas 3. Success.

Ingar grabbed Torstag, yanked him back.

A half dozen rusty iron bars slammed out of the ceiling, clanged on the stone floor, one bent slightly.

"Damn," said Torstag.

"Didn't you see the dents?" asked Ingar.

Torstag shook his head.

The bars started to retract, but the bent one jammed them just above head height.

"Step this way," said Ingar, starting to duck.

They reached the end of the tunnel, stepped *long* over the threshold, and found themselves on a raised landing. Five stone steps led down into a cavern full of skeletons, clattering as they aimlessly stamped and shuffled around. Swords and shield bosses and burnished helmets all glittered in the illumination from the everlight.

"I think we've found the source of the noise," said Torstag.

The skeletons crowded in close around the base of the platform.

CHAPTER 16: SKELETON ARMY!

Ingar considered the jostling skeletons. The curved swords looked awfully sharp, as did the spiked maces.

Skeletons. Medium speed. Hundreds. Dangerous. No room to manoeuvre.

He wasn't going to dodge or sneak his way through that lot. "Okay, we'll go up and over instead." Ingar swung his everlight over the cavern walls: smooth.

Climbing the cavern walls is a level 15 challenge.

The skeletons became agitated, clattering and swaying.

"Or not," he said, lowering the light. "How about…"

"Don't look at me," said Torstag. "It's a level four challenge just to repel one skeleton. There are hundreds of those things! It's…" He paused, obviously listening to his Tempter. "…a level nine challenge to shift that lot."

"You can do it!" said Ingar. "Level One Necromancer, right? Hammer away at your Form to get a five, gives you Performance six. Add two for whatever the feat is takes you to eight…a bit of luck takes you to nine."

Torstag shook his head. "I've only got three Potestas. I'd need to get Form five first time, so I could have more than one try at the spell. But anyway, my Necromancer feats only let me do a spell. They don't give me a boost like my Scout feats do."

"Ha!" said Ingar. He rummaged in his pocket and brought out the prize from his first attempt at the Pick Pocket feat. "Look! Old Smelly Newt's chalk!"

Torstag eyed it sceptically. "Do you think it will work?"

"I've watched him use it," said Ingar. "He never chants or prays. The spell has to be in the chalk."

"Great," said Torstag, "but what are you going to do with it?" He surveyed the cavern. "You'd be cut down before you drew anything. They'll reach over the lines, just like in the practice vault, except with swords."

"Fuck," said Ingar.

"Hang on," said Torstag. "Why's this cavern so big?"

"What do you mean?"

"It's a waste," said Torstag. "A handful of skeletons would be enough to stop intruders like us. They don't need an entire cavern."

"What if they had to hold off an army?" asked Ingar.

"Any army that got here would have to have magicians who could cope with skeletons fine…" Torstag snapped his fingers. "This *is* an army. That's the point. This is where they store the skeletons for man-hunts. This is the first place they'll come once they realise we're missing."

"Shit. We'd better get a move on," said Ingar. "What if we…?" He peered over the edge of the platform. A rough white line kept the skeletons from mounting the steps. "Well fuck me! It's just a chalk line keeping the skeletons back." A plan formed in his mind. He was…*fairly* sure it would work. He moved over to the right hand side of the platform.

The skeletons huddled into the cramped space, as if expecting him to jump off and try to get past.

Ingar raised his robe…

Testing Potestas, 3. Performance Anxiety resisted.

…and urinated. He aimed the stream not in their faces—though that was tempting—but down on the chalk at the base of the platform.

"What the hell are you doing?" asked Torstag. "You'll erase the…Oh Hell!"

Something unnatural *snapped*.

One of the skeletons moved across the steaming puddle and took a swing at Ingar's ankles.

Ingar skipped back. The other skeletons were already filing in behind the first.

He turned.

Sure enough, in moving to the right-hand side of the vault, the skeletons had cleared the left-hand side. "Come on!" he yelled. He sprang down off the platform and started running for the door at the other end. "Wheee!"

"You're mad!" panted Torstag behind him.

Ingar slammed into the door, spun to face the way he'd come.

There was no pursuit. At the other end of the vault, the skeletons were filing around the inside of the chalk, and up the steps.

As he looked on, one crossed the threshold at the far end. The entire lintel slammed down, obliterated it with an almighty crash, then banged back into place.

"So there *was* a trap," said Torstag.

As if an officer had shouted a command, the surviving skeletons about-faced and filed back down the steps. Already half a dozen skeletons were rattling down the cavern toward them.

"Bugger," said Ingar.

"How about getting this door open?"

"Holy chalk first," said Ingar. He pulled out the stick of chalk and stooped to mark the floor.

Form 3. Performing Artist at Level 3. Unlock...?

No shut the fuck up Doofus.

He drew a wide half circle from one side of the door to the other. "There."

"Hmm," said Torstag, squinting at the chalk. He positioned himself in front of the door. "I'll watch your back just in case."

"Suit yourself." Ingar crouched in front of the door and started prodding with his bent wire.

Form 3.
Performing Burglar at level 6.
Using Open Lock, cost 1 Potestas. 2 of 5 Potestas remaining.

Something clunked.

Result = 6 (Performance) + 2 (Feat) -1 (Luck) -8
(Challenge) = -1
Effect = Failure.

Ingar turned the handle and pulled. Nothing happened. There was still more work to do. "Bugger."

"Damn!" said Torstag. He bumped into Ingar's back.

Ingar pivoted in time to see Torstag throwing himself at a skeleton that had squeezed between the wall and the end of the chalk semicircle.

Torstag twisted the monster's weapon free—a short spiked mace.

The skeleton raised its round shield, but too slowly.

Torstag's commandeered mace caught the thing on the cranium, reduced the skull to dust.

Bones rained on the stone. The round shield hit the ground and rattled like a dropped coin.

Already, a second skeleton was trying to squeeze through the gap.

Torstag scooped up the shield. "The good news is I'm on Form 5 and have the advantage when they try to force their way in. The bad news is that I'm out of *Potestas* and you can't draw. How about just getting the bloody door open?"

"I'm doing my best," said Ingar. He got the wire into the right spot and twisted.

Result = 6 (Performance) +2 (Feat) +1 (Luck) -8
(Challenge) = 1
Effect = 1.
The lock moved just a little.
Result = 6 (Performance) + 2 (Feat) +1 (Luck) -8
(Challenge) = 1
Effect = 1.

There was a crash behind him. "Two down," said Torstag. "Damn…" Another crash.

Ingar forced himself to focus on the job in hand.

Behind him, Torstag grunted and there was another crash.

Ingar twisted the wire. The lock squeaked.

Result = 6 (Performance) +2 (Feat) +0 (Luck) -8
(Challenge) = 0
Effect = 0.
Result = 6 (Performance) +2 (Feat) +1 (Luck) -8
(Challenge) = -1
Effect = 0.
Result = 6 (Performance) + 2 (Feat) +0 (Luck) -8
(Challenge) = 0
Effect = 0.
Total Effect 4. Lock Opened.

Ingar rose, yanked the door open and stepped inside. "Come on!"

Torstag dived past him.

Ingar pulled the door shut.

Immediately, the handle started to turn. Ingar put his weight into holding it still. "The buggers know how to open doors."

"They were people once," said Torstag.

"They can't weigh much," said Ingar, taking one hand off. "Swap over," he said, "and I'll try to reset the lock."

Torstag stepped back and raised the spiked mace. His eyes twinkled. "I have a better idea. When I reach three, move your hands."

The mace's ball head seemed to fill Ingar's vision. "Holy Fuck you are supposed to be cautious!"

Warrior. Dangerous. Fast.

"One…

The skeletons scratched at the door, the pressure on the handle grew harder to resist. More than one skeleton must be adding its weight.

"Two…three!"

Ingar yelped and snatched his hands away.

The mace slammed into the door handle, crushed it.

There was a clang from beyond the door as the rod shot out into the skeleton cavern, taking with it the handle on the other side. The crushed door knob clanked onto the natural stone floor.

"Sorted," said Torstag.

Ingar looked beyond him.

Rank after rank of kneeling mummies filled the cavern. More tunnels led off the rear, all lined by human figures

"I see...dead people," said Ingar. "Lots of dead people."

Torstag blanched. He squared his jaw. "I'll take it from here."

Chapter 17: The Bluestocking Librarian and the Naked Barbarian

Millicent blinked into the warm air that gusted through the preternatural doorway.

It really was a naked barbarian!

Tattoos whorled over powerful muscles. Spiky hair added to his impressive stature. His clean-shaven chin and a long well-cared for moustache spoke of a certain sensual self regard.

A thick rope hobbled his ankles. His hands were clearly pinned behind his back.

Their gazes met.

Laughter lines bracketed his twinkling eyes. This was a man facing death with an ironic smile. He raised one eyebrow as if to ask what a lady were doing in such a dark place.

Beyond him stood men wearing conical hats bedecked with little bells, and ornamental-looking bronze breastplates. Each carried a spear with a leaf-bladed head in the same metal. They saw her, lifted their weapons. One man changed grip for a throw.

Millicent aimed her pistol and fired.

Form 2.
Using Skill Shooting 4. Cost 1 Potestas, 4 of 6
remaining.
Performing Shooting at Level 5.
Result = 5 (Performance) +1 (Luck) −5 (Challenge) = 1
Effect = Rope cut.

The bullet chipped the stone between the naked barbarian's ankles, ricochetted. Blood flecked from the inner thigh of a grey-bearded man who sported a felt shawl or cloak. His knee buckled. He toppled sideways.

"Damn! Sorry!" blurted Millicent. "I didn't mean…"

The hobble rope, meanwhile, had parted.

The barbarian spun on one powerful leg, lashed out with the other. His big foot slammed into a breastplate, sent a spearman crashing into his comrades.

The one using a throwing grip drew back his spear to cast.

Test of Potestas 3, declared her Voice.

"Sorry! Sorry…" said Millicent, even as she aimed and fired.

Current Form 2.
Using Skill Shooting 4. Cost 1 Potestas, 4 of 6
remaining.
Performing Shooting at Level 5.

The weapon crashed.

Pistol takes effect first.
Performing Shooting at level 9. Cost 1 Potestas, 1 of
6 remaining.
Result = 4 (Performance) −1 (Luck) −0 (Challenge) = 3
Armour 1 (2 halved) negated.
Effect = 3 (Result) +3 (Revolver) = 6.
Target slain.

A black hole appeared in the thrower's breastplate. He tumbled off the edge of what appeared to be a wooden platform. The cheering stopped. Somebody screamed into the silence.

Millicent kept on screaming.

The last two spearmen rallied and charged across the wooden deck. The barbarian flipped onto his back.

The blood rushed in Millicent's ears, making it hard to think. Like a sleepwalker, she stepped forward through the portal and out onto the platform, even as part of her realised that if the barbarian actually *needed* her help then they were both doomed.

The barbarian, however, evidently uninjured, drew in his knees, brought his bound wrists past his muscular backside and round in front of him. He kicked the knees of the nearest spearman, then rolled to his feet. A flex of his muscles and his wrist ropes snapped.

The other spearman thrust at his kidneys.

Millicent aimed and fired.

Nothing happened.

She stared at the revolver, while ice water seemed to trickle into her gut. The cylinder had four rounds left, but none of them were going to fire in this Realm because she was now well beyond the Pale.

It wasn't just the little sparks dancing over the surface of her father's revolver that told her this. It was also the scene on which the portal had opened; a wide triangular plaza lined by multi-tiered buildings with taller towers visible above the roofline. The architecture—lots of triangular columns—was unfamiliar, as was the costume of the crowd—everybody in tall conical hats with bells, men with pierced noses, women with bared bosoms and… "Ouch."

The portal in the ruined tower had clearly taken her to an entirely undocumented civilisation, one on which she had inadvertently declared war.

There was a scream and a crash. The barbarian had disarmed the man behind and used the weapon to slash the throat of the one in front.

Blood sprayed. The surviving spearman screamed and jumped off the platform into the crowd. The barbarian roared some kind of complex invective and hurled the corpse after him. It crashed into the back of one of a company of bronze-armoured soldiers who were keeping the mob back from the platform.

Everything, realised Millicent, had happened faster than they could react.

Now an officer barked orders and the soldiers about-faced.

Something drew Millicent's gaze beyond the armoured men to look over the top of the now-muted crowd.

The platform she was standing on had duplicates at the other two corners of the triangular plaza, both built around a monolith with a wooden door. The lack of fortifications suggested that each portal led to somewhere equally fatal. Even so, according to her memory of the chart, and to the strong intuitive pull she felt, she needed to get to the one on her right.

The barbarian stamped a bare foot, making the boards thud. He banged the bronze-shod spear butt on the wood.

The sound echoed back from the surrounding buildings, breaking the uncanny silence.

Still thumping the spear, he launched into something that was somewhere between a chant and a song. The language suddenly became vaguely familiar.

> Using Scholar Feat, Read Gorlakian Runes cost 1
> Potestas, 0 remaining.
> Current Form 2. Performing Scholar at level 6.
> Result = 6 (Performance) + 2 (Feat) +0 (Luck) -2
> (Spoken Language) = Understanding Gorlakian at
> level 6.

"...so know that I am Withard, son of Maeve the Cruncher, daughter of Mighty Oak King of the Lone Tower, son of..."

An order rang out.

Three soldiers detached themselves and ran up the steps to the platform.

Slash!

Stab!

Butt-strike.

Withard, son of Maeve the Cruncher despatched all three enemies without breaking the rhythm of his chant.

Another order and a solder blew a horn. An answering call rang out from somewhere beyond the plaza.

Withard, son of Maeve the Cruncher's only response was to chant louder and brandish the spear higher so that drops of blood fell like rain.

Millicent drew herself up. This was no situation for a lady. However, going back into the cold Realm entailed certain death. Unless…

She returned her revolver to her shoulder bag. Stooping, she grabbed a dropped spear—it weighed a good two pounds—and tossed it back through the portal.

The wood clattered on the scattered bones.

She did the same with the remaining three spears. Eight pounds of wood. Not enough.

A trumpet resounded from the other side of the plaza. A column of cavalry started to nudge through the crowd. Each rider carried a big recurved bow.

The platform was a creaky thing. How well put together was it?

She stooped and grabbed the edge. One good heave and a plank came loose, then another. She tossed them through the door.

The cavalry fanned out a good hundred yards from the platform. This was going to be down to archery.

The crowd streamed around the horses, getting out of the way.

The greybeard had bled out, so Millicent tore off his felt cloak.

Withard, son of Maeve the Cruncher, and—to be honest—possessor of a very fine and muscular rump—was still chanting his defiance.

Millicent half turned away, then said, "What-ho, Withard. Um, we makee strategic-um retreat-ee?"

Current form 2. Performing Virago at level 6.
Result = 6 (Performance) +0 (luck) -4 (Target Will) = 2
Tentative Practical Response.

The naked barbarian wheeled to face her.

Behind him, the mounted archers bent their bows.

It would have been ladylike to blush and avert her eyes. Instead she barked, "Come on!"

The bows rippled.

Millicent turned, threw herself through the door onto pile of scavenged timber and spears.

120

The naked barbarian landed on her.

Millicent rolled around. "Get the door closed!"

An arrow thudded into the plank she'd just vacated.

A figure appeared in the doorway.

She grabbed her bag, scrambled inside for her pistol.

The door closed shut, plunging them in darkness.

The barbarian rolled to his feet. "*Stay down, woman. Dragons!*"

"Um…" Millicent thought frantically. "*Me kill dragons with bang stick?*"

Silence. Then he said something too fast for her to understand.

Had she insulted his barbarian manhood? "Sorry! *Sorry!*"

"*I say…you like Great Cormaxaz! Warrior Queen!*"

"Oh, thank you." She stood up and shivered. "*We must be ready to fight.*"

"*Uh? Why would moose need help for such a thing? Also, where moose?*"

It was just possible she had suggested they prepare for a ritual barn raising. She repeated the sentence using a different word.

"*Oh,* fight." He laughed. "*Yes, no moose here! Ha ha!*" He hunkered down. "*No, no. This is cursed realm. They think we die.*" He sighed. "*No light. No heat. We die. How about we…*" He used a verb she didn't recognise. "*…first?*"

"Wait," she said. She rummaged in her bag and lit a match.

The flare of light illuminated the barbarian like an old oil painting. He was truly magnificent, despite the effect of the cold.

He leapt back. "*Sorcery!*"

She shook her head. "Um…*craft?*"

That seemed to quiet him.

She felt his eyes on her as she brought out the candle, lit that— "*More craft*"—then indicated the felt cloak.

He was not too proud to wrap himself in that.

She took out the heavy knife she kept for camping emergencies. She offered it to him hilt first. "*Make fire?*"

Withard worked quickly, splitting the planks lengthwise then snapping the smaller spars. He broke some into kindling and by the time Millicent got her first Potestas point back—about twenty minutes— he had a nice fire going.

The barbarian went outside to scout. He returned bearing a haunch of wyvern meat. He broke up the spare spears and added them to the fire.

Roasted wyvern turned out to be palatable enough, if a little salty.

They shared water from her canteen then sat in companionable silence until the tension became unbearable.

Potestas 1 of 6.
Form 3. Performing Virago at level 7.
Using Maelstrom+1, cost 1 Potestas, 0 of 6
remaining.

"That word you used," said Millicent. She repeated it as best she could.

"Oh," said Withard. "*Like how baby moose are made.*"

"*I'm no moose,*" she said.

His grin flashed in the half dark. "*I make you sound like one.*"

Result = 7 (Performance) +3 (Feat) +0 (Luck) +4
(Enthusiastic Target) = 14.
Effect...

As it turned out, Withard, son of Maeve the Cruncher, was no liar, though perhaps the acoustic properties of the ruin helped.

Nor was he somebody she could just abandon.

When the circle of sky grew light, Millicent showed him her chart.

Withard stabbed at one of the little circular maps, just two portals away from the central crown.

"*There,*" he said, "*big stone horse, except front legs now gone. Give me chart I get home.*"

Millicent shook her head. "I'll just have to take you there myself."

Chapter 18: Catacomb Quest!

Torstag drew himself up, squared his jaw.

Current Form 3. Performing Necromancer at Level 4. Mummies. Thousands. Inert. Enchanted.

Mummies webbed by glowing gossamer strands, to be precise. Behind them, the door thudded.

"Fuck!" said Ingar. "I thought the skeletons wanted to escape?"

"They want to kill the most number of people," said Torstag. "Since they can't escape the Catacombs, we're it."

"How do you know that?" asked Ingar.

"Um," said Torstag. "I just remembered."

"Better get this over with quickly," said Ingar.

"Yes," said Torstag. "We just follow the threads."

"Which only you can see."

"Yup," said Torstag. "It's your turn to be blind." He squinted, half-closing his eyes so he could make out the thread.

A dry breeze tickled his cheeks, warmed his limbs.

He flexed his fingers. "This way."

Current Form 3. Performing Necromancer at Level 4.
Go on...
You are Torstag, Human Warlock, Youth, Agile,
Empathic, Cautious, Marked.
Potestas 1/4. Will 2. Cowardice 2/6. Horror of the
Unquiet Dead 1/6.
Vitality 2/3. Toughness 1.
Vocations:
Warlord 1: Tea Drinking.
Warrior 1: (Brawl, Sidearm): Wrath Strike +1, Split
Shield 2/6
Scout 2 (Mountains, Forest, Jungle): Climb+1, Spider
Climb, Stalk 4/6, Forage 2/6.
Necromancer 1 (Cantrips): Repel Shade, Shade Cloak
3/6.
Various General Skills including Meditation.

While his Tempter reeled off his accomplishments, Torstag led his friend across the cavern, through row upon row of mildewed mummies, some bearing obvious wounds—even missing limbs—all sedately kneeling before a plinth on which sat a copy of the Book of Obedience in various states of decrepitude. A good proportion of them were tonsured like monks and the right sole of each bore a crudely nailed on parchment label. He stooped to read one.

Mummy. Inert. Enchanted.

"Come on," said Ingar. "We don't have time."

"We need to understand," said Torstag. He read out a date over two centuries past, then the text: "Ornhalt Corebinder, executed rebel, dedicated by City Elders of Sturmburgh. Reincarnated as Brother Nugatory." He rose and saw that the back of Ornhalt's skull had been crushed.

"'Dedicated'," said Ingar, making air quotes. "So much for having an Epiphany and dedicating *himself*."

Torstag shook his head. His eyes narrowed.

A glowing thread connected Ornhalt's mummy to its fresher-looking neighbour. He squeezed past—the mummies had the texture of dried wood—and read out a date ninety years later, then, "Brother

Nugatory, Presbyter Self-dedicated. Reincarnated as Brother Obscurity." And the next mummy was Brother Obscurity, who had reincarnated as…

"Brother Neutrality!" hissed Torstag.

"Smelly Newt liked it so much, he came back for more and more," said Ingar.

Torstag shrugged. "His choice, I suppose."

"I wonder what Ornhalt Corebinder might say, though?"

"Well, he was a rebel," said Torstag. "I mean, it's one way of taking a warlock out of the Ten Thousand Realms for a generation."

"Humph," said Ingar. "We're escaping and you're still a conformist."

Torstag frowned. There was something on the edge of his mind.

"Go on," said Ingar. "Lead the way."

The threads took them across the cavern and into one of the side tunnels. The everlights cast moving shadows from the endless rows of mummies.

One of the threads vanished.

"Stop," said Torstag. He padded around Ingar until he found the thread, now pointing backwards to a niche containing just one mummy that had toppled onto its side. "I think we've found you," he said.

Mummy. Inert.

Ingar ducked forward to read the plaque on the dead man's foot.

Torstag noticed the state of the mummy. "Wait!"

Too late! Ingar read out, "Marvon the Mutilator, tyrant. Kicked to death by the mob. Dedicated by the People's Revolutionary Council of Vitigern. Mummification Overseer, Brother Benign-Stasis." He swore. "That's bad."

"It might not mean what it says," said Torstag. "'Mutilator' might be a ritual thing."

"I'm a monster!"

"*Was* a monster. You're Ingar now."

"Am I? Fuck! What if that…person takes over a little each time I succumb to the Tempter? What if the monks are telling the truth?"

Torstag shrugged. "You were other somebodies. I'm sure some of them were quite pleasant."

"What?" said Ingar. "You mean Marvon the Impaler? Marvon the Puppy Strangler? Marvon the Kitten Drowner…"

"They wouldn't all be called Marvon," said Torstag. "And it does show you didn't have a choice. Your past self didn't 'have an epiphany and become a Dedicant', he was killed and his body sent here…"

"But that would be to stop him—me!—reincarnating as another tyrant," said Ingar. "Which on the face of it sounds quite reasonable."

"Well, you didn't, did you?" said Torstag firmly.

"He even looks like me."

"Frankly, it's hard to say what he looks like."

Though the mummy was less than two decades old, it was in a terrible state. The skull bore great dents, as did the flesh. The arms were broken in three places, with bones poking through the blackened skin. The legs weren't right either. Presumably the damage from being very thoroughly kicked to death by an angry mob had caused the mummy to collapse out of its position.

Torstag's brow furrowed. There was something else wrong as well.

Mummy. Inert.

"No enchantment," he said. "That's why you're such a rule breaker. Everybody else has a mummy kneeling before the Book of Obedience. You don't."

"Or maybe I'm just a monster," said Ingar. He sat down cross-legged. "I'll wait for you to get away then surrender myself."

Torstag regarded his friend, couldn't find the right words. He passed his mace to his shield hand, bent his knees and hauled Marvon's mummy over his shoulder. It was surprisingly light. "I'll be seeing you."

"Hey, put me down you fucker!" cried Ingar, rising. He grabbed the mummy's leg. His eyes widened. "Oh shit." He snatched his hand back and staggered. "Whoa! Oh my. Oh my…" He clutched his head. "Fuck."

Torstag took a step toward his friend, but he had his hands full.

"I'm all right—wow!—better than all right," said Ingar, steadying himself. "I had a Surge. They're only supposed to happen when you level up your top vocation."

Torstag furrowed his brow. "But I had one when the girl kissed me."

"She kissed you?" Ingar leered. "I'll bet you 'surged'."

Torstag felt his cheeks colour. "A very chaste kiss," he said. "And my Tempter called it a Surge."

"OK," said Ingar. "So you touched a girl from a past life, I touched my body from a past life…so level up or touch a relic from a previous existance and you get to surge."

"She didn't *look* like a relic," said Torstag. "But that makes sense."

"Hah," said Ingar. "I'm a level 4 Burglar, now."

"Congratulations," said Torstag. He was never going to catch up.

"Oh Gods!" Ingar bent double and vomited on a mummy's feet.

Torstag took a sharp step backwards to avoid the splash. "Come on, let's go."

"I should stay behind, for your sake," said Ingar. "For everybody's sakes. I just had a flash of Marvon wielding a hammer. He really was a mutilator."

"I…," began Torstag. There was too much to say, too little time. "I need you," he said. He set off to follow the glowing thread that still extended from his sternum.

It led them deeper into the catacombs, their footfalls now louder than the sound of the skeletons rattling at the door. They then zig-zagged through different passages and came to one with very well pre-served mummies. The warm breeze was stronger here.

"Getting close to the the portal," said Ingar.

Torstag nodded. He took three more paces and there was the mummy of a giant of a man. He was vaguely reminiscent of an old bronze tea strainer, so perforated were his upper torso and arms. Kneeling next to him was a much skinnier individual. Shimmering strands connected the pair to each other and to Torstag.

He dumped the mummy of Marvon the Mutilator across the laps of his kneeling former selves, making the dry wooden podium rock. Dust billowed from the open pages of the Book of Obedience.

"Hey! Careful with me!" said Ingar.

"My past selves," said Torstag, with a wave of the spiked mace.

Each mummy was naked and shrivelled where it mattered. Their lips had shrunken away to reveal black gums and yellow teeth. The flesh of their limbs had withered into the bones.

Torstag knelt to read the tag. The hair stood up on the back of his neck. "Berotspan son of Bruglehilda, known as 'the Marshal'. Killed while defending Yinkesia against the God Gronchard the Flayer. Self-Dedicant…"

"Gronchard the Flayer!" said Ingar. "I look after his temple. He has a really hot consort…or did. But you fought a demi-god?"

"Apparently." Torstag's shoulders slumped. "The girl mentioned we had a common enemy. But she didn't say it was a god."

"Well fuck him, and fuck her. Not our problem, remember?" said Ingar. "What about the earlier you?"

Torstag squinted at the smaller of the two husks of his former self.

"Lashton the Necromancer," he read out.

"Well that explains—" began Ingar.

Torstag read on. "Executed. Dedicated by Gronchard the Flayer. Harvesting failed."

"King Gronchard the Flayer again!" said Ingar. "You must have really pissed him off."

"*Harvesting failed*," quoted Torstag. "So Lashton-Me was executed and his body sent here. He was reborn as the Marshal…"

Ingar cut in, "But the Grey Cortège didn't manage to harvest him when he came of age."

"But he still felt the tug, and, when he was old, dedicated himself," completed Torstag. "I—he—we—didn't really choose this life, he was nudged into it."

"It's a fucking scam!" exclaimed Ingar. "Once they get one of your corpses, they have you for all eternity!"

"And I'm only a goody-two-shoes because they mummified me kneeling before the book," said Torstag. "Bastards!" He yanked at the podium. Both podium and Book of Obedience crashed into the corridor.

A weight lifted from his shoulders.

You are now: Torstag, Human, Youth, Agile, Sensitive, Bold, Marked.

"So much for *cautious*," said Torstag. "I'm my own man now. Truly."

But what did *Marked* mean?

There was a crunch.

Footsteps echoed up from further up the darkened tunnel.

"Patrol," said Ingar. "You shouldn't have made all that noise."

Three skeletons clattered out into the pool of light.

Torstag started to turn to run, but then suddenly didn't feel like retreating, not now not ever again.

"Oh shit," said Ingar.

"Hah!" said Torstag. "Let's see if this works." He glanced from mummy to mummy, from necromancer to warrior. He put his hand on the mummified head of Berotspan the Marshal.

CHAPTER 19: SMITING SKELETONS!

Power rampaged through Torstag like…oddly like a glittering column of heavy cavalry, steel plates wreathed in the glare of the desert sun while around him men fled and died and tents burned and—

9 points of Grasp Improvement available. Which Vocation?

Warrior.

First, he was going to advance the Feat that had won him the spiked mace…

Disarm 3/6 secured. 6 Points remaining.

And might as well tidy up loose ends…

Cleave Shield 2/6 secured. 2 points remaining.
Select a 5th Warrior Feat to study.

Twitch—getting in a second cut down the other side—looked useful and led on to Rampage.

Twitch unlocked at 2/6 Grasp.
You have surpassed 3 Warrior Feats.
Warrior advances to 2. 6 Feats required to secure 3rd level.
Vitality = 2 + 2 (highest applicable vocation) = 4
Select a Proficiency.

Given there were lots of them around…

"Shield" Proficiency unlocked.
2 points of Improvement available. Which Vocation?

Warrior!

Warrior, Twitch advanced to 4/6 Grasp. 0 points
remaining.
Vitality restored.
Potestas restored and boosted.
You are Torstag, Human Warlock, Youth, Agile,
Sensitive, Bold, Marked.
Potestas 8/4. Will 2. Horror of the Unquiet Dead 1/6.
Vitality 4. Toughness 2.
Vocations:
Warlord 0: Tea Drinking 2/6.
Warrior, 2 (Brawl, Sidearm, Shield): Wrath Strike +1,
Split Shield, Disarm, Twitch 4/6.
Scout 2 (Mountain, Forest, Jungle): Climb +1, Spider
Climb, Sneak
Necromancer 1 (Cantrips): Repel Shade, Shade Cloak
3/6, Manifest Shade 4/6
Various General Skills including Meditate.
Form 5.

And the clatter of skeletons echoed closer down the tunnels of the
Catacombs of Hesitation.

3 Skeletons, hostile. Natural armour. Structure 6.
Unaffected by thrusts.

Torstag wriggled his shoulders and hefted the spiked mace. Somehow he felt more himself. "Hold the everlight high," he said.

"Let's run," said Ingar.

"Let's not," said Torstag.

The skeletons came around a corner, jogging along three abreast.

"Are you going to repel them?"

"Absolutely," said Torstag, the blood rushing in his ears. He
twirled the mace, got the handle to settle into his palm.

"Oh crap," said Ingar.

You are performing Warrior at level 7.
3 Skeletons. 2 long knife, 1 hand axe. Natural
Armour, 2. Shields, 2.

The skeletons were nearly on him.

Enemy has Advantage of Numbers.
Cramped Space.

They clattered closer until Ingar's everlight illuminated the backs of their empty eye sockets.

Torstag stepped to his right, close to the wall, so as at least not to be outflanked.

Manoeuvring. Enemy advance. You stand ground. No tests.

The skeletons arrived together, but did not quite attack in unison. The one closest to the wall had a long knife. However, it shoved in with its shield raised in front as if trying to jam his mace.

War Knife outclasses Spiked Mace as melee weapon.

Torstag couldn't retreat so he sidestepped and swung his mace low.

Result = 7 (Your Performance) +1 (Luck) -3
("Outnumbered", "Heavier Weapon") -4 (Challenge) = 1
Effect = 1 (Result) +2 (Mace) = 3 damage. Target has 3
remaining Structure and Hindrance "Damaged".

The mace cracked into the ribs, sending shards of bones flying.

The second skeleton was already swinging its axe.

Torstag let the mace blow follow through, raised his hand, and whipped the weapon down diagonally, covering himself with the round shield and stepping behind the strike.

> Axe and Spiked Mace are matched as Melee
> Weapons.
> Using Feat Wrath Strike, cost 1 Potestas, 7 of 4
> remaining.
> Result = 7 (Your Performance) +0 (Luck) -2
> ("Outnumbered") -4 (Challenge) = 1
> Effect = 1 (Result) +2 (Wrath Strike) +2 (Mace) = 5.
> Target has 1 remaining structure and Hindrance
> "Damaged".

The incoming axe clanged on Torstag's shield just as his own weapon smashed into the skeleton's shoulder, cracking the white bone.

The third skeleton squeezed past the mummies and clattered off in the direction of Ingar, who swore copiously and—judging from the movement of the light—started backing away.

Again, Torstag followed through and struck down the same line at the axe wielding skeleton. This time he did not bother with a feat.

The skeleton's shield came up, but unsteadily.

> Target has 1 remaining structure and Hindrance
> "Damaged".
> Result = 7 (Your Performance) -1 (Luck) -2
> ("Outnumbered") + 2 ("Target Damaged) -4 (Challenge)
> = 2.

The spiked mace passed over the top and struck the monster's skull. It flew off and bounced off the rock wall.

> Effect = 2 (Result) +2 (Mace) = 4. Target destroyed.

With a roar of triumph, Torstag pivoted to face the skeleton that had tried to jam him with the shield.

> Target has 2 remaining structure and Hindrance
> "Damaged".
> You have Disadvantage "Outclassed Weapon".

The skeleton's long knife flashed in the uneven light.

Torstag raised his shield and hacked down behind it, letting the metal rim guard his hand.

The knife squealed down the face of the shield.

The skeleton, however, used its shield to bash the mace away.

> Result = 7 (Your Performance) -1 (Luck) -3
> ("Outnumbered", "Outclassed Weapon") +2 ("Target
> Damaged") -2 (Target Feat "Parry") -4 (Challenge) = -1
> Capped at Tie.
> Test of Potestas 7. Twitch available.

Torstag stole the momentum of the bash and whirled the mace back into another strike.

> Using Twitch 4/6, cost 1 Potestas 6 of 4 remaining.

The skeleton, however, had its knife free and brought it down to parry against Torstag's wrist.

> Enemy Feat Travel After counters Twitch.
> Effect = 1 (Luck) + 0 (Knife) = 1 Vitality Loss.
> 3 of 4 Vitality remaining.

Wet pain blossomed on his arm.

Torstag skipped backwards to get some space. Then, suddenly, he'd had enough. With an incoherent bellow, he launched himself into wild attack, flailing the heavy mace left and right, striking from one angle after the other.

> Boldness grants +2 Result. However, on a tie, it
> instead grants +2 Result to the enemy.

Again, the skeleton tried a full parry that would end in a deadly Tie. However, the third skeleton had run past, so Torstag was no longer reacting to being outnumbered. The mace drew a spiral in the gloom, missed the shield, went up and around, then down behind it.

Bone crunched.

> Result = 7 (Your Performance) +2 (Boldness) +1 (Luck) -
> 2 ("Outclassed Weapon") +2 ("Target Damaged") -2
> (Target Feat "Parry") -4 (Challenge) = 4
> Effect = 4 (Result) +2 (Mace) = 6. Target destroyed.

The skeleton's component parts scattered the floor.

"Some help, please!" yelled Ingar.

Torstag twisted. Ingar was still backing away from the third skeleton, blocking its blows with a rapidly deteriorating book stand.

Torstag's injured arm whipped the mace into a throw.

(And in the back of his mind, he heard himself talk to his Tempter:

Unlock Hurl as 5th Warrior Feat?

Yes.

Hurl unlocked at 2/6 Grasp.
Using Hurl 2/6 cost 3 Potestas. 5/4 Potestas
remaining.

The weapon spun in flight.

Ingar, eyes wide with fear but still holding up the everlight, skipped backwards, away from the onrushing skeleton.

Target is in Melee range.
Result = 7 (Performance) +2 (Feat) +4 (Enemy not
defending) +0 (Luck) -4 (Enemy Challenge) -1 (Range)=
8.

The head of the mace cracked into the monster's skull.

Effect = 8 +2 (Mace) = 10 Damage.

White bone shattered. The skeleton fell apart. The mace dropped at Ingar's feat.

1 Point of Fatigue incurred.
2 of 4 Vitality remaining.
6 of 4 Potestas remaining.

He contemplated the gash in his forearm. The everlight made the blood look black. He tucked his his right hand under his left armpit, hugging the wound to his robe. "You were a lot of help," he said.

"Fuck you," said Ingar, "I'm only Warrior zero."

Torstag just stared at him while the wound stung.

"Look," said Ingar, "It was your bloody stupid idea to fight them."

"I did, didn't I?" said Torstag. He threw back his head. The tunnel echoed with his laughter.

"And you got injured."

Torstag shrugged. He kicked one of the broken skulls. "By the Gods! I needed that!"

Ingar winced. "If that had been people it would have been…fucking disturbing."

"But it wasn't." Torstag laughed. "Oh, you were wrong about Vitality. It's two plus the 'highest applicable Vocation'. Or was for me. Warrior goes straight into it."

"Fuck," said Ingar. He chewed his lip. "So it must be half for Vocations that are kind of physical, like Burglar, but the whole whack for big tough Warriors." He cocked his head at the mummies. "Aren't you going to touch the other one?"

"The necromancer?" Torstag shook his head. "Do me a favour—rip his arm off."

"What the fuck?"

"Surge gives us five Form, doesn't it?"

"Yes."

"And heals us. So handy for later."

"Yep." Ingar nodded. He tore off the arm of Lashton the Necromancer and tucked it into his belt. "Let's get the fuck out of here."

"No, wait. Lend me the everlight," said Torstag.

"What? Sure. What are you going to do?"

Torstag placed the orb on the stone plinth, raised his mace—Morningstar, corrected his Tempter.

Ingar took a pace forward. "No!"

Torstag brought down the weapon.

The orb cracked. A sliver of flame escaped, formed itself into a tiny dragon. For a heartbeat, it hung in the air. Then it dove hungrily into the belly of the mummy of Berotspan the Marshal.

Fire whooshed. Black smoke coiled.

"Great," said Ingar. "But now we have no light."

Torstag handed the mace to Ingar. "Hang onto the mace."

"If you say," said Ingar. "What about light?"

Torstag stooped and picked up one of the long knives. It felt good in his hands. He thrust through a fold in his robe, then wrenched at the Marshal's left arm. It came off with a sickening crunch. He dipped the stump end in the fire. It caught instantly. He offered it to Ingar. "If you don't like the dark, you can hold my hand."

Coughing, Ingar took the relic by its wizened wrist. "Fucking lunatic."

The flames spread to the mummy of Marvon the Mutilator.

136

Torstag grabbed it by the head.

"Hey...! Began Ingar.

Torstag hurled the mummy across the tunnel to land amidst another pair of mummies. Fire whooshed. Black smoke now billowed over the rough-hewn vault.

The Marshal's right hand was free of flames. Torstag grabbed it— felt old scars, had flashes of cutting down his enemies like so many dogs—twisted and pulled. With a crunch, both hand and burning forearm came free.

Something buzzed past and pinged into the cavern wall.

Crossbow bolt. Off Target.

"What was...?" began Ingar.

"Crossbows!" Torstag started moving. "Jink as you run."

They turned and sprinted down the corridor, stepping left and right to make things harder for the enemy.

Somewhere behind them, a dog bayed. It was an unnaturally hollow sound that chilled Torstag to the bone.

Chapter 20: Hazardous Hospitality

"Over that pass somewhere," said Trophimus. "But we should spend the night first.

The lode bone pointed straight up the valley, but the sun was setting behind the mountains and the valley floor already in shadow.

"No fucking inn," said Cerdic, sweeping a mailed arm to indicate the scrawny village that sprawled on either side of the road. Drops of water flicked off the rings of his armour. It had been drizzling for the last hour, and the evening sky promised more rain or possibly sleet.

"That could be a problem," said Trophimus.

His little column of twelve bounty hunters had been riding for a month now, crossing through a dozen portals in that time. The training had gone well. They'd just completed a three-day stopover in an overpopulated Realm with a ready supply of practice victims, and a readily bribable local magistrate.

Readily bribable, but not *honestly* bribable, alas: clearly, they'd flashed around too much coin. They'd managed to ride off just a few moments ahead of the magistrate's henchmen. Then they had had to waste most of the day doglegging through portals to throw off pursuit. Everybody was treating it as a great joke, and would continue to do so until they remembered that in doing a runner they'd not had time to lay in supplies, nor had they picked up warmer clothing for this part of their journey.

"We'll just take what we need from the peasants," said Cerdic.

"Castle," said Trophimus. He pointed to where a walled structure seemed to fade into the rocky head of the valley just before the road climbed the pass. "I suspect the local lord would object."

Cerdic shrugged his mailed shoulders. "A place like that, there won't be proper soldiers, just servants with spears."

"Yes, but he'll be able to organise the locals," said Trophimus. "We won't sleep nearly so well as we'll eat."

"Fuck," said Cerdic. "I hate the wanker already."

Dekan leaned over in his saddle and said, "We'll ask for hospitality."

"That's for nobles," said Trophimus, slapping him down on general principle; Dekan had a tendency to speak up as if he had the same seniority as his wife.

"I beg your pardon, sir," lisped Dekan, exaggerating his patrician accent. "I am the Baron of the Vale of Hoyitt, and this is my nephew Sir Rovan who I am escorting to his wedding in the..."

"The Baronies of Oldgorge," said Cerdic. "That's through the next portal or so. Fuck me! I think this will work."

"At your service, sir," said the Kid, bowing in the saddle.

Trophimus sighed. "Right," he said "Listen up people. Axe Girl's Dekan is going to tell us how to behave like a noble's retinue."

"It's not complicated..." began Dekan.

The castle was sited to catch the last of the light. As they drew nearer, the details became apparent. It had high rough stone walls with no crenelations, and a single tower that seemed to serve both as keep and a gatehouse.

Thunder rolled. The drizzle became a downpour that rattled on Trophimus' helmet.

Somebody lit a lantern in the castle gateway.

"They have prepared a welcome!" declared Dekan.

"A castle can be a trap," said Trophimus.

"Servants with spears," said Cerdic over the din of the rain. "I think we can handle them."

It was in fact a single servant with a spear; one bored old man guarding the gate, which by all good practice he should have closed in their faces. Instead he left it ajar while he fetched his lord.

139

Lord Dreik, a stubby little man with a long white beard, appeared in the gateway. A burly servant stood behind him, holding a lantern aloft with a muscular burn-scarred arm.

"Soldier?" said Cerdic.

"Hmmm," said Trophimus.

Dekan slipped from his saddle and bowed deeply. "You are most gracious, sir. Allow me to present my nephew."

Trophimus dismounted and the others followed suit.

"Welcome, messers, an unexpected guest is a welcome one."

"Ah well, my lord," said Dekan and launched into a fictitious anecdote about their journey.

Lord Dreik ushered them into the vaulted gate tunnel. The second, inner, gate was still closed. Two additional servants waited within. These were younger and stronger looking than the old spearman, and wore long knives on their belts. They shared Dreik's thick eyebrows. Since he hadn't introduced them, it followed that they were his by-blows, bound to him by blood but not inheritance.

Cerdic jerked his head to indicate "up".

Trophimus squatted as if checking his horse's girth strap and took a good look at the vault.

It had the usual murder holes. A flame flickered. Was somebody moving up there. Now would not be a good moment for Lord Dreik to turn on them, but nor would it be a good moment to try to jump him.

Dekan and the Kid were working smoothly through the exchange of aristocratic courtesies. Dreik seemed relaxed enough, for all that the burly lantern bearer stayed close to him.

Trophimus turned to get Axe Girl's opinion. The life-worn woman was watching her nephew and younger husband with the kind of glint in the eye she normally only showed when they brought in a really big target. What was it like to feel that way?

"You and your retainers must be tired and wet," said Lord Dreik. "The servants will attend to your horses. Since my poor hall is somewhat cramped, it might be better if you left your arms on your mounts."

"I…er…" began Dekan.

Trophimus tensed. Dekan had gotten in out of his depth. He wouldn't want to surrender their weapons, but he probably didn't know about the murder holes. What hellish concoction was Lord Dreik planning to drop on their heads if they quibbled over disarming? He would have seen them advance down the valley. There was plenty of time to prepare a vat of pitch or even tallow.

Could he grab Cerdic in time? Not with Dekan and the Kid in the way. And if everybody else got singed, the mission would be a wash-out.

"Is there some problem, sir?" asked Lord Dreik. "Custom, of course, dictates that you keep your eating knives, so there will be no inconvenience."

"Um…that is…" said Dekan.

"Begging your pardon, sire," said Trophimus, putting on his best Trusted Retainer voice, "that wasn't an insult. The folks in these parts don't have weapon shrines." He started unbuckling his sword belt.

"Weapon shrines?" asked Lord Dreik.

Trophimus opened his mouth to offer an explanation, but Axe Girl's husband got their first.

"Ah yes," said Dekan. "Our people have a tradition of honouring the weapons of our guests by placing them in Shrine to Bellafortis, our War Goddess. Anything else is an insult. Hence my confusion, since you seem such a gracious host."

"Your pardon," said Lord Dreik. "You must think us very rudely provincial here."

"Not at all, sir," said Dekan smoothly. "It is I who am poorly travelled." He turned to flash a grin at Trophimus. "Hang the weapons on the horses. We regard our mounts as embodiments of honour, so none of us could take offence if our weapons shared their lodgings."

"You heard his lordship," said Trophimus. He hooked his sword belt over his saddle bow. He cocked a head at Cerdic then raised his arms so his comrade could unbuckle his scaled lamellar shirt for him. As always, Trophimus got out of his armour completely—not just the lamellar, but his greaves and vambraces—before helping Cerdic out of his mailshirt. That way, if things went bad, only one of them risked being hampered by having some piece of kit flapping around half off.

141

It took a few minutes of fuss to stow everybody's long knives and swords. The shields were already on the pack horses, along with Trophimus's thief catcher and Axe Girl's signature weapon.

Trophimus took great delight in handing armour to the old servant. "See that it is hung where it will dry. It would not do to embarrasses his lordship with a rusty escort."

The old man bobbed his head as the weight made him stagger.

"This way, messers, this way," said Lord Dreik. Somebody took that as a signal and the inner gates swung open, letting them into the rain soaked courtyard. "Be welcome!" declared the baron, striding ahead and waving his arms as if to make up for his short stature, "A warm fire awaits."

Trophimus paused under the inner arch. The rain and darkness provided a little cover, but if there were archers in the keep gatehouse then this could be suicide.

Cerdic stopped beside him. "What do you think?"

"Warm fire!" said Rufus, sliding past. "Come on!"

The Blade Bitches just pushed between them. "Out the way old men!"

"I think," said Trophimus, "that nobody has died yet."

He waited until everybody else was halfway across the courtyard then yelled, "Hey, wait for us!"

The two comrades jogged across the open space, by unspoken accord zigzagging slightly as they splashed through puddles.

There was indeed a warm fire in the hall, and a trestle table just a little larger than was needed to accommodate them all. More pertinently, for the moment Lord Dreik and his three henchmen were outnumbered with no possibility of concealed archers.

Cerdic leaned in close. "We could just…"

"I hope roasted pullets will not be too poor a supper," said Lord Dreik, moving to the head of the table.

"…wait for the pullets to be served," completed Trophimus. "Or do you want to supervise the cooks at knife point?"

"Ah," said Cerdic. "Eat first, murder and pillage second."

"Exactly. I was expecting just soup."

"Fuck," said Cerdic. "The old wanker must have had all his chickens slaughtered just to feed us. I feel almost guilty..."

Lord Dreik gestured for Dekan to sit on his right and the Kid on his left.

One of the two big henchmen appeared with a jug in which the baron daintily cleaned his fingers. More servants with more jugs appeared. The big scarred retainer, however, took station on his lord's right, just behind Dekan.

The benches creaked as everybody sat. The elderly servant had traded his spear for a lute, and struck up a pleasant melody.

"While we await the roasted pullets," continued the baron, "there is soup and bread to warm your insides, and beer to dull the ache of the journey." He clapped his hands and the servants returned with cauldrons of soup, wooden bowls, and hunks of stale bread.

Everybody remembered Dekan's hasty instructions and waited to tuck in until the baron took a spoonful of soup. He seemed to take no special precaution to avoid supping from the common cauldron. Trophimus, however, found himself glad of his own amulet that protected him from poison. The things were common enough, probably more common than actual poison, so the baron would be a fool to doctor the food in any case.

Cerdic swigged the beer. "Bugger me," he said in a low voice. "This doesn't look much like a trap. The servants are a scrawny lot except for those two lads and the big bastard. And Dreik has gone and surrounded himself."

"I don't think Axe Girl's posh toyboy and her pet gigolo count as surrounding anybody," said Trophimus.

"Hey," hissed Axe Girl.

"Just joking", said Trophimus. "Both your boys have done well."

They were evidently doing very well with the baron. The three of them seemed to be caught up in a merry banter, with much laughter on all sides.

"I have good taste," said Alice. "Do you think my axe will be okay?"

"I doubt any of the servants could lift it," said Trophimus.

She grinned at him. "Flatterer." She dropped into a whisper. "So when do we make our move? The scarred one is big, but he doesn't stand like a fighter."

Arms scarred by fire. Big. And—now Trophimus was seeing him in proper light—there were grease stains on his shirt. He wasn't any sort of warrior, he was a cook. And if the cook was guarding the lord, that meant that there were no roasted pullets and that meant. "I..."

Lord Dreik put a friendly arm around the Kid...steel flashed.

Trophimus leapt to his feet, knocking back the bench so the others fell or stood depending on their reaction time.

Dreik rose from his chair to stand behind the Kid. He had a big knife pressed to the young man's throat. The high collar would be no protection against the long blade.

The scarred cook got a meaty arm around Dekan's neck.

"Fuck," said Cerdic.

"Silence!" snapped Lord Dreik. "I have your precious groom hostage. You don't want to see him die."

Axe Girl tugged at Trophimus's arm and mouthed, "Please."

Trophimus nodded.

"But the Laws of Hospitality," squeaked Dekan, impressively managing to stay in role despite the cook's stranglehold.

"Do not apply to Pagans who worship War Gods with barbarous names," said the baron. "Now I'm not uncivilised, and I have no wish to start a war. You, Sir Dekan, may take your servants and ride to fetch a ransom. I will even let you take your sidearms for safety. Of course, whatever gifts you brought with you will be forfeit."

"I...er..." began Dekan.

"This is not a negotiation, sir," snapped the Baron. "I have your nephew hostage."

Cerdic nudged Trophimus; it would be simple just to abandon the boy, perhaps make Dekan and Alice believe they would come back for him.

Trophimus shook his head. If it had been Rufus, or one of the Blade Bitches, perhaps, given this was almost certainly his last job ever, so he no longer needed to guard his reputation. Axe Girl, however, was an old friend.

"As I said, I'm not uncivilised," said Lord Dreik. "My servants will take the boy into custody. The rest of you may finish your soup and spend the night here. There will of course be guards on the d—"

The Kid grabbed Dreik's wrist with his left hand and with his right snatched an eating knife from the table.

"No!" screamed Axe Girl, starting forward.

Lord Dreik made a slashing motion that should have half beheaded the lad.

Even so, the Kid stabbed backwards with the short eating knife.

Dreik screamed. Still screaming he staggered away toward the fireplace, clutching his abdomen while blood flowed between his beringed fingers.

The by-blows froze.

The boy flipped the blade and slashed the throat of the nearest.

Dekan meanwhile ducked free of the cook and somehow managed to throw him across the table. Wine splashed. Food spilled. Then Dekan had the man's dagger and made an end.

The ordinary servants rushed for the door. The surviving by-blow tried to drag Lord Driek for safety. A tankard thunked into the back of his head and he went down under the body of his father.

The bounty hunters took up candlesticks and stools, all except Alice who shoved aside friend and foe alike to get to the Kid.

What followed couldn't be dignified with the term, "melee".

Afterwards, they threw the bodies down the outside steps and returned to the beer and soup.

Dekan made a fuss of giving Trophimus the lord's chair.

Trophimus knew he should send people out to search the castle just to be sure, but the chair was comfortable and his gut told him that Lord Dreik had used all his men for the ambush.

"I could get used to this," he said, "we all could. But the money from this job will make us all gentry, and back home, somewhere less impoverished."

"Not a shithole, you mean," said Cerdic and everybody laughed.

Trophimus banged on the table. "A toast to the Kid—" He held up his hand. "But first, how did you know the knife was blunt?"

"*Yes...yes...*" everybody wanted to know.

"It *was* sharp," said the Kid with a smirk. "But this enchanted blade-proof shirt was a gift from the Marquis of Sodor. Very fashionable."

Alice slammed down her ale mug. "You little bastard, you should have told me!"

Trophimus raised his voice to cut off her tirade, "To the Kid!"

"To the *Invincible* Kid," corrected the Kid.

"Say," said Rufus. "What about the pullets?"

"There never were any," said Trophimus. "This was a trap from the start."

"So much for the fucking laws of hospitality," said Cerdic. He leaned in close. "Is the Kid going to get himself killed?"

Trophimus shrugged a shoulder. "He can guard the horses when we do the snatch."

Chapter 21: Bounty Hunters!

Unseen, beyond the mouth of the gulley, the desert wind plucked an eerie melody from the edge of the sword Peacebringer. A gust whirled between the rock walls and dusted sand over the surface of Zahna's tea.

She shifted to huddle into the overhanging rock, protecting her cup in her own shadow. *The Boy had better be worth all this trouble.*

Back in that odd temple of stone columns, she'd looked for any sign that he was the reincarnation of an indomitable swordsman.

Her lips quirked.

Reincarnation of an owl, more like.

A permanently startled one, judging from the way he'd stared at her.

Well, she didn't need him for a lover, just a protector. And really, she was doing him a favour in breaking the cycle of incarnations that would keep him trapped in that monastery.

The wind picked up and the sword sang louder.

Zahna had left the ancient sword planted in the ground because that was where it was needed. However, it made a good sentinel.

She closed her eyes and let her perceptions expand to fill the gulley.

Form 0.

Blame that on a poor night's sleep.

Performing Scout at Level 3.
Using Scout, Attune With Nature. 5 of 6 Potestas
remaining.
Result = 3 (Performance) +1 (Luck) +2 (Feat) +2
("Familiar Sword in Wind") = 8.
Effect = Perceiving at 8.

She shifted to kneel more comfortably, relaxed her muscles.

Form 4. 4 of 6 Potestas remaining.
Performing Scout at Level 7.
Using Scout, Attune With Nature. 3 of 6 Potestas
remaining.
Result = 7 (Performance) +1 (Luck) +2 (Feat) +2
("Familiar Sword in Wind") = 12.

The sounds became translucent, like the layers of rice paper when she was learning the Astral Geometries.

The nearby spring burbled and splashed through the rocks to feed the tiny rivulet that ran out of the canyon. Air and Water together formed a warbling accompaniement to the song of the sword. There was no regular pulse, but it had its own rules, like when the Gorvak string-flautists extemporised hours of tumbling music.

The expanded awareness carried with it a ghost memory: white grains of sand like stars on oily black tea.

Zahna looked down and saw her own face reflected back: moon pale compared to the memory.

"Who am I?"

You are Zahna, Human Warlock, Youth, Spiritual,
Perceptive, Driven, Cold.

"Thanks a lot," she said. That wasn't really a description of a nice person, but it was one who might defeat Gronchard the Flayer.

The rest was more impressive.

Potestas 4/6. Will 3. 1 Recent Ritual. 3 of 3 Prepared
Charms.

She could *feel* them, the little blocks of tea, individually wrapped in their little box: one Illuminate, and two Heals, each good for twelve doses.

She owed that to her combat skills, tested a few times on her travels.

She grimaced. "All borrowed from past selves," she said.

"Enough!"

Marvak had taught her to ride when his people came to the Plain of the Wizard's Tower for spring grazing. He had promised to teach her the bow next season, but when he rode up to the tower, he would find it burned.

Would he mourn her in the Gorvak way? Would he grow his hair out until he could plait it into death braids? Or would he shrug her off as a mere amusement? A quarry carried off by some predator, before it could be stalked and skinned.

Zahna hadn't yet learned to read a soul. Now if she ever did, it would be the quick but dangerous way: her Demon unlocking the knowledge in moments of peril, rather than her teacher patiently jogging her dead memories. She had learned to take Portents, though, but after the events of the summer, she was not sure whether it was worth using that to investigate her relationship with Morvak.

The portents for *that* day had been good—or at least according to Mistress Zinaven, to whom Zahna had been apprenticed since being fished out of a Fire Temple orphanage at the age of seven.

149

Of course, portents were useless for detecting events that were unlikely on any given day, but certain over a given time period.

The old wizard's seasonal oracle had also not provided any sort of warning: *The phoenix embraces the ashes and rises.*

They'd agreed that the phoenix was her, given her origins in a Fire Temple. Zahna had argued that the ashes represented the powers of her past selves.

The old lady, however, had suggested with a twinkle in her usually steely eye, that it was an erotic allusion. The Gorvak folk, for example, were known for their *ash* blond hair.

There were, said Mistress Zinaven, books on the upper shelves that might help her in that regard.

And Zahna had hooded her eyes and flushed, and thought, just a little, of Marvak with his archer's muscles and his short, cropped hair that was indeed ash blond.

Then the Flying Tooth Garden had appeared.

Had Marvak and his kin been there, perhaps things would have been different.

No. More people would have died, that was all.

The tower had transformed from home to trap, then, with help a little help, to an inferno. Apprentice and Mistress had climbed the great spiral stair just a few turns ahead of the attackers, trailing torches, lighting everything they passed. They reached the top-floor observatory just ahead of pursuit. They were in the act of downing tea kept for such an occasion, when the door gave and soldiers crammed into the chamber.

The old lady died.

Zahna lived.

She Walked Between to an abandoned Realm of old ruins and parched fields. That night, the dead memories came and she knew why the Flying Tooth Garden had come for her, and what she had to do.

Armed with the chart and supplies from Zinaven's secret cache, she navigated the wormholes to the Deserts of Outer Yinkesia. Her own bones had granted her a Surge, and yielded up a relic for her protector. Thence to the outskirts of Yinksi City, from where once the Grey Cortège had fetched the Marshal's body. She had leased an entire estate just so she could carry out her Great Ritual and Step Between right into their monastery—that should have been impossible, but a link from a past life pierced the formidable defences.

Then, navigating the wormholes over weeks then months, she worked her way around to the place indicated by her Backwards Remembering.

Future memories were imperfect of course; sometimes partial, always selective. However, if the boy *were* going to become a man—like Marvak perhaps—then it was going to be here…apparently.

The rhythm of the wind shifted. Somebody was coming.

More than one person. Had he brought friends?

Or had Gronchard's hunters found her?

Zahna downed her tea, refilled the little samovar and put one of her three charmed blocks of tea into it.

Tea. Charmed; "Illuminate".

The wind fanned the charcoal so it glowed visibly, even in the glare of the desert sun. The water bubbled, browned.

And she listened.

Beyond the mouth of the little canyon, harness jingled. Hooves rattled stones.

Not the boy, then. Besides, if it were him, she would have seen their bond stretched out like an old lock of hair.

Leather creaked, horses snuffled. The hunters had dismounted. Now the sounds shifted…not so much *sounds* as the presence of people muffling the wind, muting the shrill song of the sword as they closed off escape.

Her Backwards Remembering had taken her to a spot that was effectively a trap. The logical course would be to scale the rock walls and ghost away, but here was the place where she would acquire her protector—or not. In any case, they had horses and supplies, and she did not. They could starve her out, or outpace her.

The tea was ready. She wrapped a rag around the samovar's handle and poured, holding the spout low so that the wind did not divert the dark liquid as it fell.

151

Now the enemy revealed themselves in a line across the width of the blind canyon: nine men and women with clubs and shields, arranged in threes. One of the trios—all similar looking blond women—had large shields designed for stopping arrows, but no doubt handy for literally boxing in a captive; she would see if she could reduce their numbers.

Two big men strode behind the shield-warriors. One was a tall cataphract clad in head-to-toe lamellar scales, strips of steel and mail. He brandished a forked thief catcher as if it were a staff of command. The other wore a mailshirt. He had a net over one shoulder, a scabbarded bow peeking over the other.

Her eyes narrowed. That bow might be a problem for her protector.

> Current Form 4. Performing Wizard at Level 8.
> Unlock Nudge?
> Nudge unlocked at 2/6 Grasp.
> Using Cantrip Nudge 2/6, cost 3 Potestas, 1 of 6 remaining.

She sang softly to the bow, lamented that it had crossed between so many realms with different climates, regretted its long working life.

The wind carried away her words, but she felt the bow respond to them. Its fibres relaxed, gave way along fissures created by years of use.

> Result = 8 (Performance) +1 (Luck) = 9.
> Effect = Uncommon Occurrence (8)
> Cantrip Nudge advances to 3/6 Grasp.

The hunters fanned out as they closed.

Apart from the two leaders, the group all wore quilted linen jackets that had seen better days. They were hardly up to the standard of Gronchard's Myrmidons. Bounty hunters, then.

The wind picked up again, and the sword sang.

The hunters had left it untouched. That was wise of them, given that it could have been some kind of magical trap. However, in this case leaving the sword in place would mean their deaths.

Zahna rose, cup in hand, and—careful not to spill the precious tea—made a little bow and spoke over the hiss of the wind. "Welcome, friends."

They exchanged glances, then the cataphract moved to the front. He brought out a parchment and coughed. When he spoke, his steel visor gave his voice an unearthly echo. "His Divinity Gronchard, God of the Flying Tooth Garden, Emperor of the Blessed Magisterium, bids you, the Sacred Angelica, his lost beloved, come with us so that you may take your rightful place in his arms for all eternity."

Zahna gulped down the tea. It scalded the back of her throat, but the world came alive.

Tea. Charmed; "Illuminate".
Potestas reset and boosted.
12 of 6 Potestas.

The bounty hunters began to close.

New Form 5.

"A moment, of you please," she said. "Let me set down this cup— it is an heirloom."

The cataphract gestured at the youngest member of the party, a youth in a resplendently white shirt. "Go on kid. Help the Princess pack up her belongings."

On older woman, who carried an axe slung on her back, caught the boy's arm. "You be careful, love. Warlocks are slippery."

Ignoring the advancing boy, Zahna stooped to place the porcelain cup on a stone. She grabbed her staff, and rose, throat-chanting the Backwards Remembering spell.

"Oh shit," said the boy, backing away so fast he tripped on a rock.

Zahna's staff blurred with possibility so she took the hint and whirled it.

The mailed netman took a step forward. "Rush her you fucking wankers!"

CHAPTER 22: THE SCREAMING FLAME SKULL OF IMPLACABLE VENGEANCE!

Crossbow bolt. Medium Range. Off Target.

Another missile zipped past, thwacked into one of the mummies up ahead.

Ingar swore. "Probably poisoned."

Torstag held the shield to the back of his head and kept running. He and Ingar's sandals slapped the floor so that the echoes sounded like a hundred fleeing acolytes, not a mere two.

Crossbow bolt. Medium Range.
On Target.
Missile Result = 1 (Fortune)
Missile Effect = 1 (Result) +0 (Light Crossbow) -2
(Dodging) -1 (Small Shield) = 0.

A bolt clanged on the shield making the handle twist in his hand.

Torstag levelled the burning forearm of Berotspan the Marshal.

The flames streamed back toward his hand. He thrust the burning limb against the next mummy, and the next.

Now fire cast long shadows ahead of them as they hurled themselves deeper into the catacombs.

They turned into a great transverse tunnel and jogged up into a warm breeze.

Every so often, Torstag slowed to ignite another mummy. The third time he did it, a crossbow bolt struck the stone just above his head.

Crossbow bolt. On Target.
Missile Result = 3 (Fortune)
Missile Effect = 3 (Result) +0 (Light Crossbow) -2
(Dodging) = Miss.

Torstag looked at the little white patch of chipped stone. "How is the smoke not making a difference?"

"Stop fucking around and run!" cried Ingar.

The corridor curved, giving them some cover, then climbed free of the ranks of mummies into daylight. Ahead of them a patch of yellow glare illuminated on an assembly of odd contraptions. As they closed the distance, Torstag's eyes grew accustomed to the light and the machines started to resemble mechanical bats. Beyond them beckoned a disk of blue sky.

1 Exertion incurred.
1 of 4 Vitality remaining.

Torstag glanced back.

Half a dozen monks emerged from the smoke. None of them carried a source of light. Instead, each had a human eyeball mounted on the stock of his crossbow, all except for Brother Neutrality.

That monk instead carried a mummified dog's head on a stick.

The dog head howled. The sound carried with it the cold stench of the grave.

A monk dropped to one knee, raised his crossbow.

Torstag shouted. "Dodge!"

They threw themselves behind one of the leathery machines.

Crossbow bolt. On Target.
Missile Result = 2 (Fortune)
Missile Effect = 2 (Result) +0 (Light Crossbow) -3
(Dodging, Partial Cover) = -1.

There was a distant *twang!* The quarrel buzzed past harmlessly.

"Quick, while they reload," said Torstag.

They broke into a final sprint. They passed a second winged machine. A third was positioned with its nose just short of the disk of blue sky.

"Come on!" yelled Ingar.

Torstag grabbed his collar and they both came to a halt with the edge of the portal at their toes. It opened out far, far above a broken land of rock and sand that stretched to the horizon.

Torstag looked down.

Beneath him, the cliff fell away a thousand feet to a desert with rock formations like piled shards of earthenware pottery.

The cliff is a Level 12 challenge.

"TORSTAG!" Brother Neutrality's voice echoed from the cavern. The words seemed to resound in Torstag's soul. "COME HERE AND SURRENDER"

Test of Potestas, 6. Enemy attempting hostile command.
Performing Necromancer at Level 6.
Enemy Result = 8 (Challenge) +1 (Luck) -6 (Your Performance) -2 (Resisting) = 1.
Enemy Effect = 1 Potestas Lost. 5 of 4 remaining.

Torstag strained against the tug of obedience. The world became less sharp, but he resisted the call.

"Fuck you, Smelly Newt," yelled Ingar. He tossed his arm-torch onto one of the furthest machines. It caught instantly. As the flames whooshed up to engulf the stretched skin, Ingar pulled the arm of Lashton the Necromancer out of his belt and whacked Torstag with it. "And fuck the goat you rode in on."

Relic of past avatar.
Surge.

Torstag staggered.

6 points of Advancement available.
Warrior, Twitch 4/6 secured. 2 points remaining.
Select a 7th Warrior Feat to study.

On one of Warrior Tree's branches, a knight carved his way through countless enemies.

157

Rampage unlocked at 2/6 Grasp.
2 points of Advancement available. Select a
Vocation.
Warrior.
Select Hurl 4/6 or Rampage 2/6.
Hurl was an easy win, but Rampage looked more
useful.
Rampage advances to 4/6 Grasp.
Potestas reset and boosted.
Vitality reset.
You are Torstag, Human Warlock, Youth, Agile,
Sensitive, Bold, Marked.
Potestas 8/4. Will 2. Horror of the Unquiet Dead 1/6.
Vitality 4. Toughness 2.
Vocations:
Cleric, 1 (Learned): Mediation, Repel Shade 2/6.
Warlord 0: Tea Drinking 2/6.
Warrior, 2 (Brawl, Sidearm, Shield): Wrath Strike +1,
Split Shield, Disarm, Twitch, Hurl 4/6, Rampage 4/6.
Scout 2 (Mountain, Forest, Jungle): Climb +1, Spider
Climb, Sneak
Necromancer 1 (Cantrips): Repel Shade, Shade Cloak
3/6, Manifest Shade 4/6.
Various General Skills including Meditate.
Form 5.

Necromancer!

You are performing Necromancer at level 6.

The tunnel was remarkably clear of ghosts; just a single man in weird costume with a coil of rope over one shoulder and brimmed hat. Nor was the tunnel webbed by threads except those connecting him to the limbs of his past selves.

However, spectral faces roiled across the wings of the machines…faces that whimpered and groaned, "*Free us! Free us!*"

> Possessed by Shades. Enchanted.
> Wrestling with Horror of the Despairing Dead 2/6,
> cost 2 Potestas, 6 of 4 Remaining.
> Will 2 Overcome. You have Hindrance "Horrified".

Torstag dropped the burning arm of his last avatar, put his free hand over one ear. He lifted the shield and pressed his knuckles to the other ear.

It didn't help.

"TORSTAG!" Brother Neutrality repeated. "COME HERE AND SURRENDER"

> Test of Potestas, 8. Enemy attempting hostile command.
> Performing Necromancer at Level 6.
> Enemy Result = 8 (Challenge) +0 (Luck) -6 (Your Performance) -2 (Resisting) +2 (You are Horrified) = 2.
> Enemy Effect = 2 Potestas loss, 4 of 4 Remaining.

"Don't just stand there. Fucking do something!" yelled Ingar.

> Crossbow bolt. On Target.

A crossbow bolt whipped past beween raised forearm and neck, tore a strip out of his cheek. Pain sheeted over his face.

> Missile Effect = 3 (Fortune) + 0 (Light Crossbow) -2 (Cover) = 1.
> Test of Toughness 2. Poison resisted.
> 3 out of 4 Vitality remaining.

Blood spilled down his neck, soaked his chest.

Beyond the smoke most of the monks were reloading their crossbows. Brother Neutrality, however, strode towards them.

Torstag tossed the torch.

Fire crackled from the wing and spread out. The shades screamed and writhed into the smoke, which blew back down the tunnel toward the monks.

"Come on!" yelled Ingar.

Somehow, he mastered himself just enough to function. Torstag caught Ingar's arm. "Into this one."

Still clutching the spiked mace, Ingar squirmed into the seat. "Can you make it fly?"

"Absolutely!" Torstag ditched his shield.

He clambered in next to his friend. The wickerwork supports creaked ominously.

"You're too heavy!" said Ingar.

A crossbow bolt skimmed the stone floor. Another went up through the wing above their heads.

"Shades!" bellowed Torstag. "Fly us out of here!"

Performing Necromancer at level 6.

The shades screamed. "Free us! Free us!" Unwanted memories squirmed into his head.

Torstag threw back his head and bellowed, "*FLY YOU DOGS, FLY!*"

Tormented shades howling, the Tomb Bat flapped its wings once, twice, and took off.

"Out of here!"

The Tomb Bat lurched through the portal and soared out under the desert sky while the hot wind howled around them, and the distant ground became more distant.

Torstag roared with a mix of terror and glee while his heart tried to hammer its way out of his ribcage and his wounded cheek throbbed.

The Tomb Bat levelled off.

Torstag sat back. "We escaped!"

"But where to?" asked Ingar.

Whatever Realm they were in, it was late afternoon and the sun cast a shadow ahead of them on the rock-strewn ground far below. A glowing thread connected Torstag's sternum with something concealed by an outcrop of rocky badlands that rose out of the desert to the east of them.

"Follow that thread," ordered Torstag.

The Tomb Bat swung to obey.

"What thread?" asked Ingar over the roar of wind. "If it's a thread it will lead to the Girl!"

"We'll survive five minutes in a desert without supplies. Do you have any better ideas?"

Ingar turned away. He twisted in his seat and shouted something incoherent

Torstag risked a glance.

Behind, the portal was a dark circle in the side of a weathered spire of rock that seemed ready to catch the setting sun on its summit.

Links webbed the air. One of them—a writhing thing of teeth and bones—was particularly strong. It connected their Tomb Bat to another Tomb Bat that seemed to be catching up fast.

Ingar leaned close. "They're after us!" he yelled. "We should have wrecked all the machines."

"Watch this," said Torstag. "Turn back."

The Tomb Bat swung around to face west and the spire of rock.

Ingar grabbed his arm. "What the fuck are you doing?"

Torstag ignored him and focussed on the distant enemy.

Using Necromancy Cantrip Manifest Shade 4/6, cost 2 Potestas. 3 Potestas Remaining.
Challenge = 0 (Shades) +2 (Dozens) +2 (As Poltergeists) +0 (Existing Link) = 4
Result = 6 (Performance) +0 (Luck) -4 (Challenge) = 2.
Effect = Shades manifest as poltergeists for a watch or so.
Manifest Shade advanced to 5/6.

He had a sense of the captive shades tearing themselves free of the construction, then the link was gone.

The other Tomb Bat fell out of the sky.

"Fuck you Smelly Newt!" said Ingar over the roar of the wind.

It smashed into the rocks. Something flashed.

Torstag. "They'll haul his body back to the catacombs and snag him when he reincarnates."

"So basically he's fucked for all eternity," said Ingar.

Torstag raised his voice. "Return to following the thread again."

"We'll return to the monastery some day," yelled Ingar.

"With fire and steel!" replied Torstag.

"What?" said Ingar, leaning close.

"Um…" said Torstag. "That just seemed appropriate."

The Tomb Bat swung back to an easterly course. Torstag squirmed around to keep an eye on the crash site.

The wicker supports groaned and bowed.

"Be careful," said Ingar. Then louder, "What the fuck is *that?*"

Something bounced out of the wreckage of Brother Neutrality's craft; something that trailed smoke.

Screaming Flame Skull of Implacable Vengeance.

"Screaming Flame Skull of Implacable Vengeance," repeated Torstag.

"Oh, that's all right then," said Ingar. "No, wait…it's not! Make this thing go faster."

"*Faster*", ordered Torstag.

The Tomb Bat wings kept up their steady beat.

The flaming skull bounced closer across the landscape, trailing fire as it went, steadily gaining on them.

"Not going to work," he said.

"We're fucked!" said Ingar.

"We'll handle it. *More details.*"

The Screaming Flame Skull of Implacable Vengeance is a Necromantic enchantment deriving its power from the death of the caster. It pursues and attacks unremittingly until either it or the slayer is destroyed. Repelling it is a level 10 challenge.

"Bad news," said Torstag. "It's higher level than I can cope with. Good news, it's only after me."

"Yes," said Ingar, "but I'm sitting next to you, and you're the one person that can steer this hell bird."

"Bat," said Torstag. "It's a Tomb Bat, not 'Bird'." He slipped the war knife out of his belt. "I'm sure we can dodge the skull."

The thing bounced up out of the landscape, drawing an arc of smoke behind it.

Torstag raised the knife. "*When I say dodge—damn!*"

162

It really was Brother Neutrality's skull, except now it had pale, flaking, skin and wide eyes that blazed as red as the flames that now served as hair.

**Wrestling with Horror of the Despairing Dead 2/6,
cost 3 Potestas, 0/4 remaining.
Will 2 overcome.
Hindrance, "Disquieted" incurred.**

"Dodge!"

Nothing happened.

He had the fleeting thought that the Tomb Bat would only respond to very specific commands. Then Brother Neutrality's grinning face bobbed up in front of him and screamed, a sound like icicles being hammered into his teeth. Flames streamed back and tickled the human parchment making up the underside of the wings.

A burning tongue shot out from Brother Neutrality's distended lips.

Torstag hacked at it with his knife—

**Current Form 5.
Performing Warrior at level 7.
Result = 7 (Performance) -2 ("Disquieted") +1 (Luck) -6
(Enemy Challenge) = 0.
Enemy uses Entangle Feat as a tiebreaker.
Enemy Result = 6 (Challenge) +2 (Feat) -1 (Luck) +2
(You are "Disquieted" -7 (Your Performance) = 2**

The tongue, whipped around his neck, seared his flesh.

**Enemy Effect = 2 Vitality lost,
1 out of 4 Vitality remaining.**

"Get it off get it off!"

Ingar twisted in his seat, wafted his spiked mace ineffectually.

The head released Torstag and wrapped its tongue around Ingar like a bolas.

Ingar screamed and, with a twist in his seat, threw a punch. His fist connected, stopped the Screaming Skull.

The thing squirmed uncannily and fastened on Ingar's arm. "Fuck fuck fuck!"

Torstag tried for a Wrath Strike, but being seated seemed to make that impossible. Instead he screamed and hacked at it while the desert floor rushed past below.

Result = 7 (Performance) +2 (Boldness) +1 (Luck) +2 (Target Immobile) -2 ("Disquieted") -6 (Enemy Challenge) = 4.
Damage = 4 -3 (Armour) = 1.

The blade struck above the thing just above the ear, sank in an inch.

With a scream, Brother Neutrality's flaming skull recoiled. It unwound its tongue and latched onto the wickerwork. Now the flames billowed along the underside of wings. The trapped shades of the Tomb Bat howled in agony.

"Oh shit," yelled Ingar. "Do something!"

Still obediently following the thread, the burning Tomb Bat was about to plough into the badlands, specifically into a little group of figures that seemed to be dancing in the mouth of a canyon with a silvery brook running through its bottom.

A hand clutched Torstag's heart.

Not dancing, fighting.

Performing Warlord at Level 5.

Suddenly the situation made sense.

A tall woman—*the* girl—whirled a staff to hold off a dozen attackers...not attackers, hunters. Most of them carried cudgels, but relied on their big round shields for defence as they worked to hem in the Girl while a mailed man with a net tried to get into position to capture her.

The staff flicked out. A hunter spun out of the fight, dropped their shield and splashed face-first into the stream.

"Fuck!" said Ingar. "Don't land in the middle of that."

The Screaming Skull emitted an appalling wail.

The attackers turned to look.

The Girl took advantage of the distraction, broke through the cordon of shield-bearers and ran toward the open where—bizarrely—a sword stood stuck in the ground.

Her enemies remembered themselves and sprinted in pursuit. Steel armour flashed in the desert sun as a second armoured man strode along behind the line of hunters, waving some kind of staff weapon to urge them on. The man with the net unslung a bow from his back; if she got too far they would wing her rather than let her escape. Presumably that was why she had not try to climb the canyon walls.

The burning Tomb Bat lurched, dropped fifty feet, skidded into the ground. Timber crashed. Captive shades screamed,

Torstag tumbled clear. He lost his grip on his long knife.

> Form 5. You are Agile.
> Performing Crash Survival at Level 5.
> Crash Result = 10 (Challenge) +1 (Luck) -5 (Performance) = 6.

Torstag glimpsed the girl skipping out of the way, then he somersaulted.

He landed on his back, his right let bent under him, the breath knocked from his lungs.

Gasping, he tried to sit up, found his right arm wasn't working. Pain spiked his spine. The world spun.

> Crash Result = 6 Slam.
> Slam Effect = "Knocked Sprawling" (4 points) +2 Vitality loss.
> You have Disadvantage "Knocked Sprawling."
> Toughness 2 overcome. You have Hindrance "Stunned". Form 0. No Feats available.
> Vitality -1 of 4.
> You have Hindrance "Debilitated."

Torstag put his weight on his left hand. His tendons blazed—he'd done something to his left arm. He rolled onto his knees.

The Screaming Skull bounded towards him, bringing with it the reek of burned meat.

Somehow Torstag got onto his feet. He looked around for his war knife, instead spotted the sword.

The width of its crossguard suggested it was a long-bladed greatsword. The weapon was still stuck down in the dirt, too far away to reach.

His left ankle collapsed under him. He started to fall.

The girl sprinted across his field of view.

"Idiot!"

She flicked her staff, caught the sword's crossguard, flipped it into the air. The blade flashing in the harsh sun, the weapon cartwheeled toward Torstag.

Torstag reached for it, feeling as if his left arm were wrapped in wet carpet.

Current Form 0.
Performing Warrior at Level 2.
Result = 2 (Performance) -3 ("Stunned", "Debilitated")
-1 (Luck) -4 (Challenge) = -6
Sword is "Undroppable".
Effect = Good Catch.

The grip smacked into his palm. He closed his fingers and felt home.

Peacebringer (Undroppable), the Greatsword of
Berotspan the Marshal.
Relic of Past Avatar.
Surge.

CHAPTER 23: PEACEBRINGER

The sharkskin sword grip was warm in the hand.

For an instant, Torstag's muscles relaxed. Then dead memories whirled out to envelop him in blood and battles and mayhem and a crinkle-eyed lady with perspiration beading her sand-brown skin and a voice that wanted to be louder.

The surge took him.

> 8 points of Advancement available.
> Warrior Hurl 4/6 secured. 6 Points remaining.
> Rampage 4/6 secured. 4 Points remaining.
> Select a 9th Feat to study.

Once again, the Warrior Tree unrolled, only now each figure wielded a greatsword.

Torstag's eye fell on Wrath Strike. He could select it for a third time, make it even more decisive, as illustrated by a swordsman cheerfully carving diagonal chunks out of a variety of targets, human, animal and Gods-knew-what.

> Wrath Strike+2 unlocked at 2/6 Grasp.
> Wrath Strike+2 advanced to 6/6 Grasp and Secured.
> No points remaining.
> You have secured a 6th Warrior Feat. Warrior Level 3 secured. You have 6 Warrior Feats. 10 Feats required to secure level 4.
> Warrior Level 3 is your highest ranked Vocation. You have levelled up.
> Select a Proficiency.

Damn. If he had not already been surging, he could have had an extra surge out of levelling up.

Select a Proficiency.

I can take a hint.

He picked the one that covered everything from long-handled bastard sword through to man-sized double-hander, in short any sword wielded in two hands.

Longsword!

The map faded and he became aware of the warm-handled greatsword.

Peacebringer, Enchanted Greatsword, Undroppable. Warrior Level 3 unlocks a feat. Select from Cleave Armour, Smite Undead, Shear Magic, Parry Arrows.

Smite Undead.

Smite Undead unlocked. Next feat unlocks at Warrior Level 4.

Red hot fingers pushed through Torstag's flesh. They yanked at his injured arm and leg, stretching him. They punched his spine, setting it ablaze. They pinched the edges of his cheek wound, suturing it with liquid fire.

He screamed.

Wounds nullified. Vitality reset and enhanced to 5.
Potestas reset, enhanced to 5 and boosted.
You are: Torstag, Human Warlock, Youth, Agile,
Empathic, Bold, Marked.
Potestas 10/5. Will 2.
Vitality 5. Toughness 2.
Vocations:
Warrior 3 (Sidearm, Shield, Brawling, Longsword):
Wrath Strike +2, Split Shield, Disarm, Twitch,
Rampage, Hurl, Onset Thrust 3/6.
Warlord 0: Tea Drinking 2/6.
Scout 2 (Mountain, Forest, Jungle): Climb +1, Spider
Climb, Stalk.
Necromancer 1 (Cantrips): Repel Shade, Shade Cloak
3/6, Manifest Shade 4/6
Various General Skills including Meditate.
Form 5.

Torstag raised the greatsword high.

Screaming Flame Skull of Implacable Vengeance.
Hostile. On Fire.

Brother Neutrality's burning head bounced toward him, kicking up the dust, trailing smoke. It landed just short of him, then arced up toward his throat.

He brought the sword back down in a diagonal cut, putting his whole body into the strike. "Hah!"

Bold Attack.
Using Wrath Strike +2, cost 1. 9 of 5 Potestas
remaining.

The sword caught Brother Neutrality's head above the ear—

Using Sword Feat Smite Undead. Cost 1 Potestas. 5
Potestas Remaining.

—sheared clean through the eye and the jaw on the other side.

Result = 7 (Performance) +2 (Boldness) +1 (Luck) -6
(Enemy Challenge) = 4.
Effect = 4 +4 (Feat) +4 (Smite Undead) +2 (Greatsword)
-3 (Natural Armour) = 11.
Target destroyed.

The Screaming Skull split diagonally into two halves. Burning brains scattered like embers across the rocky ground.

Torstag kicked the top half of the skull. "That's for…"

Everything. A thousand moments of cruelty not just to Torstag, but to his friend…

"Ingar?"

Heart pounding, Torstag squinted against the sun. A shock of red hair caught his eye.

Ingar lay to the west, sprawled face down on the ground a few paces from the still smouldering Tomb Bat.

"Ingar!"

Ingar drew in his arms, tried to lift his head.

Torstag took a pace toward him.

The Girl cried, "Yah!"

Torstag turned in time to see her whirl through the hunters, smacking shields. She escaped the canyon mouth, skipped over the brook and sprinted south, to his right.

Nine hunters jogged after her: seven fast moving club and shield fighters in padded jacks, and two more heavily-armoured men bringing up the rear.

The girl reached a rock plug twice her height and simply went up the side as if this were her normal way of getting about.

She was playing for time, realised Torstag. She needed his help.

How am I doing?

Current Form 5.
Warrior Level 3.
Performing Warrior at Level 8.
9 of 5 Potestas remaining.
Warrior 3: (Sidearm, Shield, Brawling, Longsword):
Wrath Strike +2, Split Shield, Disarm, Twitch,
Rampage, Hurl.

As if reading his mind, the armoured pair turned his way. One wore mail with an open faced helmet.

Medium Armour, 2. Net. Sword. Dagger. Bow.

The other wore full cataphract armour, and brandished an odd weapon that looked like a barbed pitchfork. A greatsword hung from his belt.

Heavy Armour, 3. Knife. Greatsword. Thief Catcher.

So that was what it was!

Torstag raised Peacebringer above his head. He bent his knees, settled into a stance that seemed right.

A cold part of his mind sized up the enemy, wondered how long it would take to secure those two additional feats to get to 4th level and what Sword Feats might be on offer.

"Run away, boy!" said Thief Catcher, his visor making his voice come out oddly muffled. He advanced on Torstag, banging the iron shod butt on the stone for emphasis. Windblown sand hissed across his armour. Its burnished plates flashed sunlight with every pace. "This woman belongs to Gronchard the Flayer."

The blood rushed in Torstag's ears. He opened his mouth to say something clever and heroic, but only managed, "Go to Hell."

"Fucking warlocks," said Net Man. "How old is he? Twelve? Shit." He reached over his shoulder to unsling his bow.

Should Torstag run? He would be an easy target. Charge against two seasoned fighters? That seemed a bad option.

Net Man nocked an arrow and all choice was gone.

Time seemed to slow down and Torstag knew he must sidestep sharply then charge.

Net Man drew back the arrow.

The bow stave creaked, snapped. One limb clanged on the man's helmet. "Fuck!" He let the bow drop and cast away the arrow. "Fucking warlocks," he repeated. He bellowed. "Axe Girl! Deal with this piece of shit!"

There was a flurry of movement off right.

Torstag stole a glance.

The girl was at bay on the stone platform, tossing stones down at the hunters. However, only a half dozen remained. Two were recrossing the brook back in Torstag's direction.

> **Club and shield. Light armour.**
> **Club and shield. Light armour.**
> **You are "Outnumbered".**

The armoured leaders had already turned their attention to the girl, leaving Torstag to the new pair.

The women approaching on the left had to be "Axe Girl". She had been pretty once, perhaps, but now she was terrifying. It wasn't the scars or the way she had an axe slung on her back so the head was positioned like a trained parrot. It was the look of shear glee on her face.

The man on the right had a ridiculous red codpiece, more of a hat for the privates than a modesty garment; intended as misdirection, perhaps.

Ingar's voice cut through the sound of the wind. "Torstag, behind you!"

"Kid, no!" cried Axe Girl.

Torstag spun, bringing his raised fists forward so they shielded his eyes from the sun.

A youth—younger than Torstag, practically a boy—was lunging in with a dagger extended, his long hair whipping in the wind. "Gotcha!"

> **Dagger. Light armour. Attacking Boldly.**
> **You have Disadvantage "Outmanoeuvred".**
> **Greatsword against Dagger has Advantage "First**
> **Strike" during Onset.**
> **First Strike cancels "Outmanoeuvred."**

And Torstag…*remembered.*

Screaming, he pivoted back and slashed Peacebringer diagonally into the space he'd just left, putting everything into the cut.

Bold counter-attack cancels Bold attack.

The boy yelped, "Oh shit!" He tried to veer away while meeting the greatsword with the cross of his dagger.

He was blurringly fast.

**Using Wrath Strike+2, cost 1 Potestas. 8 of 5
Potestas Remaining.
Result = 8 (Performance) + 1 (Luck) -2 (Enemy
Challenge) = 7.
Armour 1 Negated.
Enchanted Greatsword negates Enchanted Shirt.
Effect = 7 +4 (Feat) +2 (Greatsword) = 13**

Peacebringer bypassed the dagger, cracked into the boy's shoulder, passed through his quilted armour, his rib cage, came out in a spray of blood and gore.

Head, shoulder and arm fell away. Lungs glistened in the desert sun. Exposed bones shone a bloodied white.

"Damn!" Torstag had wasted Potestas on a Feat he had not needed to use.

What was left of the boy toppled onto the rocky ground, spilling offal like a broken canopic jar.

Somebody wailed, "Kid!"

Torstag temples seemed to clamp. He had cut down what was little more than a child, and there he was calculating the opportunities it had cost him. Were warlocks monsters that deserved to be locked up in places like the Monastery, after all?

A woman screamed in anguish. Wood resounded on the rocky ground.

Torstag turned, raised his sword.

Net Man bellowed, "Catch her you fuckers!"

The girl appeared from nowhere, whirling her staff. She smacked Red Codpiece's shield.

Codpiece skipped backwards to avoid her strokes, yelling, "Alice! No! Alice it's a warlock. No! I love you! No! Oof!"

The staff caught him in the belly and he went down.

The girl skipped over the prone man and sprinted away, across the gulley mouth, heading for the broken ground to the north.

Once again, the hunters jogged after her, Thief Catcher and Net Man bringing up the rear.

One hunter stayed behind.

The thud of wood had been Axe Girl—Alice?—dropping her shield and club. The tide of the fight had left Torstag alone with her. She already had her axe unslung and cradled in both hands.

Tears ran down her wrinkled cheeks but her eyes were cold. "He was just a boy. You fucking murdered him. You didn't even have to learn how to use your sword. Somebody else did the work and you just *remembered*."

That was…That was *unfair*. But what words would he say?

Blood trickled down Peacebringer's raised blade, dripped onto Torstag's fingers. The boy's blood.

Current Form 5. Performing Warlord at Level 5. Unlock Warlord, Confront?

No! Torstag wasn't going to waste Potestas on an unmastered Feat. Warlord would have to do on its own.

"A boy with a dagger who died well," said Torstag. "If you mourn him, tend to his corpse. We have no further quarrel."

Result = 5 (Performance) +1 (Luck) -4 (Challenge) -10 ("You just killed her beloved nephew") = -8, Aggressive Proactive Hostile Response.

"Alice! No!" yelled Red Codpiece, now unsteadily on his feet.

Axe Girl ignored him. "Fucking Warlocks! Trophimus was right. Let's see how you do with an adult."

War Axe. Light Armour. Greatsword and War Axe are matched in the Onset.

Torstag edged closer. "Yes, let's find out." How could he sound so calm?

Axe Girl's eyes dilated little, as if she were spreading her focus. She spun the axe like a juggler; left, right and back. She grinned through her tears. "Come on then, boy, where's the opening? Round and round the axe goes, where she lands nobody knows…"

The movement tugged Torstag's gaze with it. When was the right moment to attack?

Enemy using Flourish.
Test of Potestas, 8. Form Maintained.

That was nice, but he still didn't feel like getting any closer without his own edge.

Come on Tempter, I know I can study two feats at a time.

Unlock Onset Thrust or Waiting Guard as 9th Warrior Feat.

There wasn't time for standing around. "Onset Thrust."

Warrior, Onset Thrust unlocked at 2/6 Grasp.

Axe Girl was still whirling her axe when Torstag thrust at her chest, pivoting forward behind the blade to give the attack more reach.

Using Onset Thrust 2/6 at cost 3 Potestas. 5 Potestas remaining.
Onset Thrust is Unpredictable.
Result = 8 (Performance) -2 (Unpredictable) +2 (Enemy performing Flourish) -4 (Enemy Challenge) = 4

She saw him coming too late, tried to back-step and sweep her axe…

Armour 1 Negated.
Effect = 4 (Result) +2 (Greatsword) = 6

Axe Girl's quilted armour did her no good. Her ribs crackled as Peacebringer sank a good handsbreadth into her torso.

Her eyes widened enough to stretch her wrinkles flat and Torstag saw she had once looked angelic with a round face and big eyes. "How the fuck…?" she gasped, the coughed.

Blood sprayed Torstag's face. The light went from her eyes. The corpse toppled, the surprised look forever fixed on her tear-streaked face. Somewhere, a man sobbed.

Enemy Slain.
Onset Thrust advances to 3/6 Grip.

"Holy—" began Torstag.

A net draped over him, tightened around his arms.

"Surprised."
Enemy Result = 5 (Performance) +2 (Feat) +2 (Net in
Onset) +3 ("Tactical Advantage", "Target Distracted") −
8 (Your Performance) = 4.
Enemy Effect = Successful Netting.
Test of Potestas, 5. Form lost.

Torstag cursed and tried to break out.

New Form 2.
Performing Warrior at Level 5.
Result = 5 (Performance) +1 (Luck) −15 (Net) = −9
Effect = None. Still netted.

Finally, Torstag twisted against its tether to face Net Man.

The mailed hunter merely tugged at the rope, tightening it further, pinning Torstag's upper arms. "Got you, you little fucker. You fucking killed Axe Girl and the fucking Kid. Now I'm going to fucking make you fucking die slow and painful, you fucking fucker. Then I'm going to give your body to Gronchard the Fucking Flayer so he can bring you back as some fucked up undead thing and fucking fuck you up some more."

You have disadvantages "Netted", "Leashed",
"Outreached."

CHAPTER 24: INGAR TO THE RESCUE!

Ingar's vision spun.

Test of Will, 3. Still Dazed.

Torstag yelled. Metal clattered. Wood thudded.

Ingar raised his head into a warm breeze that whipped sand into face. Everything hurt. "What the actual fuck?"

You incurred 4 Vitality Loss: 3 on crashing—which surpassed your Toughness, incurring 1 Wound and Hindrances "Stunned" and "Wounded"—then 1 additional point from fire. Vitality was reduced to 0, resulting in Hindrance "Debilitated". Form and Feats were rendered unavailable.
Disadvantage "Knocked Sprawling".

The two halves of Brother Neutrality's split skull lay not far off like a broken theatre mask. The remaining eye still twitched. Smoke seeped from the hair and spread out across the rocky ground.

The side of Ingar's head throbbed. His left arm stung—the skin was red and blistered. He lowered his face, rested it on the backs of his hands while the world whirled.

OK Doofus, where am I at?

> You are Ingar, Human, Youth, Quick Witted, Nimble
> Fingered, Hedonistic, Sensitive.
> Potestas 12/6. Will 3.
> Vitality 0/4. Toughness 2. 1 Wound. Hindrances
> "Stunned", "Wounded", "Debilitated".

He'd been really pleased back in the Catacombs when raising his Burglar level had finally boosted his Vitality—it really did take two levels per point. It had not, however, really done him any good.

> Vocations:
> Burglar 4: Hide, Climb +1, Spider Climb, Move Silently,
> Stalk, Pick Pocket, Open Lock, Detect Trap, Stalk
> Close 3/6, Disarm Trap 2/6.
> Cleric 1: (learned): Meditation. Repel Shade, 1/6.
> Entertainer 2: (Learned): Tout, Recite, Acrobatics,
> Sing.
> Artist 0: Visualisation 4/6.
> Disadvantage "Knocked Sprawling".
> Sand stung his cheeks. "Gnugh," said Ingar.

Again, he tried to get up, or at least get his face above the mini-sandstorm that swept across the ground at ankle height.

> Test of Will 3. Hindrance "Stunned" shaken off.
> Hindrances "Wounded", "Debilitated" remain.
> New Form 3.

His arms collapsed under him.

"Bugger fuck."

He struggled onto his side and saw that the girl was skipping around the top of a big rock, throwing stones at her hunters.

Ingar twisted his head—his neck hurt from the crash—to find Torstag.

His friend now wielded a really big sword and looking frankly dazed as two hunters approached him from the front.

A kid a bit younger than him crept up behind. A dagger flashed silver in the desert sun.

Ingar yelled a warning. Torstag seemed to come to himself. He spun. The sword cracked down. Blood sprayed. The boy...fell into two pieces.

Ingar's gorge rose.

One of the hunters, an older woman with a lined face, dropped her shield and club, pulled an axe off her shoulder and went for Torstag.

Her companion—a man with a silly red codpiece—yelled something.

The girl whirled past, drove him back, whacked him in the belly. He doubled over and she ran on, the other hunters trailing behind.

A wave of nausea caused Ingar to sink back to the rock. When he looked again, Torstag already had his sword embedded in the chest of the axe woman.

She went down like an old sack. The man with the silly codpiece stumbled toward the corpse, sobbing.

A net draped over Torstag, tightened. A rope tugged him off balance.

Blearily, Ingar traced the rope to the hands of a mailed man who wore a nasty looking sword on his belt.

It was all happening so very fast.

"Fuck," said Ingar.

Vitality 0 of 4. Toughness 2. 1 Wound.
Hindrances "Debilitated", "Wounded" Remain.

Yeah, thanks for the reminder Doofus. Now shut the fuck up for a while.

Ingar flopped onto his front and crawled across the rocky ground toward the dropped axe. His head swam, his right arm blazed as if it were still on fire. Waves of windblown sand stung his hands and wrists.

Everybody, however, seemed distracted. Just perhaps…

Chapter 25: Going Down Fighting!

The mouth of the net tightened around Torstag's arms, pinned them to his side. He strained his muscles until the blood ran to his face and his forehead hurt. At last, the rope scraped up his skin, then lodged in the crook of his elbow. Now he could just manage to heave Peacebringer up to horizontal. He yelled and ran at his captor.

Laughing, Net Man sidestepped and yanked.

Enemy greatly outreaches you.
Result = 5 (Performance) +2 (Boldness) -1 (Luck) -4 ("Netted", "Leashed", "Outreached") -5 (Enemy Challenge) = -3. Fail.
Enemy Result = 3 (Result) +2 (Your Boldness, since you failed) = 5.
Enemy Slam Effect = 5 (Result) = Knocked Over (4) + 1 Vitality loss.

Torstag lost his footing, crashed sideways into the grit and stones. Pain blazed in his shoulder and flank.

4 of 5 Vitality remaining.
Test of Potestas, 5. Form 2 Preserved. You have Disadvantage "Knocked Sprawling".

He managed to wriggle around onto his hip.

The mailed hunter had drawn a sword that seemed like the bastard offspring of a barbed fishhook and a darning needle. He hunched down as he advanced. "Got you now you little prick."

With a yell, the girl sailed in from nowhere, staff extended. It caught the Net Man in the throat. Her weight was behind the staff. Bone crunched and he flopped to the ground.

A muffled voice shouted, "Gods! No! Cerdic!"

The girl landed nimbly, whirled her weapon and—with a long step to the North—struck at her returning pursuers.

She caught one by surprise, flicked the staff into the back of her head. Bone crunched. Teeth sprayed into the scalding desert air. The body of a beautiful young woman tumbled into the ground, long blond hair trailing behind her like a winter comet.

The surviving two front-rankers—both also blond women—blocked with their shields and fell back, while two male fighters with bigger shields slipped East to flank the girl. One of them shouted, "Trophimus you old fart! You've fucked up!"

"This is not the time, Rufus!" growled Thief Catcher.

Torstag let go of Peacebringer and strained to get a fingerhold on the net.

Test of Toughness, 2. Fail.

The cataphract appeared behind the girl, an apparition rendered in steel. He thrust the thief-catcher at her neck.

Torstag yelled, "Watch out…" He didn't know her name. "…*my lady!*"

The girl turned just in time for the fork to catch her under the chin. The tines bracketed her neck and spring-loaded bars snapped into place, trapping her.

The cataphract tugged her forward. His voice cracked. "You killed Cerdic!"

The girl whirled her staff at him but he only pulled her off balance.

"Your man killed Axe Girl and the Kid," continued the cataphract. "Rufus! Blade Bitches! Come on. Get her!"

The four remaining shield-and-club fighters closed in.

The girl grabbed the shaft of the fork with her left hand, flourished her staff one-handed, low.

The hunters scattered like startled pigeons.

Again the girl whirled the staff.

The cataphract shoved, making the blow go wild. "I'm going to watch Gronchard peel your soul back like an onion and I'm going to laugh." He looked past Torstag. "Come on Dekan, disarm this one then I'll help you torture that one properly. I know tricks to make it really last…"

Torstag rolled over and found that Red Codpiece was standing over him. The man had his sidesword poised to thrust, but his eyes were glazed with tears and he was mumbling to himself, "Beautiful beautiful she was beautiful…"

"Dekan!" snapped the Thief Catcher.

Red Codpiece kicked Peacebringer out of reach. "Later, scum," he said, voice aristocratic despite its rawness.

The girl started chanting.

The cataphract shoved her forward by the throat, choking her off. "No you don't with your damned wizardry."

Torstag strained against the net, thrashed his legs.

Test of Toughness, 2. Fail.

Red Codpiece sheathed his sidesword, ducked in, yanked the staff out of her hands.

The girl snap-kicked him in the crotch.

He collapsed.

The cataphract yanked the thief catcher.

The girl grabbed the shaft with both hands. She skipped with the motion, keeping her feet but still making choking sounds.

Torstag brought his hands up as much as he could, bent his neck, and hooked his fingers into the mesh of the net. He tugged and the net shifted up his biceps, scouring the skin.

The four hunters closed in on the disarmed girl. She hopped and kicked, but they only laughed and bashed her with their shields.

A growl welled up in Torstag's throat. Muscles blazing, he raised his arms against the constraining rope and cord. The net caught his chin, scuffed his neck, lacerated his nose, and it was off.

Test of Toughness, 2. Success.

He grabbed Peacebringer and, still growling, rolled to his feet and charged, point forward.

Performing Warrior at Level 5.
Club and shield. Light armour. You have the Tactical Advantage.
Club and shield. Light armour. You have the Tactical Advantage.
Greatsword has First Strike.

Thief Catcher barked, "Bitches! Ware left!"

The two blond women turned as he closed, dressed their shields toward him. Behind them, the girl and the cataphract kept up an odd dance; her trying to yank the fork out of his hands, him pushing and shoving to keep her off balance while the other two men with big shields tried to box her in.

Tactical Advantage Lost.

Torstag frowned. He should have attacked immediately, perhaps risked an Onset Thrust.

Club and shield. Light armour.
Club and shield. Light armour.
Great Sword has First Strike.
First Strike negates disadvantage "Outnumbered" during Onset.

Grinning mirthlessly, Torstag cut diagonally at the woman on the right, stepping to put his weight behind the blow.

Using Feat Cleave Shield, cost 1 Potestas. 4 Potestas remaining.

His target lifted her shield to block.

Torstag changed his angle to catch the edge of the shield.

The four-foot blade clove the wooden shield, glanced off the woman's helmet, severed a blond pigtail, caught the base of the neck, cracked through the collar bone, splashed blood. Her head flopped onto the opposite shoulder and the body fell sideways.

The second blond woman was already on him, grunting as she shoved her shield to block his arm.

Torstag pivoted back and struck diagonally, again catching the shield's rim.

Peacebringer split the shield, swept off her hand. She stumbled away, sinking as blood spurted from the stump.

Ingar's voice rang off the cliffs. "Torstag. Behind you!"
Torstag turned.
The two remaining shield and club fighters were on him, bigger shields well to the front to form a barrier.

Enemy Combined attack.
Club and large shield. Light armour.
Club and large shield. Light armour.
You have disadvantage "Outnumbered".
Large Shield in Combined Attack outclasses
Greatsword for Melee.
Enemy have manoeuvred to negate your "First
Strike".
Result = 4 (Performance) +0 (Luck) -5 (Enemy
Challenge)- 4 ("Outnumbered", "Combined Attack",
"Weapon Outclassed") = -5.
Enemy Effect = Feat "Arm Pin" (cost 2) + 3 Vitality
loss.

One jammed his shield under Torstag's elbows to stop him cutting. The other clubbed him in the ribs. Something cracked. A stabbing pain drove the wind out of him.

3 Vitality Lost.
1 of 5 Vitality remaining.
Toughness 3 Surpassed.
1 Wound incurred.
Hindrances, "Stunned" and "Wounded".
Form lost. Feats unavailable.
New Form 0. You are Performing Warrior at Level 3.

Torstag gasped for breath. He stumbled backwards trying to get away, trailing Peacebringer.

Disengaging is Unpredictable.
Result = 3 (Performance) +2 (Disengaging) -3
("Stunned", "Wounded") -2 (Outnumbered) -2
(Unpredictable) -4 (Enemy challenge) = -7.
Effect = -5. Retreat unsuccessful. Enemy has
"Tactical Advantage"

His heel bumped a rock. He'd trapped himself against the wall of the canyon.

Chapter 26: It Looks Like a ****ing Axe to Me!

Ingar's hands were sticky.

He turned his palm and saw it was caked with blood and dust. He was crawling in gore.

He shuddered. "Man up! Man up man up!"

You are Sensitive.
Test of Will 3. Issue, "Horror of Murder" acquired at 1/6 Hardening.
Wrestling with Horror of Murder 1/6, cost 2 Potestas, 10 Remaining.
Hindrance "Horrified" evaded.

"Fucking marvellous."

Ingar willed himself to keep crawling, hands then knees sticking to the tacky surface.

And there was the axe.

He reached out, grasped it and had a memory of plying a similar weapon on the stern of a dragon-prowed ship while arrows rattled off his scale armour. "Fuck!"

Unlock Warrior, Halberd Proficiency.

Ingar screwed up his eyes against his growing headache. "Halberd?"

Weapons tumbled across his mind's eye, all chopping blades on long handles, some sophisticated confections of spikes and flanges, some not so far from what you'd chop wood with, and some so primitive that the 'blades' were basically chunks of rock.

"It just looks like a fucking axe to me," said Ingar. "But okay Doofus."

Vocation Warrior unlocked at Level 0. You need to secure 1 Feat to secure Level 1. Proficiency Halberd unlocked.
Select a 1st Warrior feat.

Doofus started to bring up an image of tree with people fighting. *Look, I just want to use the axe, not marry it. Give me something that just puts the other fucker down.*

Wrath Strike adds +2 Effect.

That sounds like it will put the other fucker down. Yes.

Warrior, Wrath Strike unlocked at 1/6 Grasp.
You may have 4 Vocations. Cleric vocation Abandoned. Supernatural feat lost. Meditation retained as Skill.
You are Ingar, Human, Youth, Quick Witted, Nimble Fingered, Hedonistic, Sensitive.
Potestas 10/6. Will 3. Issue "Horror of Murder" 1/6.
Vitality 0/4. Toughness 2. 1 Wound. Hindrances "Stunned", "Dazed", "Debilitated".
Vocations:
Burglar 4: Hide, Climb +1, Spider Climb, Move Silently, Stalk, Pick Pocket, Open Lock, Detect Trap, Stalk Close 3/6, Disarm Trap 2/6.
Warrior 1 (Halberds): Wrath Strike 1/6.
Entertainer 2: (Learned): Tout, Recite, Acrobatics, Sing.
Artist 0: Visualisation 4/6.
Various Skills including Meditation.
Current Form 3. Hindrances "Stunned", "Dazed", "Debilitated".
Disadvantage "Knocked Sprawling".

"Thanks Doofus."

The situation had changed.

The girl was now trapped by a fork—the term **thief catcher** popped into Ingar's mind—but Torstag was free of the net.

Ingar relaxed. His friend would manage fine without him.

Torstag split a pair of shields as if they were rotten wood, splashed blood on the rock. Two hunters fell, both women.

Wrestling with Horror of Murder 1/6, cost 2 Potestas. 6 of 6 Potestas Remaining.

Two ordinary bounty hunters remained, this time with big shields. They slammed into Torstag. One of the clubs cracked home.

Ingar's friend stumbled away, ineffectually dragging his sword like a wounded limb. He bumped into the rock wall of the canyon.

"Fuck fuck fuck fucketty fuck." Ingar used the axe—

Halberd.

Axe to lever himself to his feet. The effort seemed to make his brains try to escape via the bruise on his head.

**Form 3. 5 of 6 Potestas remaining.
Performing Burglar at level 7.
Using Feat Stalk Close 3/6, cost 1 Potestas. 5 of 6 Potestas remaining.**

Suddenly, he was aware of everybody's field of view…more specifically the shifting spaces where they weren't looking.

Don't mind me, don't mind me.

**Result = 7 (Performance) + 2 (Feat) -3 ("Debilitated", "Wounded") = Stalking Close 6
Effect= 6 (Stalking Close) +1 (Luck) -5 (Enemy Challenge) -2 (Outnumbered) +2 (Enemy Distracted) = 2. Tactical Advantage.**

That was the armoured man who had the girl by the neck. Let her take her chances; this was none of Ingar's business.

Result = 6 (Stalking Close) +0 Luck -5 (Enemy Challenge) -2 (Outnumbered) + 3 (Enemy "Distracted", "Looking the Wrong Direction") = 3. Tactical Advantage.

That was the shield fighter about to club Torstag.

He rose up and put everything he had into a cut to the nearest hunter's head. "Fuck you!"

You have Warrior level 0.
Current Form 3. Performing Warrior at Level 3.
Attacking Boldly.
Using Warrior, Wrath Strike 1/6 cost 2 Potestas. 3 of
6 Potestas remaining.
Result = 3 (Performance) +5 ("Tactical Advantage",
"Surprise", "Enemy Distracted", "Enemy's Back
Turned") + 2 (Bold Attack) +1 (Luck) -3 ("Debilitated",
"Wounded") -5 (Enemy Challenge) = 3
Armour 1 Negated.
Effect = 4 +2 (Feat) +3 (War Axe) -2 (Shield) = 7
damage.

The double handed axe clanged into the helmet above the ear, split the iron, passed through the skull, tore off the opposite jaw bone on the way out, then and clipped a disk of flesh out of the shoulder, before drawing sparks from the rock.

The body crumpled like a rat-eaten mattress cast out from the dorms. The ruined upper portion of the head gathered dust as it rolled on the stone. It came to a stop against Ingar's sandalled toe.

Target is dead.

No shit!

Wrath Strike advances to 2/6 Grip.

Ingar stared at the wreck of what had been a person.

Wrestling with Horror of Murder 1/6, cost 3
Potestas. 0 of 5 Potestas Remaining.
Will 2 overcome. You have Hindrance "Horrified".
Form 0. No Feats available.

A wreck he'd created.

Wrestling with Horror of Murder 1/6, cost 3
Potestas. -3 of 5 Potestas Remaining.
Will 3 overcome.
You have Hindrance "Fugue State"
Potestas below 0. You have Hindrance "Stunned".
You now have Hindrances "Stunned", "Debilitated",
"Wounded", "Horrified", and "Fugue State".

The surviving man rounded on him, club raised.

Ingar wanted to turn and run, but for some reason his legs wouldn't obey.

Chapter 27: Marked!

The shields hemmed Torstag against the rock. He raised his sword but the effort made his chest muscles spasm. Agony to exploded in his cracked ribs.

Ingar appeared as if out of thin air, brandishing a double-handed axe. Screaming, he brought it around and down, partially decapitating one of the two shieldmen.

Blood splashed the face of the second man. He turned, raised his club—

And Ingar just stood there, staring stupidly.

> Test of Will 2. "Stunned" Hindrance shrugged off.
> Vitality 1 of 5. Hindrance "Wounded" remains.
> New Form 3.
> Performing Warrior at Level 6.
> 3 of 5 Potestas remaining.

Torstag drove his sword into second man's back. The effort seemed to make something snap in his chest. He gasped as the blade sank in.

> Result = 6 (Performance) +2 (Boldness) -2 ("Wounded")
> -1 (Luck) +4 (Double Tactical Advantage) -4 (Enemy
> Challenge) = 5.
> Shield Outflanked. Armour 1 Negated.
> Effect = 5 (Result) + 2 (Greatsword) = 7.
> Enemy Slain.

Thief Catcher's visor-muffled voice again: "Dekan, *no!*"

Torstag whirled around to face the new sound.

The cataphract still had the girl by the throat. However, the unlucky man with the stupid red codpiece had again drawn his sidesword and was advancing on Torstag.

Light armour. Sidesword. "Wounded". "Distraught".
Sidesword outclasses Greatsword in Clash.

Red Codpiece was in a bad state: one side of his head bloody, lips bruised, teeth missing; the girl's handiwork. He was also muttering to himself. That did not, however, make the long-bladed cut-and-thrust sword look any less deadly. It would be a really bad idea to spend time with the blades crossed.

As he closed on Torstag, he said, "Her name was Alice and she was my wife you treated her like a lump of meat. I'm going to hamstring you and cut off your balls and make you eat your own…"

A terrible calm gripped Torstag. It didn't make his vision less fuzzy or his broken ribs less painful, but somehow seeing straight didn't matter.

He intercepted the grieving man with a diagonal Wrath Strike and for an instant everything was perfect; the sword sliced forward, his body came on behind it, muscles fluid, every joint lined up to impart power to the strike.

Red Codpiece saw death coming, raised his hand to thrust into the cut. The point flew toward Torstag's eye.

Bold attack.
Enemy making Bold counter attack.
A tie will result in a Double Hit.
Using Wrath Strike +2, cost 1 Potestas, 2 of 5
remaining.
Result = 6 (Performance) -2 ("Wounded") -2 ("Weapon
Outclassed") +1 (Luck) +3 (Enemy "Wounded",
"Distraught") -6 (Enemy Challenge) = Tie.

The greatsword clanged into the strong part of the sidesword, just short of the guard, while he stepped offline to avoid the point.

Neither weapon struck home.

So much for delivering a Wrath Strike.

Test of Potestas 2. Twitch or Disarm available.

Torstag flinched from putting his hand anywhere near that flickering blade so flowed into a Twitch instead.

Using Twitch, cost 1 Potestas, 1 of 5 remaining.

Red Codpiece tried to continue the thrust, but Torstag whirled his blade clear and with a step *out* left, delivered a cut to head.
Peacebringer clanged into the helmet, leaving a dent.

**Result = 0 (Tie) +1 Luck = 1.
Effect = 1 (Result) +2 (Greatsword) -1 (Armour) = 2
Vitality Loss.
Enemy "Stunned".**

Red Codpiece slurred, "Alice!" He flicked his lighter sword around for a slashing cut.

**Now in Clash. Sidesword outclasses Greatsword.
Both still fighting Boldly.**

Torstag thrust his heavier weapon into the cut, angling his crossguard to protect his fingers while trying to skip back out of range so he could use another Wrath Strike.

**Attempting Disengagement. Armour matches. Result will be Unpredictable.
Result = 6 (Performance) -2 ("Wounded") -2 ("Weapon Outclassed") +2 (Disengaging) -2 (Unpredictability) +4 (Enemy "Wounded", "Distraught", "Stunned") -6 (Enemy Challenge) = 1.
Effect = 1. Disengagement successful.
Somehow the pain in his chest took the spring out of his step. Even so he was now clear of the sidesword.**

"Bastard," growled Red Codpiece, lunging after Torstag.
Torstag threw a Wrath Strike into the lunge, stepping left so that the blades crossed even as his sought the other man's throat.

Enemy making bold attack.
You are making bold Counter Attack.
Using Wrath Strike +2, cost 1 Potestas, 1 of 5
remaining.
Result = 6 (Performance) -2 ("Wounded") +0 (Luck) +3
(Enemy "Wounded", "Distraught") -6 (Enemy
Challenge) = 1

The greatsword swept aside the sidesword, caught Red Codpiece on the shoulder.

Effect = 1 (Result) +2 (Greatsword) -1 (Armour) = 2
Vitality Loss.
Enemy "Debilitated."

Peacebringer sliced padding and skidded across Red Codpiece's collar bone, slicing open the armour in a spray of blood.

Red Codpiece brandished his sidesword like a whip, brought it down at Torstag's face.

Attempting Disengagement. Armour matches. Result
will be Unpredictable.
Result = 6 (Performance) -2 ("Wounded") -2 ("Weapon
Outclassed") +2 (Disengaging) +3 (Unpredictability) +5
(Enemy "Wounded", "Distraught", "Stunned",
"Debilitated") -6 (Enemy Challenge) = 4.
Effect = 4. Disengagement successful. Back to
Manoeuvring.

Blood now soaked Red Codpiece's shoulder and chest. "Come back and fight, you coward." He raised his sidesword into a thrusting guard.

There were too many boulders to make it possible to manoeuvre for advantage. "As you wish, sir," said Torstag, stepping closer.

The girl made a choking noise.

Once again, Red Codpiece lunged.

Enemy making bold attack.
You are making bold Counter Attack.
Using Wrath Strike +2, cost 1 Potestas, 0 of 5
remaining.

Torstag responded by cutting into the thrust with a Wrath Strike, this time slamming his fists down to this hip while keeping the point up.

The heavier greatsword intercepted the sidesword, bounced it away, stopped with the tip aligned with Red Codpiece's face.

Torstag followed up with a thrust to the chest.

Red Codpiece tried to bring his sidesword back in a parry, tried to flinch away.

Peacebringer caught him in the cheek, passed up into his braincase.

Result = 6 (Performance) -2 ("Wounded") +0 (Luck) +5
(Enemy "Wounded", "Distraught", "Stunned",
"Debilitated") -6 (Enemy Challenge) = 3
Effect = 3 (Result) +2 (Greatsword) +3 (Feat) -1
(Armour) = 8 Vitality Loss.

"Alice!" The man tottered a pace toward's Axe Girl's corpse, then collapsed.

Target Killed.

Now only the cataphract who had the girl in a thief catcher remained.

Her face was drawn. She was breathing hard and looked utterly spent.

As Torstag approached, the Thief Catcher swung the forked device around, forcing the lighter girl to tiptoe between them as a shield.

"Leave be, boy, and we'll split the reward. What is she to you?"

Cataphract. Heavy Armour. Armour Advantage.
Hindrance "Wounded" remains.

"Yeah…" said Torstag. "Shut up."

Torstag had no remaining Potestas and felt their absence. The pain in his chest was like a flag snapping in the wind. Everything was just a little blurry around the edges. There was no way he was going to rise to this challenge.

He glanced at Ingar.

His friend was sitting on his haunches, throwing up.

"Here, have her, then," said the cataphract. He shoved at the fork. Something clicked. The girl toppled free and into Torstag.

Torstag caught her with his left hand.

The forked weapon clanged on the stone. The cataphract drew his own greatsword, raised it.

Swords are matched. Enemy has "Heavier Armour".

The girl was light, but not so light given that Torstag was wounded. He could drag her away, but not far, not fast enough.

Nor did Torstag have the Potestas to put up a fight.

Instead, he stooped, laid her down, then chastely kissed her on the lips.

"That's right, say bye bye," said the Cataphract. "You—Oh shit."

You are Marked.
Spurred on!
Potestas restored to 5.
Hindrance "Wounded" temporarily in abeyance.
Form 6. Feats are free.
Performing Warrior at level 9

The Cataphract started to raise his sword.

As the pain dropped away, Torstag realised that his lack of armour would be an advantage if he went for speed. He dipped Peacebringer and propelled himself into an Onset Thrust, aiming for the square eyeholes in the Cataphract's visor.

Using Onset Thrust 3/6, cost 0 Potestas. 5 Potestas
remaining.
Onset Thrust is Unpredictable
You have "Much Lighter Armour."
Result = 9 (Performance) +2 "Much Lighter Armour" -
2 (Unpredictable) -6 (Enemy Challenge) -2 (Squinting
Strike) = 1.

Torstag half-expected the cataphract to ignore the attack and rely on his armour. He didn't. Instead he cut low into the thrust, using an odd rotated grip.

The blades clashed, but Torstag's point caught the other man under the chin where only ringmail protected him.

Damage = 1 (Result) + 2 (Greatsword) -4 (Cataphract
Armour) = 0

The point connected, but the armour held.

Onset Thrust advances to 4/6 Grasp.

Torstag drew his blade back to ward while he disengaged, then realised he was so much better than his enemy that he didn't need to risk the unpredictability. Instead, he cut for what looked like a weak spot where only mail covered the gap between shoulder defences and upper arm.

You have disadvantage "Much Lighter Armour"

Now the difference was working against him. It didn't matter. The swords met in a shower of sparks.

Result = 9 -1 (Luck) -2 (Much Lighter Armour) -6
(Enemy Challenge) = 0.
Tie.
Test of Potestas 5. Success. Disarm available.
Using feat Disarm. Cost 0 Potestas. 5 Potestas
remaining.

Torstag took his left hand off his sword, let the blade sink under the cataphract's pressure.

He pivoted in, grabbed the other man's blade close to the hilt and twisted the weapon free.

Enemy fails Potestas test.

They stood facing each other, breathing hard.

Torstag flung the other man's sword behind him, returned his hand to his own sword. "Go home," he panted. "Pass the word. The girl belongs only to herself."

The cataphract grated, "Damned warlocks. You're just a boy. You killed my best friend. You killed Axe Girl. Who are you to take my blade?" He lunged for one of the dropped swords that now scattered the ground.

Torstag started to follow.

The girl screamed out of the sky, feet first.

Torstag had time to think, *Magic?*

Then she struck the back of the cataphract's helmet. His head cracked forward. As he fell, the girl spun in mid air and landed like a cat.

The cataphract crashed into the stone.

Enemy Dead.
Current Form 6. Performing Warlord at Level 6.

Torstag surveyed the battlefield.

Ingar was sitting on a stone, not badly hurt, but rocking backward and forward sobbing, casting a long shadow in the setting sun.

Corpses littered the broken ground, each with its own dark patch.

11 slain. Notable loot includes one greatsword, cataphract armour, mailshirt, arrows for a horseman's war bow, long knives, a sidesword, several shields. No surviving enemy.

The Tomb Bat was glowing ashes now and Brother Neutrality's Screaming Skull was just a patch of embers. Black smoke billowed up the face of the rock spire. The entrance to the monastery's portal glowed red. Nobody was coming out of that any time soon, and if they did they it would be the hard way without the use of Tomb Bats.

Torstag relaxed and started to feel his injuries press in on him: not just the cracked ribs, but a dozen bruises and scrapes he'd forgotten about. He should go to Ingar.

"You kissed me," said the girl, her eyes alive. The thief catcher had left a red welt on her long neck.

"It...I'm 'Marked'?" managed Torstag, taking a step closer, and suddenly she was the hidden horizon beyond the mountains that called for him, the home he'd lost that most likely no longer existed, the Untrodden Valley he'd yearned to walk.

Zahna's eyes became beads of black amber. "Yes you are." She took his hand. "Come."

Her voice sounded different. Older.

Chapter 28: Lament for Angelica

"What the actual fuck!" said Ingar.

Torstag blinked into the glare of the everlight. It was dark and cold and everything hurt. He struggled to his feet. His ribs blazed white in his mind's eye. The desert night prickled his bare skin.

"I must have fallen asleep."

The girl groaned, sat up. A deep bruise marred her upper right arm, and another splotched her left hipbone. Her elbows were bloodied and scabbed.

She saw Ingar, yelped and bundled her kaftan to cover her breasts.

New Skills: Ascending Elephant, Rampant Butterfly
3/6, Cascading Mountain 3/6.
Vitality -2 of 5. 1 Wounds. 1 Fatigue incurred.
Hindrance "Wounded" restored.
Hindrance "Debilitated" and "Fatigued."
You have superficial scratches on your back. You
have abrasions on your...

"Stop!"

"Stop what?" asked Ingar. He was standing in the entrance the rocky nook with the pitch dark behind him. There was blood on his face, his arm looked scorched. "You've *already* stopped."

"I was speaking to my Tempter," said Torstag. He winced. His broken ribs didn't want him to speak.

"*She* isn't doing anything."

"She," said the girl, "has a name."

The girl got her arms into her kaftan, buttoned it closed, then rolled over and messed with a tinder box.

"What the fuck are you doing?" asked Ingar.

"Making tea," she said in a flat voice that could have hidden any emotion.

"Oh great," said Ingar. "We literally murdered a dozen or so people. Now let's have cup of tea. That will make it all better."

"I suppose you know what they were planning for me?" said the girl.

The tinder caught.

Ingar's glare bored into Torstag. "You don't know it, do you? Her name."

Torstag flushed.

"It's Zahna," said the girl. She reached for her britches, then seem to think the better of it. She wrapped the kaftan closed as she rose. Somehow she managed to fill the space with her presence. Her normally sharp cheeks dimpled. "Oh, you two aren't lovers are you? I haven't come between you? It was just business from a previous incarnation. It happens from time to time. Apparently."

A stone formed in Torstag's stomach.

"Nothing like that," Ingar was saying. "Just that my best friend left me for dead. I came round in the dark surrounded by corpses."

"We got carried away," said Torstag. "Anyway, I knew you were all right. You'd just freaked out."

"Yes, I think I may have done just that," said Ingar his voice rising. "Let me see, was it the fucking disembodied head of my old teacher trying to eat my fucking face? Or perhaps having to whack some poor fucker *in his* head to keep you alive? You tell me."

"You saved my life," said Torstag. He reached for his robes.

"Why were you even *in* the fight?" asked Ingar. "It was none of our business."

"He was saving me," said Zahna. The everlight made the pale skin of her neck glow like marble.

The last hours jumbled through Torstag's mind and his shoulders slumped. His past avatar might have been worthy of her, but not this one.

Ingar shook his head. "We were supposed to be escaping *together*."

"We also have a common enemy," said Torstag.

"Gronchard the Flayer," said Ingar. "Not my enemy."

"But we're friends," said Torstag.

"Yes we are. But I'm no killer like you. If this is your quest, count me out."

"We should check the bodies," said Zahna.

"I just did check the bodies," said Ingar. "I didn't want to get stabbed in the back when I was looking for you. And I can confirm that they are indeed bodies, as in 'corpses of recently deceased persons'."

"Um, great?" said Torstag. "Did you find anything interesting?"

"Oh yes, I *almost* forgot," said Ingar. He fished in the pocket of his robe and brought out a glass orb. "My Tempter tells me this reeks of magic."

"No!" said Zahna. "Put it away. Destroy it."

"Exactly," said Ingar. "If Gronchard can so easily hand out magic items like this, then you haven't a hope of taking him—*seriously what the actual fuck?*"

There was a flash and a ghostly blond youth appeared, standing over the crystal ball. His light illuminated the little cove.

Ingar yelped and dropped the globe.

It struck the stone and rolled toward Torstag, taking the image sliding with it.

"You're Gronchard!" blurted Torstag, rising. His chest muscles spasmed. He bit his lip to avoid crying out.

The giant phantom youth sneered down at him. He turned to inspect Zahna. "Angelica, I know you are in there, trapped in this...this harlot."

"*She's* Angelica?" blurted Ingar. "But I used to..." Was he blushing?

Zahna squared her shoulders. She raised her hand as if about to cast magic.

Torstag shifted to put himself in front of her.

"Please, queen of my heart," said Gronchard, speaking over his head. "I have missed you so badly these centuries. Stay where you are, my people will come and bring you to me. I will flay away the uncouth soul-shells to free your True Soul to inhabit this not unpleasing body in love and kindness."

Hence Gronchard the *Flayer*, realised Torstag, a dead memory stirring. This monster was going to erase Zahna's current self to flay her soul back to somebody she once was.

"Over my burning corpse," said Zahna, behind him.

"Be Silent…" Gronchard wrinkled his nose. "…*Shell Person*. I have waited lifetimes to be reunited with my true love. I can wait more. *I know you're in there Angelica! Please!*"

"Holy Fuck but you're a creepy little fucker!" said Ingar. He picked up the orb and hurled it against the gulley's rock walls. Fragments of crystal tinkled on the ground.

Once again, only his swinging everlight illuminated the little cove.

"He's dead," said Torstag, with total certainty.

"Idiot!" said Zahna. "Of course he isn't. Your friend smashed the projector, that's all."

Torstag shook his head. "No," he said, "I mean I am personally going to kill him."

Zahna cocked her head to one side, eyes twinkling in the everlight. "Because of what we just did?"

"No. On general principle."

Zahna nodded. "That's exactly my plan."

"How?" said Ingar. "He's immortal. You're completely fucking crazy. The girl has fucked with your head."

Torstag put a hand to his forehead as if that would leave any telltale bumps. He already knew, however, he was "Marked".

Zahna returned to her samovar. She rose and handed each of them an enamelled cup full of liquid that glistened behind a veil of steam.

"He's a warlock like us, no more," she said. "Drink."

Torstag did as he was told.

A pair of molten iron hands seemed to reform his broken ribcage. He gasped but could not scream.

**Vitality reset. 1 Wound healed. Hindrances
"Wounded", "Debilitated" and "Fatigued" shed.**

Ingar staggered drunkenly. "Fuck fuck fuck."

Zahna plucked the cup from his fingers. "Better?"

Ingar squeaked.

"So," said Zahna. "Each time Gronchard dies, his followers kidnap the next avatar and flay back his soul to reveal Gronchard."

"That's…" Torstag couldn't think of the right word. "Worse than murder."

"Really fucked up," said Ingar, speaking at the same moment.

Zahna nodded. "So help me defeat him."

"Sure, since you asked so nicely," said Ingar. "Oh wait a moment, he's some kind of God and has his very own Flying Tooth Garden, whatever the fuck that is. You are insane. Come on Torstag. Say good bye to the nice lady. We'll try to find you another one…you know, that's not utterly barking."

"How?" asked Torstag, ignoring his friend, which was pretty easy to do with Zahna standing before him like the kind of dream he used to have back in the monastery.

"To the Jungle Tomb of the Ice Queen," she said. "The Ice Queen once repulsed Gronchard and his Flying Tooth Garden."

"And that will help, how?" asked Torstag.

"I thought you might ask her how she did it," said Zahna. "You are a necromancer, after all."

Torstag chewed his lip. "I wanted to leave that behind."

"Oh?" said Zahna. Her eyes twinkled. "You seem to have no problem *creating* dead people—how is talking to them so much worse?"

"I will do it," said Torstag, "if that's what it takes."

"Fuck," said Ingar. "Seriously?"

"As you said, it's my quest, not yours," said Torstag. "We can pick a place to meet up after."

"Come with me," said Ingar. "Between us we can live well."

"Live well by burgling tombs, you mean," said Zahna. "Why not start with this one? There will be treasure."

"I…we…how did you know my Vocation?" said Ingar. "Torstag did *you* tell her?"

"No," said Torstag. "We didn't talk."

Ingar glanced meaningfully at the bedding roll. "I guess not."

"Treasure," prompted Zahna.

"There'll be treasure?" said Ingar.

"The Ice Queen will have her things buried with her to ensure reincarnation to a similar status," said Zahna.

Ingar glanced at Torstag.

"I have to do this," said Torstag, "and I need you."

"Fuck," said Ingar. "Okay. Just this once, then you'll have to choose."

"Sure," said Torstag.

"Good," said Zahna. "Now Gronchard is onto us, we don't have much time."

Chapter 29: Gronchard in the Manifestorium

Pain blazed behind Gronchard's eyes. His fingers stung from the shattering of the manifestation egg. He rose to his feet, making the dragon eggs rattle and rustle. That noise seemed to break the dam of his emotions and he screamed at the top of his voice, "Angelica!"

The voice of the Saint Omnipresence rang out, "The Divinity is hurt!"

Eggs clashed and crashed as Seraphim plunged down the steps into the Manifestorium.

Gronchard thrashed his arms, causing painted eggs to fly free and bounce across the surface of the pit. "No you idiots. Get back! A blasphemer destroyed an Egg of Manifestation, that is all."

The Seraphim halted.

A sob escaped Gronchard's chest. "Curse this young body and its youthful humours!"

"Divinity!" said Saint Omnipresence—another old retainer, noted Gronchard—"You should rest."

1 Vitality lost. 3 of 4 remaining.
6 of 6 Potestas remaining.

"Saint?" said Gronchard, tears drying. "Do you presume to tell me I am weak? Bring me the egg for the bounty hunters nearest the Broken Realm."

"No, Divinity. Yes, Divinity."

Gronchard shifted to sink back down under the surface. There was something comfortingly womb-like about the Manifestorium. The

206

indestructible but light eggs enclosed and supported him, but without generating any pressure.

Only shock had worked to preserve his dignity during his manifestation. What other man had seen his true love in the arms of another, still dishevelled from her lovemaking? And yet, had he not manifested, he would not have seen her at all. Nor would he have any clues as to where she had gone.

Should he summon Saint Prescience to advise him?

No, he, Gronchard the Flayer had a thousand lives of wisdom to draw on. He did not need an old man knowing that he was a cuckold. He just needed to focus himself.

What had he seen?

Angelica half-dressed...

Yes that, but also two youths the same age as his own vessel, one naked, the other wearing a blood spattered habit like a monk's...like a monk of the Order of the Grey Cortège.

A hand seemed to clutch Gronchard's vitals. "No! That would be unfair. She couldn't have..."

He stood up. "Forget the bounty hunters, bring me the egg for the Monastery of the Untrodden Valley."

They fetched the egg and had a Lesser Angel fly it out to where Gronchard lay. Rather than an eye, this egg bore a simple number for identification.

Clutching it in two hands, he wriggled beneath the surface.

Using Manifestation Pit. 2nd Circle Spell. Cost 4 Potestas, 2 of 6 remaining.

Gronchard found himself standing in a deserted chapel at what could be dawn or dusk.

It was definitely *his* chapel: there was a triptych displaying three of his more prominent vessels, and an icon of the Sacred Angelica. However, the place was dusty, with old leaves on the floor. The candles had not been lit in so long they had cobwebs on them. Small wonder then there was no reservoir of Potestas for him to draw on, though Angelica's shrine had at least the aura of having been worshipped properly.

He turned his attention to the gong.

The metal dish clanged sonorously.

At last, a youth came running in, saw Gronchard's manifestation, yelped, then ran away.

Eventually an old man limped through the entrance.

"Abbot!" thundered Gronchard. "What kind of welcome is this for a God? Look at the state of my chapel!"

The old man regarded him unblinkingly. "Incense and candles, both, have been of too poor a quality, this year. To use them would have been an insult. Also, to my shame, the current cohort of acolytes are insufficiently pure for the work of tending to your Sacred Shrine."

Absolute rubbish, of course, and the old man knew that Gronchard knew. Gronchard, however, had yet to regain his full powers and he sensed that his Cynosure Charismatic Presence would not work on this white-haired cleric.

"Are you," he asked, "perhaps missing an Acolyte or two, Abbot?"

"What?" said the Abbot. "Oh, yes, now you come to mention it a couple did abscond last night. I'm sure we'll catch them."

"Which two Acolytes?" asked Gronchard. "By which I mean, who were they when they were dedicants?"

Some boys rushed in with candles and incense.

"Here, Deity," said the Abbot, "let me makes some offerings to you." The old man fussed around lighting candles and filling sensors.

Soon light flickered on clouds of fragrant smoke. There was no real devotion in it, but it did improve the interior and cast particularly good light on the icon of Angelica.

"So," said Gronchard.

"Deity?"

"You were telling me about the two escapees and how one of them was Berotspan the Marshal."

"Oh," said the Abbot, "is that who they were? Thank you, Divinity. Unfortunately they caused a small fire on absconding, damaging our records. Had we known it was Nee Berotspan we would of course we would have informed you immediately."

"Of course," said Gronchard, "because I seem to recall that I previously gave Berotspan into your keeping when he was Lashton the Necromancer, and he would never have been able to defy me at Yinkesia had you managed to harvest him."

The Abbot shrugged expansively, raising both hands. "What can one do, Divinity? Sometimes Warlocks have a destiny that cannot be denied. However, we did harvest him this time around."

"And let him escape."

"If he had not been a formidable soul, your Divine Providence would not have troubled to entrust him to us. Nevertheless, he will be recaptured."

"When? He has kidnapped my Sacred Angelica." That last came out as a whine. Gronchard blushed and hated his youthful body all the more.

"Soon," soothed the Abbot. "We have a small army of skeletons, houndheads to do the tracking, and not inconsiderable magic granted to us by the Ineffable One."

"With all that power," said Gronchard, "it seems strange that you have not already recaptured him."

"Unfortunately, the fire damaged our means of entering the Broken Lands—which is where they fled."

Gronchard had a memory of entering the Monastery via a portal high up on a rock pillar. Which lifetime had that been? Angelica had been beside him, holding his hand, and there had been arcane flying machines. "He destroyed your Tomb Bats, didn't he?"

"They will be replaced, Divinity."

"But not any time soon," said Gronchard.

"No, Divinity. And between our main portal and the Broken Lands lie many weeks journey."

"So you have a party in transit?"

The Abbot shook his head. "The trail would have gone cold by the time my people arrived."

"What about the Cortège?"

"We would need the remains of his previous avatar."

"You have those!" said Gronchard. "I. Gave. Them. To. You."

The Abbot grimaced. "The fire, Divinity."

"So you have nothing," said Gronchard, his voice rising. "No way to chase him or locate him. And yet you said he would be recaptured."

"Of course, Divinity. He is pledged to the Ineffable One. When he dies, the Cortège will Step Between to retrieve his remains, which in turn will enable us to harvest his new avatar, and thus the Great Circle will be restored. Ultimately, there is no escape for Acolytes."

"And what of my Angelica?"

"The mission of the Cortège is constrained by our pact with the Ineffable One."

"And what of *our* Pact, Abbot?"

"But Divinity, you yourself reneged on it by not warning us that he would have a rescuer."

"Rescuer?"

"Clearly the Sacred Angelica's current avatar—"

"Vessel!" corrected Gronchard.

"—current *vessel* intruded on our holy precinct in order to entice away Nee Berotspan for her own nefarious purposes."

Gronchard bit back a gasp. So that was what Angelica's vessel had been up to! She had Stepped Between from Yinkesia to the Monastery and back. This was all part of some plan. What could she hope to achieve??

If the vessel had just wanted to evade capture, she would focus on putting distance between herself and Gronchard's realms. Not only would that make her exponentially harder to find, it would also—eventually—place her outside the range of his Mausoleum.

Instead, she had lingered on his borders, first in Yinkesia, which was closer to his Magisterium than the realm where he had first located her, then worked her way around to the Broken Realm.

The vessel must intend going on the offensive, and that in turn meant that she had some plan for attacking Gronchard. If he could work out what that was, he could intercept her and bring back his Angelica.

"Divinity?" prompted the Abbot.

"Next time you have Nee Berotspan, see that you keep him," said Gronchard and ended the manifestation.

Chapter 30: Virago!

Zahna paused at the portal's threshold and let the cool dry air flow around her.

Beyond the portal, crumbling steps wound through towering shards of rock. Behind her, a decaying wooden causeway snaked through an insect-ridden marsh with leather-winged pterodactyls wheeling overhead.

"Come on," she said. "We can camp on the other side."

Form 2. Performing Virago at Level 3.

Torstag did not meet her gaze as he trudged closer, boards creaking under his weight.

He was tall and broad, broader than when she had first sought him out—levelling up tended to do that to warlocks with physical vocations. However, there was still a puppydog boyishness about him. Would that fade as he grew into his warlock self?

Zahna wasn't sure what she'd expected of her first time with a man, other than that it would be with Marvak, and not this stranger. She certainly hadn't expected it to be quite so...*acrobatic*? Or so hungry and vulnerable all at once...

Which is what had led her to say yes to unlocking the Virago vocation...that and the way Torstag's Mark had seemed to call it out of her.

Zahna's fingers clenched on her staff.

All these years, she'd carefully kept that last Vocation slot empty! The other three had been filled for her. Mistress Zinaven hadn't asked permission to awaken her as a Wizard, nor had she given her a choice about becoming a Flow Fighter. Their tea-making expeditions had also made it impossible not to embrace Scout.

Zahna didn't resent any of that.

Without Mistress Zinhaven, Zahna would have ended up stuck as a temple virgin, tending the Sacred Flame in some backwater Realm.

However, that *fourth* Vocation slot had always been Zahna's to fill. She would lie awake at night floating in dead memories considering becoming a musician, a farmer, or a great architect, or maybe adding another magical vocation…she had rather fancied being a fireball-flinging Goeticist.

And then suddenly she'd found herself with the gormless Boy staring at her like a startled owl and that precious last Vocation slot was filled by…She wasn't sure she wanted to know what a Virago was.

Mind you, it did seem to help her get her way.

Commanding Presence had quelled Ingar well enough back in the canyon, though she had qualms at using it on somebody who had fought for her, however unwillingly.

"Couldn't we have kept the horses?" groaned Ingar. A plank gave under his right foot, which plunged through the rotten wood. "Fuck."

Torstag laughed. "You answered your own question."

"Fuck you," said Ingar. He offered his new axe to his friend.

Torstag flinched but took the weapon. He seemed to wilt under the extra weight.

He was wearing the lamellar body armour and helmet of the cataphract she'd killed—the limb defences, hadn't fit—and, to be fair, Zahna *had* dragged him from desert to tundra to mountains to rice fields to icecap. Even so, it seemed more than that.

Ingar stooped to haul on his sandal strap. Foot and sandal came free in an explosion of soggy brown splinters. "I'd kill for some proper boots."

"You did, only you were too squeamish to take them," said Torstag, studiously not looking at the axe.

"Where are *your* new boots, then?" asked Ingar. "You don't give a shit about dead bodies."

Torstag's smile became thin. "For a necromancer, walking a mile in another man's shoes has implications, especially if the man is dead."

"Fuck," said Ingar. "My axe isn't haunted?"

"What?" said Torstag. "No, not at all. Totally clean." He offered it back while seeming to find something interesting to stare at in the swamp.

Ingar hefted the weapon over his shoulder. He glared at Zahna. "What are you looking at?"

Something splashed in the water under the causway.

"Come on," she repeated. "We need to keep moving."

"If we are in such a rush," said Ingar. "How come we're taking the long way round?"

Zahna sighed. "Each portal multiplies the possibilities, makes us harder to track using magic."

"What about dogs?" asked Torstag, raising his gaze to meet hers. He immediately looked away.

"I kept using a purifying spell on our scent," she said.

"That explains the weird chanting," said Ingar.

She looked at him, fought back the urge to say something cutting. "Yes, the weird chanting is how I do magic." She started to turn back to the portal. "Come on, we—"

"—have to multiply the possibilities," completed Ingar. "I get it. But what if we just fucked off our separate ways?" He nudged Torstag. "Come on mate, you wanted to be your own man. This isn't it."

"I…" said Torstag. He looked Zahna in the eye. "What does Marked mean?"

Zahna felt herself flush. "Nothing *I* did. Something my past self put on the Marshal."

"She's flannelling," said Ingar.

"I…" began Zahna. Her jaw clenched. She shouldn't have to recite the whole business of the flaying again. What was she? A damsel in distress?

She squared her shoulders.

**New Form 3. Cost 1 Potestas, 5 remaining.
Performing Virago at Level 4.**

"Torstag. You're coming because it's your destiny. Ingar, you *say* you're coming for the treasure, but really it's because your Torstag's friend. Isn't that enough for both of you?"

**Using Virago, Commanding Presence 3/6, cost 3
Potestas, 1 remaining.
Result = 4 (Performance) +2 (Feat) = Commanding at 6.
Effect on Burglar: 6 (Commanding) -3 (Will) -1 (Luck) =
2 (Tentative Practical Response)**

"Fuck, she has a point," said Ingar. "But are you really going along with all this 'champion' crap?"

**Effect on Warrior: 6 (Commanding) -0 (Will Negated
by "Marked") +1 (Luck) = 7 (Purposeful Practical
Response)**

Torstag lifted his head. His eyes twinkled. "Ha! Apparently it's who I am. Come on, lead on, my lady."

**Virago, Commanding Presence advances to 4/6
Grasp.**

Yes, thought Zahna. Whatever it was, Virago certainly helped her get her way. If only she felt good about it.

Chapter 31: Council of Saints

The sacrifices ran the gauntlet of the shrubs. Every so often one of the plants bit off a chunk of flesh. Blood sprayed and splashed, but nobody screamed.

"You see?" said Gronchard to his Saints, who were lined up along the balcony. "Wiring their jaws closed stops their screams disturbing my repose, and yet the plants still enjoy a good chase."

Saint Prescience flushed and lowered his eyes.

Gronchard led them inside to the council chamber. "I am immortal, not moribund. As I come into Myself, there will be changes. Now…" He settled in his throne and clapped for them to sit, "I need the counsel of My Saints. Angelica's vessel has some plan to attack Me."

They all looked at him in silence.

Gronchard sighed. "So, counsel Me. What are My weaknesses?"

Nobody said anything.

"Let's start with you, Saint Incarnation."

Saint Incarnation screwed up his face in concentration.

"Well…?" prompted Gronchard.

"Your physical form is well guarded, Divinity," Saint Incarnation. "If an assassin could infiltrate the Flying Tooth Garden, he still could not reach your Divinity. There is always at least one Seraphim Wizard on guard using Backwards Remembering. An army, Divinity?" He made an open palm gesture. "An army would still have to breach the defences. May I ask, Divinity, does Angelica's Vessel have an army?"

Gronchard shook his head. "She has but two followers."

"An immediate direct attack seems unlikely, then," said Saint Incarnation. "Perhaps she plays the long game."

"Fool! If that were so," said Gronchard, "then she would have fled far away with the plan to return once she had built her strength." He surveyed the table. "Saint Mausoleus?"

"Divinity, if the vessel's primary goal is to…keep the Holy Angelica imprisoned, then her objective may be to destroy the contents of the Mausoleum."

Saint Incarnation raised a hand. "By your leave, Divinity, I shall assign Seraphim Wizards to guarding the Mausoleum."

"That should already have been done," said Gronchard. "Saint Prescience? You have witnessed my scrying of her. What do you say?"

"Divinity, if she has gathered so few followers, it must mean that she intends to move quickly while travelling light. That suggests that whatever she plans requires the completion of a quest."

"At last," said Gronchard. "A useful contribution. So she—the vessel—quests for something that may harm me. What might that be?"

Again Saint Incarnation raised a hand. "Attacking your Divinity directly seems impossible, as does attacking the Mausoleum. However, what if she had a way to attack the Flying Tooth Garden?"

"What?" said Gronchard. He laughed. "How is that even possible?"

The table exploded into mirth.

Gronchard snapped his fingers at one of the Seraphim. "You. Kill this Saint, take his Angel. You are the new Saint Incarnation."

The Seraphim drew his sword and advanced.

"Wait," cried Saint Incarnation, "You do not even know where the Flying Tooth Garden came from, do you?"

"An excellent point," said Gronchard. He nodded at the Seraphim, who ran his sword through Saint Incarnation, detailed some other Seraphim to take away the carcass and then smoothly assumed his place at the table.

"So," continued Gronchard, "what do we know of the origins of the Flying Tooth Garden?"

"Nothing, Divinity," said Saint Prescience. "We are all mere latecomers to your immortal lifetime."

"I…" began Gronchard. A hand seemed to clutch his heart.

216

He simply didn't remember.

Had he created the Flying Tooth Garden?

Found it?

Stolen it?

His Saints continued to sit in silence, waiting for him to finish his sentence.

"...am disappointed in you all," he said.

The silence continued, broken only by the wind and the sound of the shrubs rending the flesh of the sacrifices. It turned out that humans could make quite a lot of noise without opening their mouths after all. Gronchard still rated this as an improvement on full-throated screams.

"Divinity," said the new Saint Incarnation. A drop of blood trickled into his eye. He wiped it off with the back of his hand, making an unsightly smear. "Surely what matters is what she—the vessel—knows."

"Go on..." prompted Gronchard.

"Well, Divinity," said Saint Incarnation, "though my predecessor failed to rescue Angelica from the wizard's tower, he did confiscate the wizard's library. Perhaps there is some clue to be had there."

Gronchard opened his mouth to have Saint Remembrance initiate a search, then realised that it would be best to keep the knowledge to himself.

"Have the books brought to my Heaven. And gather up any of the archivists who have inspected them and feed them to the shrubs."

It took Gronchard two weeks to get through the wizard's library. He found neither spells nor esoteric accounts relating to the Flying Tooth Garden. In fact the only reference to it was in a chronicle, which told the story of Gronchard's brief war with the Queen Rasinta, known as the Ice Queen.

As he recalled, he had broken into her realms and started salting her cities, but she in turn had discovered how to send attackers Stepping Through to the Flying Tooth Garden until he withdrew—her bleak northern kingdom hardly merited a fight to the utterance.

Gronchard had never discovered how she did it. Eventually, in passing from one vessel to another, he lost interest in the question.

The Ice Queen had died long ago. No trace of her empire remained. Even so, perhaps there was a clue to be found in her tomb.

He called for Saint Remembrance.

At length, a young man he didn't recognise hurried in and prostrated himself.

"You've changed, Saint Remembrance," remarked Gronchard.

"My predecessor was among those who viewed the forbidden tomes."

"Enough of all that," said Gronchard. "Find me the location of the Tomb of the Ice Queen."

Chapter 32: Irritated by People Stuff

They passed out of the portal into heat and gloom beneath a dark green canopy. Leaves squelched underfoot.

A big insect buzzed at Zahna's face.

Torstag backhanded it out of the air.

She blinked away sweat. The perspiration just lay on her skin as if it had nowhere to go. "We're here."

"Treasure!" said Ingar. "Fuck!" he slapped his neck, flapped his monkish robes. "What the fuck?"

"Jungle," said Zahna, laughing.

"As in Jungle Tomb of the Ice Queen," said Torstag, flicking away another insect.

Zahna glanced at him. That was the most he'd said in days.

He met her gaze then looked away.

Zahna unshouldered her pack and took her time in extracting the samovar.

What was going on in Torstag's head? He'd been avoiding talking to her since she'd used her Virago vocation.

"Where is it?" asked Ingar.

"Further off." She brought out the samovar. "Stay covered up while I make tea."

"Tea...?" said Ingar. "I thought we were in a rush?"

"*Magic* tea."

Torstag leaned back against a tree, letting it take his armour's weight. Zahna felt his eyes on her as she loaded up the charcoal and got it lit. She broke off a brick of black tea, set it to brew as a base.

"Right," she said. "Torstag. Don't let this boil. Just simmer gently. Close the vent to control the temperature."

"Don't abandon us!" said Ingar. "We don't know the portals."

"I won't be long," she said, turning as she rose to hide her smile. For all that Torstag was behaving oddly, she had established her leadership. The raid on the tomb should go smoothly, and perhaps Ingar would see the benefits of tagging along for more treasure. His skills would be handy but also she wasn't—she realised—ready for it to be just her and Torstag.

Torstag slapped at yet another insect. He contemplated the patch of blood on his palm. "Where *are* you going?"

"Foraging," she said.

Which was mostly true.

You have 5 of 5 Potestas.

She began to chant.

Using Tea Making, Walk Unhindered, cost 1 Potestas.
4 of 5 Potestas remaining.
Challenge = 5 +2 ("Natural Environment") = 6
Form 3.
Performing Wizard at level 7.

Not good enough!

The handy thing about Tea Making was that she could improve her form before completing the spell.

New Form 2. Cost 1 Potestas. 3 of 5 Potestas remaining.

Even Worse!

Zahna drew in her focus, tried again.

New Form 5. Cost 1 Potestas. 2 of 5 Potestas remaining.
Performing Wizard at level 9.

Now, she half-closed her eyes and started weaving around the muddy jungle floor. The Sight came over her and the jungle lit up with meanings. She was dancing now.

A piece of moss drew her attention. She pounced. "Ha!"

Then a fern, then some oddly shaped fungi.

Zahna glanced back through the trees, picked out the orange glow in the gloom. The scent of smoke drew her back to the waiting boys.

Chanting loudly now, Zahna pushed her finds into the samovar, then sat on her haunches to wait.

As the tea simmered, gossamer strands webbed out to connect everything in the jungle: the insects, the trees, even the droplets of humidity condensing on Torstag's armour.

Result = 9 (Performance) +0 (Luck) -6 (Challenge) = 3.
Effect = A dozen doses. Spell duration is about 2
watches. Tea maintains potency for a couple of days.

The Gods were with her today!

Zahna laid out the enamel cups and wrapped her hand in a cloth. She poured a cup of tea and took a slurp. The insects danced away. Her pores opened. Her skin tingled. She nodded. "Drink," she said.

"Is it safe?" asked Ingar. The boy's red hair was plastered to his scalp and the humidity had brought out a flush that made his freckles look pale.

"What?"

"Last time you gave us a potion, it hurt," said Torstag.

"Of course it's safe…" grated Zahna.

You are "Cold".
Test of Will 3. Failed.
You have Issue "Irritated by People Stuff" at 1
Hardening.
Wrestling with Irritated by People Stuff (1/6) cost 3
Potestas, -1 of 5 Potestas remaining.
Will 3 overcome. You have Hindrance "Infuriated."
Potestas -1. You have Hindrance "Emotionally
Exhausted."
Form lost. New Form 0.
Performing Virago at Level 1.

Zahna took a deep breath.

Nearby a frog chirped. Further off, something screeched.

**Test of Will 3. Hindrance "Infuriated" shaken off.
Hindrance "Emotionally Exhausted" remains.**

She sighed. That wasn't going to go away until she got her Potestas back up above zero. Just growling at them wasn't going to work. "The tea," she said, her voice flat to her own ears, "will let you pass through the jungle unhindered for two watches—say eight hours."

"Unhindered as in un-feasted-on?" said Ingar, slapping at his arm. "I'm in." He squatted and knocked back the drink

"Thank you," said Torstag, following suit. He shook out his shoulders, making the lamellar plates rattle. "Much better. Now what?"

Zahna decanted the tea into a flask. It would keep its potency for a day or so. She used her knife to dig a hole in the loam, then nudged the glowing charcoal into it. Finally she packed up her bag. "Uphill from here, pretty much in a straight line and there's the Tomb of the Ice Queen. What are you waiting for? Come on."

The tea continued to work as they climbed steadily through the gloom, occasional shafts of light revealing clouds of insects between the trees. The ground slowly tilted up to become a gentle hillside. Here and there, rocks reared out of the mud, making clearings where sunlight pooled.

Just as Zahna got back up to two Potestas, something ahead of them flickered in her Sight.

"Halt," said Zahna. "Magic."

Torstag unsheathed his sword. Ingar hefted his new axe.

New Form 2. Performing Scout at level 5.

Moving lethargically, they stalked forward, Torstag and Zahna in perfect silence, Ingar blundering and cursing under his breath. "Fucking jungle."

They needn't have bothered with stealth.

They came on a middle-aged woman in heavy woollen clothing, propped against a stone door in the side of a low cliff with trees overflowing its edge. From its curve, it looked very much like an old quarry cut into the hillside.

222

Warlock.

Zahna held up her hand. "Careful. She might be dangerous."

Torstag nodded and unsheathed his sword.

"Bollocks," said Ingar. "She needs our help." He crashed through the vegetation toward the woman.

"Wait," said Torstag, blundering to catch up with him, armour letting him brush through thorny growths and foliage.

"Gah," said Zahna. She slipped after them, ranging out to the flank just in case.

The woman blinked up at the two men, eyes narrow above insect-puffed cheeks. "Oh good," she said. "Savages. You can take my money. Just make sure you put me out of my misery first."

"Tea," said Ingar, looking directly at where Zahna was trying to lurk. "Now."

Zahna stepped out of hiding.

The woman's head snapped around.

Virago. Challenge, 4.

"Oh," said the woman. "You're another…lady."

Chapter 33: Tea and Sympathy

The woman wrinkled her nose. "Lukewarm tea. Don't you have coffee?"

"It will make you feel better," said Ingar.

She managed a smile and the jungle seemed to light up. "You're being awfully kind to me."

Because I'm not Marvon the Mutilator, thought Ingar. "It's just nice to meet somebody who's not trying to kill us," he said.

The woman took a deeper sip. Her insect bites started to fade. Her face lost its puffiness. "Interesting," she said. "What *was* in that?"

"Ask Zahna," said Ingar. "She made it."

The woman drew in a knee and shuffled up into a more upright position. The movement caused her right leg to briefly emerge from her long skirt, revealing a muscular calf and a laced ankle boot.

Ingar was suddenly reminded that this was only the second girl—*woman!*—he'd met since the Grey Cortège took him. There was certainly more of her than there was of Zahna, but Ingar didn't think that was a bad thing. He wondered what she'd look like—

Unlock Companion, Gallantry?

"Ahem," she said.

He flushed, couldn't think of anything to say.

Unlock Companion, Gallantry?

Fuck yes. Please. Gallantry.

You are Quick Witted so Gallantry Feats start at 2
Grasp.
Companion, Gallantry at 2/6 Grasp.
You may have 4 Vocations. Entertainer vocation
Abandoned. Tout, Recite, Acrobatics and Sing
retained as Skills.

Wait! What?

"Is something wrong?" asked the woman.

Ingar flushed and shook her head. He could hardly tell this stranger that he'd just given up everything from his childhood just so he could flirt with her.

"Then perhaps you should introduce yourself? Who exactly are you?"

"Who am I?"

You are Ingar, Human, Youth, Quick Witted, Nimble
Fingered, Hedonistic, Sensitive.
Potestas 6/6. Will 3. Issue "Horror of Murder" 1/6.
Vitality 4/4. Toughness 2.
Vocations:
Burglar 4: Hide, Climb +1, Spider Climb, Move Silently,
Stalk, Pick Pocket, Open Lock, Detect Trap, Stalk
Close 3/6, Disarm Trap 2/6.
Warrior 1 (Halberds): Wrath Strike 1/6.
Companion 0: Gallantry 2/6.
Artist 0: Visualisation 4/6.
Various capabilities including Tout 2, Recite 2,
Acrobatics 2, Sing 2 and Meditation.

Ingar exhaled. The skills he'd learned growing up were still there, just shifted a little.

The woman's eyes twinkled, obviously enjoying his discomfort.

Go on then. Make me gallant!

Ingar bowed flamboyantly. "Permit me to introduce myself. I am
Ingar the Burglar, at your service my lady."

**Result = 3 (Performance) +2 (Feat) +1 (Luck) −6
(Challenge) = 0
Effect = Mild Tug (0).**

The woman fanned herself with her hand. "A burglar? How *ro-guish*!"

Companion, Gallantry advances to 3/6 Grasp.

"Miss Millicent Tomarda," she said, extending her hand for a kiss.
"Delighted I'm sure, Master Ingar."

"Very pleased to meet you, Miss Millicent. This is Zahna and…"
He glanced around and located his friend lurking a little distance off,
watching over them like a sheepdog. "…that's Torstag. Might I ask
where you are from?"

"Why, the City of Timbandria!" She seemed to read his expression.
"We're famous for our libraries. Libraries and steam engines I suppose."

"Not a sorcerer or a warrior, then?" prompted Zahna, who had
moved to sit on her haunches nearby.

Miss Millicent raised a limp arm and let it drop. "I really am beyond the Pale aren't I?"

"Pale, as in bucket?" asked Ingar.

"Pale as in the Pale of Rationality," corrected Miss Millicent. "We
must be positively surrounded by gremlins." Her expression sharpened. "I'm a librarian," she said. "What am I doing here?" Her eyebrows rose. "Did you *kidnap* me?"

"No, really, Miss Millicent," said Ingar, "we didn't." He poured
her more tea. "So what *are* you doing here, Miss Millicent?"

"The chart!" she said, scrabbling in her things. "Ah…" She pulled
out a rather floppy roll of parchment. "I should have copied it onto
paper. How was I to know about the humidity?"

"May I?" asked Ingar. "Hmmm."

It was a portal map familiar from the monastery geography lessons. It was easy to trace their route from the "Broken Lands" to a portal in the middle of the chart, marked with a crown.

"I am an *experienced* spelunker," declared Miss Millicent. "In fact, I am a founder member of the League of Lady Spelunkers and Trailblazers. And I was cautious at first." She blinked at them. "Are you...*natives*? It's just that you look as if you come from two different cultures."

"Ingar and I are former monks," said Torstag, striding over. "Zahna..."

"I travel a lot," said Zahna.

Ingar offered her the cup.

Millicent sipped. "Odd taste. Where was I?"

"The League of Lady Spelunkers and Trailblazers," prompted Zahna, her eyes narrow.

"Oh yes," said Miss Millicent. "When I discovered this chart in an antique desk, I thought 'How fabulous to surprise everybody with a new route for our Summer Expedition'. But there were dragons, and I rescued this naked barbarian who turned out to be a king and wanted to marry me so I slipped away and I should have headed home but it was only two portals from the crown and I thought I had come this far, just a quick look around...Which reminds me..." She fished in her bag, opened a small wooden box took out a pill. "I have to take these...for my voices."

"Voices?" said Ingar.

"Well, just one voice...why am I telling you this?"

"Do the pills work?" asked Ingar, putting a gentle hand on her arm. He caught Zahna's eye, trying to put a question into the look.

"Not entirely," said Millicent, "But they do muffle it somewhat."

Zahna coughed. "You should absolutely..." She glanced at Torstag, who was watching her. Her eyebrows raised a little. "...absolutely *not* risk taking them," she completed. "You don't know what effect the humidity will have on the medicine."

What *was* going on there? Having Zahna along made everything complicated. He and Torstag should be in some tavern by now, flush with loot from some old tomb. *I'm going to fuck all the women, drink all—*

Millicent blinked owlishly, which somehow captured all his attention. "Oh. Good point, I suppose. I can always tell it to shut up. That works, but then people think I'm mad. Do you think I'm mad?"

"No," said Ingar.

"Then what happened?" Zahna leaned forward. "Once you reached the jungle?"

"Then somehow I just kept walking. It was as if I was being towed. And here I am, days from the portal." She laughed. "It sounds really quite foolish now I say it aloud. Perhaps I should ask Dr Joyous for new pills when I get home? Finally I saw something through the trees and I thought *Oh Thank Goodness! I've found an Underground Station.* But instead it's some kind of tomb and I can't get in—though why I should want to I don't know, I mean disturbing the archaeology is bad—and I am too exhausted to backtrack but at least the stone is cold for some reason."

"Will you excuse us for a moment?" said Zahna, rising.

"Of course," said Miss Millicent. "I imagine you'll want to talk about what to do with me."

"Nothing like that," protested Ingar.

"Go on," said Miss Millicent. "People make stupid decisions when they can't discuss them properly."

"Actually," said Torstag. "Ingar will stay with you while Zahna and I find a spot to make camp."

"Will he now?" said Ingar.

Torstag gave him a meaningful look.

"Sure," said Ingar and turned his attention back to Miss Millicent.

Chapter 34: Beware the Virago

Sweat streamed down Torstag's face as he scrambled up the rocky rise to the right of the cliff. The overlapping plates of his lamellar made it hard to bend far enough forward to lean into the climb.

Zahna got to the top ahead of him. She lent on her staff and stood looking down at him with the lush green behind her.

As he reached her, she turned and strolled over to the cliff top overlooking the tomb entrance where Ingar now sat next to Miss Millicent.

"Good spot to camp," she said. "Dry."

Form 1. Performing Scout at Level 2.

The area behind the cliff top was a mostly flat. Low bushes had sprung up wherever a crack or crevice would hold soil. Otherwise, it was an expanse of exposed stone.

"Wouldn't take long to clear a camp," she said.

Torstag shook his head. "I think we need to make some kind of raised platform."

Zahna's eyebrows steepled. "Why would we do that?"

"Um," said Torstag. He cast around and spotted a column of ants crossing a bare patch. "Insects?"

"My tea deals with that," she said without looking his way.

Zahna was watching Ingar talking to Miss Millicent. Torstag's friend seemed particularly animated by the conversation: bobbing this way and that, alternately stooping and straightening. Sure, there was an age difference, but from this distance it didn't look *that* complicated.

"Magic," said Torstag.

"Yes, magic tea," said Zahna.

"Yes," said Torstag, then realised that wasn't what he meant. He unbuckled his helmet and mopped his brow.

The cliffs were just high enough that he could see over the treetops and beyond hills that undulated like great green waves all the way to the horizon. How far would he have to walk before he found any other people?

A giggle echoed up from below.

"Your magic," he said.

"Well, obviously," she said.

Torstag put the helmet down on a rock—a dead memory told him he would have to check it for insects and snakes later—then started on the straps of his cuirass.

"What is it?" said Zahna.

"When I brought up my Necromancer Sight back then, it said you and Miss Millicent are both...Viragos?"

"Yes," said Zahna. "I am. I'm not honestly sure what that means."

"But it's like Warlord," said Torstag. "It gets people to do what you want. Specifically men."

She didn't respond.

"That's why you were going to tell her to take her pills," he said.

"I...you can see what she's doing to Ingar," Zahna. "Was I so wrong?"

Torstag got the last buckle. The cuirass opened out. Laughter drifted up from the tomb entrance. Should he be dashing back down to protect his friend?

The lamellar clattered as he draped it over the helmet. "It wasn't Ingar you were worried about."

"No," she said. "If you could hear my Demon you'd know I'm 'driven' and 'cold'. You would be too, if Gronchard wanted you for his slave."

Torstag straightened and stood while the sweat dripped from his robe. It would be good to just strip off. "So Virago lets you manipulate men."

"Yes," she said. "It seems to work that way."

"So how do I know..." Torstag struggled for the words. "Back after that fight, did you use magic to make me...?"

Zahna rounded on him. "Of course not. I don't think Virago is magic anyway."

Test of Potestas 5. Influence detected.
You are Level 3 (Warrior). Current Form 1.
Result = 4 (Performance) +2 ("Irritated") -1 (Luck) -3
(Challenge) = 6.
Effect = Resisted.

"You just tried it!" said Torstag.

"Yes...no...I didn't mean to." Zahna crossed her ankles, uncrossed them. "It's not Magic any more than a pretty face or a well-turned ankle is magic. If I were built like Miss Millicent—all breasts and hips and legs—would you be having this conversation?" She shifted, bracing her legs.

It looked as if she were poised to drop into a fighting stance, but the interplay of bone and sinew took Torstag back to their fierce coupling.

Her eyes twinkled knowingly.

It would be all too easy for him to blame his mood on the heat and move on to other concerns. Torstag, however, was his own man.

"How can I tell?" he said. "I'm 'Marked'."

Zahna sighed. "I didn't do that."

"It doesn't matter, though, does it?" said Torstag. "I will never know whether what I feel is real."

"What you *feel?*" said Zahna.

He remembered her shrugging off their encounter as the business of past lives.

"What I *feel* right now," said Torstag, "Is that I should help you get what you need from this tomb, and then we should part company."

Vegetation crashed. Ingar was blundering out of the undergrowth to join them. "You two are scheming to get rid of her."

"She's a—" began Zahna.

"—warlock and doesn't know it," said Torstag, suddenly not wanting to burst his friend's bubble.

"Well that's obvious," said Ingar.

"I saw links binding her to something in that tomb," said Torstag.

"She has no idea," said Zahna. "This Pale of Miss Millicent's must be a Reservation."

"To keep people in?" asked Ingar.

Zahna shook her head. "To keep Gremlins out. Without them, people rely on machines and forget all about magic. Even so, perhaps Miss Millicent can help us get inside."

"Absolutely not," said Ingar. "She deserves to get back to her life. You don't know what it's like—"

"To be taken away from your life by powerful forces outside your control," completed Zahna. "Yes I do. But—"

"No buts," said Ingar.

Zahna shrugged. "Cleaning out the tomb will break its power over her. We'll do that without her help then get her to safety. Right now we need to make camp and recover from the journey."

Ingar frowned at her. "Who died and put you in charge?"

"I did," said Torstag. "Apparently."

CHAPTER 35: ATTACK OF THE FLYING TOOTH GARDEN!

The sky above the edge of the Flying Tooth Garden changed from the blue pink of the last realm—a place of calm seas and palm groves—to a wall of black mountainsides.

Translocation complete. Flying Tooth Garden is hungry. 0 of 4 translocations available. 1000 Sacrifices required.

Gronchard squared his shoulders. Judging from their body language, his Saints had not much liked his gamble; rushing the Flying Tooth Garden through three all-but empty Realms, gambling everything on finding more sacrifices in this one. However, the charts indicated the city of Ironhaven was sited near this ley nexus. How hard could it be to round up a few sacrifices?

One of the seraphim pointed North. "Divinity! Look!"

A big stone appeared over the rim of the Flying Tooth Garden. It seemed to hover for a moment, then dropped.

Gronchard stared at it stupidly.

The stone fell a few tens of feet and crushed a patch of squirming shrubs. The tooth plants screamed.

The Peril Gong resounded across garden.

The mingled sounds dispelled Gronchard's mental paralysis. He left the balcony and strode out for the the bridge that connected his Heaven with the Temple of Incarnation. As he crossed the colonnaded span, he glanced north.

Another stone followed the first, then another.

Each was almost at the top of its arc as it passed the rim, so did not have much momentum when it struck the garden. Even so, Saint Incarnation should be responding by now.

Gronchard swept into the sanctuary in time to see a seraphim cast a handful of grains over the central sandbox.

As they fell, some grains stuck and outlining a translucent phantom of the Flying Tooth Garden hanging between steep mountain sides. One wall of the valley was bare except for a scattering of trees. The other bore a vast city, well-guarded by thick ramparts and dozens of sturdy bastions, each of which bore a huge trebuchet.

Form 5. Performing Cynosure at Level 9.

All eyes turned to Gronchard. All activity ceased.

He snapped, "Get back to casting sand, boy!"

Another cast of sand and great stones now hung in the air like wingless hummingbirds. On the bastions and long trebuchet arms were caught frozen in the moment after the slings whipped their missiles high into the air.

Gronchard's eyes narrowed. Something was missing. "Why aren't we shooting back?"

Saint Incarnation bowed. "The range is too great, Divinity."

"Well then," blazed Gronchard, "get us closer."

"We can't, Divinity, not without risking grounding. We need more sacrifices."

Without answering, Gronchard strolled to the observation platform on the far side of the chamber. It looked out onto the Garden's central well. Hundreds of feet deep, and wide enough to contain a small town, the well framed a limited view of the landscape below the Flying Tooth Garden.

At this moment, a foaming river ran down the middle of the valley. Rising up on either side were terraced orchards and stone-walled rice fields.

"Who are these people to defy our will?"

"The Republic of Ironhaven, Divinity," said Saint Prescience. "They have grown arrogant on the riches won by mining these mountains."

"None defy me," said Gronchard. "Saint Incarnation—the denizens of the Immaculate Hall of the Holy Concubines will no doubt gladly give their lives so we can prevail. Send men to make that so—tell them no need to wire the jaws shut this time, since the need is pressing."

Saint Incarnation despatched a Seraphim.

Gronchard's brow furrowed. He'd wiled away long hours in the Immaculate Hall and it did seem a waste—his surgeons had spent months sculpting the concubines into the likenesses of Angelica's various vessels.

However, his sensed that it might be difficult to explain the concubines to Angelica herself, so this seemed a fitting resolution to the problem.

The Flying Tooth Garden has been fed. Some movement now possible.

That was quick! The shrubs must be sentient enough to know they were in peril—a thought worth investigating later…or did he already know all about that?

"Set course for that city. Position the Garden directly above its heart."

It would be much harder—probably impossible—for the enemy stone casters to shoot vertically.

Current Form 5. Performing Warlord at Level 7. Saint Incarnation barked orders. The Flying Tooth Garden swung into motion.

The ground below the Well slid past.

It wasn't going much faster than walking pace.

A great crash came from outside.

The seraphim cast another handful of sand.

Another trebuchet had come into play. This one stood in its own plaza in the midst of the buildings. It was had a shorter arm than those on the wall, but was build far more robustly, with a massive counterweight. Clearly this was designed to throw very large boulders.

There were also now little smoky streaks marring the space between the city and the Flying Tooth Garden.

"The enemy have bolt throwers," said Gronchard, since nobody else seemed to understand what they were seeing. "They are shooting incendiary missiles."

"The fire fighting companies are already on standby, Divinity," said Saint Incarnation.

"Of course," said Gronchard.

He considered the phantom city. Did he want to add it to his Magisterium, or merely harvest sacrifices?

Another crash. Tiles fell from the ceiling.

Using Feat Airborne Assault 3/6, cost 1 Potestas. 5 of 6 remaining.
Result = 7 (Performance) +2 (Feat) -1 (Luck) = Planning at Level 8.

Now he could see several options.

"Saint Incarnation, attend me."

The young saint edged a pace toward the sand box.

Gronchard sighed. "Fool. Come in close by me, I don't bite."

Saint Incarnation obeyed but did not speak.

Gronchard nodded. Unlike his veteran predecessor, this Saint Incarnation knew to keep his mouth shut and listen to the wisdom of his Living God. "The objective," said Gronchard, "is force the city into submission without overly damaging its ability to produce revenues."

"Yes, Divinity."

"So, the cherubim will swarm the siege engines. Once they are engaged, half the Myrmidons will winch down. Once the Myrmidons are deployed, the cherubim will break contact and sweep the road, forcing all refugees to travel south, up into that steep the pass. The resulting fatigue will make it easy for us to harvest them."

Saint Incarnation was regarding him strangely.

Gronchard had seen the look before, every time he'd had to go through adolescence. People would see the skinny youth and forget that his age was measured in tens of thousands of years. He had learned—if he remembered correctly—to savour that moment, rather than punish its belatedness. After all, if he had Saint Incarnation executed, he would have to go through the same tedious process with his successor.

"Go on then," said Gronchard, "make it so."

The distinctive thud of the Garden's own artillery resounded in the temple.

Gronchard straightened from the sandbox and gestured at the sand seraphim. "Go on then."

The grains fell, capturing the Tooth Garden's engines in the act of reloading, and stones falling and bouncing around the city's heavy trebuchet.

The gunner captains had chosen their target well. That had to be the only engine that could attack the Garden until it was almost over the city.

A trumpet blew. Gronchard turned to watch a flock of cherubim dive down the well. With good fortune they should silence the heavy trebuchet.

He strode over to the observation platform and realised he felt more truly himself than he had since coming to conciousness in the Flaying Room.

He'd left himself notes, of course, and among other things they had advised him to leave off conquest until his vessel was at least twenty one years of age. However, clearly he had been too cautious.

At last the Flying Tooth Garden moved over the city.

The light was fading now. The darkened townscape was alive with flickering lights.

"Saint Incarnation! What *is* this? I did not order the use of incendiaries!"

The military saint stammered for a few moments then said, "They are not ours, Divinity."

"What then?" asked Gronchard. "Do they burn their own city?"

"I...I don't..." began the Saint. "They're getting bigger!"

Not bigger, *closer*.

The lights swelled as they rose.

"Fire lanterns, Divinity," said the Saint.

"I can see that," snapped Gronchard. "Do something about them."

The Saint ran to the edge of the platform and bellowed, "Archers!"

There were, of course, archers stationed to prevent a counter-attack via the well. These now loosed their arrows.

The angle, however, was clearly difficult until the last moment, and the steam of paper balloons fast moving. When arrows did strike, they passed right through, and the balloon kept rising.

One exploded, scattering hissing embers. Some in turn struck other balloons, which burst into flames.

Most passed through the well into the sky above the Flying Tooth Garden. Some flashed as they climbed and more embers rained down. Others drifted out of view over the deck.

Bells rang.

2 Roofs on fire in main plaza. 3 Tooth Plants damaged by embers.

"Divinity," said Saint Incarnation, "the fire lanterns are raining embers on the deck."

"Fool, I know—what is *that?*"

A glowing ball trailed fire as it whooshed past up the well.

Flaming Carcass.

Gronchard leaned over the rail and tried to pick out where it had come from.

There was an odd timber construction directly below.

Incendiary has struck Tooth Plant bed. Fire damage. Risk of fire spreading

"Drop rocks," ordered Gronchard.

"But the city…" began Saint Incarnation. "Yes Divinity."

He barked orders. Rocks started tumbling back down the well.

The launcher disgorged a ball of burning material. This one bumped the side of the well, rose high, then fell back the way it had come.

It landed in a plaza, casting long shadows on the rocks that lay scattered around the siege machine. Oddly, none of them had actually landed near it.

As Gronchard looked on, more rocks fell, all *just happening* to miss the one spot where they needed to strike.

"There's a wizard down there. Redirect the cherubim!" ordered Gronchard. "Silence that engine. Bring me the wizard's corpse for my mausoleum."

Saint Incarnation folded his arms and stood in silence for a moment. "It is done, Divinity."

Golden-winged cherubim swept into view over the rooftops, converging on the weapon. Something broke their rush. Individuals flitted off in the wrong direction, or crashed into rooftops.

"Killer wasps, Divinity."

"What?" Rage boiled through Gronchard. "Lower two companies of Myrmidons onto the plaza."

"But the enemy engines…" Saint Incarnation caught Gronchard's look. "Yes, Divinity."

A short pause, then two boxy platforms dropped through the well, winches paying out double cables as they fell. They braked as they approached the ground.

A cable snapped. One of the platform plummeted. It smashed into the plaza, scattering Myrmidons like a burst coin purse.

197 Myrmidons killed. 3 Wounded.

A fifth of his fighting force wiped out just like that.

Another burning missile launched. It lost speed as it climbed, then fell back down to—somehow—land on the deck of the surviving elevator platform, the one that was packed with Gronchard's Myrmidons.

Chaos irrupted. Burning men leapt over the side. Fire flared on the cables. The platform dropped and landed near the first one. This time, armoured figures crawled away from the burning wreckage.

102 Myrmidons killed. 98 Wounded.

Gronchard felt it like a punch in the gut.

Current Form 5. Performing Theurge at Level 9.
Using Great Miracle Salt City 2/6, cost 3 Potestas, 6
Vitality, 6 Will.
Result = 9 (Performance) + 1 (Luck) -5 (Base Difficulty)
= 5.
Effect = Salination Attack level 5.
Average Will in the Target is 4.

Below, it was as if a sudden snow fall had dusted the city white. The big stone thrower collapsed, sending out an expanding cloud of dust. Cherubim dropped. Roofs shattered.

City: Around 2500 mortalities and 2500 survivors.
Cherubim: 154 casualties. 44 remaining
3 of 6 Potestas remaining.
-2 of 4 Vitality remaining. You have Hindrance
"Debilitated"
Toughness 2 Surpassed twice. You have 4 Wounds.
You have Hindrances "Wounded," "Stunned" and
"Dazed". Form Lost. No Stunts available.
-3 of 3 Will remaining. You have Hindrances
"Discombobulated", "Mentally Depleted".

"Uh, wow," said Gronchard, legs buckling under him. "Uh."

You have hindrances "Debilitated", "Wounded",
"Stunned", "Dazed", "Discombobulated", "Mentally
Depleted" conferring a penalty of -7.

Hands caught him, kept him upright.

The noise of the Sanctum pressed in. There were orders he should give, decisions he should make.

"Divinity?" prompted Saint Incarnation. "What now?"

"I...uh...," said Gronchard. "I need to...uh...rest. Take me to my...Angelica..." His brow furrowed. Where was he supposed to be? "Concubines. Take me to my concubines."

"You had them sacrificed, Divinity."

"I meant to my Heaven! Take me to my Heaven!"

> Will -7.
> You still have Hindrances "Debilitated", "Wounded",
> "Stunned", "Dazed", "Discombobulated", "Mentally
> Depleted" conferring a penalty of -7.

"Quick," said somebody. Was it Saint Prescience? "Carry his Divinity to his Throne of Praise."

"But Angelica..."

Saint Incarnation saluted. "Do not worry, Divinity. We will harvest the sacrifices then get under way. We should be at the Tomb of the Ice Queen within a day."

CHAPTER 36: TARPIT TOMB

Morning found Millicent standing on the cliff top where it overlooked the approach to the tomb, nursing a fresh cup of Miss Zahna's tea. Now the insects had stopped pestering her, the jungle's deep green and lush primary colours were quite enchanting, but not as enchanting as the delightful trio of youths trying to get the tomb door open.

The one with the sword had nice muscles, but had eyes only for the girl…

Warrior Level 3. Marked.

…which seemed reasonable since she had a certain magnetism that belied her years.

Virago Level 1.

But no!

Silence!

No hearing voices today.

Millicent really didn't want to have to take a pill. Even if the girl was wrong about the effect of the humidity—there'd been something shifty about her when she said that—it was actually a relief to be able to hear her voice properly, rather than have it mumbling in the background like an attic-bound mad aunt.

An insect buzzed past.

Millicent took a good gulp of the tea. It wasn't coffee, but it packed a punch—well to be quite honest it tasted completely foul, as if made from mashed fern and random moss and mushrooms and goodness knows what—but it really did seem to do the job.

In the same way, the red haired boy—Ingar—wasn't her usual lost young scholar type—the kind who'd blink at her like a rabbit in a night hunter's lantern—but there was an alluring vulnerability behind his cheeky persona. It was also…intriguing to watch him run his hands over the stone door and its frame. It added a certain frisson that he was a member of a party of rogues who could have leapt from the pages of some penny dreadful.

Millicent told herself that she wasn't quite spying on them, just observing from where they weren't looking.

Ingar stepped back from the stone door, hands raised in defeat.

Level 4 Burglar. Youth, amorous, frustrated.

Oh do be quiet.

"There's no way to open this fucking thing," said Ingar. "Are you sure it's even a real door?"

"This is definitely the way in," said Miss Zahna, who—as far as Millicent could gather—was some sort of traditional healer, and, being a Virago, albeit an inexperienced one, the natural leader of the party.

I could do that, thought Millicent and remembered childhood dreams of marble halls and faithful servants.

"How do you know this is the way in?" asked Ingar.

"Magic."

Millicent raised an eyebrow. Not just healer, but some kind of shamanic practicioner. She leaned forward a little. This was a rare opportunity to gather folklore from Beyond the Pale.

"Well then why don't you magic the thing open?" said Ingar.

"Hmm, I suppose it's come to that," said Miss Zahna. "Flip should do it." The girl drew a knife and started scraping the stone, gathering the resulting powder in a little fold of leather.

"What are you doing?" asked Torstag.

"Making tea," said Miss Zahna.

"What the fuck?" said Ingar.

"Flip is a 2nd Circle Spell," said the girl. "That means doing it as a Ritual. I make the tea from the door, I become the door, it does what I want it to do."

Millicent stalked over to where her handbag hung on a cleft stick along with their other belongings—something about avoiding ants, she recalled. She rummaged for her notebook then stopped.

This wasn't about ethnology or folklore; this was about her own survival.

She turned away and carefully negotiated the slope down to ground level.

Miss Zahna was still scraping at the stone.

"Will this take long?" asked Torstag.

"All day," said Zahna. "It's a difficult spell. And I'll be mentally fatigued until I've slept the night."

"What if more bounty hunters come?" hissed Torstag.

"Then," said Miss Zahna, without looking up, "You can hit them with your sword."

"Or Gronchard and his Flying Tooth Garden?"

Zahna shrugged one bony shoulder.

Were these young people fugitives? Millicent's brow furrowed. That put a different complexion on things.

Torstag turned to his friend and put a hand on his arm. He spoke low voiced, but not so low that Millicent's keen ears did not pick up the conversation. "Ingar. You're supposed to be a Burglar."

"Yes," hissed Ingar, "that's how I know there's probably no trap there."

"Probably?" said Torstag.

"Why don't you try," said Ingar. "Hit it with your sword, since you think that solves everything."

You are Virago Level 4.
Form 2.
Performing Virago at Level 6.

Millicent's Voice again. Whenever it started talking about her being a Virago, men started looking at her. Perhaps this was a bad idea. She reached for her pills, then instead manoeuvred down the slope to join the others. "What on Earth is going on?"

Ingar said, "What are you doing Miss Millicent? It's not safe for you."

"Don't be silly," she said.

Result = 6 -1 (Luck) -3 (Target Will) = 2.
Effect = Tentative Practical Response.

The red-haired youth tilted his head. "Well I suppose if you stayed back…"

Amazing, thought Millicent. She should have started really listening to her Voice earlier.

"Bad idea," said Torstag. He waved, shooing her. "Sorry Miss Millicent, this really isn't safe."

Unlock Quell +1?

"What? Oh…" Her Voice often said that whenever she had any kind of confrontation.

Besides, despite what her doctor said, saying yes to her Voice usually had good results, especially with Maelstrom and Amorous Impunity, which had kept her in lovers and out of any sort of lady's trouble for a good twenty years.

Oh, go on then.

Virago, Quell+1 unlocked at 2/6 Grasp.
Using Quell+1 2/6, cost 3 Potestas. 3 out of 6
Potestas remaining.

She turned her gaze on Torstag. "I am *quite* old enough to look after myself."

Result = 6 (Performance) + 3 (Feat) +1 (Luck) -3 (Target
Will) = 7.
Target is Marked.
Effect = 0.

Torstag shrugged.

"With respect, Miss Millicent," said Miss Zahna. "That was not entirely true when we found you."

Level 1 Virago.

Yes, I do remember.

What her Voice called "Virago Feats"—an odd choice of word that made her think of circus performers—appeared to work on most men and a very particular type of woman that could be entertaining for a night or two, but never ever on other Viragos. However, Millicent had been here before. She grinned. "You have me there, Miss Zahna. However, I shall only really be safe once I have returned back to the Pale, which will only happen once you are done here. So, let me help you—please?"

Miss Zahna's eyes narrowed.

"Perhaps Miss Millicent will remember something?" said Torstag.

Zahna nodded.

Millicent raised an eyebrow. "Remember?"

Before Miss Zahna could respond, Ingar cut in, "There's no hidden catch or opening mechanism."

"Well of course," said Millicent. "Otherwise I would have found a way in—though the Gods alone know why I should want to. Are you quite sure the door isn't simply sealed?"

Miss Zahna shook her head. "It has to be possible for a solo avatar to get inside. That's the nature of these tombs." She turned to Millicent. "What does your De—the voice in your head say?"

Millicent flushed. "I don't want to talk about…"

But the voice was saying something, something very specific. She took a pace forward, coughed and addressed the door. "Open up, for I am Millicent nee Lintar nee Frontisia nee…" The names went on for a while. Just as her voice grew horse, she reached a crescendo: "…nee Rasinta the Ice Queen!"

With a squeal of ancient hinges, the stone door swung up until it stuck out at right angles like the roof of a particularly stark portico.

Cool air gusted out of the void beyond.

Millicent stumbled toward the darkened threshold.

Ingar grabbed her arm. "Wait."

Relic Structure. Surge.

Sensation flooded through her.

> Potestas restored and boosted.
> Vitality restored.
> 9 points of advancement available.
> Quell +1 3/6 secured. 6 points remaining.
> Select an 11th Virago Feat.

And Millicent found herself treading the carpets of a rich palace, contemplating the pictures.

She paused at one entitled, Sacred Orgy, but then noticed the one next to it, which was even more lurid, for all it had fewer participants. *Yes, that was perfect.*

> Tsunami +1 unlocked at 2/6 Grasp. Secured. 2 points remaining.
> Select a 12th Virago Feat.

Now for something more practical…

> Brush Aside unlocked at 2/6 Grasp. Advanced to 4/6 Grasp.
> You have secured 11 Virago Feats. 14 are required to secure Level 5.

Her Voice seemed to take a deep breath.

> You are Millicent, Human Warlock, Middle Aged, Outgoing, Forceful, Hedonistic, Self Hating.
> Potestas 12 of 6. Will 3.
> Vitality 5. Toughness 2.
> Virago 4:   Maelstrom +1, Amorous Impunity, Tsunami +1, Icestorm, Commanding Presence +1, Quell +1, Eye of the Tornado, Sweep Along, Brush Aside 4/6.
> Scholar 4 (Learned): Erudition, Research, Debate, Locate, Conservation, Restoration, Source Criticism, Read Old Imperial, Read Gorlakian Runes, Read Squamafian, Identify Art, Identify Architecture.
> Skills include: Mountaineering 3, Shooting 4.

She opened her eyes to find she was now standing a good few feet from the entrance.

Torstag was staring past her through the tunnel. Ingar, however was all-but hopping from foot to foot.

"Is something the matter?" asked Millicent, sweetly.

Ingar flushed delightfully. "Hang on," he said, "I'll be back." He plunged off up into the jungle.

A moment later there were chopping sounds.

Miss Zahna's eyes twinkled. "You just surged, Miss Millicent."

"Oh is *that* what that was?" said Millicent, fanning herself. "But what does it *mean*?"

"It means you were involved in creating this tomb," said Torstag.

"I would think," said Millicent, "I might remember doing that."

"You did," said Miss Zahna. "All that 'Open up for I am Millicent nee…'"

"Oh, balderdash," said Millicent. "I don't believe in reincarnation."

Zahna shrugged.

"Right," said Ingar, crashing out of the jungle. He now held a freshly cut branch.

"You appear to have wood, young man," said Millicent.

"Ten-foot pole," he said, flushing. "Long and light but not too whippy." He frowned at it. "It makes sense now I have one my hand." He approached the door.

Millicent shielded her eyes from the daylight and peered within. Firewood was heaped up beyond the door. No, not firewood, bones. Bones and black-eyed skulls. "There appear to be human remains," she said.

"Probable trap," said Ingar. "Stand back." He positioned himself to the side of the door, then poked the ten-foot pole around corner into the passage and prodded the floor.

Something clicked. A bronze grating swung down and crashed into place, filling the entrance like a cat flap from hell. Long spikes protruded from the armoured back of a corpse that had been fresh perhaps forty or so years before.

It was literally a nightmare come true.

Millicent shuddered and set her jaw. She was damned if she was going to scream.

After a moment, Miss Zahna said, "I think we know what happened to Lintar."

"That's me!" said Millicent, speaking over the rush of blood to her ears. "I dreamt this. I was creeping inside then, slam! I... *What is happening to me?*"

"It's a Tarpit Tomb," said Zahna. "Watch. It will reset."

With a creak, the bronze grille swung back up from the doorway.

The armoured skeleton slid off the spikes, clattered onto the floor just beyond the threshold.

Millicent flinched. "Is that *me?*"

The spiked grille reached the ceiling with a clunk.

"See?" said Zahna.

A patch of floor gave under the skeletons weight. There was another click. Once again, the bronze grille slammed back down. This time the lower edge clipped the corpse and kicked it out into the jungle.

It landed in pieces at Millicent's feet.

As if in a dream, she knelt and touched the skull.

"Brace yourself," said Torstag.

"Pardon?"

"If you touch the remains of a past avatar, you get a surge," said Zahna. "Just like when you opened the door."

They all stood around waiting.

At length Millicent stood up and brushed down her skirts. "You said it was me."

"They all are," said Torstag. "And you should have surged."

"Perhaps another avatar took the surge," said Zahna. "Remains aren't like structures. They run out."

Millicent considered the pile of bones where it lay in the dark. The hairs stood up on the back of her neck. "Are all of them *me?*" "How?"

Miss Zahna asked, "What are grave goods for?"

"Grave goods?" Millicent straightened and turned to tower over the girl...except they were—annoyingly—the same height. "To ensure a good afterlife, or so I read."

"So it's a form of sympathetic magic," said Zahna.

"Why yes," said Millicent. Where was this going? "If you put it like that."

"Hang on," said Ingar. "What's sympathetic magic?"

"Well…" began Miss Zahna.

Millicent got there first. "A magical ritual which depicts the desired result as closely as possible. Make a doll of your enemy, stick pins in it. Make a model of your house, fill it with coins."

"I was going say, *backwards art*," said Zahna.

"That's certainly more succinct," said Millicent. "So where does this take us?"

"What if the afterlife took place not in some heaven, but through being reborn in the Many Realms?"

"Reincarnation, you mean," said Millicent. She thought for a moment. "Yes, logically—if sympathetic magic worked—the grave goods would affect the next life…"

"Bury a man with a sword," said Zahna, "he's reborn as a warrior."

"But that's just superstition."

"So," said Miss Zahna. "Suppose you wanted to make sure the next *you* would get that sword?"

"Well then," said Millicent, too curious to resist the girl's attempt to take the lead, "you would leave a note to yourself."

"How would you do that?"

"Oh, you couldn't, could you…?" Millicent didn't like being back to bottom of the class. "But you *could* hope that your new self would feel the pull from the remains of your old self…Oh…" She tilted her head to peer into the tomb. She shivered despite the heat of the jungle. "I'm buried in there, aren't I?" she said. "But why the traps?"

"You tell me," said Miss Zahna.

"To protect your treasure," said Millicent. "Of course! You'd expect your new self to remember them, like I remembered the…spell to open the door."

"And did *your* last self—we say *avatar*—remember the trap?" Zahna indicated the corpse.

"On balance, looking at the available evidence—"

"Her corpse, you mean," put in Miss Zahna.

"—-no she did not," said Millicent. Now a wave of nausea went through her. "Oh Gods she *is* me."

"So what happens when the tomb contains two sets of remains, all of the same person?"

"I suppose the pull doubles." Millicent winced. It was suddenly hard to think.

"Indeed," said Miss Zahna, way too cheerfully. "And so a third avatar comes. Does *this* avatar remember the trap?"

"Bugger," said Millicent, catching up. "I'm not the third, am I?"

Miss Zahna shook her head. "If a grave determines the status of the next avatar through sympathetic magic, what happens?"

"Each avatar is born into metaphorical traps and dark places…" Millicent didn't like where this was going. "They are increasingly ill equipped to deal with the tomb. You called it a tarpit, didn't you? An animal gets stuck in the tar, its distress cries attract a predator, that gets stuck and dies. Scavengers come. They get stuck…"

"So help us clear this one of your remains," said Miss Zahna.

Millicent regarded the girl. "What's in it for you?"

"An item from the treasure will aid me on my quest."

"Hmm," said Ingar. He was contemplating the corpse. "It's not exactly what you'd call safe, is it?"

"Nonsense," said Millicent. "It will be a fabulous…adventure." She winked.

> Using Sweep Along, cost 1 Potestas, 11 of 6
> remaining.
> Current Form 5. Performing Virago at Level 9.
> Result = 9 (Performance) +2 (Feat) +1 (Luck) -3 (Target
> Will) = 9
> Effect = Purposeful Practical Response (Cost 4) + For a
> Watch (Cost 4)

A delicious blush appeared behind Ingar's freckles. The boy straightened his shoulders and squared his jaw. He grinned. "Sure. What's a bit of danger to a Warlock, eh?"

"Let's get our kit," said Miss Zahna.

Together they scrambled back up to the camp.

Torstag stooped to pick up his armour. "Somebody help me get this on."

"I will," said Miss Zahna. "Who's going to carry the rope?"

"That's the Burglar's job," said Ingar. "Am I the only one with an everlight?"

"No…" began Miss Zahna.

As she watched the young people equip themselves, a stone seemed to settle in Millicent's gut.

You are Self Hating.
You have incurred Issue "Guilt at Using People" at 1 Hardening.

Damn! Another issue! She'd only just gotten over the delightful "Feeling Ugly on the Inside". The damn things kept popping up as quickly as she nailed them down. The worst of it was—given the circumstances—that this particular issue would be hard to discuss with her Dr Joyeous.

It was unfair anyway! The boy was clearly part of some quest. It was his own choice, wasn't it?

Wrestling with Guilt at Using People 1/6, cost 3
Potestas 6 remaining.
Will 3 Negated
You have Hindrance, "Feeling Guilty."

Millicent sighed. This was going to become inconvenient.

Chapter 37: Dark Awakening!

"I am Rasinta the Ice Queen!"

Who said that!

A clang echoed through the stone chamber.

She opened her eyes and somewhere in the dark, parchment crumpled.

She was not hot, not cold, but nor was she numb.

Another clang.

She flexed her fingers. Again parchment crumpled.

Had some animal slipped into her chamber? Was she in peril from an assassin? And, how was it she felt so calm?

There was no quickening of the pulse, no urge to gasp in fear.

Why was her heart not hammering in anticipation of the fight!

But then, if an assassin had come, she would be dead by now.

"Slave! Light the lamps!"

As she spoke, some animal emitted a hollow croaking, drowning her voice.

And the word *soul thief* came to her.

She did not fear the soul thief any more than she did the assassin; rather she welcomed her...which on the face of it seemed strange, though perhaps since she could not remember her own name, the soul thief had been and gone.

Her brow tried to furrow, tighten, refused.

"Slave!" she repeated. "Light the lamps!"

Her words sounded only in her head.

She herself was the source of the hollow sound, and still there was no light, only translucent strands, some of them drifting across her field of vision.

"Where am I?"

The words came out as a croaking wheeze, like old bellows working in an abandoned forge.

She rose and whatever chair she was sitting on must be very ancient indeed, because wood, or something very like wood, creaked and groaned.

There was still darkness, but in the darkness ghost treasures lay stacked around the wall of her chamber; golden figurines of the animals of her ice kingdom, caskets of jewels, contour hugging gowns of silver mail, all allure and no protection…

Panic flooded her mind, but again there was quickening neither of breath nor pulse. Nor was there the rise and fall of the chest, nor indeed the presence of heartbeat.

"*What* am I?"

Rasinta the Ice Queen. Lich. Level 10.

Will 1 of 10.

Potestas 1 of 10. Potestas Reservoir 27.

Vocations:

Lich, 10…

"Enough!"

The memory came back to her like a shroud.

Queen Rasinta sank into her throne, tried not to hear the protest of mummified skin as it flexed, of parched joints as they bent.

Weeping phantom tears from shrivelled ducts, she settled against the backboard and listened…more than listened, she *felt*; felt the thrum of the translucent strands, then felt her…abode as if it were an extension of herself.

It *was* an extension of herself; for shade creatures like a Lich, the symbol of the thing *is* the thing.

One of the strands thickened and tugged at her sternum, and she knew the other end was fastened in the chest of the soul thief herself.

Queen Rasinta reached with both hands for the strand. The ghost of her fingers passed through the translucent filament.

Her hands collided. Bone and withered skin touched in the dark.

She snatched them apart and shuddered. Soon she would be able to haul on that filament, find her freedom, but not yet.

The memory came to her of the first time a soul thief had approached her tomb.

Rasinta had been oh-so-eager to feel the wind again, to embrace lovers, or to revel in the touch of her handmaidens. She had tugged hard, and the soul thief had moved too quickly for the dead memories to catch up. The easily evaded first trap had sprung and the strand had snapped back into Rasinta's sternum bringing with it a burst of Potestas, but no soul.

The second time a soul thief answered the call of the tomb, Rasinta had sat and waited in the not-dark.

This soul thief flinched from the first trap, but the interval of one incarnation had evidently erased the dead memories of the second trap.

And so it went. Every generation a soul thief arrived, and each time, through ignorance, she failed to bring her precious cargo as far as the Refectory.

If her worshippers had not kept her fed all these centuries, Rasinta would have faded away, all her splendour lost, her memories surrendered to her hateful successors.

The strand thrummed and Rasinta experienced a numb echo of desire.

For the first time, it seemed, the soul thief had arrived in company. For obvious reasons, the tomb's magic had not been configured for this. However, though companions might add complexity, they might also ensure that the soul thief survive the several traps.

That was enough.

Rasinta's consciousness flowed from her like a silken gown and extended to embrace her tomb.

While she waited to come into her full powers, she would use what little strength she had to keep the soul thief alive.

Chapter 38: The Green Door

Ingar peered into the gloom of the tomb's entrance tunnel.

Burglar Level 4. 12 Potestas. Form 5.
Performing Burglar at Level 9.

He mopped his brow with the back of his hand. "That heap of bones certainly helps focus the mind."

"Good," grunted Torstag, who was hefting a log they'd trimmed using their long knives.

"About there," said Ingar, indicating with the butt of his axe.

Torstag dropped one end onto the spot, then pushed the log upright so it jammed the big stone hatch into place the way a column holds up a temple porch roof.

Ingar rapped his knuckles on the wood.

"It's solid," said Torstag, and Ingar felt he didn't recognise his old friend. The lamellar armour and helmet belonged on his broad frame, as did the big sword that sat comfortably on his steel-covered hip.

"Yeah," said Ingar. "Take my axe, will you?"

Torstag flinched back. "No…I mean I need to keep my hands free for my sword."

"Fuck!" said Ingar. "You look like you saw a ghost."

"Ghost?" said Torstag. He drew himself up. "No, nothing like that."

Ingar turned and offered his weapon instead to Millicent. "Miss Millicent, would you mind looking after my axe."

"Axe?" said Millicent. "Isn't it technically a halberd?"

"Pedant," said Ingar. He took a deep breath then stepped into the shadow of the open hatch. Cool air bathed his face but no instant death descended on him. He played the everlight over the tomb's entrance passage.

> **Performing Burglar at Level 9.**
> **Result = 9 (Performance) +0 (Luck) +4 (Trap Witnessed)**
> **−10 (Challenge) = 3**
> **Trigger Plate trap detected.**

Sure enough there was a seam in the stone two paces beyond the threshold. Interesting that he didn't need a feat for this.

Tell me something I don't know, Doofus!

> **You are Ingar, Human Warlock, Youth, Quick Witted,**
> **Nimble Fingered, Hedonistic, Sensitive.**
> **Potestas 12/6. Will 3. Horror of Murder 1/6.**

Morning meditation had been worth it, but nothing seemed to remove his Issue…not that it needed removing, really.

> **Vitality 4/4. Toughness 2.**
> **Vocations:**
> **Burglar 4: Hide, Climb +1, Spider Climb, Move Silently,**
> **Stalk, Pick Pocket, Open Lock, Detect Trap, Stalk**
> **Close 3/6, Disarm Trap 2/6.**
> **Warrior 1 (Halberds): Wrath Strike 1/6.**
> **Companion 0: Gallantry 2/6.**
> **Artist 0: Visualisation 4/6.**
> **Various capabilities including Meditation.**

I knew all that!

"Be careful," said Zahna behind him.

"Do let the artist work in peace," said Millicent.

"Because somebody is going to get hurt," said Zahna.

"Hey! Thanks for the vote of confidence," said Ingar.

"The portents," said Zahna. "That's why I brewed some healing tea."

"Well that's okay then," said Ingar.

"Tea won't help you regrow a hand…or a head," said Zahna.

Ingar peered into the darkness beyond the glow of the everlight.

"What are you all talking about?" said Millicent. "Portents. Healing tea? Mumbo jumbo."

A thought came to Ingar. "Chalk."

"Chalk what?"

"Does anybody have some?"

Millicent harrumphed and rummaged in her hand bag. She produced a big stick. "Have you actually done this before?"

Ingar's Form was good. Let's try Gallantry again.

Performing Companion at level 5.
Using Gallantry 3/6, cost 3 Potestas, 8 of 6 Potestas remaining.

He probably shouldn't be burning through his Potestas just to flirt.

"Experience is overrated," said Ingar, rising. He caught hold of the stick of chalk, and for a moment both were gripping it.

He found himself glancing at the chalk suggestively—which was idiotic, because what was suggestive about a stick of chalk and immediately wished he could bite back the words. Surely he had gone too far?

Miss Millicent's eyes twinkled. "I'm sure I could change your mind about that."

"There's only one way to find out," he said.

"You might end up…plunging in out of your depth," she said.

"I'm sure it would be great fun looking for traps."

The older woman pursed her lips.

Ingar held his breath, trying not to flinch.

She grinned. "Some traps are more welcoming than others."

"But still basically dangerous," said Ingar.

Millicent laughed.

Result = 5 (Performance) +1 (Luck) +4 (Enthusiastic Target) = 10
Effect = Purposeful Practical Response (4) lasting about 4 hours (4)
Gallantry advances to 3/6 Grasp.

It was suddenly inevitable that something should happen between them, and the worst of it was Ingar didn't care that Warlock Feats were at work. He was also very glad that his monk's habit was quite so roomy.

"Ahem," said Zahna. "Traps? Tomb robbing?"

"Spoilsport," said Ingar and risked a cheeky smile.

Performing Companion at level 5.
Result = 5 (Performance) +1 (Luck) -5 (Target
Performance) =1.
Effect = 1 -3 (Will) = -2. Abject failure.

Zahna gave him a withering look.

"I'm doing it, I'm doing it!" Ingar marked the near and far edge of the trigger for the spiked grille. Careful not to lean out, he extended the ten-foot pole and—holding his breath—tapped at the space between the bones and the trigger plate.

"Nothing," said Millicent.

"Nothing is good," said Ingar.

He kicked off his sandals and tucked them in his belt next to the long knife they had looted from the bounty hunters. Barefoot now, he stepped over the trigger and let his weight settle slowly. The stone was cool on his soles, covered in tiny fracture lines like a mosaic. "Don't worry folks."

Using Burglar, Detect Trap. 1 Potestas expended.
7 of 6 Potestas remaining.
Form 5.
Performing Burglar at Level 9.

Starting the day on top form! Thanks Doofus.

Detecting Traps at 9 (Performance) +2 (Feat) = 11.

So the feat gave him a bit of a boost. How significant was a "+2"?

There was something not quite right about the floor beyond the bones.

Success = 11 (Detecting Traps) +1 (Luck) -12
(Challenge) = 0
Effect: Possible Trap spotted.

"I've spotted one. See, no worries?"

He shivered. The air was certainly cooler in the tunnel.

"Is this going to take long?" asked Millicent.

Ingar glanced over his shoulder.

260

The buxom woman was leaning on the log column, looking bored. It shifted under her weight. She stood up straight as if nothing had happened. "Only," she said, "I have just remembered that I am supposed to be home for a meeting of the Trustees."

Ingar dropped to his haunches and peered beyond the pile of bones. The change of angle cast long shadows from irregularities in the rock-cut floor. It also showed up where teeth and bits of bone littered the tunnel.

"These bodies aren't all from the first trap," said Ingar. "Somebody's been moving the kills from the next one, and perhaps some others and piling them up in the entrance."

"You mean this tomb has a…a *janitor*?" exclaimed Millicent.

"Not one you'd want to meet," said Torstag.

"Well it's perfectly safe right now," said Ingar, considering whether to leap over the bones or push them aside. Something clunked. His left and right foot each sank just a little. The fragments of stone started to tilt. Dozens of sharp points pricked his soles.

**Success = 11 (Detecting Traps) -1 (Luck) -12
(Challenge) = -2
Result = Trap Triggered.**

"Bugger fuck I missed one! Fuuuu…"

Test of 7 Potestas. Dodging.

Even as he cursed, his muscles twitched and hurled him backwards towards the entrance. Time seemed to slow down.

He sailed out over the threshold. "…uuuuuuu…"

**Success = 9 (Performance) +1 (Luck) -8 (Challenge) = 0
Effect = Near Miss.**

As Torstag yelled his name, Ingar crashed into Miss Millicent, then sprawled in the mud at her ankle-high boots. "…uuuuck!" He curled up and hugged his feet that had so nearly been impaled. "Fuck fuck fuck fuck. FUCK!"

The librarian peered down at him over the top of her corseted bosom. "Is the profanity aspirational, or are you merely badly injured?"

261

Ingar grinned up at her. "Keep a good hold on my weapon, just in case."

"Ingar!" Torstag dropped to kneel beside him.

Ingar sat up. "I'm fine! Really."

There was a metallic squeal from the tunnel.

Spikes had risen from the floor like a malign hedgehog, displacing all the little stone scales. Now they were retracting again.

Success = 11 (Detecting Traps) +0 (Luck) +4 (Trap Witnessed) -12 (Challenge) = 3

"Why the fuck didn't I spot it in time?"

Double Trigger Plate Detected. Trap triggers on simultaneous pressure on two locations.

"Bloody marvellous," said Ingar.

"Who are you talking to?" asked Miss Millicent. "Oh."

"We're *all* warlocks," said Ingar, picking himself up. He leaned into the tunnel and retrieved his ten-foot pole. He banged the second trigger plate, left right, forward back. "I think we're okay if we stand on one leg."

"I have a better idea," said Zahna. She closed her eyes and started her weird throat chanting.

"Fascinating," said Miss Millicent. "What *is* that?"

"Shush," said Torstag without turning his gaze from the tall girl.

"Magic," said Ingar, "obviously."

"There's no such thing as magic," said Miss Millicent in a stage whisper. "Perhaps psychic powers, and I will certainly now grant the strong possibility of reincarnation, but not actual magic."

Zahna stopped chanting. Her eyes snapped open. "Give me the chalk."

Ingar tossed it to her. "If it makes you happy."

Zahna caught it, in turn tossed her staff to Torstag, then strode up to the tomb entrance.

"Careful!" said Torstag, who now carried both weapons.

Zahna ignored him, stepped over the first and second trigger plates to kick bones out of the way. "Bones are safe," she said. She stooped to draw two circles on the floor beyond the pile. "And it's safe going through the middle," she said.

"Your magic shows you traps!" said Ingar. "So much for all that crap about needing me."

Zahna shook her head. "I can see safe paths, that's all. It doesn't tell me how to disarm traps or open locks." She strode further down the tunnel, then squatted and drew around another patch. "Not safe there."

"Come on," said Torstag.

Millicent handed him his axe.

"Bloody marvellous," said Ingar, slinging the weapon over one shoulder.

"Oh don't be a brat," said Millicent. She slapped his buttocks. "I am sure your time will come."

Ingar started forward, even though the whole thing seemed like a stupid way to get killed.

He checked just past the threshold. Why was he doing this? Was Millicent influencing him?

"Hurry up," she said, then made the kind of double-clicking noise more appropriate for urging on a horse.

Ingar laughed. "What the fuck? Let's do this."

CHAPTER 39: FIRE IN THE DEEP!

Zahna stared down the tunnel, Remembering Backwards. She'd bound her everlight to the top of her staff so it worked like a flameless torch. This gave her a good view of the tunnel, as of right now. She was, however, more interested in *as of in a few moments.*

Behind her, bones clattered and crunched. "No surge here, either," said Millicent.

"One of your avatars got lucky," said Ingar.

"Imagine having dozens of…surges one after the other," purred Millicent.

"Shush!" snapped Zahna. She should probably have left Ingar to do his job, but honestly, *that* woman was turning him into a liability. It would have been better if she'd taken hrt damn pills…except there'd been that look in Torstag's eyes. *I'm not a bad person, I'm just Driven.*

> You are Cold. Wrestling with issue Irritated by People
> Stuff 1/6, Cost 1 Potestas. 7 of 6 remaining.
> Loss falls short of Will 3. Hindrance avoided.

"Let me concentrate!" She squinted at the tunnel.
How am I doing?

> Current Form 3
> Performing Wizard at level 9.
> Backwards Remembering for an hour or so.
> 7 of 6 Potestas remaining.

Zahna had burned three Potestas on attempts just to get her Form to above one. It was as if the mere presence of the older woman was enough to spoil things. Worse, taking portents had already cost her one Potestas, and Backwards Remembering had cost her another. At least making up a flask of pre-enchanted healing tea had not cost her anything.

Fortunately, she had enough form to see the possibilities of grisly death floating around the first two traps. Further off there was also a sense of falling.

Zahna strode over to the dangerous spot and drew a chalk line around it. "Keep to the left."

"Pit trap," said Ingar, his voice echoing.

"Show off!" said Miss Millicent. "Does it really matter what it is?"

"It does," said Ingar. "There's probably one or two of you down there."

"Ugh," said Miss Millicent.

An odd sort of courtship, thought Zahna as she advanced deeper into the tunnel. But thinking about that brought up the subject of what to do with Torstag. She shook her head.

As if prompted by her thoughts, Torstag said, "Just one."

"How do you know?" asked Miss Millicent.

"I can see the threads connecting the dead with the living."

"Double ugh," said Miss Millicent. "Brrr, even."

"Hang on…there's a pit," said Zahna. A few paces ahead was what looked like an unfenced well. She approached the edge and, stooping, held her everlight over the drop. After about three feet, the hole seemed to open out into what had to be a room. About fifteen feet below lay a wide stone floor, scattered with human bones. "Not a pit, a shaft leading down to the next level."

"The tunnel seems to end," said Ingar. "Is that a door?"

Zahna straightened.

Ingar had adjusted his everlight to shine down the length of what remained of the passage. It went on a good twenty feet further, then ended in a bronze door, green with age. This time there was a sense of spraying blood.

"A mysterious green door," said Millicent. "I wonder what's behind it?"

"It's trapped," said Zahna.

"No shit," said Ingar. "Let's try the hole."

"But which one?" said Miss Millicent.

265

Ingar laughed.

Torstag said, "*All* Miss Millicent's links lead back to the traps, except for one strong link, which leads down. This has to be where we'll find the Ice Queen."

He moved to stand beside Zahna. He looked every bit the seasoned warrior in the helmet and lamellar coat. However, he had his visor up and his eyes were big and wide like when they'd…like…except right now she detected horror. "What can you see?" she asked.

"Dead people," he said.

Miss Millicent snorted. "I'm not sure I can take this Spiritualist malarkey seriously."

"It's okay," said Ingar, "Torstag will be the only one to see them anyway."

"Thanks a lot," said Torstag.

"So," said Miss Millicent, "it's through the Green Door of Death or down the Shaft into the Chamber of Bones."

Ingar hunkered down near the edge and held out his everlight. "I'm getting *possible trap*. Look at that slot."

Zahna glanced down. No memories. "The hole seems safe."

Everybody peered at the sides of the hole. Sure enough, there was a finger-width slot about half way down the narrow section.

"Could be ornamental," said Miss Millicent.

"You're *supposed* to be on my side," said Ingar. "Right. Hang on a moment."

At length, Miss Millicent leaned over the shaft to peer at the bones. "Those are all me, aren't they?"

Torstag shook his head. "Like I said, just one link."

"Oh," said Miss Millicent.

Zahna took a better look.

The older bones—green tinged by algae—seemed scattered randomly. However, the shaft framed two almost complete skeletons, each with scraps of clothing and black strands of skin and sinew. On was missing a head and arm. The the other had its ribcage shattered.

"What would do that?" said Torstag.

"Perhaps they were killed before being dropped down," said Zahna. She glanced around. "I don't see an altar."

"Perhaps," said Miss Millicent, "this is an osuary for fallen warriors."

"No," said Torstag. "Those aren't warriors."

"How ever can you know that?" asked Miss Millicent.

Performing Scout at level 6. Possible aftermath of Bear Attack.

Zahna laughed. *Hah, no!*

"I hardly think this is a laughing matter," said Miss Millicent.

"Something my…" began Zahna. But she was not going to explain herself to this woman. "Torstag can see dead people."

"I keep forgetting," said Miss Millicent, her voice amplified by the stone walls of the passage. "Well, doubtless some kind of scavenger got into the tomb the last time it was opened."

"It's possible," said Torstag.

"Sacrifices," said Zahna. "They must help prevent the attraction from fading."

"I am beginning to really dislike myself," said Miss Millicent.

It's always about you, thought Zahna. There was something about the way the librarian filled the confined space with her personality that made Zahna want to throw her down the hole.

"Brrr," continued Miss Millicent. "How very beastly!"

"Cultists generally are," said Zahna. She played her light over the floor on the other side of the hole. There were old muddy footprints leading too and fro from the green door.

Torstag shifted, his hand went to his sword.

"What?" asked Ingar. He was tying the rope to one end of his ten-foot pole.

"Footprints," said Torstag. He gestured down the tunnel toward the mysterious entrance. "Somebody uses the green door."

"Cultists!" exclaimed Millicent. "How exciting!"

"Fuck," said Ingar. "They won't be pleased if they catch us."

"Well you should have bloody checked for that," said Torstag. "You're our burglar."

"Keep your voices down!" said Zahna. "There might be a portal behind the door leading to a temple with people in it."

"Right, yes," said Ingar. He'd tied the rope to his 10-foot pole. "Out of the way." He tossed it harpoon-like down to the hole. It thumped the stone floor beneath, crunching some old bones.

"Nothing," he said. He yanked it up, dropped it, making it dance around the floor below. "Still nothing."

Something hissed across the hole. The rope went slack.

"Fuck! And fuck again," said Ingar, holding up the severed end of the rope. "I was right!"

"Language!" exclaimed Millicent in a stage whisper.

"Aspiration," shot back Ingar.

Torstag sighed, then turned to Zahna. "I thought you said the path was safe?"

Zahna felt herself blush. "There was no *immediate* threat."

"Yes," said Torstag, "but if we'd roped down there, we'd have been stuck."

"Hence at least some of the the bones," said Millicent. "I contrived to starve tomb robbers to death multiple times. I don't think I can have been very nice." There was a false brightness to her tone.

"Not you," said Ingar. "The Ice Queen. Past lives don't count."

Zahna squared her shoulders, tried to look in charge. "Whoever designed this tomb knew about Remembering Backwards."

"So we try the green door instead," said Torstag. "Perhaps it leads to the lower level."

"Or angry cultists," said Zahna.

"Torstag can hit them with his sword," said Ingar.

"Wait a moment," hissed Millicent. "If they are cultists, then they worship the Ice Queen, which means me. I'm their Goddess! Perhaps I should simply present myself to them?"

"That makes a certain amount of crazy sense," said Ingar.

Zahna shook her head. "Why have the tomb in this Realm, then? I don't think you're supposed to meet the cultists. Perhaps the traps are actually to stop the cultists from exploring the tomb."

"Why wouldn't I want myself to meet my own worshippers?" asked Millicent.

"You don't know how they worship," said Zahna. "Perhaps they keep goddesses in cages?"

"Oh," said Millicent.

"Let's try down," said Ingar. "We'll drag in another log and jam the blade."

"It would have to be a long log," said Torstag.

"*No*, I mean braced *across* the hole," said Ingar.

"Pardon me," whispered Millicent, "but wouldn't that make a lot of noise?"

"It would take too long, anyway," said Zahna. "For all we know we've already set off an alarm."

"What about the spell you were going to try on the entrance?" asked Torstag.

Suddenly everybody was looking at her.

Zahna shook her head. "Flip would take all day. I don't think we have that much time."

They fell into silence, staring into the hole as if it were a camp fire.

"Oh," said Millicent. "Oh. Hang on a moment." Her eyes went unfocused; the sign of somebody communing with their Demon. She thrust her open hand toward the hole and intoned some resonant gibberish followed by the word, "*SALAMANDER!*"

A flaming lizard formed in her hand. With a hiss, it dove into the hole, veered into the slot, then shot back out to land on the floor beneath, setting some old bones smouldering.

"Oh my goodness," said Miss Millicent, fanning herself with her hand.

"Do you believe in magic now?" asked Ingar.

Miss Millicent grinned. "Did you *see* that? It appears I am a..." She cocked her head. "*Goeticist.*"

Zahna glanced at Torstag. "Of course you are."

And Zahna would never be a powerful Goeticist. One moment of abandon and an entire school of magic was closed to her until she'd spent years levelling up.

The librarian raised her hand for another spell.

Ingar caught her wrist. "You'll burn through your Potestas is what you'll do."

"Oh," said Miss Millicent, she lowered her arm, 'just happening' to brush Ingar's fingers she did.

The boy's green eyes went as wide as slingstones.

Zahna sighed. "Did you see how the salamander rebounded? The blade has magical protection. Miss Millicent, you are simply not powerful enough to overcome that."

"Yet," said the older women. She contemplated her hand. "Not powerful enough *yet*."

"We're missing something," said Ingar. "None of this makes sense."

"This is shambollic," said Torstag.

"Logic," said Miss Millicent, firmly. The librarian took off her glasses and blinked in the gloom. "How am I supposed to leave? I mean…" She started polishing the lenses. "Imagine I remember all the traps and magic words, and I get down there and find the treasure. If the rope is cut, how do I leave?"

"Maybe," said Ingar, "there's a password for the trap."

Miss Millicent shook her head. "My Voice would have told me."

"Perhaps there's a lever down there that switches it off?" said Ingar.

Millicent harrumphed. "I really can't see *myself* setting myself up to heft treasure up and down a rope and I imagine the Ice Queen would be even more averse to setting her future self up for manual labour…"

"Given the Queen part of that name," said Ingar.

"My point is," said Millicent raising her voice a little. This somehow grabbed the entire attention of both men. "There must be another exit. Which means there's another way in."

"There's only one door in the hill," said Zahna, keen to shut down this nonsense. "Perhaps the other way in and out leads to whatever is beyond the green door."

"Didn't you say that I probably didn't want to meet my worshippers?"

Zahna chewed her lip.

"So logically, the exit has to be somewhere in this tunnel," continued Millicent.

"A secret door leading to stairs," said Ingar. He started working his way back up the tunnel, tapping on the wall with his axe-butt.

"I…" began Zahna.

"Shush," said Ingar.

Ingar's axe thudded on the stonework, again and again as he worked his way up one wall of the tunnel, the back down the other.

"Nothing," said Zahna.

"What about that pit trap?" said Miss Millicent.

"I am an idiot," said Ingar.

"Yes," said Miss Millicent, "It's a good thing I'm here to organise you young people."

"We don't need organising," said Zahna.

"Yes you do," said Millicent. "Besides, this is my tomb. You are technically my guests."

"If it gets things over with," said Torstag. "Why not?"

Zahna sighed.

Chapter 40: The Realm of the Ice Queen

Gronchard woke to screaming. Agony clawed his spine.

Something warm squirted in his face.

He opened his eyes, saw red, tasted blood.

Somebody cried, "He wakes!" and hundreds of voices echoed the words; "He wakes! He wakes!"

More screaming.

A damp cloth wiped away the blood. Gronchard's Temple came into focus.

Gronchard blinked and located the source of the screaming: a sacrifice writhing on the altar at the foot of his dais.

His back spasmed.

The marble Throne of Praise had revived him, but it was built for a taller avatar. It had left his back in excruciating discomfort and his neck stiff.

The sacrifice went mercifully silent.

That was one thing at least. He could do without a headache on top of the other pain.

Gronchard started to rise and hands helped him to his feet. The choir began to sing, and hymns echoed from the high vault.

6 of 6 Potestas.
3 of 4 Vitality remaining. You have Hindrance "Sore back"
2 of 3 Will remaining.

From long habit, he looked to his right, seeking Angelica.

And there she was, rendered in marble, exquisitely painted. The flicker from the braziers lent her life so every curve invited touch. She was indeed the perfect reference for the imperfect efforts of the surgeons. Hopefully the present Saint Sanguineous had held back some suitable candidates for the Immaculate Hall of the Holy Concubines. Sometimes the loneliness was unbearable.

"I hurt," said Gronchard. "Everything hurts."

The chorus drowned out his voice and the statue was implacable. Even so, it was easy to imagine Angelica crooning soothing words, taking his head on her ample lap, stroking his hair.

But now the singing really was making his head hurt.

He composed himself.

> **Form 3.**
> **Performing Theurge at level 7.**
> **Using Feed on Adulation, cost 1 Potestas. 5 of 6 remaining.**
> **Result = 5 (Performance) +1 (Luck) -5 (Challenge) = 1.**
> **Effect = 6 (Result) +5 (Hundreds) = 6.**
> **Potestas now 9 of 6.**

"Better!" He held up his hands to signal silence, and contemplated his Temple.

Servitors had already dragged away the latest sacrifice and were mopping down the altar. The Saints and Seraphim filled the apse. All was as it should be.

Gronchard reached out to his surroundings.

> **Translocation complete. 2 of 4 translocations available. 500 Sacrifices required.**

"Are we there yet?"

Saint Incarnation prostrated himself so quickly that his angel toppled and had to scramble and flutter back onto his shoulder.

"Well?" prompted Gronchard, indicating that he could rise. "Are we there yet?"

Saint Incarnation merely raised his forehead from the damp mosaic floor. "Divinity, we have indeed arrived at the Tomb of the Ice Queen in the midst of the Winter Lands."

But Gronchard was already striding down the aisle, his worshippers prostrating as they passed.

Cherubim flung open the great doors and he stepped out into a light snowfall. Cold air prickled his skin.

Attendants caught up and draped him in a fur cloak.

Gronchard slowed to let them fasten it, then turned onto the bridge and picked up speed, not caring when he skidded on icy patches. He was running by the time he burst into the sanctuary of the Temple of Incarnation.

The seraphim within prostrated themselves, except for the one scattering grains over the sandbox.

Gronchard peered at the living diorama.

The suspended sand showed the Flying Tooth Garden poised over a mountain valley. There were no settlements. However, two columns of standing stones processed to where a big latticework figure dominated the valley. At this point, the west facing valley wall was a shear cliff…shear except for a craggy promontory with a cave entrance behind.

He had found the tomb! But where was Angelica?

Gronchard marched out onto the viewing platform overlooking the Great Well.

Far bellow, the land was snowbound, except around the latticework figure—a giant wicker man—where the feet of workers had evidently trodden through to the heather beneath.

It was late afternoon, and the sun cast barred shadows from the carved balustrade that marked the edge of the craggy promontory. The cave mouth was not visible from this angle, but the snow-covered top of the promontory was clearly flat. All was as described in the ancient travelogue that Saint Remembrance had unearthed from his archives.

"The Tomb of the Ice Queen!" declared Gronchard. "But where is my Sacred Angelica?"

Somebody coughed next to him; Saint Prescience. "Divinity," said the portly saint, "this is indeed the Tomb of the Ice Queen. However, there is no trace of the Sacred Angelica."

"What? No!" blurted Gronchard. "I am never wrong."

"But Divinity…" began Saint Prescience.

Gronchard seized him by the collar.

Form 3.
Performing Warrior at Level 5.
Result = 5 (Performance) +1 (Luck) +2 (Advantage of
"Surprise") −3 (Challenge) = 5
Effect = Throw (4).

The old man screamed as he toppled over the barrier into the Great Well. Increasing distance muted the sound as he spun toward the snow beneath.

His angel fluttered back and alighted on the shoulder of one of the Seraphim of the Temple of Prescience.

"Divinity," said the new Saint Prescience, a much younger and more deferential individual, "would you like the lodebone?"

"Yes, yes of course," snapped Gronchard. He rubbed his temples. All this stress was worsening his headache.

The former Saint was now a speck on the snow. There was still no sign of the natives. Presumably they had disrespectfully fled the valley. It was amazing how easily Gronchard had penetrated the Ice Queen's realm, when her name only recalled memories of hard fought battles and an ultimate uneasy truce. "I am clearly better than I was," declared Gronchard.

"Yes, Divinity," said Saint Prescience.

"I have achieved what my past avatars have not!" continued Gronchard, then realised such boasting was unseemly for a god. "Give me the lodebone."

Tenderly, he took the thigh bone that had once been graced with his beloved's flesh and suspended it by its silken cord.

It spun clockwise, then anticlockwise…

Gronchard held his breath.

…then back clockwise again.

For several minutes he could only stare as the bone swung back and forward with no sense of anything pulling it. At length he came back to himself. "Saint Mausoleus!"

The Saint in charge of necromantic operations stepped forward. "Divinity?"

Gronchard wrinkled his nose. The old man always smelled of rotten meat and embalming fluid. "What do you see?"

"Nothing, Divinity," said Saint Mausoleus, "other than some ghosts prowling the landscape around that wicker man, and others haunting the top of that promontory. Alas, the only links from the lodebone point back to the Mausoleum."

"I was wrong," wailed Gronchard. "And now the Vessel has escaped with my Angelica!"

Chapter 41: Millicent in Charge

"Go on," said Millicent. She raised the glowing jewel he'd given her higher to better illuminate his efforts. "Give it a poke."

The boy burglar stuck his tongue out at her. "I *do* know how to do this." He stomped on the square of stone. It swung down, then back up again.

There was a clunk.

Ingar flung himself sideways. Torstag shoved Zahna out the way.

Something arrived with a whir and slammed into Millicent's chest. She looked down at it—a small stubby arrow now protruded from her bosom, casting a shadow like a sundial. "Now where did *that* come from?"

Ingar slid past the trap door. "Millicent!"

She laughed and pinged the arrow to make it thrum. "My stays caught it." She handed him the everlight and tore off the remnants of her blouse to reveal her corset.

Miss Zahna, who had picked herself up, scrutinised it. "This seems incomplete for armour. Rather too much unprotected flesh."

"*Moral* armour," said Millicent.

Ingar laughed.

Millicent shot him a Quelling Glance, and ignored her Voice's patter, except when it said, **8 of 6 Potestas remaining.**

He flushed. "I mean, I'm glad you are okay."

"Well," said Millicent. "Pull it out while I brace."

Now blushing bright red, the boy yanked on the arrow while she clamped the corset with her hands to stop it tearing open.

"Lucky," he said. "A little higher and it would have missed the…undergarment, hit you between the—"

"Far too lucky," said Miss Zahna.

"Well," said Millicent, "it is *my* tomb after all."

"That worked so well for your past selves," said Zahna.

"Where did it come from?" asked Torstag.

"One way to find out," said Ingar. "Everybody stand clear this time."

The boy returned to his former position. This time he squatted by the edge of the trapdoor and pushed with his hands, once, twice—each time triggering another arrow which appeared to be coming from above the mysterious door at the end of the passage. He pushed a third time, hard, almost toppling into the hole.

The shove was enough to cause the trapdoor to swing down all the way. There was another, deeper clunk and the trapdoor remained in the *down* position.

Ingar directed his everlight into trap. "Oh, I don't think you want to see this."

"Nonsense," said Millicent striding over.

"You don't," said Torstag.

The shaft went down a good ten feet to a bed of long metal spikes. There was enough space between them to accommodate the the skulls and other bones that lay around the base. A single skeleton was propped up against the walls, both feet and one shin bone impaled on the wicked needles.

Millicent shuddered. "She probably bled to death, poor thing," she said, "alone in this pit…at least I was doing this to myself."

Test of Guilt at Using People 1/6, cost 0 Potestas
Guilt at Using People advances to 2/6 Hardening.

"Hah!" said Millicent.

Everybody looked at her. She shook her head. She really needed to remember that other people couldn't hear her Voice.

"Look," said Ingar, gesturing down.

Sure enough, there were iron rungs set into the side of shaft.

"Miss Zahna?" prompted Millicent.

The girl with the magic powers strode over and peered over the side. "Seems safe." She shrugged one shoulder. "For the next few moments."

"Hmm," said Millicent. "If this is supposed to be my egress from the lower level, I am not impressed. Imagine climbing up that ladder laden with treasure."

"Ah, but if the treasure is a spell book or amulet," said Miss Zahna, "then it would be easy to return later with hirelings and clean the place out."

Torstag loosened his sword belt.

"What are you doing?" asked Zahna.

"Going first." He wound the belt around the scabbard, then slung it over his armoured shoulders so that the big sword was strapped to his back.

"My," said Millicent, "you look quite the dashing hero now."

"You look like an idiot," said Zahna. "You'll never draw it like that."

Torstag nodded. "Just don't want to get tangled." He edged around the pit then climbed over the side. There was enough space between the spikes and the pit walls for him to squeeze around. "Tunnel," he said. "Empty. Right direction. Ingar?"

"Hang on then," said Ingar, making a move to follow.

Millicent shook her head. "Miss Zahna next."

Ingar and Zahna glanced at each other. The girl shrugged. She passed her staff down to Torstag, the light-orb-thingy still tied to its top. Then she swarmed down to join him. After a moment, she called up. "Looks safe."

"You next, milady," said Ingar. He bowed theatrically. "I'll bring up the *rear*."

"I'll thank you to keep your hands to yourself," said Millicent, being sure to bump him as she slid past. "For now."

Though Millicent prided herself on her strong legs, her arms were weak. It was no fun climbing down the iron rungs with their abrasive patina of rust, especially not with a bed of spikes waiting for if she fell. Nor was it any better squeezing between the spikes and the cold stone wall, boots crunching her own mouldering bones.

279

She was breathing hard by the time she joined the wizard and the warrior in the lower tunnel.

Ingar handed her his halberd, then shimmied down with both hands free. As he sidled around the spikes to join them, he plucked a shin bone.

That felt obscurely like an act of violation. "Hey!" she protested.

"You might need a surge later," said Ingar. He winked and slipped the bone into his belt.

The tunnel widened as it sloped down into the rock.

"How are we doing, Zahna?" asked Millicent.

"Still safe."

"Well let's get this over with! I must confess I'm not looking forward to meeting myself even if I am dead."

Ingar caught her arm. "Give me my axe, I need to go first."

Millicent relinquished the weapon. "Technically it's a halberd."

Ingar laughed and slipped between the others to take the lead.

They descended the slope in silence, except for the steady tapping of the young man's halberd-butt.

About half way down. Zahna's voice echoed back up the tunnel: "Why a ramp and not stairs?"

"To facilitate the use of wheelbarrows, I imagine," said Millicent. "All that treasure."

Something clunked.

"Fuck," said Ingar, halting. "I think we just armed a trap."

"We?" said Torstag. "Zahna what can you see?"

The girl called back, "The path still looks safe, all the way to the door."

"Phew," said Ingar. "False alarm. Or —fuck!—perhaps it set off an alarm and the cultists are coming."

"I think..." began Millicent.

Behind her, falling stones plinked and rattled. She turned in time to see great slabs of masonry crash to the floor behind a curtain of dust. A hollow roar rattled her teeth and resounded in her gut.

Miss Zahna shouted, "What have you done, you silly woman?"

"...that..." continued Millicent.

It suddenly came to her that for all her worldly experience, she might possibly be out of her depth leading a party set on burglarising an ancient tomb, beset with traps.

"…the architect knew all about your Remembering Backwards," she completed.

Something vast and furry fell through the dust and landed with a deep thud, filling the passage from side to side with its bulk. Its eyes burned red. It tossed its single great horn and let out another roar, propelling the cloying stench of embalming fluid down the tunnel like a wave of nausea.

And yet…and yet Millicent recognised the creature from the Science Museum. "But you're extinct. Preposterous!"

Ingar appeared at her arm. "What in the name of all fuck is that?"

As if in a dream, Millicent heard herself answer, "Woolly rhinoceros."

"*Zombie* woolly rhinoceros," corrected Torstag pushing past. He raised his sword. "Get the next door open. I'll deal with this."

The monster snorted. It pawed the floor, crunching rubble, then charged.

"Or we could all just run screaming," said Ingar.

Chapter 42: Fauna of the Ice Kingdom

Zombie Woolly Rhinoceros, hostile, charging.

Torstag cocked Peacebringer over his shoulder and gestured with his left hand. "BACK!"

Form 1.
Performing Necromancer at Level 2.
Using Repel Shade, cost 1 Potestas. 9 out of 5 Potestas remaining.
Result = 2 (Performance) +2 (Feat) -15 (Challenge) = -11.
Failure.

Still carrying Peacebringer one-handed, Torstag turned and ran from the thunderous echoes of the beast's hooves.

The others were barely ahead of him.

"Go! Go! Go!"

With each pace, Torstag's lamellar armour jingled and his helmet tried to bob off his head. Neither he nor the armour were built for running.

"I'll get the door!" cried Ingar, voice vibrating as he sprinted on ahead.

The ghost of Axe Girl sprinted with him. She grabbed at the axe. Her fingers passed through it.

Wrestling with—

Warrior! Not Necromancer!

Test of Potestas 9. Third Eye closed.

The ghost vanished. She was still there, of course, but that didn't really matter right now.

Millicent yelled, "Wait for me!". She puffed and panted, ankle boots clattering on the stone, but didn't seem to be able to go any faster. "I know!" she gasped. "*Open up, for I am Millicent nee Lintar...*"

Torstag risked a glance over his shoulder.

The undead creature rumbled closer, matted legs eating up their initial lead as it picked up speed from the slope.

"No luck!" yelled Ingar, his voice juddering as he ran. "Try again."

Torstag pushed the librarian between the shoulder blades. "Faster!"

"I'm trying!"

"Faster!"

Ingar reached the door first, gave it a shove, then started screaming obscenities while hacking at it with his axe.

Zahna caught up in long strides, collided with Ingar and knocked him against the door.

And still Millicent lumbered along as best she could. "*Open up...*"

Torstag halted and turned to face the onrushing monster.

Its eyes blazed red. Its hooves thundered on the rock-cut floor.

Torstag raised his sword into a high guard. Perhaps if he split its skull...

"Torstag, no!" shouted Zahna, more of a command than a plea.

"Humph," said Miss Millicent, appearing next to Torstag.

"Run," said Torstag. "I'm saving you!"

"No," said the librarian, "*I* am the one saving us." She extended her hand. "SALAMANDER!"

A fat fire lizard sprang into existence, uncoiled and hurled itself at the undead creature.

Flame splashed over the fur, black smoke billowed.

Zombie woolly rhinoceros. Hostile. Charging. On Fire.

Flames and oily smoke now billowing from its back, the zombie woolly rhinoceros continued to close on them.

"Bugger," said Millicent. She turned and fled, leaving Torstag to stand between the burning monster and his friends.

A great peace came over him. He wasn't going to survive this, but perhaps if he could cut off one of its legs he might just slow it down and save his friends. The sword's Smite Undead feat should at least help.

He swung the greatsword behind himself in what a little voice told him was "Tail Guard" and tried to concentrate.

1 Potestas Expended. 8 out of 5 Potestas remaining.
Form 2. Performing Warrior at Level 5.
The flaming zombie woolly rhinoceros is Challenging
at 4, Charging.

That would have to do. The monster thundered closer, filling the tunnel. It dipped its long horn and Torstag knew this wasn't going to work. No Wrath Strike was going to stop that thing, let alone take out a leg. Its hide would be thick, and the thing was dead anyway.

What about destroying one of the glowing red eyes? Undead didn't perceive the world through their sense organs, but their senses relied on being anchored to whatever was put in their place. Even blinding it down one side would give his friends a fighting chance.

When the monster was still two sword lengths away, he whipped Peacebringer forward and pivoted into a thrust. His armour rattled as his front foot smacked the sloping stone floor.

Everything seemed to slow down. He braced his back leg and lined the wobbling tip of the sword up on the glowing red orb that served as the monster's left eye, knowing that the horn would surely pierce his armour shortly after the blade pierced its target.

Eye as target requires 5 Finesse.
Thrust structural damage is capped.

No point in using Smite Undead, then.

Using Onset Thrust 3/5, cost 1 Potestas. 7 of 5
Potestas Remaining.
You have advantages "First Strike" and "Superior
Performance."
Your Medium Armour and the Monster's
Manoeuvrability are matched.
Onset Thrust is Unpredictable.
Result = 5 (Performance) +2 ("First Strike"), +2
(Unpredictable) -4 (Enemy Challenge) = 5
Effect = 5 (Result) +2 (Greatsword) -5 (Finesse) = 2

His sword tip struck the eye socket, displaced a red glass ball, then lodged in the bone.

Left eye destroyed.
Thrust. Structural Damage reduced to 1.
Onset Thrust advances to 5/6.

Caught between the thing's skull and Torstag's iron grip, the sword blade actually bowed. The tip of the rhino horn reached within a hands-breadth of the rectangular plates covering his belly, then he skidded backwards.

Enemy Result = 4 (Challenge) +4 (Charging) +1 (Luck) -
2 ("Left Eye Missing") -5 (Your Performance) = 2.

Torstag's sandals slid over the stone floor as, spewing black smoke, the charging burning zombie woolly rhinoceros shoved him backwards.

Enemy Slam Result = 2 (Success) +6 (Enemy Slam
Factor) = 8.

Peacebringer's grip slipped in his fingers so the cross guard pressed into his right hand. His elbows started to bend.

Now the massive rhino horn pressed into the metal plates protecting his gut.

His belly muscles tensed, as if they could escape what was about to happen.

And still the tunnel floor slid under his sandals, warming his feet through the leather soles.

Torstag heard himself scream, and then his friends joining in, Ingar emitting one loud long, "Fuuuuuuuuck!"

Zahna somersaulted overhead and vanished through the curtain of smoke.

The pressure collapsed his arms, drove the sword pommel into his armoured sternum, knocked the wind out of him. He lost his footing.

With a mighty *boing!* the sword straightened, hurled him back.

The lamellar plates crashed into the wood.

The door gave, slammed open.

He glimpsed Ingar and Millicent, each pressed up against the door-posts.

Torstag fell back into darkness, found himself staring up at a vaulted ceiling bathed in the orange light of the burning woolly rhinoceros.

Something crunched against his armour. His helmet bumped the ground.

Enemy Slam Effect = 8 (Slam Result) -4 (Knocked
Sprawling) -3 (Your Armour) = 1 Vitality loss.
4 of 5 Vitality remaining.
You have Disadvantage, "Knocked Sprawling".

The monster kept coming. The remaining eye blazed red. The great horn came down, in an instant it would hook against the plates of his armour.

The flaming zombie woolly rhinoceros is Challenging
at 4, charging.
Your Medium Armour and the Monster's
Manoeuvrability are matched.

There was no time to get up, so Torstag tried to roll out of the way. Bones crunched. The world spun.

Performing Warrior at Level 5.
Manoeuvring.
Result = 5 (Performance) +0 (Luck) -2 (Knocked
Sprawling) +2 (Enemy "Left Eye Missing") -4 (Enemy
Challenge) = 1
Effect = Successful Evasion.

The monster crashed past, grinding bones under its hooves, enveloping Torstag with choking smoke.

Torstag, however, was still sprawled amongst the skeletons.

Clutching Peacebringer, Torstag rolled to his feet, tottered, drew himself up. He shook his head to clear his vision.

Just beyond the doorway, Ingar flapped at his robes ineffectually, which had caught fire, while Millicent yelled at him. Zahna, meanwhile, ran toward Torstag. "Behind you!"

Torstag spun, nearly fell over again.

The monster was completing its turn. In a moment, it would charge again.

Once again, Torstag pivoted into a surprise thrust.

Using Feat Onset Thrust 5/6, cost 1 Potestas. 5 of 5
Potestas remaining.
You have advantages "First Strike" and "Enemy
Caught Turning."
Your Medium Armour and the Monster's
Manoeuvrability are matched.
Onset Thrust is Unpredictable.

His front foot skidded on powdered bone—

Test of Performance 5. Passed. Skid avoided.

—but then grounded nicely against the rock-cut floor.

Result = 5 (Performance) +3 ("First Strike", "Enemy
Caught Turning") +0 (Unpredictable) +2 (Enemy "Left
Eye Missing") -4 (Enemy Challenge) = 6
Required Finesse 5.
Effect = 6 (Result) +2 (Greatsword) -5 (Finesse) = 3
Right Eye destroyed.

Again, his tip struck the eye socket. A second red orb tumbled to shatter amongst the bones…

Onset Thrust secured. Select a 10th Warrior Feat?

The creature finished turning. It inhaled through shrivelled nostrils, snorted and came at Torstag like a nightmare pillar of fire.

Unlock Crooked Strike?

"Oh yes."

Crooked Strike unlocked at 2/6 grasp. Securing this
Feat will advance Warrior Vocation to level 4.
Crooked Strike is "Unpredictable" so doubly affected
by Luck.
Crooked Strike is "Weak", so has -2 applied to
Damage.
Manoeuvring Advantages and Disadvantages Apply.
A successful Crooked Strike confers "Tactical
Advantage".

As the burning zombie rhino rumbled toward him, he hurled himself out of the way and windmilled his sword into the space he had just left.

Using Crooked strike 2/6, cost 1 Potestas, 3 of 5
Potestas remaining.
Crooked Strike is Unpredictable.
Test of Performance 5. Passed. Skid avoided.
Attacking Boldly.
Result = 7 (Performance) +2 (Bold attack) +4 (Enemy
relying on scent) +1 (Unpredictable) -4 (Enemy
Challenge) = 10
Natural Armour 4 negated.
Using Sword Feat "Smite Undead" cost 1 Potestas 2
of 5 remaining.
Damage = 8 +2 (Greatsword) -2 (Weak) +4 (Smite
Undead) = 14.

The blade caught the creature behind the neck, stripped a flap of smouldering fur and flesh to expose yellow-white bones.

Target Toughness 8 surpassed.
Target has Hindrance "Damaged"
Crooked Strike Advances to 3/6 Grasp.
You have "Tactical Advantage".

The undead woolly rhinoceros trundled past, deeper into the chamber, trailing black smoke. The flames on its back illuminated an artificial cavern about thirty paces across; as large as the monastery refectory.

The blinded monster crossed the bone-strewn floor and thumped into the far wall at an angle, skidded to crash lengthwise into the carved stonework.

The façade bowed and collapsed.

Ingar—now naked except for his breach-clout—charged after it screaming, "Fuck you you great hairy dead lummox you!"

The rhino rolled back onto his its stubby legs, bringing down yet more masonry, revealing the rock behind.

Ingar swung his axe at the burning monster.

Zahna appeared from nowhere. As she ran past, she yelled, "Zombie cave bears!"

Behind her bounded a huge creature with patchy fur, red glowing eyes, and massive yellow teeth.

CHAPTER 43: DARK HUNGER

Rasinta snarled into the link-webbed dark.

Bad enough that the soul thief's minions had damaged her first guardian. Worse, that they had made her *feel* it.

Rasinta the Ice Queen. Lich. Level 10.
Will 4 of 10.
Potestas 4 of 10. Potestas Reservoir 24.

She was almost ready to face them.

The link to the soul thief quivered and Rasinta felt a hollow yearning.

If only the soul thief would cross the threshold into the Refectory, *then* Rasinta could close the door and trap her for good.

Rasinta frowned, and tried to ignore the way the expression tore the skin of her forehead.

It was the tall warrior who was to blame!

He should have been dead by now, trampled by her first guardian. But when ill fortune saw him pushed back onto the others, she had been forced to open the door and let them *all* into her Refectory.

Even so, it should not be a problem as long as the soul thief did not get herself killed. The stupid woman had already forced Rasinta to burn potestas to divert a crossbow bolt.

Soon.

Rasinta rose from her throne. Boot leather—yes, let it be boot leather and not mummified skin, not dried joints barely muffled by her furs—creaked as she paced her burial chamber and took position by the threshold of.

She stroked the filament connecting her sternum to the soul thief.

Why not? Just a little encouragement.

#

Millicent took a step after Ingar, then checked just short of the threshold.

What could she do? Ingar had told her to stay put and stop the door from closing.

The chamber echoed with thuds as the youth swung his halberd, laying into the burning woolly rhinoceros. Meanwhile at least two giant bears had somehow joined the fight.

How could she intervene in all that?

She glanced down at Ingar's still smouldering robe. Tossing magical fire around had not gone well.

No, she should stay put.

**Wrestling with guilt at Using People 2/6 Hardening.
Cost 2 Potestas, 5 of 6 remaining.**

"Damn you."

But there was her shin bone, the one Ingar had salvaged. More power, more feats. Perfect.

She scooped it up. "Come on, will you, surge!"

Nothing.

"I can't just stand here!"

Ingar had wanted to protect her, but she was doomed if the monsters could not be defeated; she could not outpace the woolly rhinoceros, and even if she did, she would not get up the iron rungs before the bears tore her apart.

"Bugger this for a game of soldiers."

Millicent bundled up the robes, crammed them into the open hinge of the door. Clutching the shinbone like a primitive warclub, she marched into the fray, and not a moment too soon.

Chapter 44: Could Have Been a Bull Dancer

The burning zombie woolly rhinoceros rolled away from the wall, bringing down the remains of the facade.

Naked dancers and garlanded bulls jumbled across Ingar's mind's eye.

Unlock Companion, Bull Dancer?

Flames and smoke roaring from its back, the monster turned and lunged for Ingar, hooking with a horn that was almost as long as Torstag's new sword.

"Fuck you Doofus! And fuck you too, you great lummox!" Ingar skipped out of the way. The movement made his shoulder throb where his burning robes had seared his flesh.

Form 2.
Performing Warrior at 2.
Light Armour has the advantage over Cumbersome.

Light armour? A breech-clout counts as light armour, now does it?

Manoeuvre Result = 6 (Performance) +2 (Lighter Armour) +0 (Luck) +5 (Enemy "Relying on scent", "Damaged") −4 (Challenge) = 9.
Effect = Successful evade + Tactical Advantage (2).

His foot slipped.

Test of Performance 2. Skid avoided.

Ingar regained his balance, stepped inside the monster's turning circle. He swung his axe at the back leg.

Great Axe gets First Strike.
Using Wrath Strike 3/6, cost 2 Potestas. 0 of 6
Potestas remaining.
Result = 4 (Performance) +2 (Boldness) +3 (Lighter
Armour, Tactical Advantage) +1 (Luck) +5 (Enemy
"Relying on scent", "Damaged") -4 (Challenge) = 13.
Natural Armour 4 negated.

The axe slammed into the leg. The smack of the blow stung Ingar's hands.

Effect = 13 + 3 (Great Axe) + 2 (Feat) = 18.

Target Toughness 8 surpassed.
Target has Hindrance "Damaged+1".
Wrath Strike advances to 4/6.

The creature came at him.

He yanked back the axe and dodged.

Manoeuvre Result = 6 (Performance) -1 (Luck) +6
(Enemy "Relying on scent", "Damaged+1") -4
(Challenge) = 7
Result = Successful Evade + Tactical Advantage (2)
Test of Performance 2. Skid avoided.
Great Axe gets First Strike.

"Fuck you!"

Again, he swung the axe, this time with an ordinary blow, which was the best he could do with no remaining Potestas.

The blade caught the monster between the ears.

Result = 2 (Performance) + 0 (Luck) +6 (Hindrances
"Missing Right Eye", "Missing Left Eye", "Relying on
scent", "Damaged+1") -4 (Challenge) = 4.
Effect = 8 (Result) +3 (Great Axe) -4 (Natural Armour) =
7.

The creature bellowed, scythed with its horn. Smoke enveloped him.

Manoeuvre Result = 6 (Performance) +1 (Luck) +5
(Hindrances "Missing Right Eye", "Missing Left Eye",
"Relying on scent", "Damaged+1") -4 (Challenge) = 9
Test of Performance 2. Failed.

His bare foot slipped. Something clawed his ankles. He had stepped into a rib cage and now it was working like a mantrap.

You have disadvantage "Landed Sprawling".
Test of Potestas 0 of 6. You have lost your weapon.

His legs slipped out from under him. He let go of the axe, windmilled his arms, landed amidst broken bones. Shards stuck into his back, spiked his thighs.

He caught sight of Millicent cradling the thighbone he'd saved. She blinked and hurled the remains of her past avatar at the monster. "You leave him alone!"

And the flaming undead woolly rhinoceros came for him.

Ingar let out a long yell of, "Fuck!", tucked his legs under himself and ran.

Manoeuvre Result = 6 (Performance) +1 (Luck) +5
(Hindrances "Missing Right Eye", "Missing Left Eye",
"Relying on scent", "Damaged+1") -4 (Challenge) = 9
Effect = Successful Disengage and Tactical
Advantage (2).

CHAPTER 45: TRAPPED!

Torstag raised his sword as the massive zombie cave bear bounded after Zahna, splashing dried bones across the floor.

You have Tactical Advantage.

As the thing passed, Torstag whacked it with a diagonal cut. He drove the blow from his legs, put his hips and shoulders into it. The greatsword caught the monster behind the head.

Attacking Boldly.
Current Form 4. Performing Warrior at level 7.
Using Wrath Strike +2, cost 1 Potestas. 2 of 5
Potestas remaining.
Result = 7 (Performance) +2 (Bold Attack) +2 (Tactical
Advantage) +4 (Enemy Charging) -1 (Luck) -5
(Challenge) = 9
Natural Armour 4 Negated.
Using Sword Feat, Smite Undead, cost 1 Potestas. 1
of 5 Potestas remaining.
Effect = 9 (Result) +4 (Smite Undead) +2 (Greatsword)
+4 (Wrathstrike+2) = 19.
Target Toughness 9 surpassed twice.
Undead Cave Bear has Hindrance, "Damaged +1".

A great flap of dead flesh flopped back, unleashing a foul smell. Exposed vertebrae flashed white in the light of the burning woolly rhinoceros. Seemingly unperturbed, the undead cave bear continued its rush into the chamber of bones, however, it was now moving more clumsily.

The rush became a spring aimed at Zahna.

Even as he called her name, the girl whirled out of the way and smashed her staff into its skull.

It lumbered around and, still on all fours, charged her.

Torstag swerved to intercept it and repeated, "Zahna!"

You have Tactical Advantage.

He aimed for the spot he'd already hit.

This time he had but one point of Potestas left. He was going to husband it.

Result = 7 (Performance) +2 (Bold Attack) +2 (Tactical
Advantage) +4 (Full Attack) -1 (Luck) +3 (Enemy
Damaged +1) -5 (Challenge) = 8
Armour 4 Negated.
Finesse 4 Negated.
Effect = 8 (Result) +2 (Greatsword) +4 (Smite Undead)
= 14
Target Toughness 9 surpassed.
Successful Revisit adds damage.
Target has Hindrance "Damaged+3"

The blade hit the exposed spine, bit deep into a vertebra.

Now the thing could reach him. It reared up and swiped with a vast paw.

Torstag roared and stepped in. He raised his fists so that his sword draped down his left shoulder like a cloak, not blocking the attack, just redirecting it.

The paw slid down past.

Now Torstag sidestepped and again cut for the same spot.

Result = 7 (Performance) +2 (Bold Attack) +5 (Target
Damaged +3) +1 (Luck) -5 (Challenge) = 10.
Armour 4 Negated.
Finesse 4 Negated.
Damage = 10 +2 (Greatsword) = 12.
Target Toughness 9 Surpassed.
Zombie Cave Bear has hindrance Damaged +4.

Peacebringer cracked into the exposed vertebra. The zombie cave bear's head flopped forward. It crashed on its side, sending old bones skittering across the floor.

Eyes watering, Torstag raised Peacebringer.

The zombie cave bear rolled away and came to a stop against the wall where the facade still survived. The dancing flames from the zombie rhinoceros illuminated a door carved in granite and set in into the wall.

Torstag glanced to check that Ingar was still keeping the rhino busy, then strode in to complete the decapitation. He did not need his Tempter's background chatter to tell him it was an easy task.

Still snapping, the head rolled clear then was still.

Zombie Cave Bear Destroyed.

From somewhere nearby, Zahna's yelled, "Torstag!"

He turned in time to see a second undead cave bear swat at him.

The great paw brushed aside his sword and smashed the plates of his right shoulder and upper arm...

Enemy Result = 5 (Challenge) +2 (Surprise) +2 (Tactical
Advantage) +1 (Luck) -7 (Your Performance) = 4.
Enemy Effect = 4 (Result) +2 (Undead Cave Bear) -3
(Your armour) = 3.
3 Vitality Loss, 0 Vitality Remaining.
Toughness 2 Negated.
You have Hindrance "Stunned".
Form lost. Feats unavailable.
Toughness 2 surpassed. 1 Wound. You have
Hindrance "Wounded".
Vitality 0 of 4.
You have Hindrance "Debilitated".
Slam Effect = 4 (Enemy Result) +2 (Cave Bear Paw) =
Knocked Sprawling (4) +2 Damage.
Enemy Damage = 2 (Damage from Slam) -3 (Armour) =
0
You have Disadvantage, "Knocked Sprawling".

...sending him sprawling on his back.

You have Hindrances "Stunned", "Debilitated" and
"Wounded".
You have Disadvantage "Knocked Sprawling".
Feats unavailable. Form lost.
Vitality 0 of 5.
Potestas 1 of 5.

The second undead cave bear let out a hollow roar and reared up over him.

# # #

The soul thief had entered the Refectory!

Using Feat Control Tomb, cost 1 Potestas, 3
remaining.
Will 3 of 10.
Potestas Reservoir 24.
Result = 3 (Power Level) +1 (Luck) = 4.
Effect = None. Door Jammed.
Rasinta clenched her fists until the skin cracked and
the bone crackled. "What have you done?"

One of the links jerked.

Second Guardian has hindrance "Damaged +4."

She shuddered.

No.

She picked out the link and tugged it.

She sensed the embattled cave bear rolling toward her hiding place. It thudded against the granite door.

Close enough!

Finger bones crackling, the skin on her palm tearing, Rasinta pressed her hand flat against the stone.

Form 3.
Performing Liche at level 6.
Using Liche, Regenerate Undead Guardian, cost 1
Potestas, 2 of 10 remaining.
Effect—

Pain.
She felt pain.

Second Guardian Destroyed.
Rage now, rage and pain.

But the soul thief was so very close…close enough to eat.
Rasinta pushed at the stone door.
It refused to budge.
The undead cave bear had fallen against the door.
She was trapped inside her own burial chamber.

Chapter 46: Undine!

Heart pumping, Ingar sprinted away from the burning zombie woolly rhinoceros while the monster clattered along close enough to send old bones flying into the back of his heels.

Manoeuvre Result = 6 (Performance) -2 ("Knocked Sprawling") +1 (Luck) -4 (Challenge) = 1. Effect = Retreating successfully.

And there was Torstag on the ground, the cave bear rearing above him while Zahna flailed at it futilely with her staff.

With another scream of, "Fuck!" he dove between the bear's massive hind legs.

Manoeuvre Result = 6 (Performance) +1 (Luck) +2 (Surprise) -5 (Challenge) -4 (Difficulty of Manoeuvre) +2 (Floor is slippery with bone dust) = 2.

He skidded on his bare stomach. Bones and slimy grit scraped his skin. He crashed into the prone Torstag.

"Fuck that hurts."

1 Vitality lost. 2 of 4 Vitality remaining.

Behind him, there was a weird thud-crunch and a rising cacophony of hollow growls and roars.

Torstag scrambled backward, still trying to rise, gaping wordlessly.

Ingar rolled to his feet.

The horn of the zombie woolly rhinoceros now projected obscenely from belly of the cave bear.

Ingar realised where the point of entry must be and winced.

The burning undead rhino shook its head, trying to shed the writhing bear. Firelight flared on the vaulted ceiling. Black smoke streamed from the undead bear's posterior.

Undead Cave Bear has Hindrance Damaged +3.
Undead Cave Bear is "On Fire".

Ingar got Torstag under his arms—the plates of his armour were sharp on his fingers—and dragged him away. "Come on get up get up get up!"

The undead rhino tilted its horn, hurled the now-burning cave bear onto its back. Flames still dancing on its own hide, the rhino aimed itself at Ingar and Torstag.

Ingar knew he should let go and run, but he wasn't going to leave his friend; not now, perhaps not ever. He tried to heave Torstag to the side, but the rhino just tracked them.

He looked for his axe, but it was out of reach and half buried in bones. Zahna, meanwhile, was whacking the bear as it tried to pick itself up.

Weaponless, not remotely strong enough, all Ingar he could do was pull harder. "Get up you great fucking wanker you! Up!"

The rhino trundled closer, dipped its horn. The stench of burning meat became unbearable. Perhaps he could distract it, lead it off…

Millicent stepped between him and the monster. She pointed her hand and intoned, "UNDINE!"

Ingar leaned out just in time to see a mermaid uncoil from her hand. With an unearthly scream, it flew across the space, bounced off the floor and vanished up into the monster's mouth. A flick of silvery tail and it was gone.

"What was the point of—" began Ingar.

The undead woolly rhinoceros halted in its tracks. White steam billowed from its nostrils then its vacant eyes holes.

There was a thunderclap. Great hunks of mummified flesh trailed smoke and flames across the chamber.

Zahna shouted, "Help me!"

The now burning cave bear had picked itself up and was bounding after her on all fours.

Torstag heaved himself upright with a clatter of armour. Somehow he'd kept hold of his sword. "Zahna! Head for me!"

Chapter 47: Bloody Shambles!

Torstag raised his sword. He was breathing heavily and his right upper arm was throbbing. At least he'd shrugged off being "Stunned".

Zahna sprinted closer in long strides. Now trailing black smoke, the massive mummified cave bear bounded along behind her.

Torstag, Human Warlock, Youth, Agile, Empathic, Bold, Marked.
Potestas 1 of 5. Will 2 Horror of the Unquiet Dead 2/6.
Vitality 0 of 5. Toughness 2. Wounds 1.
Vocations:
Warlord 0: Tea Drinking 2/6.
Warrior 3 (Sidearm, Shield, Brawling, Longsword): Wrath Strike +2, Split Shield, Disarm, Twitch, Rampage, Hurl, Onset Thrust, Crooked Strike 3/6
Scout 2 (Mountain, Forest, Jungle): Climb +1, Spider Climb, Sneak
Necromancer 1 (Cantrips): Repel Shade, Shade Cloak 3/6, Manifest Shade 4/6
Various General Skills including Meditation.
You have Hindrances "Debilitated", "Wounded"

He set his chin, bent his legs, readied himself. One Potestas…he would use it wisely.

New Form 5.

That was good fortune indeed.

Zahna was almost on him, normally narrowed eyes distended with fear.

Behind her, the bear picked up speed, bounding in graceful arcs that made the flames whoosh.

Torstag yelled, "Dodge right!"

She skipped right—to his left. The bear tracked her.

You have the Tactical Advantage.

And Torstag struck.

Form 5.
Performing Warrior at level 8.
Using Sword Feat, Smite Undead, cost 1 Potestas. 0 of 5 Potestas Remaining.
Result = 8 (Performance) +2 (Tactical Advantage) +4 (Enemy Damaged +3) +4 (Neglecting Defence) +1 (Luck) -3 (Debilitated, Wounded) -5 (Challenge) = 12 Natural Armour 4 Negated.
Damage = 12 +2 (Greatsword) +4 (Smite Undead) = 18.
Toughness 9 Surpassed.
Enemy has Hindrance Damaged +5

The blade caught the undead creature behind the head, sheared through the spine.

The huge head flopped forward.

The rest of the monster tripped on its own head, went over on its back and lay there with the flames licking around its flanks.

Zahna's eyes reflected the firelight. "I was helpless and you saved me."

Torstag lowered his sword and took a step towards her.

She turned away and swung her staff to thud into the burning carcass. "That," she pronounced, "is the last time I'm ever going to feel like that."

Torstag's his muscles quivered. He leaned on his sword and watched Zahna kick and hit the hulk of the undead bear. It was the first time she'd used her staff when somebody wasn't distracting him by trying to kill him.

Zahna was power in motion, stringy-muscles propelling the staff with perfect form as she stepped and whirled and sprang.

It was hard to believe that they had been lovers, if a post-combat tussle counted. It was not so hard to believe that Fate had bound him to her in some way.

You are "Marked".

He wasn't so sure how he felt about that.

He wasn't sure about how he felt about any of this.

He could be sure of just one thing.

"Bloody shambles," he said.

"What?" said Ingar.

Current Form 5. Performing Warlord at Level 5.

"How did we come so close to all dying?" said Torstag over the sound of Zahna hitting the dead undead beast.

"Can you blame us?" said Ingar. "What kind of fucking lunatic fills a tomb with zombie bears and rhinos?"

"Me, so it seems," said Millicent. She heaved herself to her feet. Her face was flushed behind soot marks. She removed her glasses and started to clean them. "We were *literally* battling for our lives."

"Battle implies some order," said Torstag. "Not running around individually, yelling and hacking." He raised his voice. "Zahna. Stop."

Zahna stopped whacking the bear carcass, and turned, eyebrows raised in surprise. "What?"

"Bloody shambles," said Torstag.

Chapter 48: Postmortem in an Unquiet Tomb

"Bloody shambles," repeated Torstag.

There was silence except for the crackle of the burning zombie. The cave bear carcasses smouldered where they lay. There were bits of mummified rhino flesh scattered around the floor. Thankfully, the oily smoke poured up through the shaft and out of the vault.

Everybody was battered and dirty.

Everybody was looking at Torstag.

Performing Warlord at Level 5.
Result = 5 (Performance) +0 (Luck) +3 ("Self Evident
Need for Leadership", Party Injured) -5 (Average Will)
= 3 (Tenative Practical Response).

He flexed against the weight of his armour. "Zahna. How about that healing tea?"

Zahna shrugged. She trudged off to the doorway, and Torstag saw she had dropped her pack there when she vaulted over the rhino.

"This place gives me the heebiejeebies," said Millicent. "I feel...watched. All the dead me's, I suppose."

"Enjoying all that existential horror, then?" said Ingar.

Millicent pushed off the wall and gave him a playful punch. "I think you're the horror, young man."

Ingar sobered. "There's only one way in or out."

"If your 'surge' thingy had worked," said Millicent, "we'd have been fine."

"Surge didn't work...?" began Zahna, handing out cups. "But that implies that one of your avatars found the skeleton on the pit trap, surged, then left."

"How very perspicacious of her," said Millicent.

"But you're okay now?" asked Ingar.

The librarian nodded. "Some rot about being out of Potestas and having Hindrance..." she made air quotes... "*Stunned*. Casting that last spell left me discombobulated so I sat down for a while." She put a hand to her mouth. "Oh My God. Here I am talking about casting spells like some mountebank...and now my Voice is talking about Grasp? I feel I have lost that."

Zahna poured the lukewarm tea. "Drink up."

"Fuck that hurts," whimpered Ingar.

"Ouch!" exclaimed Millicent. "Ouch!"

Torstag braced himself then sipped.

The magic seared through him, healing his injuries...and it hurt as badly as the making of them, except all at one go. He tried to speak, tried to even whimper, but the pain was paralysing.

"Bloody hell," said Ingar. "Look at Mr Stoical. Not even a squeak."

Sweat beaded Torstag's brow.

> **Wounding reset. Vitality restored to 5. Potestas restored to 5. Form lost.**

"Impressive," said Millicent. "Do you use some traditional spiritual practice to transcend the pain?"

"Something like that," said Torstag, glad that the dancing firelight hid his trembling. He handed back the cup and turned away so she would not see how his hands shook.

"Now what?" said Millicent.

"Now Torstag speaks to dead people," said Zahna.

> **Current Form 4.**
> **You are performing Necromancer at Level 4.**
> **Potestas 5 of 5.**
> **Skeletons, inert. Ghosts, scores.**

Torstag frowned. It was as if his Tempter were ignoring him and listening to Zahna.

Glowing ghosts filled the vaulted room, ghosts that wriggled in their bonds like chrysalises, ghosts that tried to run with their hands tied behind their back, ghosts that knelt and pleaded…

Torstag tried to ignore the ghosts and focussed on the strong link that extended from the librarian's ample chest to the patch of wall behind the remains of the zombie bear that he had dispatched. The outline of a door was clearly visible.

"I've found the burial chamber, I think," he said.

One-by-one, the ghosts saw him, stilled and spoke wordlessly.

Torstag shuddered, but at least he still had Channel Shade blocked by his two uncompleted Necromancer feats.

"What do you see?" asked Ingar.

Torstag glanced his way, and wished he hadn't.

The ghost of Axe Girl was still trying to wrest the two-handed axe from out of Ingar's grip. She left off, turned to face Torstag, opened her mouth to speak.

Wrestling with Horror of the Unquiet Dead 2/6. Cost 1 Potestas. 4 remaining.

Enough.

His sight closed, the ghosts vanished.

Torstag chewed his lip. "I don't think I'd want to be trapped down here."

Zahna hefted her staff. "Where is it?"

Torstag pointed to cave bear. "Behind that."

Ingar bowed. "Will you hold my axe, Miss Hunter?"

"Technically a halberd," said the Librarian as she took the weapon.

Ingar crunched over and examined the wall with his everlight. "Yep, there's definitely a door here. "A door. I think it opens out."

"We need to get the bear out of the way," said Torstag.

"Perhaps…" began Millicent.

"No," said Torstag, "you cannot set it on fire. We'll take it in turn with the axe."

"Technically a halberd," said Millicent. "I will have first go , if you don't mind."

The middle-aged librarian didn't last long. However, between them they managed to cut the zombie bear into sections and drag them away from the door.

"This had better have been bloody worth it," said Ingar as Zahna started chanting.

Zahna cast around. "No immediate danger."

"That's me through there?" asked Millicent.

"The tomb of your avatar," said Zahna.

"Well then." Millicent straightened her shoulders and strode forward. "*Open up, for I am Millicent nee Lintar nee Frontisia nee…*"

A slab of stone rotated out of the wall.

Ingar yelled "Fuck!" and skipped out of the way. "You could have bloody warned me."

Beyond the new entrance, gold and silver glittered in the light from the burning zombie rhino.

"Still safe," said Zahna.

Millicent took a pace forward.

"Right," said Torstag. "Enough chaos. We're going to do this carefully."

Everybody turned to look at him.

"Well?" prompted Zahna.

Torstag flushed. "Ingar, grab your axe—"

"Halberd," corrected Miss Millicent.

"—and you stand to the left, I'll stand to the right. Miss Millicent, you stand ready to throw fire. Zahna…" He frowned, but what he was about to suggest made sense. "…you have your Remembering Backwards, so you get to look inside."

"Makes perfect sense," said Zahna. She took out her everlight.

Ingar nodded.

Torstag and his friend each took up his position. The librarian made herself ready. Then Zahna looked inside.

Torstag held his breath.

"All safe," she said.

The four of them crammed into the doorway.

Zahna's everlight shone into a small square chamber with mouldering tapestries around the walls, gilded furniture, intriguing chests and a silver throne on which sat the mummified corpse of a woman. Her parched figure was decked out in white furs and silver jewellery. Diamond eyes reflected Zahna's everlight.

"And there she is," said Zahna. "The Ice Queen."

The librarian started to past into the chamber. "She's magnificent! So well preserved…"

There was something not right about the mummy.

Form 5.
You are performing Necromancer at Level 6.
Lich.

"Folks," began Torstag, raising Peacebringer. "I think…Damn."

The lich rose and extended withered arms. She grasped the thread that connected her to Millicent and pulled.

Chapter 49: Queen's Move

Torstag backed away slowly, as if that would help.

The lich curled her arm. The bones across the floor rustled. Miss Millicent gasped as if stabbed. She tottered closer to the lich.

"Get her clear!" ordered Torstag.

Ingar already had the librarian by one arm. Zahna took the other. Together they dragged her away from the door.

"She's following," said Zahna.

"It's fine," said Torstag. "I've got this!" He whipped his sword up, sprang boldly forward to drive a diagonal strike at the undead queen's neck just above the shoulder.

> Current Form 5.
> You are performing Warrior at Level 8.
> Using Wrath Strike+2, Cost 1 Potestas. 3 of 5 Potestas remaining.
> The blade caught the lich's neck and simply clanged to a stop.
> Result = 8 (Performance) +2 (Boldness) +0 (Luck) +4 (Enemy neglects defence) -5 (Challenge) = 5
> Using Sword Feat Smite Undead, cost 1 Potestas. 3 of 5 Potestas remaining.
> Effect = 5 +2 (Greatsword) +4 (Wrath Strike +2) +4 (Smite Undead) = 15
> Effect x 0 (Target invulnerable) = 0.

"What?"

The lich turned to face Torstag. Her diamond eyes glinted. She thrust with her right hand.

You are making no defence.
Enemy Result = 5 (Challenge) +4 (No Defence) +1
(Luck) -8 (Your performance) = 2
Effect = Air Punch on Target.
You are performing Necromancer at level 6.
Enemy Result = 12 (Challenge) +0 (Luck) -4 (Your
Performance) = 6.
Enemy Slam Effect = 6 +0 (Slam Factor) = 4
(Knockdown) +2 Damage Effect.
Actual Damage = 2 (Damage Effect) -3 (Armour) = 0
You have Disadvantage "Knocked Sprawling".

An invisible fist shoved Torstag to the ground. He skidded two body lengths and crashed into the still burning torso of the undead cave bear.

The ghosts of all the sacrifices gathered round to stand over him, mouthing words he could not hear.

Beyond them, Zahna let go of Miss Millicent, took a running jump and hit the Ice Queen with both feet.

She bounced off, fell backwards into the carpet of old bones.

The undead Ice Queen paced after Miss Millicent.

"Fuck!" cried Ingar. "Fucketty fuck!" He dragged the big librarian through the door.

As he got her over the threshold, the lich paced after them at slightly faster than walking place, each step making her limbs squeak and rustle.

The door slammed closed behind her.

Zahna reached the door just after and started examining the frame.

Torstag got to his feet. "Open it! We have to save them."

Zahna shook her head. "My Flip spell should do it, but I'd need most of the day. Sorry."

Torstag lined himself up. "Out the way I'll shoulder charge it..."

Zahna put her back to the door and folded her arms. "You will not. It's solid oak and opens *into* the room, remember?"

"Perhaps I can drill through with my sword."

> You are performing Warlord at Level 5.
> Lich travelling at walking pace takes about 5 minutes
> to reach the tomb exit. Burglar and Virago travelling
> at a jog will arrive first.

"Apparently not." He brightened. "But they'll outrun her, lose her in the jungle and come back for us."

Zahna shook her head.

"What?"

"Liches become more powerful as they awake," she said. "But I can't remember how quickly, or whether that makes them faster. But the main thing is they can't leave their tomb. When she gets to the entrance, she'll turn back."

> 1 Potestas restored.
> 4 of 5 Potestas remaining.
> Lich due in about 5 minutes.

"I'm afraid it's not going to be much of a conversation," said Torstag, suddenly certain about what he had to do.

"What?"

"You wanted me to ask her how she beat off Gronchard."

"Let's just focus on getting out of here," said Zahna.

"I have it covered," said Torstag, not exactly lying. "Go look. Perhaps there's a weapon in her burial chamber."

Zahna's eyes narrowed. She nodded and slipped away toward the empty burial chamber.

Torstag tapped at the door with Peacebringer's pommel, probed for secret catches. Nothing.

Zahna's voiced echoed behind him. "There's a second door at the back of the burial chamber!"

Torstag's heart lifted. Just perhaps…

"No," said Zahna. "Solid stone. Won't open."

Torstag gave up hope and relaxed into his choice.

Tell me about my Warrior Vocation.

Warrior 3 (Sidearm, Shield, Brawling, Longsword): Wrath Strike++, Split Shield, Disarm, Twitch, Rampage, Hurl, Onset Thrust, Crooked Strike 3/6

He counted the Feats as his Tempter recited them.

1, 2, 3…10 including Crooked Strike.

Securing Crooked Strike will increase Warrior to Level 4.

Zahna appeared beside him. "Got it." She held out a small wooden box then stuffed it in her satchel, which she jingled. "Plus loot to keep Ingar happy."

A stone settled in Torstag's gut. "Look after him."

Shock dragged itself across Zahna's face. "What?"

"Right," said Torstag. He took the satchel from Zahna, strode over to the shaft and lobbed it up to the next level. A thud echoed down to them.

"What are you doing?" asked Zahna.

"What I always do," said Torstag. He snatched her staff, tossed that up and through too.

"But…" she said.

He made a cradle of his hands. "When the door opens, I'll boost you into the shaft. You can chimney climb out. She can't fly, so you should be able to make it out."

"No," she said. "We'll work together to get past her."

Torstag shook his head. "If you die, Gronchard will find your body and enslave your next avatar."

"What about you?" she said. "Even if you can get round her, there's no cover in the passage. She'll have an easy time hitting you with her Air Punch."

"*Air Punch?* Is that what it's called." Torstag shrugged. "I have a plan."

"I bet it's not a very good plan."

He shrugged. "No, it is not."

Zahna's eyes glistened in the light of the burning zombie cave bear. She nodded. "I'll see you again."

"One way or another," said Torstag.

Zahna kicked off her soft leather boots, revealing sleek feet that didn't belong in the grime and debris of the tomb. "Unless Gronchard gets me anyway."

"If so, I will find you."

She kissed his forehead then threw the boots up through the hole. "I'm ready. What now?"

"We wait."

"I have a better idea." She stooped and kissed him full on the mouth.

He put his hands around her waist and drew her close, though he could feel nothing through the plates of his lamellar.

Time became endless sensation.

All thought dropped away. His awareness expanded until he could hear everything…the hiss of Zahna's breath on his cheek, the drip of water, and the Lich Queen's boots clacking on the stone, getting closer and closer down the tunnel toward them. Now the ringing of metal as she climbed down the ladder into the pit trap. Now her steady footfalls as she returned.

1 Potestas restored.
5 of 5 Potestas remaining.

That was five minutes gone.

The footfalls were behind the door now.

"Go," said Torstag, gently pushing her away.

Zahna kicked some bones out of the way, moved back a few paces, then ran at him.

The girl didn't so much get on his shoulders as run up his body: one foot in his hands, the next on his shoulder, the last one actually on his helmet.

He had a fleeting impression of her heat on his face then, with a yell, she was above him in the shaft.

He looked up in time to see her wedge back against the shaft walls and walk herself up. At the top she twisted and vaulted free.

The blade scythed across the hole.

His heart lurched, but there was no splash of blood, no scream.

"I made it."

"Run!" he said.

He caught a murmured, "Farewell." Then the soft tread of Zahna's feet as she fled the tunnel toward the daylight.

The door creaked like an aged executioner raising his axe.

Torstag jogged over to take position behind it. He dropped into Barrier Guard; left foot forward, sword held out in front, point down. The blood rushed in Torstag's ears, his limbs trembled. He concentrated on breathing.

The lich queen swept into the chamber, pivoted, fixed him with her diamond eyes. Her laughter was like icicles pressed into the ears. "I may not be reborn this day, but at least I shall feed well."

Lich. Hostile. Slow. Melee Distance.

"That remains to be seen."

CHAPTER 50: SHEAR MAGIC!

The lich queen extended a hand.

> Enemy Attacking Boldly.
> New Form 4. Performing Warrior at level 7.

Torstag bellowed, "Yah!"

> Using Crooked Strike 3/6, Cost 2 Potestas. 3 of 5
> Potestas remaining.

Torstag sprang to the side. As he moved, he crossed his hands, windmilling the sword into the space he'd just vacated, but angled forward.

> Crooked Strike defends by Evasion.
> Attacking Boldly negates Enemy Boldness.
> "More Heavily Armoured" negates "Slower Enemy".
> Test of Performance 7. Passed. Skid avoided.
> Crooked Strike counts as a Dodge.
> Result = 7 (Performance) +2 (Unpredictable) -5
> (Enemy Challenge) = 4

Her Air Punch prickled past. Behind him, stone crashed; the miss had wrecked some of the chamber's carved façade.

His sword tip struck her wrist.

It bounced off.

> Effect = 4 (Result) + 2 (Greatsword) -2 (Weak) = 4 x 0
> (Invulnerable) = 0
> Crooked Strike advances to 4/6 Grip.

Torstag had landed well to the right, but still in melee range. As long as he stayed close, she couldn't just knock him down with her Air Punch; she had to fence.

> You have "Tactical Advantage".

She turned, tracking him with the hand, diamond eyes flickering in the firelight.

Again he sprang out of the way and windmilled the blade at the threatening limb.

> Crooked Strike defends by Evasion.
> Attacking Boldly negates Enemy Boldness.
> Using Crooked Strike 4/6, Cost 2 Potestas. 1 of 5
> Potestas remaining.
> Test of Performance 7. Passed. Skid avoided.
> Result = 7 (Performance) +2 (Tactical Advantage) -1
> (Unpredictable) -5 (Enemy Challenge) = 1

The blade clanged off her shoulder.

> Effect = 1 (Result) +2 (Greatsword) -2 (Weak) = 1 x 0
> (Invulnerable) = 0
> Crooked Strike advances to 5/6 Grasp.
> You have "Tactical Advantage".

He was actually between her and the door now. He could turn and run. However, he didn't think he would get very far.

Instead of tracking him, the lich pivoted backwards, away from him. He took a long stride after her, stepping offline as he closed.

Manoeuvring.
Retreating negates your Tactical Advantage.
"Slower Enemy" cancels out "More Heavily
Armoured".
Result = 7 (Performance) -1 (Luck) -5 (Enemy
Challenge) -2 (Enemy Retreating) = -1
"Tactical Advantage" lost.
Melee Distance maintained.

Torstag laughed. "Too slow. You can't get away."

The lich let her arms fall by her side. She drew herself up and Torstag saw that she had once been beautiful.

"You cannot harm me," she hissed. Her tone changed to something huskier and more human. "Why not...love me instead?"

Suddenly, she was as she had been...as she was now—not cold, like Zahna but as warm and welcoming as a hot spring in a snow storm.

Test of Potestas 1, Failed.
Enemy Result = 11 (Challenge) +1 (Luck) -5 (Your Will)
= 7 = 7 x 0 (Marked) = 0.

"What?" blurted Torstag.

"I said...*love me*," purred the lich.

Enemy Result = 11 (Challenge) +1 (Luck) -5 (Your Will)
= 7 = 7 x 0 (Marked) = 0.

There it was again; *Marked.*

She screamed "Marked!" The beauty dissolved. She came at him, arms outstretched. "I am going to drink you down."

Once again, Torstag sprang to the side and crossed his wrists to windmill the blade at her hands.

Using Crooked Strike 5/6, Cost 1 Potestas. 0 of 5
Potestas remaining.
Crooked Strike is Unpredictable.
Test of Performance 4. Passed. Skid avoided.
Crooked Strike defends by Evasion.
Attacking Boldly negates Enemy Boldness.
Result = 7 (Performance) -2 (Unpredictable) -5 (Enemy
Challenge) = 0. Tie. Both parties are Bold and have
Result 2.
Effect = 2 (Result) + 2 (Greatsword) = 4 x 0
(Invulnerable) = 0

"Damn!"

The blade struck, rebounded.
Her Airpunch caught him as he landed.
Enemy Result = 2.
Enemy Effect = Air Punch On Target.

The magical force crushed the plates of his cuirass into his chest…

Current Form 4.
You are performing Necromancer at level 5.
Enemy Result = 12 (Challenge) +1 (Luck) -4 (Your
Performance) = 7.
Enemy Slam Effect = 7 +0 (Slam Factor) = 4
(Knockdown) +3 Damage Effect.

…threw him off his feet.

Damage = 3 (Damage Effect) -3 (Armour) = 0
You have Disadvantage "Knocked Sprawling".

He thumped onto his back, crunching old bones with his armour.
The lich laughed.

Crooked Strike advances to 6/6 Grasp.
Crooked Strike Secured.
Select another…

Busy right now. Get to sword feats.

You have 10 Warrior Feats.
Warrior advances to Level 4.
Level 4 unlocks a second Sword Feat. Select from
Cleave Armour, Smite Undead, Shear Magic, Parry
Arrows.

That one!

Shear Magic unlocked. Next feat unlocks at Warrior
5.

His Tempter seemed to take a deep breath.
Time stopped.

New highest level vocation.
Level Up Surge.
Vitality reset.
Potestas resent.
4 Points of Grasp Advancement available.

What? A mere four points. Surges seemed to be entirely random.

Select a Vocation.

He remembered the shambles that had gotten them into this mess.
Warlord.

Warlord, Tea Drinking secured. 0 points left.
Warlord advances to Level 1.
Unlock a 2nd Warlord Feat.

Something to avoid another shambles.

Dead memories flitted through his minds eye, commanding armies, defending fortresses, planning assaults…and leading a small part of warriors up a moonlit riverbank.

There had to be a way of making less of a pig's breakfast of things. That.

Small Unit Tactics unlocked at 1/6 Grasp.
You are: Torstag, Human Warlock, Youth, Agile,
Empathic, Bold, Marked.
Issue, Horror of the Despairing Dead 2/6.
New Potestas   6. New Will 3.
New Vitality 6. New Toughness 3.
The Sword Peacebringer (Undroppable): Smite
Undead, Shear Magic. Next feat unlocks at Warrior 5.
Vocations:
Warlord 1: Tea Drinking, Small Unit Tactics 1/6.
Warrior, 4 (Sidearm, Shield, Longsword): Wrath
Strike++, Cleave Shield, Disarm, Twitch, Onset Thrust,
Crooked Strike.
Scout 2 (Mountains, Forest, Jungle): Climb +1, Spider
Climb, Stalk 2/6.
Necromancer 1 (Cantrips): Repel Shade, Shade Cloak
3/6, Manifest Shade 5/6
Various General Skills.
Form 5.
Potestas Boosted to 12.

And he was back with the lich queen.

For an instant, Torstag was tempted to throw everything at her: both sword feats, a good Wrath Strike and all the boldness he could muster.

By the time he'd decided it was a stupid idea, however, he had rolled to his feet and was running clean past the lich.

He sensed her wheel to take another shot at him.

Current form 5. Performing Warrior at Level 9.
Manoeuvre Result = 9 (Performance) -2 (Knocked
Sprawling) +2 (Retreating) -1 (Luck) -5 (Challenge) = 3
Manoeuvre Effect = Retreat successful

As he passed the open door, he raised his fist, dipped the greatsword so it rested on his armoured shoulder and hung over his back. His shoulders tensed in the expectation of another one of her invisible punches.

> Enemy Targeting = 5 (Challenge) +2 (No room to
> dodge) +1 (Luck) -2 (Throwing Range) = 6. On Target.
> Using Sword Feat, Shear Magic, cost 1 Potestas. 11
> of 12 Potestas remaining.
> Shear Magic shifts magical defence to Warrior
> Performance.
> Result = 13 (Challenge) +0 (Luck) -9 (Your
> Performance) = 3
> Effect = "Staggered" (2)

It was like being butted by a horse. He stumbled, almost fell, but he was through the door, into the sloping tunnel. Light spilled from the trap entrance up ahead.

He ran harder, legs churning, armour rattling.

Voices echoed down the tunnel to greet him. *"Torstag! Come on! Leg it you wanker!"*

That was Zahna and his friends.

They couldn't help him, though.

Torstag tried to weave as he ran, bumped the sidewalls, gave up and just ran for it.

A burst of raw power whooshed past.

Masonry crashed from the ceiling.

Peacebringer, he realised, couldn't protect him from the secondary effects of magic.

> Falling Rubble Result = 4 (Hazard) +1 (Luck) -2 (You are
> moving) = 3.
> Falling Rubble Effect = 3 (Success) +2 (Damage Factor)
> -3 (Armour) = 2

A rock clanged off his helmet, bumped the plates of his shoulder.

> Vitality 2 of 6.

Here I go, stunned.

But no, his Toughness was three now.

He was almost on the bed of spikes with the remains of Millicent's avatar, still skewered through the shin bones. He couldn't jump it while carrying his sword, couldn't pause to go round to make himself a target.

Without breaking stride, he whipped Peacebringer back and around, hurled the sword ahead of himself and leapt.

> Current Form 5.
> Performing Scout at level 7.
> Result = 7 (Performance) +0 (Luck) -2 ("Medium armour") -4 (Difficulty) = 1
> Effect = Success

He crashed into the ladder, immediately snatched his hand back. Peacebringer's hilt smacked into his hand.

> Peacebringer (Undroppable).

Another whoosh of power.

> Enemy Targeting = 5 (Challenge) +2 (No room to dodge) -1 (Luck) -2 (Throwing Range) = 4. On Target.
> Using Sword Feat, Shear Magic, cost 1 Potestas. 10 of 12 Potestas remaining.
> Shear Magic shifts magical defence to Warrior Performance.
> Result = 13 (Challenge) + 0 (Luck) -9 (Your Performance) = 3
> Effect = "Staggered" (2)

An invisible hand shoved him into the ladder.

And Zahna was singing.

Rock crashed.

Torstag pressed himself against the ladder, tensed in anticipation of the tonnes of stone swatting him onto the spikes then crushing him into them.

Nothing.

Torstag twisted to look back.

"The tunnel happened to collapse," said Zahna above him.

"Impressive," said Miss Millicent.

"Just a Nudge," said Zahna. "Good for things that are already likely."

"Oh," said Miss Millicent. "I can *feel* her winding up to shift the rubble."

"Come on Torstag," said Ingar, "give me your sword and let's get you the fuck out of there."

CHAPTER 51: UNREPENTANT!

Outside, warm rain poured through the jungle canopy. Millicent exhaled and felt strangely clean.

They were all slumped against the bowl of a tree, all except for the big warrior who was removing his armour.

As she wiped her glasses, Millicent tried to work out whether she now felt relieved or exhilarated. *Who am I?*

> You are Millicent, Human Warlock, Middle Aged,
> Outgoing, Forceful, Hedonistic, Self Hating.
> Guilt at Using People 2/6 Hardening.
> Potestas 2 of 6. Will 3.

Millicent shuddered. The Ice Queen had simply scooped off a handful of her Potestas.

> Vitality 5.
> Goeticist 0 (Power Words): Manifest 3/6.
> Virago 4: Maelstrom +1, Amorous Impunity, Tsunami
> +1, Icestorm, Commanding Presence +1, Quell +1, Eye
> of the Tornado, Sweep Along, Brush Aside 2/6.
> Scholar 4 (Learned): Erudition, Research, Debate,
> Locate, Conservation, Restoration, Source Criticism,
> Read Old Imperial, Read Gorlakian Runes, Read
> Squamafian, Identify Art, Identify Architecture.
> Skills include: Hiker (Learned) 3, Throwing (Learned)
> 4...

Millicent listened while it prattled through the meagre sum of her life to date. Apparently, she was good at "Cataloguing": who would have thought? There were even half-forgotten accomplishments like

"Cross Stitch" that took her back to stuffy beige classrooms while the sun beckoned through too-high windows.

At length she could bear it no longer. "What *was* that thing? I mean, if I'm me then who is she?"

"A lich," said Zahna.

"Oh well that explains it all." Millicent dug out her flask, took a gulp and passed it to Ingar.

"Bloody shambles," said Torstag, hanging his sword on the tree. He shook his head at Ingar, who passed the flask to the girl.

Warlord, commented her voice.

Interesting. That was new.

And interesting that her Voice was useful now she was listening to it. No more little pills for her, ever.

"Yes, it *was* rather a shambles," said Millicent, deciding to see where this development would lead.

Zahna shook her head. "We succeeded." She swigged the liquor. "Good stuff." She brought out a wooden box.

Form 2.
Performing Scholar at Level 4.

Millicent polished her glasses then read out the Gorlakian script: "Remember that *I Rasinta, Queen/Empress/Chief of the Icelands*...Oh she's not really an actual 'Ice' Queen...*repelled the Flying Tooth Garden*." She sat back. "What a preposterous name."

"What's in the box?" asked Ingar.

Zahna slipped the hook-catch and flipped back the lid.

It was full of beans.

"What the fuck?" said Ingar. "All those jewels and you managed to grab some magic beans? "

"Feel free to go back and loot the place," said Torstag. He draped his scaled armour over a handy branch and balanced his helmet on it.

"Fuck you!" said Ingar.

Zahna dipped a hand in her satchel and produced a handful of silver necklaces. "That won't be necessary."

Performing Virago at Level 6.

"Excuse me!" said Millicent. "That's my tomb. *My* jewels."

"It doesn't work that way," said Zahna. "You get a share, that's all."

Millicent rounded on her. "Did you not promise you would clean out my tarpit tomb'?"

Zahna shook her head. "It's not a tarpit tomb. It's a lich's bower."

"I *thought* you were on a quest to defeat evil?"

"An evil warlock," said Torstag. "So we can be free." He glanced at Zahna. "Once we've done that, we could come back."

"Sure," said Zahna. "If we can level up enough to beat Gronchard, it will be trivial to finish off here."

"Finish off *her*, you mean?" said Millicent. "Which takes me back to my question; if I'm me, who's she?"

"A lich," said Zahna.

Millicent didn't bother to hide her irritation. "A little expansion, if you please."

Zahna grinned, acknowledging she'd been caught out being deliberately obtuse. "The Ice Queen was one of your previous avatars. Her shade now inhabits the preserved corpse."

"Shade?" Millicent thought back through all the folklore she knew. "So even though I'm me, there are ghosts of my past selves?"

"Ghosts are just a particular kind of shade," said Torstag.

"But…but, I'm here right now. How can I have a *shade* knocking around?"

"Ah," said Torstag. "You are your soul and the body it inhabits. Between you, you develop a shade. It's…"

"A *persona*," said Zahna.

"Yes," said Torstag. "When you die, your soul reincarnates, but your shade remains, fading over the centuries…unless it ends up animating its own remains. Which, um, takes magic."

Necromancer.

So we all know how that can happen. Millicent caught his eye and he looked away. "So the lich is like a zombie?" she prompted. "Brrr."

"No, much more self aware than that," said Zahna. "More like a vampire that feeds on shades. Hence the sacrifices."

"What would have happened if…?"

"If she'd eaten your actual soul," said Zahna, "then she would come not-life…for a while. When you ran out, it would be back to the tomb to wait for the next avatar."

Millicent shuddered despite the heat. "What about the past me's? Why didn't she feed on them?"

"I think she needed to eat them in that chamber where we fought," said Torstag. "None of you got that far. She'd have gotten a surge each time one died."

"So, that's why the bones were all duds!" said Ingar.

Millicent held up a hand to cut off any more technical discussion. "I never *liked* myself very much," she said, "and the more I learn, the less there is to like."

"Oh, that's just the sympathetic magic at work," said Zahna. "Stuff like that is going to echo in your psyche."

"What?" A stone seemed to settle in Millicent's belly. It was hard to breathe. "But…years of psychoanalysis…" She had to get some air. She heaved herself to her feet. "You mean I don't like myself because it so happens that, incarnation after incarnation, I've been literally eating myself and not in a good way."

"Yes," said Zahna. "Welcome to being a warlock."

"That's fucked up," said Ingar.

"But…" Millicent got up and walked out into the rain.

The vegetation rustled behind her.

Torstag called out, "Leave her be."

Ingar replied from much closer. "Oh shut up."

Millicent didn't stop to let the boy catch up. She marched onwards through the sodden vegetation while her mind raced in circles. It was because she disliked herself that she didn't really expect anybody to like her so just got what she wanted by being unlikable, which was why she didn't like herself…

"Millicent," called Ingar. "Slow down."

Her blouse was soaked so she tore it off. Now warm rain splashed her shoulders, ran down her chin and dripped into the front into her corset.

She tugged the laces open, let the damaged corset drop behind her.

She inhaled deeply. "I never really realised how restrictive that thing was."

The heavy skirt was next. The girl's magic still seemed to be keeping the insects off and the silk chemise was more than enough in the oppressive heat.

She didn't trust the magic to protect her from the twigs and briars of the jungle floor, so the boots and woollen stockings stayed.

Thunder crashed. Not so far away, a tree exploded in a sheet of white flame.

"Millicent," called Ingar.

Now she did stop and turn.

Naif. Youth.
Form 2. You are performing Virago at level 6.

Why not?

Using Feat Maelstrom +1, cost 1 Potestas. 2 of Potestas remaining.

"Whoa," said Ingar. He slowed down, but did not stop advancing. "You're using some kind of magic."

"Maelstrom," said Millicent. "A great whirlpool, with me at the centre." The silk chemise was wet now, so off that went.

Ingar's blue eyes widened. He didn't seem to know where to feast his eyes. "I can feel its pull."

"And just *where* are you feeling it?" asked Millicent.

He halted just short of her, his red hair plastered to his head, his breech clout wilted against his youthful body. "Nowhere I'd name to a lady."

She kissed him lightly on the lips. "You'll have to show me then," she said. She tugged at the wet fabric. He was young, but his legs were muscular rather than skinny. Overall, she rated him 'not unpleasing'.

"Wait, you're much older than me," said Ingar.

"Meaning you can sow your wild oats without fear of romantic entanglement," said Millicent. "Isn't that what young men want?"

"And you're using magic on me," he said.

She untied the strip of linen protecting his modesty and let it fall. "Don't all women, in a way?"

He made no effort to cover himself. "Good point," he said.
"So it seems," she said.

You are Millicent, Human Warlock, Middle Aged,
Outgoing, Forceful, Hedonistic...Unrepentant.

Chapter 52: The Marshal and the Queen

The rain hissed on the lush green canopy and Torstag found himself looking into Zahna's twinkling eyes. He wanted to touch her…to hold her…but it felt as if they had all the time in the world.

Unlock Warlord, Formal Courtship?

Hah no, I am not wasting that slot. Perhaps if he moved just a little closer…?

A bellowing cry penetrated the rain-sodden jungle.

Torstag started to rise. "What in the Thirteen Hells was that? Some kind of carnivorous moose? They're in trouble!"

Zahna pulled him back. "No, really they're not. That's Miss Millicent."

"But." Torstag felt himself flush. "Oh."

The cry trailed off into a whimper then repeated, louder.

Torstag glanced at Zahna, but she wasn't looking his way.

Lighting flashed. Thunder rumbled hard on its heels.

"The storm's passing over," he said.

Millicent cried out again, triumph and pleasure mingled.

"Not for our lost librarian," said Zahna.

"Um," said Torstag. "What do we do with the beans?"

"We?" said Zahna,

"I don't know whether it's destiny or choice," said Torstag. "Plus Ingar was right about Gronchard…he is a creepy fucker…"

"A wise man once said, 'Some people need killing'."

"I…" began Torstag.

More cries from Miss Millicent.

It was Zahna's turn to look away.

"I was the Marshal," said Torstag. "And you were my queen."

"I was Zenobia of Yinkesia, yes," she said.

"I nearly sacrificed myself to save you from the lich."

"I tried to share the risk," she said. "But you insisted."

"You didn't argue very hard," he said.

Zahna shrugged. "You heard Gronchard. A thousand rebirths, a thousand painful growths into womanhood, each rewarded by being taken and flayed back to Princess bloody Angelica."

"This is the first time you've broken the cycle," said Torstag.

Zahna nodded and he could not tell whether it was rain or tears that ran down her cheeks. "One avatar managed to die where he could not retrieve her body for his mausoleum. The next was Queen Zenobia. She repelled Gronchard's legions, the Marshal slew Gronchard before he died."

"But Gronchard didn't stay dead."

"His priests found his next avatar and flayed the child to reveal the soul of their Living God. So no, I didn't argue with you very hard."

"It seems…" began Torstag, not sure whether to be annoyed or amused. "It seems that you are going to use me, because you have to."

"Yes."

"Not even a 'sorry'?"

Zahna let out a curt laugh. "Would that make a difference?

"Do either of us have a choice?" he asked.

She said nothing, so he kissed her

CHAPTER 53: TO THE RESCUE!

"Ahem, Divinity," said the young Saint Prescience. His angel flapped nervously, as well it might.

"Yes," said Gronchard, flushing. He picked himself up from the cold floor of the Temple of Incarnation.

He shivered. How long had he been lying there? Snow was pouring down the Great Well. A blizzard would be bad for the shrubs. Why had nobody moved him?

Gronchard opened his mouth to order everybody executed.

Saint Prescience coughed. "If I may, Divinity, You are indeed never wrong, Divinity. The tomb contains a portal leading out of the Winter Lands. Perhaps the Sacred Angelica's vessel is to be found at the other end?"

"Yes!" cried Gronchard. "My intuition is never wrong, just misinterpreted on occasion." He raised his voice. "Follow that portal. We're going to rescue my Angelica!"

About the Author

A self-described "Howling Medievalist", M Harold Page believes in "write what you know", hence the sword scar, the study with rather more than the average number of grimoires and edged weapons, and the battered set of plate armour in the loft crated up for the next generation to grow into (his teenage daughter is somewhat scary).

Martin—that's the "M"—is old enough to have grown up playing AD&D, Runequest, and first edition Traveller, and young enough to study and teach Historical European Martial Arts with the Dawn Duellists Society, of Edinburgh, one of the world's first HEMA clubs.

He specialises in German Longsword, partly because it's a rich and satisfying system, but mostly because its technical terms are frankly just more Metal than those of the Italian system, e.g. Zornhau versus Fendente... which sounds more dangerous? He's spent a lot of his life exploring ruined castles and tramping old battlefields. He once tried to get down the sixteenth century mine and countermine at St Andrews Castle while wearing full plate armour.

Level Up publishing specialises in LitRPG and GameLit books. If you have enjoyed *The Jungle Tomb of the Ice Queen* you might be interested in our other titles, which can be found at www.levelup.pub/books

To join our mailing list for news about forthcoming books and opportunities to be an ARC reader, just fill in the form on that page.

You can also find us on:
Facebook @LUPublishing
Twitter @LevelUpPub
And by searching for Level Up WhatsApp group